A TEAM OF THREE

THE UNSANCTIONED ASSET SERIES BOOK 3

BRAD LEE

PART 1

THURSDAY MORNING, DECEMBER 29

1

THE RESCUE

Outside Soto La Marina
Tamaulipas, Mexico
Three Hours South of Brownsville, Texas

The two armed guards in the dune buggy weren't supposed to be there. Axe hadn't expected any patrols until he had gained access to the compound.

I wonder what else we got wrong about this op, he thought.

Flat on his stomach, Axe calmed his mind and made himself disappear into the sand. A sharp stone dug into his kneecap. He ignored it. With the moonless night sky and the undulating desert landscape, he would be difficult to see, especially in stealth mode.

Unless they dismount and walk around. Or their lights shine on me.

Then he'd be dead, shot first and questions asked later.

And he couldn't shoot back.

Why did I agree to come unarmed?

The fourth patrol in an hour continued bouncing across the desert straight toward him. The dune buggy's headlights and three glaring roof-mounted floodlights probed the darkness. The light shone weakly where he lay in a shallow depression in the ground, more of a groove than a ditch, but grew brighter by the second.

Turn.

Through mostly closed eyes, he could see the two men riding in the souped-up dune buggy. With its extra-large tires and roll cage design, it had no trouble with the rough terrain. The headlights washed over him.

Turn, damn it!

In his black technical pants, shoes, shirt, and black backpack disguised with branches from the prevalent local bushes, he blended in perfectly… in the dark. Lit up, he'd look at first like a rock or scraggly plant. Then he would be exposed as a dangerous infiltrator and either run over or shot.

Or both.

He had a knife and a stun gun. Neither would be effective against the vehicle or the men. But he wouldn't give up.

As long as they don't shoot the second they notice me, I have a chance.

The guards in the dune buggy came on fast. The desert around him shone in the powerful lights. He had only a few seconds until they saw him or ran him over.

Turn. Come on, turn!

One of the guards shouted, excited.

Axe tensed, ready to jump up, draw his knife, and take his chances.

They swerved to his left and sped up, trying to run down a small animal bounding away in a panic.

They're just driving wherever they want. Chasing animals, playing around. No pattern, no discipline.

The noise of the vehicle had warned him of their approach and gave him time to disappear into sniper mode. Their reliance on the bright lights instead of using NVGs made his stealth approach to the compound possible. But the randomness of their driving made the mission more dangerous. At any moment, they could run him over or notice him. Every exposure to their haphazard search risked the mission.

He had to get over the wall of the compound before they came through again.

Axe pulled himself forward, faster than he had earlier. There could be other guards patrolling the surrounding desert on foot, but he had to risk it.

Ahead of him loomed the high wall surrounding the compound. If anyone watched from there with thermal imaging, they could already see him. His body had warmed up over the past hour after cooling considerably during his river swim insertion.

They could be observing me right now, laughing at my slow progress.

It wouldn't surprise him if this was yet another ambush.

His career as a SEAL had been filled with stealthy approaches toward enemies who knew he was coming.

Moving forward at a steady pace, his hand avoided a small hole in the side of the gully. During the initial planning of the op, he had worried about rattlesnakes. If bitten, he wouldn't get to a hospital in time unless he stood and got the attention of the enemy in the compound, which would only get him killed more quickly than the bite.

Besides, he doubted a rural Mexican hospital three hours from the Texas border would have anti-venom.

But in researching the issue for him, Haley discovered it wouldn't be a problem. Rattlesnakes were common to the area but should be hibernating for the winter.

Should be. Let's hope the nights haven't been warm enough to tempt them out of their holes.

Axe moved forward another few feet, then froze. After counting to ten, listening and extending his senses but picking up no nearby danger, he continued.

Down by the river, the dune buggy turned and angled to Axe's right, toward the highway in the distance, continuing their large loop around the compound.

He pushed himself to risk moving even faster. He'd already been crawling for two hours—an hour longer than he had expected for the short distance from the river. But he hadn't counted on the frequent patrols.

Rule one: the intel is always wrong.

This time, the inaccurate intelligence landed squarely on him. He and Haley had looked at several days of satellite images together and agreed the three-building compound looked lightly guarded. They had seen no patrols. The only guards were near the compound's main gate.

We didn't see the dune buggy. I hope we weren't wrong about the hibernation of snakes, too.

They could have taken more time to plan the operation, but decided it had to be tonight. Heavy clouds would hide the bright moon. It would be the darkest night for a while. Anyone with half a brain would use the weather to their advantage.

Axe took a chance. He raised to a crouch and hustled through the night. If there were more guards than he'd seen via satellite, it could be deadly. But if he didn't get going, the dune buggy patrol—and coming dawn—would catch him. Ahead, the last hundred yards between the desert and the wall had been cleared of the small bushes, cacti, and natural depressions he had used to hide his approach so far.

No hiding there.

And he still had to rescue his target and escape back the way he'd just come—with an untrained civilian. In the dark, with the patrols. Then make it to the river, all without being spotted or her captors noticing she was missing.

His only backup—another untrained civilian—had orders to leave him behind if trouble came up.

Axe was unarmed, way behind enemy lines, and he had too much to accomplish before the sun came up and took away all his cover.

He fought back a smile.

I love this shit!

The impossible mission, saving lives, taking out bad guys—he was born for this.

In the green glow of the goggles, the desert floor showed its hollows and undulations. Axe followed a dip and raised from a crouch to sprint farther and faster than he normally would, trading stealth for speed. Getting over the wall before the men in the dune buggy came back required it.

In our defense, we didn't have a dedicated satellite or drone. Looking at still images from a commercial satellite isn't ideal for planning an operation.

After saving the world twice in the last year, he was once again an unsanctioned asset. Tonight, he was tasked with a rescue operation at a compound in the middle of the northeastern Mexican state of Tamaulipas.

He heard a noise and dropped, ignoring the rocks poking his body and the sand which infiltrated his clothes and shoes. No SEAL was a stranger to being coated with sand. "Wet and sandy!" was still a common command at BUD/S, the basic training course for SEALs, these many years after Axe attended. The students would run into the crashing surf off Coronado Island near San Diego. They'd fully immerse themselves in the frigid saltwater. Then they sprinted to the dry sand of the beach where they dropped, rolled, and flung armfuls of sand onto their bodies to turn themselves into, as their instructors called them, "sugar cookies."

The sand stuck to their skin and clothing, lodging in every nook, cranny, and orifice. It would chafe as they drilled and exercised for hours. At frequent intervals, both for reprimands and to teach recruits how to be mentally tough, the instructors would once again yell, "Wet and sandy!" and they'd be off to repeat the procedure.

Tonight's stealthy crawl was nothing compared to being a sugar cookie for weeks on end.

After listening intently, but not hearing the noise again and seeing no danger, Axe checked his watch. If the patrol pattern continued as it had for the past two hours, the dune buggy with the guards would be on the far side of the compound. He could barely hear it, which he took as a good sign.

They're driving around the desert, avoiding cacti, chasing animals. I have just enough time.

Axe hurried to the base of the wall and shrugged off his large backpack, avoiding the branches which helped break up his silhouette in the dark. Moving with practiced speed, he removed a small telescoping ladder and extended it—silent except for a small click as it locked into place. He leaned it against the thick block wall, donned the backpack, and slipped on coated, cut-resistant gloves from his front cargo pocket. As he had seen from the satellite view, glass shards and broken bottles had been embedded into the wall to keep people from scaling it.

Climbing the ladder smoothly and silently, Axe heard the growl of the dune buggy as he pulled himself to the top of the wall.

The guards were early.

I bet they're patrolling the cleared area near the wall before venturing farther out.

Driving along the open area, free of obstacles, had taken less time than other patrol routes. And it would allow them to go faster and skid around the corners—more fun for the men.

They'd changed their pattern at the most inopportune moment. Instead of driving randomly through the sand and scrub, then along the riverbank, they were headed directly for him again.

Some ops are like this: bad luck. Murphy's Law.

No problem.

The only easy day was yesterday.

Hurrying, he pressed with his arms, mantling the wall like he was getting out of a swimming pool. He placed one foot on either side of the sharp glass shards embedded in the wall, waiting to slice him. He crouched, arms straight out for balance, aware of how close the glass was to his legs and groin.

Axe grabbed the ladder and started pulling it up. The shift in balance made his left foot slip. His right leg took all his weight, and he windmilled his free arm wildly for balance. The ladder came dangerously close to clanging against the wall, but he caught it at the last second.

A sharp piece of glass pressed against his upper inner thigh.

No, no, no, not there.

He carefully got his left foot back on the wall and stood, relieved he hadn't gotten cut in the worst place possible for a man.

If anyone is watching me, they're laughing their asses off at this.

The bright lights of the dune buggy neared the corner, ready to turn in his direction. In seconds, he would be exposed, then shot.

A heartbeat before the lights caught him, he collapsed the ladder and jumped over the wall.

Normally, he would roll after a jump from this height, but the ladder and backpack made it impossible.

He hit the ground hard, jarring his knees but keeping the ladder quiet. At two in the morning, sound carried, and dropping the aluminum ladder would have been as obvious as a siren going off announcing his presence.

One of my least graceful approaches, but if the guards in the dune buggy didn't notice me, I'm in undetected, and good to go. I love this job... but it sure takes a toll on the body.

He refused to let his mind review his concerns about being too old for this kind of work. He'd have plenty of time for that once the mission was complete.

With his knees protesting, Axe rushed forward twenty feet to the edge of the nearest building—a workshop or garage, they had guessed from the satellite view. He would need his hands free to silence any guards he came across, so he took a second to remove the gloves and stash the ladder in the backpack.

Ready for part two of the plan, he looked around the corner of the building and saw the main gate, three hundred yards away. A long barn with a low-angle roof and a wide awning stretched several hundred feet on the right. He couldn't tell in the darkness through the NVGs but knew from his earlier research it looked well maintained and had a green metal roof, red walls, and bright white trim.

On the left sat a modest single-story house in the same color scheme, looking homey and welcoming, not at all like the home of a drug cartel captain.

Where would they hold the prisoner? In the house or the barn? He and Haley hadn't been able to determine her location.

The house. She's a 'guest,' so they'll treat her like one.

He started forward, slow and silent, a shadow in the night, making his way toward the house. After only a few steps, he froze in the open. He sensed a presence nearby.

A tall young man emerged from the backyard of the house, moving slowly, looking down, playing soccer with a small rock.

Axe stepped back smoothly and stood against the front of the workshop, merging with its shadows. The man, carrying an M4 slung on his shoulder, walked through the fifty-foot gap between the back of the house and the side of the building, kicking his rock the whole way, switching feet as he went.

Damn. Roving patrols inside as well. Though not expecting trouble, judging from his inattentiveness.

Axe resumed his approach to the house, quickly arriving at the front door.

What are the odds it's unlocked? Pretty good is my guess.

Bad guys around the world protected themselves with guards, fences, dogs, and guns. Then they went and left their doors unlocked. The SEALs didn't mind. It made their jobs easier.

Axe tried the knob. Locked, which surprised him but posed no real problem. It would only slow him down a few seconds.

He took out a compact lock pick gun from his cargo pants pocket, inserted it into the lock, and triggered the mechanism. With a soft click, the tumblers released.

As he turned the knob, he faintly heard a toilet flush carry through the quiet night from the workshop building near the back wall. He held in place, waiting to hear more.

If there's another guard who I missed because of his bathroom break, it cuts off my planned exfil.

A few seconds later, he heard a door open and softly close.

Now that's a very dangerous man—he didn't wash his hands.

He chuckled silently at his joke, knowing Haley wouldn't appreciate it if she were here with him.

He waited to see if the suspected guard patrolled or stayed on station. After several more seconds, Axe caught the faint smell of cigarette smoke.

I got in unseen because of the man's bowels.

Sometimes, it took luck to accomplish the mission. While he never relied on it, he'd take it when offered. Unfortunately, unless he wanted to deal with the guard on the way out, the exfil had to change.

But first, the rescue. Axe entered the house and moved through it like a ghost, guided by instinct. He guessed the master suite would be on the left, farthest from the front gate. On the right would be the spare bedrooms. He went right, through a nicely furnished great room. A Christmas tree stood in the corner with lights blinking merrily.

Even drug dealers celebrate the holidays.

He entered a long hallway. The first two bedroom doors were open. The third was locked from the outside. Someone had put the locking knob on the exterior instead of the interior.

Found her.

He unlocked the door and opened it. A woman sat up in bed, looking at him with a sleepy frown as she clutched the quilt to her body.

He knew how he looked. Dressed all in black, with NVGs looking like binoculars strapped to his eyes. His face, including the bushy beard, was covered with camouflage paint. Sand coated his clothes, which smelled of the river he used as his approach. Thankfully, he didn't look at all like the men who patrolled the area. She would know he wasn't a guard.

"Carol?" he whispered as he eased the door mostly shut behind him. The woman, in her late sixties, nodded. "Your brother sent me."

She let out a quiet sigh of relief, her shoulders relaxing.

"You ready to get out of here?"

She nodded and slid out of bed. Modestly, she turned away from him as she put on the jeans laying on the arm of the chair near the bed, then pulled a sweatshirt over her t-shirt. Though stocky, she moved gracefully, especially after being woken suddenly in the middle of the night. She sat on the bed to put on socks and running shoes, then stood and nodded again, all without saying a word.

No needless questions or noise. She's solid.

Carol proved adept at moving quietly, making their exit from the house easier than expected. As they neared the front door, Axe considered going with his original plan. He could take out the guard, then they could climb the wall at the rear of the compound and make their way to the river, escaping the same way he had approached.

It was a good plan, simple, despite the challenge of getting the woman over the tall wall and avoiding the dune buggy. But unless he killed the guard, they wouldn't make it to the river before the alert went out. They would be caught.

What are the odds they have a guard on the other sides of the compound—behind the house and the barn, too?

He glanced back at Carol, her hand on his shoulder so he could guide her through the dark. He didn't want to be wandering around the compound with her, checking on other guards, but getting over the wall—undetected—was the best plan.

I'll check behind the house. If there's no guard, we'll go over the wall there.

They left through the front door and went toward the back of the compound. Carol moved more quietly than Axe had expected—a bonus.

They neared the edge of the house. Axe flattened against the wall. Carol copied him without question. She'd heard it too. They waited for a few seconds. The tall guard appeared, still kicking his stone.

Axe drew his stun gun—the only weapon he had aside from a knife—and waited until the man walked obliviously past the corner of the house where they hid.

He's clueless. I can let him go by.

Then the rock being used as a soccer ball rolled toward Axe, landing a few feet in front of him.

The guard switched direction, intent on continuing his game.

As he came closer, he looked up. He didn't notice Axe, but his eyes widened when he noticed Carol against the wall.

Axe closed the distance between them, unseen, and held the stun gun to the man's exposed neck before he could yell out. The guard shook and dropped to the ground, out cold.

The zapping sound seemed to echo through the compound.

Time for Plan B. We'll do this the old-fashioned way—with brute force and dumb luck.

He quickly picked up the guard's M4 and spare magazines from his pocket. Admiral Nalen had insisted on no guns, but when the plan changes, the rules needed to change, too.

Non-lethal is all well and good, but I'm not going into a real battle with only a knife and a stun gun.

2

FOX 2

Soto La Marina River
Soto La Marina
Tamaulipas, Mexico

Kelton eased the throttle back on the large fishing boat, letting it drift under the modern concrete and metal bridge. The river's lazy current helped him to the perfect position to wait.

He glanced at the cheap watch Axe had given him before the op. No fancy bells or whistles that could make noise and no GPS to be tracked. The hands glowed in the dark and the plastic chafed his wrist. It had been a long time since he'd worn a watch this inexpensive. Still, he treasured it. Getting asked to participate in the operation had both thrilled and terrified him. But so far, he'd done well. He felt better than he had in years. Instead of pacing an office, plotting and scheming a way to reclaim his former CEO position, he relished being out on the water, doing important work instead of obsessing over the sudden changes in his world.

I'm helping to save a life tonight.

The realization that he also risked his own life made the joyful grin falter. But after being fired as the CEO and chairman of the board of the company he founded, what else was there to do? He had been asked for help, and he'd answered the call.

I owe my life to Axe. If he wants me to risk it to help him save the nurse, so be it.

His time on Earth would have ended eight months before if it weren't for the Navy SEAL's intervention on his superyacht off the coast of Long Island. Any days alive since then were a bonus.

Axe would arrive in a few minutes. He and the American nurse would work their way down the short hill next to the bridge, climb on the boat, and Kelton would motor them safely home.

He smiled as he reversed the throttle, keeping the boat pointed downstream and hidden under the bridge.

Unlike Axe, Kelton wasn't dressed all in black and didn't have his face and hands camouflaged. Instead, he wore a wild print Hawaiian shirt—though the colors were dark green, black, and red, making it blend well in the dark—black jeans, and a black floppy hat to hide his features.

He looked the part—a gringo fisherman from a few hours up the coast, slumming on the Mexican beaches. Fishing in the daytime, drinking cheap beer at night, and making no effort to blend in. With the scraggly beard and the long, unkempt hair, no one had looked twice or wondered what one of the world's formerly richest men was doing in their area.

He grinned, turning the wheel of the boat slightly and feathering the throttle to maintain his position. He not only had a Navy SEAL as a buddy showing him the ropes, he also was on an op and using his childhood boating skills to help the mission.

This is so great!

3

ADAPT

Axe watched Carol hesitate, staring down at the zapped guard, looking like she wanted to help the man.

Her nursing instincts, even for an enemy.

He pulled her close and whispered in her ear.

"We have to hurry—he'll be fine in a minute. New plan. We use one of their vehicles. You drive, I'll get the gate. Follow my lead."

He headed back the way they'd come, toward the front gate and the line of black vehicles neatly lined up near it. A guard sat in a cheap white plastic patio chair by the gate, his legs stretched out and chin touching his chest.

She held his hand and wouldn't let him go.

What the hell?

Carol pulled him close and whispered in his ear. "I can get us out. I've seen how they leave. Trust me!"

Instead of waiting for an answer, she rushed along the front of the house toward the closest SUV, catching him off guard. He hurried after her, wanting to argue, but she seemed to have a plan.

She's been held here for weeks. Maybe she knows what she's doing.

He hated turning over his rescue operation to the rescuee, but the

SEAL command structure is different than other fighting units. While they have an established leadership hierarchy, every member of the Team is expected to know the operation and be fully prepared to take over in the event of an emergency. It made them a stronger, more deadly force.

So instead of arguing, Axe fell in behind her.

She must have planned this escape for the last few weeks of captivity.

Just like she had engineered her own rescue. Before she had traveled to Mexico, she had planned for the possibility of being kidnapped and gave her brother a list of trigger words and phrases. Then, a few weeks ago, her brother had received a Merry Christmas email with benign-sounding code words indicating she had been abducted.

It's logical to think she's figured out a way to escape—once she got a little help.

The brother had reported his concerns to the FBI, and it had quickly landed on Haley's desk. Haley had worked her magic, found the likely location of the imprisoned nurse, and she and Axe had planned the mission.

There hadn't been time—or desire—to loop in the FBI. They would only drag their feet, attempt a diplomatic solution, risking Carol's captors moving or killing her. No—it was the perfect op for Nalen's team to handle... as long as they didn't get caught or create an international incident. Drug dealers or not, Axe still couldn't go in shooting.

As they neared the gate, Axe saw five full-size SUVs lined up neatly on the far side of the house, facing out, ready to go.

Just like the satellite showed. At least we got one thing right.

Carol gestured to the passenger door of the one farthest from the gate. Axe should get in while she drove. The guard by the gate snored. He'd be easy to take out silently, but Axe would have to find the keys, unlock the gate, and open it. Or he could go along with Carol's plan.

What the hell. 'Life is either a daring adventure or nothing.'

Axe opened the heavy truck door on the passenger side. Its weight made him think the vehicle was bulletproof.

There's that, at least.

Carol slid into the driver's side seat. The keys were in the ignition, as he had hoped. No one wanted to have to search for the person with the keys when they needed to go. Carol started the truck, the throaty roar of the big SUV's powerful engine loud in the darkness. Not only would the zapped guard be coming around any second to sound the alarm, but whoever was in charge would investigate an SUV starting in the middle of the night.

But even the beast of a truck couldn't ram through the heavy front gate. Axe looked at the nurse, praying she had a workable plan.

Carol pulled forward, not rushing, and turned toward the guard who now stood with his M4 held casually in one hand, trying to look awake and alert.

Carol slowed and flicked her high beams twice, blinding the man while signaling to open the gate.

Exactly like the higher-ups have done to him countless times before. Brilliant.

The guard hesitated, torn between following protocol and pleasing whichever bigshot drove the vehicle.

Carol flashed the lights again, holding the high beams a touch longer, showing impatience. She also tooted the horn twice, not nicely, like, "When you have a second, I'm ready to leave," but more of a "Get going, you jerk!"

The horn did it. The guard bobbed his head in apology, gave a little wave, and fumbled with a key to the large padlock through the thick chain around the gate.

Lights came on in the house behind them.

The lock fell open and the older man pushed, leaning into it to make the gate swing open.

Carol waited until the gap widened barely enough for the truck, then shot through, driving as Axe guessed she'd seen her captors drive.

Axe looked back. The guard worked to push the gates closed. Behind him, a burly man in pajamas and slippers emerged from the front door of the house, waving his arms angrily, questioning the early morning disruption.

Then the gate swung shut and the old guard replaced the chain and padlock.

Carol drove the vehicle expertly down the packed dirt road, going fast.

Not bad, all things considered.

"Well done, Carol. I'm Alex. Axe for short. Stop at the intersection ahead. I'll drive using the night vision goggles. It'll make it harder for them to follow. We can chat as we drive, but right now I have to check in."

Carol nodded in the glow of the dash lights. She looked tense but grateful. "Thanks for coming to get me. Sorry for the trouble."

"No problem." He clicked his long-range radio. "Fox One to Fox Two?"

Kelton Kellison's voice, sounding focused, responded instantly. The boat idled in the background.

"Fox Two to Fox One. Go ahead."

"Change of plans. Exfil location two, six minutes. Me and guest."

Miles away, on the river, Kelton confirmed. "Location two, six minutes."

"Out."

Soto La Marina River
Soto La Marina
Tamaulipas, Mexico

Kelton pushed the throttle forward. Instantly, the rented fishing boat sped downstream toward the bend in the river.

Trouble.

The fallback position meant a switch from an easy rescue to a difficult one. The river wound its way east to the coast, and the road to the north ran parallel to it for miles, coming within sight of it often.

If the pursuers sped up and got lucky, they could shoot at them from the road. Or get in front of them and set up an ambush.

If they learned about the boat.

The extraction revolved around getting to the boat cleanly and keeping it a secret.

He sped up, pushing the boat. His night vision goggles helped, but he had little experience with them, making the rush down the river nerve-wracking. Still, he had to make it around the bend long before Axe's pursuers came close enough to see him.

I've got this.

He stayed in the middle of the river, following the few channel markers showing the safe passageway to the other drunk tourists that frequented the area.

His years of experience on lakes and rivers with the family speed boat long before he got rich were finally paying off. As the big boat swung safely around the bend in the river, hidden in plenty of time, his smile lit up the night.

He throttled back and sought a place to wait—deep enough for the boat yet out of the main channel. Axe and the nurse would come to him, then it would be an easy trip down the river to the ocean and from there, home.

I wonder if all his ops are this easy.

Soto La Marina

Tamaulipas, Mexico

When Carol stopped at the T intersection, Axe slid over, and they awkwardly switched places. He turned off the lights and turned right onto the paved highway as they both buckled in.

"Here's the plan. We'll stop on the far side of the bridge ahead. You know it?"

Carol nodded, easy to see in his NVGs.

"We're meeting a boat. It will take us down the river to the ocean, then home."

"I don't have my passport. They took it."

"Not a problem. We'll—"

Axe saw headlights from the compound, behind them and to the right across the dark desert terrain.

"Looks like we have company. Someone doesn't want you to leave." Over the low scrub brush, the compound gate opened. An SUV shot through, scraping its sides on the gate with a shower of sparks.

A second truck followed, and a third, then the last one, all moving fast up the road.

The lights of Axe's SUV were off and the night was dark. The pursuers wouldn't know if they turned right or left at the T intersection, so the smart play would be to send two vehicles in each direction. Axe could handle two. He'd done it before.

He smiled at the memory of the night he had rescued Haley and started his new life as an essential member of Nalen's team.

Besides, they had a decent head start. At this speed, they would reach the bridge—and Kelton's boat—in less than five minutes. It would be close, but it should be fine.

Then, from behind the compound, the dune buggy's lights bounced crazily across the desert at them on an intercept course.

4

THE BRIDGE

Axe gripped the steering wheel tightly and pushed the SUV hard.

The two guards in the dune buggy came on fast. The lightweight machine bounced crazily over the desert, weaving around bigger bushes and a few scraggly trees, but always aiming for a spot on the road ahead where they were sure to meet the SUV.

If the truck is bulletproof, what do they think they're going to accomplish? Are they seriously going to ram us?

The dune buggy would intercept them soon. And all four of the other SUVs had turned right at the intersection, onto the paved road, following them.

NVGs? Or did they guess correctly?

He could stay ahead of the SUVs. It would be tight, but he already had an idea for the bridge. The guys in the dune buggy, though, were another story. Axe would do tremendous damage to it if they rammed him. They had to be too smart to try it. But no matter what, he had to lose them. For his plan to work, he needed to be out of sight of his pursuers for a minute. Thirty seconds at a minimum.

Axe eyed Carol sitting calmly next to him, looking like a grandmother out for a ride to the grocery store. From the file Haley had put together, he knew she had been an emergency room nurse for over forty years, all of them spent at big-city hospitals in New York. She'd retired at sixty-two and went on a Caribbean cruise vacation.

Then she got back to work, volunteering in Mexico, helping in small villages or wherever a nurse was needed.

She might look frumpy, but she could handle herself. With her short-cropped, straight gray hair and suntanned face, she radiated calm competence.

The dune buggy barreled toward them, going airborne every few feet. Carol chuckled as she looked out the window at the spectacle, sounding even more like a dear, sweet grandmother. "That would be Jorge and Enrique. Brothers. Not the brightest bulbs. Hotheads. They patrol at night together because no one can stand them, for one. Two—if they weren't working, they'd be partying all night and sleeping half the day. The dune buggy was the boss' idea. A toy to make their job interesting so they'd pay attention and do it."

Axe pushed the SUV as fast as it would go. The speedometer displayed kilometers per hour, and he didn't take the time to do the calculation, but they were flying.

"Dollars to donuts you don't have to worry about them," she added.

As she finished speaking, the dune buggy hit an unexpected dip, too deep for the large wheels and off-road suspension to handle. The nose slammed into the ground and the back end kept going, flipping into the air.

The vehicle landed upside down on its roll bars, wheels still spinning, nose pointed back in the direction it had come. Its headlights lit up the desert, though the three bright lights mounted to the roll bar must have been crushed.

A few seconds later, two figures fell out of the seats and staggered to their feet.

One joined the other on his side and they squatted, attempting to push the vehicle back onto its wheels.

Seriously?

Then Axe and Carol flashed by.

"They're too dumb to give up," Carol said. "And that dune buggy is top of the line. They've flipped it before. It won't be long before they're back at it."

"Shouldn't matter. We're almost there."

"What's the plan?"

"I'll drop you on the bridge and drive the truck into the ditch. Hopefully, it will distract them—looking for us in the desert—long enough to buy us the time we need. We jump into the river. It's deep enough. We'll swim downstream, staying hidden and letting the current do much of the work. Our boat is waiting around the first bend."

Carol's previously calm demeanor vanished instantly. She crossed her arms, hugging herself tightly. It might have been a trick of the night vision goggles, but he swore her face went pale.

"Problem?" He could see the bridge ahead. He checked behind them. The four SUVs were far back. The dune buggy was upright again and nearing the road, the headlights skewed instead of pointing straight ahead.

She glanced at him, struggling to keep it together. "I can't swim."

"At all? You never learned?"

"I grew up in New York City. Never had the opportunity."

He flashed back to his first op with Haley, months before, when he slipped to safety into the water after being bitten—for a second time—by a vicious guard dog.

"It wasn't a priority for my family," Carol continued. "We were poor and lived in the Bronx. The ocean might as well have been another world."

"Okay, it's easy. I'll be right there with you, like a lifeguard."

She squirmed in her seat.

There must be more.

"I'm also kind of afraid of the water… more like terrified."

The road curved slightly. Just enough, he hoped, to screen them from the pursuers. "How terrified? Like respectful fear—or phobia?"

"Pretty close to phobia, but not quite." She hesitated, then whispered, "Maybe."

"Then this will be an interesting night for both of us."

Not even a smile? That was a good one.

They were near the bridge. "Get ready. Stand near the railing and I'll be right back."

She nodded in the darkness, still hugging herself. She took a few deep breaths, though, and seemed to calm down.

They reached the bridge. "Hold on."

Axe slammed on the brakes, flinging both of them hard against the seat belts. The SUV shuddered to a stop.

"Out, now!" Carol already had her belt undone and the door open. As soon as she stepped clear, Axe accelerated while undoing his seat belt.

Past the edge of the bridge, he hit the button on the dash to set the cruise control and pointed the SUV down the road.

This is going to hurt.

He jumped out, hitting the asphalt and rolling to dissipate the energy. His knees screamed at him. His body would be black and blue for days.

That's going to leave a mark.

The SUV continued down the straight road, tracking true. A right-hand curve a half-mile ahead, east toward the ocean, would stop it if it didn't drift into the ditch before then.

Axe ran back to the bridge at a full sprint. They didn't have a moment to waste. In the green glow of the NVGs, he saw Carol mumbling, giving herself a pep talk.

"Stand on the railing!"

She looked at him. For a second, he worried she would refuse. He didn't have a backup plan. He had a knife, the stun gun, and the guard's M4 slung on his back. But the admiral had insisted—no killing unless they couldn't help it. No international incidents. He and Kelton were private citizens, unsanctioned assets. If they got into trouble, the weight would fall squarely—only—on themselves. There would be no rescue, no diplomatic negotiations. If caught by the authorities, they would rot in a Mexico jail... until the cartel had them killed. Or they would die tonight and vanish into a shallow grave in the desert.

Instead of refusing him, Carol hesitantly stepped onto the narrow railing, her short legs struggling to reach.

He could see the glow from the lights of the trucks and dune buggy approaching. They were out of time.

Carol carefully pushed herself fully onto the railing, ending in an awkward squat. She clung to it with one hand and glanced back at Axe, running full tilt toward her. "I don't think—"

He didn't hear the rest. He barely slowed when he grabbed her, flinging them both into the air as the light of the dune buggy started around the corner up the road.

Axe rolled their bodies so he would take the brunt of the impact. Ideally, he would have jumped feet first from this height.

Life is hard.

He held Carol in a bear hug as they hit the water. The impact took his breath away. As he sank, refusing to let go of the nurse, he flashed back to his SEAL training. During the second phase, after Hell Week, they took dive training. One of their many challenges had been to fix problems with their breathing apparatus—from the mouthpiece to the tank—while blindfolded. The instructors delighted in messing up the gear and making them struggle, their breath running out, fighting desperately to keep calm and work the problem.

The instructors also frequently "helped" by slapping and jostling them. It taught focus and how to control fear in the face of adversity.

Like now—underwater, out of breath, pursued by dangerous criminals, holding onto a terrified woman who desperately wanted out of the water and had the strength of two SEAL instructors.

Axe kicked to the surface.

I hope I don't have to knock her out.

Carol struggled furiously in his arms, slippery as an eel. With an extra push, she slid out of his grasp, panicked and fighting for her life. Her elbow caught his forehead, a glancing, underwater blow that still hurt.

Then one of her flailing legs connected with his groin as she kicked for the surface. He lost what little air he had left, doubling over underwater.

Her running shoe connected with his chin as she shot upward past him.

Embrace the suck.

He had to accept how bad the situation was and deal with the problem. First, though, he had to breathe.

Almost as important, he had to stop the nurse from swallowing half the river, drawing their pursuers to them by making noise, or drowning him.

Not necessarily in that order.

He kicked away, getting more separation from the terrified woman. With his stomach heaving, desperate for air, he still didn't panic. He'd been in trouble underwater before and knew he had time.

His head broke the surface to hear the sounds of Carol gasping, sputtering, crying, and splashing.

"Quiet!" he hissed from a few feet away. "Focus and relax. You're fine."

His words didn't get through to her. The whites of her eyes shone in the night, easy to see even with the NVGs dangling around his neck.

Nope, not healthy fear of the water. Definitely paranoia.

"Help me!"

"Not so loud!" he said, too loudly himself. Above and behind him, on the bridge, the roar of the pursuing vehicles got louder.

He moved closer to her warily—for good reason. As soon as he came within reach, she grabbed him, pushing him under to keep her head above water.

This time, he kept his body turned to the side, so his thigh took the kick from her leg, instead of his crotch.

I don't have time to calm her down. She's going to hate me after this...

Axe swam away underwater, then surfaced and quickly moved closer to her from behind. He snaked his arm around her neck and pulled her close, keeping her head above water—which she liked. She stopped struggling so much, but still made too much noise, gasping and splashing.

He increased the pressure—which she didn't like. In a flash, Carol realized what he was doing. Or thought she did, at least.

"I'm not killing you to save myself. I'm only knocking you out. Sorry."

She had no leverage and didn't want her face to go underwater, so she could only flail as he choked her unconscious. It took a few seconds but felt longer as truck after truck sailed by on the bridge behind them.

The nurse went limp, making her much easier to handle. Axe supported her body like a lifeguard, keeping her face out of the water. He kicked hard, guiding them closer to the riverbank.

He'd gotten them near it when she came to with a shudder.

"Carol," he whispered. "Relax. You're safe and floating. Do not struggle. If you do, we die."

Did I time it right?

Axe wanted to reach her mind while she regained consciousness. Not too early, or she wouldn't comprehend what he said. Too late and she would have already entered panic mode.

She tensed but didn't struggle.

"Perfect. I've got you."

He kept kicking, moving them swiftly downstream, away from discovery.

"You okay?" he whispered, knowing how well sound traveled over water.

"I can't believe I'm doing this."

"You're doing great."

Like the trauma nurse she had been, she adapted quickly to the challenging situation. They made good time with Axe swimming quietly, towing her along.

He glanced back every few strokes but saw no one searching the riverbank. Yet. The empty SUV and lack of footprints in the sand around where it had crashed wouldn't fool them long. The river would be the next place they looked.

But with any luck, they wouldn't immediately consider the possibility of a boat so far upstream from the ocean and downstream from the nearest town. Axe hated relying on luck for an op, but with his team limited to Haley and himself, supported by the inexperienced former billionaire Kelton Kellison, it was what it was. A hodgepodge team of three.

Good times.

They rounded the sharp bend in the river. Axe guided them closer to the bank. The hulking shape of the fishing boat loomed in front of them, exactly where it should be. Kelton stood at the stern, watching for them.

A minute later they were on the boat, moving slowly and quietly downstream. Kelton handled it expertly while Axe took Carol into the tiny forward cabin. She stood, shivering and hugging herself.

"You did well," he said. "Thanks for trusting me. Towel and dry clothes for you here. I'll be up top helping navigate and prepping in case we're followed. Stay here and out of sight. How much effort do you think they'll make hunting for you?"

Carol toweled off her face and short hair, looking very relieved to be out of the water. "I have no idea. I don't even know why they took me prisoner. I'm just a nurse helping poor villagers." She turned her back and stripped off her dripping sweatshirt, wrapping herself in a towel. "Thanks for rescuing me. And in the river." She looked over her shoulder at him. "You choked me out!"

"Yeah, sorry."

Not really, though.

"No, it's fine. It worked."

"Get changed and warmed up. I have to help up top. We're not out of this yet."

Axe gave her privacy and joined Kelton on deck. The night protected them as they motored quietly downstream, balancing speed with the noise level of the engines. Soon, their pursuers would realize the nurse hadn't escaped into the desert on foot. They would consider the possibility of a second vehicle first and send trucks down the road... which occasionally paralleled the river.

If they were smart, they'd also search the river, both along the bank and in the water.

But how smart are they? Will they guess we had a boat waiting? If they do, will they have a boat at their disposal to look for us?

And would they waste time searching on their own, or call it into their bosses right away?

They were far enough away from the bridge. "Gun it," Axe ordered.

The boat surged forward, with Kelton's huge smile glowing in Axe's NVGs.

5

THE CAG

Haley needed desperately to move. Pacing would be perfect. But she couldn't draw attention to herself in the office, so she sat quietly, hiding the turmoil inside.

The stress of knowing she had placed Axe and Kelton in harm's way felt heavy on her shoulders. Her mind, normally incredibly focused, bounced from one fear to another.

What have I missed? Could I have created a better plan? What if they get hurt, captured, or killed?

Despite her best efforts, the biggest question of all kept spilling into conscious thought.

What the hell am I—a twenty-one-year-old analyst—doing running an unsanctioned international operation to rescue an American citizen held hostage by a Mexican drug cartel?

She abruptly stood in her tiny gray-fabric cubicle and looked around the room. The night shift analysts worked, many with headphones on to better focus, though the room was quiet, as always. The clatter of keyboards and mouse clicks competed only with the hum of the bright fluorescent lights overhead. A few of her colleagues glanced up from their screens to look at her. Over the past year, she had gained a reputation as a renegade who had been right on every major prediction. She had an uncanny knack for finding threats long before anyone else. She was going places.

Even in the tight-lipped, secrecy-filled upper echelon of the CAG, rumors abounded. She'd overheard a few. She had the boss's ear. True. Gregory had started to respect her talents more in the past few months.

Another rumor claimed her analytical powers verged on magical. Also true, though overly dramatic. She had incredible focus and trusted her instincts—then used them to work the problem harder than ever. It paid off.

Haley had been told the final rumor by Gregory himself, who had been told by someone on the staff who bravely asked for confirmation or denial, which he refused to provide. It claimed she had killed countless people on an unsanctioned—but ultimately successful—secret mission.

Which, again, was so very true. Her mind flashed to the soccer stadium on the island of St. John, where she had slashed and stabbed enemy guards with a stolen knife.

Don't think about the body count. Focus on the present.

What else could she do to help Axe?

Nothing. He's on his own.

She held her phone, silenced, hoping it would vibrate with a message confirming the successful rescue of the nurse. The woman held a secret. The next piece in the puzzle. Haley could feel it.

Getting the nurse home safely was not only the right thing to do. They needed to debrief the woman to discover the latest threat to the country. But had Haley sabotaged the mission from the onset by suggesting Kelton Kellison as Axe's helper instead of going herself?

Is Kelton an asset or a liability to Axe?

Her first choice had been to send Cody on the operation, but as the new leader—Pioneer—of the Movement, a back-to-nature cult-like organization she, Axe, and Cody had infiltrated a few months before, he couldn't be spared.

She had wanted to go along instead, but Admiral Nalen had dissuaded her. She didn't have the boat-handling skills for the mission. And he said her looks, an advantage infiltrating Stefan Conroy's cult on the last mission, would be a liability on this one.

Axe and Kelton needed to be in stealth mode for this trip. She could have joined them as Kelton's girlfriend again, but Nalen didn't want her noticed and remembered. For the plan to work, they had to get in, get the nurse, and sneak back out.

"No international incidents," Nalen had demanded.

Easier said than done with a man like Axe.

Haley smoothed the wrinkled khakis and blouse she had put on thirty-six hours before and wondered about body odor. She would have to change clothes and sleep at some point—when the op was done and Axe, Kelton, and Carol were safe. Then she could clean up and rest.

Haley didn't make eye contact with the colleagues who glanced her way. She didn't know the night shift crew well—or the day shift, either. A year ago, many ignored the junior analyst in their midst. At best, some had been politely welcoming.

After her recent successes and meteoric rise, a few had offered congratulations for a job well done. Others seemed jealous of her success.

Several were uneasy around her. She overheard one calling her "The Witch."

She couldn't decide if she had earned the nickname because of her winning personality, which she needed to work on, or her ability to picture the entire puzzle after seeing only a few of the pieces—an ability none of the other analysts came close to matching... or understanding.

Haley wondered what her nickname—and reputation—would be if they knew about her most recent operation. They would probably call her "The Killer," if they learned the total body count of bad guys whose lives she had ended. But Gregory, her boss, plus Nancy and Dave, her small team of analysts, had kept their mouths shut. And she had kept many details of the week out of her report.

Her coworkers had a better idea of what she had done nearly a year before on her first operation. Haley had been abducted, thrust from analyst to field agent overnight, killed two men, managed an unsanctioned asset, and provided the warning that saved the New York City area from a catastrophe at the nearby nuclear power plant.

Not to mention writing a report for the President of the United States which caused the "suicide" of the vice president.

Then she had threatened her boss with the same fate as the VP if he was a mole.

Luckily, only the fact she had worked in the field and helped avert a disaster was known. Again, in writing the report of her adventures, she'd kept it simple and left out most of the gory details. People just didn't need to know.

While she couldn't pace without giving away her nervousness and causing the rest of the office to wonder what had her so spun up, she could power walk to the bathroom, then the small employee kitchen. She filled a mug with boiling water and returned to her desk to choose from her stash of herbal teas. No way could her tension level handle caffeine right now.

What were Axe and Kelton doing? By this time, they should have rescued the nurse. They were probably on the boat, escaping down the river.

She could only wait.

But no more sitting around. I have to get to the bottom of this puzzle.

She immersed herself in the data. It was the only way to bring relief.

The tea sat untouched, cooling as she vacuumed up information. Her mind collated data and connected dots. She ran various scenarios the way a chess Grandmaster would analyze potential moves, planning several steps ahead. How did the pieces fit together? What if this connected to that?

She lost herself, speed-reading reports, rumors, and raw data. Reported sightings of suspected terrorists, the home life of political figures—both allies and enemies. Intercepted phone calls, dispatches from ambassadors, personal email, and recorded phone calls from around the world which the AI had flagged for review. Hundreds of reports from spies and informants.

Plus the local newspapers, which often had a better handle on actions, activities, and trends than could be found in America's extensive data collection network.

From it all, the pieces sat, somehow connected. A threat was out there.

Mexico.

China.

Drugs.

Money.

Her skin tingled and her heart pounded.

This is real. Danger is coming.

What scared her most, aside from having no real clue what it meant, was her sense of dread when she considered the data.

She couldn't shake the feeling. An attack on the country was in the works. It threatened the lives of Americans. But she had a feeling it was bigger than that.

We almost had World War Three a few months ago, brought on by Stefan "Pioneer" Conroy. Am I seeing ghosts, or is there another threat to world peace coming?

If she and the other analysts couldn't figure it out soon, an unspeakable horror would engulf her beloved country, and possibly the world, if she believed her hunch.

Haley finally took a break, pushing away from the keyboard and sipping her cold tea. She couldn't find any new pieces for the puzzle. For the time being, she could go no further. She had to wait for Axe to report. The nurse—Carol—would provide more data. It might be enough to pull it all together and stop the attack.

She hoped.

6

THE CALL

Mansion of Arturo Ruiz
Outside Aldama
Tamaulipas, Mexico
Five Hours South of Brownsville, Texas

The cell phone's unique ringtone woke Arturo Ruiz instantly, despite the early morning hour.

He didn't panic, though his heart pounded the instant he recognized the sound. It meant one of his people had experienced an emergency that not only required waking him but was deemed worth the risk of electronic communication to report.

He pressed the green button on the phone's screen without putting on his glasses, though he sat up and swung his legs out of bed in case he had to leave immediately. His middle-aged body surged with adrenaline.

He didn't speak. No doubt his voiceprint had been identified in the past fifteen years of running one of Mexico's notorious drug cartels.

"Mama, the puppy has run away! We cannot find her anywhere," a young woman's near-hysterical voice sobbed.

He could picture the scene. One of his captains would have enlisted a daughter or maid to make the call to confuse any potential listeners—like the United States Drug Enforcement Agency or the few Mexican authorities who hadn't accepted his bribes.

While he and his men had not established a specific code, he only had one female captive at the moment: the American nurse who had seen too much.

He hung up the phone without comment, ran a hand through his thick, salt-and-pepper hair, smoothing it into place as he contemplated plans of action, then stood and padded to the door. He released the deadbolt as quietly as he could to not bother his wife any more than the phone already had, then swung open the reinforced steel door. His night guard stood at the ready.

"Someone shall drive to town immediately. There, they will call the General and tell him to use his helicopters to search the area of Soto la Marina for our missing guest. He is to work with the area captain. Do you understand?"

"Yes, *Jefe*," the guard said with a small bow, his respect bordering on reverence.

Arturo stepped back inside the spacious bedroom and locked the door. The guard would maintain his post. He took his role as bodyguard seriously, standing armed and alert the entire night, ready to die defending his boss.

Instead, he would use the short-range radio to call a runner, who would come to him, receive the message, and take it to a responsible lieutenant to act upon. The message would safely be called in from the center of the nearby town of Aldama within fifteen minutes.

Arturo lay down in bed and pulled the covers over him. His wife liked the room chilly. She stirred but had either not woken or had gone quickly back to sleep.

He lay awake, considering his problems.

There was no doubt America's National Security Agency had recorded the call. But the odds of the artificial intelligence software flagging a routine call for human analysis were slim.

For safety, the woman who called him would place another call to a number similar to his. That phone was in a room in Monterey, Mexico, in a large, crowded apartment building. The young woman would repeat the message, asking why she had been hung up on by her mother. The phone call would be handled by the woman on duty, one of many well-trained actresses employed exclusively by his organization. They sat in the comfortable apartment, reading or watching TV their entire shifts, waiting for the rare chance to perform an improvised sketch for an exclusive audience: the men and women of America's and Mexico's law enforcement who sought to catch and punish him.

It cost him a few thousand dollars per month for the emergency "wrong number" precaution, but the money was worth it. His foes in America were persistent and intelligent. All his predecessors had underestimated their determination to rid their country of illegal drugs. Even while the hypocritical United States doctors prescribed more and more pharmaceuticals to a population that, inexplicably, desired escape from what his countrymen and women would consider a life of ease and leisure.

The Americans blamed him—and the others like him—for their own problem.

But in this situation, the drugs didn't matter. In exchange for much-needed cash, he had agreed to provide security services and handle the messier tasks of a secretive organization. So far, they had been asked to procure "volunteers" for medical experiments, then disposed of the bodies. They had also been asked to hold the nurse securely, allow her to communicate occasionally via censored email, and not harm her. A trusted captain had housed her in his own home for the past weeks.

The Americans would not find the call suspicious, but losing the nurse could be catastrophic. His local captain believed she did not know the importance of the knowledge she possessed. But if she had been rescued from the compound two hours north, it meant someone was either on the trail of the information or a relative had hired a competent team to extract her.

Perhaps the General's helicopters would find her. If so, he would authorize a permanent solution to the problem. The time had come.

Better to apologize for the loss of her life than admit she had almost gone free.

If she wasn't found? He would deal with it if necessary. He and the other cartel leaders were at a critical juncture. This problem could not be allowed to derail their secret plans.

7

THE RIVER

Soto La Marina River
Tamaulipas, Mexico

A military helicopter flew up the river in front of Axe and Kelton, gaining elevation as it approached. Axe considered alternatives while Kelton kept the boat expertly positioned next to a large concrete support pylon in the darkness under the bridge.

The helicopter flew without searchlights, meaning the pilots and spotters had night vision goggles. Axe had a defense against those—three incredibly bright lights mounted together to temporarily blind a pilot, but it had to be a last resort.

I could shoot them.

He still had the young guard's M4, slung on his back during the swim. But harming a military helicopter with it would be difficult. Killing the pilots would be his only hope.

And then hello, international incident.

Nalen would be pissed.

But we'd be alive and free instead of captured or dead.

No, the best move was to hide.

Everyone wants to kick in doors and blow shit up, but it's not always the right way to go.

In the SEAL Ethos, the creed he lived by still, they called themselves the "quiet professionals."

That has to extend to missions, too. We don't just blow up all we see. We bring violence of action when needed—but we're not afraid to sneak in, get the job done, and get out without firing a shot if it benefits the mission.

But at some point soon, the cartel would add patrol boats to the hunt.

I might have to shoot my way out, after all. Sorry, Admiral.

The bridge they hid under was the last one until the open ocean a few miles away. The stealth approach wouldn't work much longer.

Driving the SUV into the ditch had fooled their pursuers for a while, at least. But the helicopter meant they were serious about finding the woman. The enemy had figured an escape to the river made the most sense.

"I'm surprised it took them so long," Kelton whispered, reading his mind. His voice quavered with fear.

The man's smart and perceptive, but I don't think he's cut out for this lifestyle.

"They might have had to call for permission—or find military units with helicopters they could bribe."

The helicopter banked right, then a few seconds later turned left to follow the road, going low and slow, probably scanning the scrub desert for signs they were on foot.

Their hiding place under the bridge had worked.

Axe made an impulsive decision. "Go for it. As fast as you can for a few minutes until we see or hear another chopper."

Kelton gunned it and the twin engines throbbed. "Our wake is easy to see at these speeds," he yelled over the noise.

"We have to risk it. We're out of time." He clung to the rail. The boat tilted hard as Kelton swung it around the latest tight bend in the river. Axe looked at the former billionaire's face as he concentrated on his task. Kelton had changed in the last few months. Losing his homes, megayacht, and company had left him adrift. When Axe and Haley had approached him about helping on the op, he had agreed, taking the planning incredibly seriously. He found a renewed sense of purpose in being America's newest unsanctioned asset.

They swung around another tight bend at a speed Axe wasn't at all comfortable with. But Kelton claimed to have memorized the river from the bay to the city upstream from the compound. He stood, focused but not tense, handling the large boat with ease.

"Cut it!" Axe had a feeling. Time to hide. He hadn't heard anything—he couldn't, not over the engines. And he hadn't seen anything, either. But his well-honed sense of danger told him it was time to change tactics.

Or am I too cautious? Getting old and slowing down?

Kelton responded instantly, throttling back the engines to idle and aiming for the side of the river. A large tree stood at an angle, jutting over the water. At a different time, Axe would have loved to set up a rope swing. He could easily spend an afternoon leaping from the river's edge, swinging, then letting go to splash into the cool water before climbing the bank, having more beer, and doing it again.

Not tonight. Right now, they had to risk running into submerged rocks, logs, or getting stuck in the mud.

They drifted smoothly into place. Kelton goosed the engine every few seconds to keep them pointed downstream while remaining under the many tree branches. They were well hidden.

Will the wake point them right to us?

Faintly, he heard a helicopter approaching. This one came from ahead of them and to their left, following the road a half-mile away from the river.

The bird flew low and slow, like the last one. If the men in it stayed focused on the road, they were safe. If it turned south, it would fly right over them.

They're serious about getting Carol back—they have at least two choppers hunting us.

Kelton glanced at him, looking much more afraid.

It's finally sinking in. This is life and death.

"How did you know to stop?" His whisper was so quiet, Axe could barely hear the tiny tremble of fear.

After years of combat experience, every man in the Teams had developed a feeling for danger. When to run, when to stop. None of them could explain it. Many claimed it was God's hand protecting them. Others shrugged and laughed it off, not caring what, how, or why—as long as it worked. Axe figured it might be dumb luck. He had no way to test whether his hunches were correct. He'd lost count of the times he'd had a feeling, stopped, and nothing happened. Did he stay safe because he stopped, or was there no danger to begin with?

But he still relied on his gut. If it told him to hold up and hide because another helicopter was coming, he listened.

The helicopter banked toward them, leaving the road behind.

"Don't move an inch," Axe whispered through clenched teeth.

The helicopter passed two hundred yards behind them, then banked sharply, flying up the river, slowly following every bend.

The pilot had made a mistake. Instead of covering the river from the bay a few miles downstream, the pilot had focused on the road first, then switched to the river, just missing them.

But both helicopters would turn around at some point and search again.

"Let's go," Axe said.

It took Kelton several seconds to painstakingly work the boat safely away from the shore. Then he gunned it again, speeding down the river in the glow of their night vision goggles, getting closer to freedom with every second.

"Coming up to the bay, just around the next bend," Kelton yelled. The man truly knew the river.

He'll be back in business—and a billionaire again—in no time. I'm lucky to have used him tonight. This would have been vastly more difficult on my own, driving a jet ski, or with Haley piloting the boat.

Ahead lay open water and the marina where they'd rented a dock for the night.

Kelton glanced at him. "Full throttle," Axe said.

If a helicopter appeared, or he sensed one, they would ease off and—hopefully—make it to the marina to hide in plain sight. They could slip out with the rest of the boats at dawn, less than an hour away.

But no choppers appeared as they gunned it across the bay, skirting the no-wake zone of the marina.

The chopper that flew over the bridge covered the lower river, then switched to the road. The second one covered the road, then switched to the river. We were in exactly the right place at the right time for them to miss us.

Several minutes later, they were in the Gulf, heading straight out to sea to put as much distance between them and land as possible. After a while, they would turn left, north, and cruise home with fishing lines out. Maybe they could catch dinner on the way. The trip back to Brownsville would take several hours, but at least they were safe. By noon they'd have Carol back in the United States.

When in cell phone range, they'd get on coms for a debrief with Haley. She needed intel and Carol had it… even if she didn't know what it was.

The nurse lay curled on the bed, asleep despite the pounding of the boat over the predawn swell. He hoped Haley could access whatever knowledge lay trapped in Carol's mind, work her magic, and figure out the next step.

If Haley's worried about a threat, so am I.

8

ROJO

Ruiz Cartel Drug Lab *Rojo*
Near Sierra De Tamaulipas Mountain Range
Tamaulipas, Mexico
Four hours south of Brownsville, Texas

The police helicopters appeared over the Sierra De Tamaulipas mountain range at dawn. The lookout posted on the mountain radioed in.

While the specific date and time were unexpected, a raid on the lab was not a complete surprise. The national government had been cracking down on the Ruiz cartel, working with the American Drug Enforcement Agency, using AI to predict likely lab locations and satellite surveillance to narrow down suspected sites.

And the dark clouds guaranteed tonight would be an excellent night for a hit on the lab.

Within two minutes of the warning, the workers evacuated the underground lab. They hurried into their designated off-road SUVs, hidden from surveillance in the back of the cattle barn.

Each truck's assigned driver drove their cross-country route to avoid the government vehicles approaching on the one road leading to the ranch.

The workers would be dropped at out-of-the-way safe houses—in the countryside and the nearby town of Soto la Marina—where they would remain hidden until given the all-clear.

Every shift practiced the escape and evasion plan at least twice a month. Each worker knew the risks of capture—not as much from the government, who would interrogate them and apply pressure to talk. Few worried about their tactics, as uncomfortable as they could be.

The punishment from Señor Ruiz for being captured was much, much worse, whether or not they gave up information.

One team, however, did not evacuate. They sat silently, every light and power supply turned off, including the ventilation system which brought fresh air from the surface down to the lab buried deep underground.

Luis Angelo, chief of security of the Ruiz cartel's drug Lab *Rojo*, sat locked in the control room for his usual six PM to six AM shift. In front of him in the dark were three blinking red buttons. He alternated between watching them flash and looking through the old-fashioned periscope. Starting at eye level, it extended through the concrete ceiling, forty feet of dirt, and nearly twenty feet of cow shit composting in an enormous pile four hundred yards from the barn housing the other drug lab. The periscope used no power, to help prevent detection. It could survey three-hundred-sixty degrees, and easily remained hidden by the tires holding down the white tarp covering the manure.

Despite Luis' lofty title of security chief, he had one function. The government would raid the lab in the barn, then they would destroy it. It was how the game was played between the cartels and the police—at least, the ones *Señor* Ruiz couldn't bribe.

But to dissuade them from future assaults, they would be punished.

It was a new escalation from *Jefe* himself. Anyone in the government, army, or police not willing to take bribes would be dealt with severely. More so, even, than in the past.

If the authorities raided the barn and found the lab underneath, Luis would destroy it all.

If the police were at the ranch for more than just the first laboratory and found his hidden, secondary lab for making the more profitable drug, he would blow it—and himself—as well.

If he didn't, his mother and father, his wife, son, and daughter, and every other relative, would be tortured. Their agony would be on his head.

He knew what the cartel would do to them. His own life meant nothing in comparison. His finger moved to the clear plastic cover over the left button and flipped it up, preparing to kill himself. He would not hesitate if needed.

Upon hearing the early warning from the sentry in the mountains, he had shut down his underground bunker and given the evacuation order to the regular lab.

As he watched through the periscope, government armored vehicles sped toward the barn and other buildings of the ranch. He waited, hoping, and breathed a sigh of relief when the helicopters hovered over the field behind the barn housing the main lab. Six black-clad police slid expertly down ropes there instead of approaching his location.

Captain Hernandez, commander of the operation, watched the action at the barn from the helicopter as it rose and moved to safety after dropping off the men. He sat in the copilot's seat wearing assault gear that matched what his men wore—camouflage fatigues, armored plate carrier with extra magazines, and an assault rifle. His role this morning, however, was strictly command and control.

"Prepare for the assault," he spoke into his radio microphone. The men knew exactly what to do, but some of them would be nervous. The orders of a confident leader would settle them down.

Today we take down a lab, at least.

At best, they would gain the valuable information he hoped for.

Luis flipped up the plastic cover on the other two buttons and held his finger over the middle one.

The police from the vehicles rushed to the front of the barn, lining up along the wall near the door.

The men from the helicopter did the same at the rear.

"Breech the barn," Hernandez ordered. The area looked deserted, but you never knew.

Could they have been tipped off? Did they know we were coming?

Below him, his men executed the plan perfectly, entering both from the front and rear.

Luis watched, impressed, as both teams entered simultaneously.

There is no doubt. They will find the lab.

When all the enemy had breached the barn—except a small contingent forming a security perimeter—he pushed the middle button without remorse.

The explosives hidden throughout—shaped to direct their damage inward—detonated with a force that shook the ground inside his small safe room, leaving the barn remarkably intact but decimating everything and everyone inside.

Smoke poured out both the front and back doors.

The pilot banked the helicopter away from the explosion and smoke, which made it impossible for Hernandez to see the barn.

"Turn back, turn back!" he yelled.

Over the radio, the screams of his wounded men went quiet quickly.

The ones not killed instantly are already dead.

"Get in there," he ordered over the radio. "Search for survivors. Medics to the barn."

Luis shook his head at the scene, resigned to the order but regretting the loss of life, even if the men were the enemy. The police who had remained outside had probably been bitterly disappointed to not be part of the main assault, but now they ran toward the building to attempt a rescue.

After they entered, he pushed the second button. More explosives detonated, though he didn't feel it. The secondary bombs sent shrapnel flying through the space. The remaining men would die also, but more slowly.

Their leaders would hesitate before raiding a Ruiz compound again.

Hernandez wanted to tear off his headset to avoid hearing the screams of agony coming from his men after the second explosion.

I should have been there.

He worked the radio, calling up the quick reaction force and medical helicopters, but there wasn't much he could do.

"Get me on the ground," he told the pilot. The man looked at him with fear in his eyes and hesitated.

Hernandez moved his hand, subtly angling the assault rifle hanging from the chest strap to point at the pilot.

"Now."

The chopper moved to an open area and dropped him off. With a prayer, he rushed into the barn to render what first aid and comfort he could to his dying men.

Luis stood and took two minutes to creep in a circle, looking through the periscope. As unlikely as it was that anyone was still alive on the ground, or for the helicopter pilot to watch his area in the middle of the catastrophic raid, it paid to be cautious.

He had to see if more soldiers were coming. The lives of everyone he loved depended on it.

Nothing stirred nearby.

When he returned to his original view, he saw another helicopter arriving behind the barn. Six more men slid down ropes. In the front, more armored vehicles had pulled up. The men moved cautiously into the barn to render aid to their injured comrades.

Luis sat, waiting. He had done his part. There were no more explosives.

While the police investigated the incident, he and his colleagues would remain safely hidden under the manure.

It would be a day or two before he could relax. In the meantime, he would stand every few minutes and slowly turn the periscope. He would snack, pee in a bottle at his post, and pray the devastation at the barn would occupy the authorities completely. He hoped no one had sold them out, and that none of the soldiers would be interested in investigating the gigantic pile of cow shit with the hidden entrance to his lab in the back.

Once the authorities left, the others in his lab would get back to work, preparing the expensive drugs the cartel desperately needed to sell.

9

THE REPORT

Compound of Arturo Miguel Hidalgo Ruiz
Outside Aldama
Tamaulipas, Mexico

Arturo's trusted right-hand man, Hugo, stood in front of him. The shorter, thin man with a lopsided goatee shifted his weight and squirmed under Arturo's steady gaze. Being the ruthless leader of one of the five drug cartels in Mexico made all who reported to Arturo hesitate to tell him bad news, though he would never harm Hugo.

He is more nervous than I have ever seen, Arturo thought.

"What is it?" Arturo asked.

"*Jefe*, I have bad news. Last night—or rather, this morning—was not good to us. Our operations were hit twice."

Twice? No wonder he is scared.

"I will not shoot the messenger, Hugo," he reassured the man. "Just tell me what happened."

"First, the phone call you received. The nurse got away, and we have not found her. She was rescued by one man."

"One man?"

Hugo opened the plain manila folder in his hands and offered a large, professionally printed, color security camera photo. The detail from the 4K system was remarkable. The picture showed a bearded man, his face covered by camouflage paint, wearing night-vision goggles. Although tinted green because of the night vision security camera, the intruder showed plain as day. He looked like an experienced, professional soldier.

"This man avoided the roving guard patrols, snuck into the captain's compound, rescued the woman, and subdued a man before stealing a vehicle and bluffing his way out of the compound. The man and the nurse were either picked up by another vehicle or escaped down the river. The helicopters found nothing. They vanished, *Jefe*."

Arturo frowned. "People do not vanish."

"Yes, *Jefe*. We continue to search the area. They could be swimming downstream, hiding from our patrols. The local captain is confident they will be found, but I doubt it. Too much time has passed, and the rescuer would have a better plan than simply walking away."

He held the photo. "No weapon?"

"He used a stun gun on the guard in the compound."

"The police, the army, the DEA, none would send one man alone."

Who could it be? A mercenary?

The woman's rescue was a problem. How the authorities—or whoever—had found her was another.

"What is the other bad news?"

Hugo hesitated, then spoke. "Lab *Rojo* was hit last night. But just section One. Two was undetected. The barn was blown up as per standing orders. Approximately eighteen police are dead."

Arturo had grown up in the cartel, starting as an outpost guard and working his way up to *jefe*, boss. He had seen much. Good and bad luck. The twin setbacks of the previous night were concerning, but not catastrophic. Unless...

If we have a mole, infiltrator, or a leak, the situation is very bad.

Hugo must have had the same idea. "An informant may have alerted the authorities—perhaps the Americans—about the nurse. They could have hit the lab to distract us, not understanding your decentralized approach. Or they could have rescued the nurse to cover for the attack on the lab."

Arturo considered the information. It made sense but felt off. The timing wasn't right.

"I have ordered a doubling of the guards at the hotel, in case it is the client who is under attack, and not us," Hugo continued. "Or, if we have a mole in your inner circle..." He trailed off. "I felt it best to have extra protection. If the police should attack, the hotel needs to be defended long enough for the contingency plan."

"You have done well, Hugo. Run a check on the plan at the hotel site. In the event of an attack, whether they are after us or the client, I will not be linked to whatever chaos the client has in the works. We cannot have our plans jeopardized, lucrative as the assignment has been."

Not now. We are so close.

He and the other cartel leaders had been working hard for five years, preparing for the time when they would achieve their greatest victory. The finish line was less than a year away. They had needed the money from guarding the nurse, providing "volunteers" for the scientists in the basement of the hotel, and taking care of the bodies afterward. The job had helped fund their terribly expensive long-term project. But with the finish line so close, he would gladly cut ties with his American client to protect his own interests.

I'll wait to notify the American.

There was a chance, however small, the nurse would be recaptured.

"Flood the area around the compound, the river, and the coast with people to supplement the search for this man and the nurse. Get this picture, and hers, to all our people. And if she cannot be found by this afternoon..."

His look said it all. No one responsible for her loss would live long. Their screams of agony would serve as a reminder to any who were allowed to live: do not fail *El Jefe*.

10

BARANOV BRANDS
EIGHT WEEKS EARLIER

Baranov Brands Headquarters
Las Vegas, Nevada

Victor Baranov unbuttoned his suit coat and placed it carefully on its hanger. He left the vest in place. As a concession to the late hour, however, he undid the top button of his starched dress shirt and loosened his tie slightly.

One must keep up appearances, no matter how early in the morning.

He sat primly in his battered leather chair—a true family heirloom. His grandfather had purchased it over one hundred years ago. It had been passed down to his son, and then to himself when he took over the presidency of the company from his father.

In time, he would have passed it along to his son.

If I could stop him from doing drugs in nightclubs until dawn.

By now, Nickie—

Nicholas, he prefers. I must make the effort.

Nicholas should be working at the desk across the long room from him. Taking over divisions of Baranov Brands one by one, gaining familiarity with the company's many parts. He should be making minor mistakes now to avoid harmful ones later when he ran the entire company. Like Nicholas' father, grandfather, and great-grandfather before him.

Instead, he screwed around.

Victor neatened his vest, redid the button, and tightened his tie.

I must be diligent and disciplined. Unlike Nicholas.

As usual, it was late—or rather, early—and while tired, he wasn't sleepy. He moved his mouse to wake the computer, then entered his complex password. He had work to do.

Another hour, then maybe I'll be able to rest.

His mind drifted as the computer connected to the secure video app. At fifty-five, he should be perfecting his golf and tennis games. Traveling. Spoiling grandchildren. But with Nicholas a hard-partying bachelor, none of that could happen.

Probably for the best, given what is coming. The changes will be drastic to my life—and Nicholas'.

His son would be shocked by the upcoming challenges. Keeping him in the dark about his family's secret past had been prudent.

The end game to Victor's life was about to begin, whether he wanted it to or not.

The video feed came online. He watched the scientists at the research site in Mexico as they tested the latest version of the drug.

He leaned closer to the screen, intent on the proceedings.

The plan will probably work without a Level 5 product. But having it will please the ones pushing so hard to produce it in time for whatever chaos they have planned for New Year's Eve.

Research Facility Alpha
In the Basement of the Hotel Riviera Especial de China
Near the town of China
Nuevo Leon, Mexico

Dr. Edgars licked his lips and smoothed his wild white hair. With his full gray beard, tall but stooped frame, and soft belly, he looked every bit his sixty-eight years. He resisted the temptation to look at the dark plastic half-circle on the ceiling behind him. It, and the many others, housed security cameras. Despite the late hour, he knew Mr. Baranov would watch the experiment. There was too much at stake for him not to.

This time it will work. It has to—for both of us.

After a successful career at the biggest pharmaceutical company in the world, researching drugs—and funneling their secrets to his Russian handler—he had been told to quit and join Baranov Brands. His talents were needed on an urgent project.

And despite his efforts over the past year in the state-of-the-art lab, they were behind schedule. The batches of the product had failed for one reason or another. This would be their last chance. The patience of their handler, and whoever he reported to, had run out. Their debt was past due and must be paid now. Their lives, freedom, and honor were at stake.

Through the glass of the one-way mirror, Edgars watched two American college freshmen. They sat on basic straight-back wooden chairs in the observation room, twitching. Agitated. Edgars made a check mark on his chart.

Next to him, six of his colleagues did the same.

It had been twenty-eight minutes since the final consumption of the drug.

The scientists had a detailed pool on a large sheet of paper taped to the nearby wall—out of sight of the surveillance cameras. Listed on the side were the names Lucas and Benjamin—the two students. Across the top, the time was marked in thirty-second intervals. The small squares formed by the grid lines contained the initials of the men of the research team.

Each square allowed the bettor to select both a winner and the amount of time for him to kill the other young man.

Earlier, there had been a fuss when none of the scientists wanted to bet on squares past the four-minute mark. They had to tear up the first paper and create a new one, switching from one-minute increments to thirty-second squares. This allowed bets on more specific timing.

Only one young man would leave the room. As both were evenly matched—healthy, though not athletic, closer to nerds than jocks—the survivor would be a tossup. The trick was to choose the time until death.

Each square cost ten dollars. The winner would come out with a tidy sum, though it didn't matter. They were handsomely paid already but hadn't been allowed out of the research facility in the year since they'd arrived—a surprise to all except Edgars, who had ordered it.

They wouldn't be allowed to leave until they had perfected the drug. And then only after whatever his handler had planned for it on New Year's Eve.

But more than likely, they will all end up in a shallow mass grave nearby.

Luckily, his skills were too essential and debt too great for him to be killed. He would continue to serve Russia, whether at this project or another.

As long as I have my laboratory and research, I don't care. I'll happily do what I'm told. Not only do I owe it to them, it's what I love.

He already had a great idea for the next version of the drug. But first, this level had to be perfected.

The scientists watched through the glass as the eighth member of their group—Jacob, who as the youngest had once again been given the most dangerous assignment—addressed the two men. His white skin blended in with his official-looking white lab coat. After weeks of experiments with different subjects from the local area, the scientists were relatively confident the two freshmen were under control for another few minutes. But you never knew. Hence Jacob's tense and unhappy body language. His position of safety close to the door was an illusion. He knew it, and so did they. The door could only be unlocked from the outside.

Jacob began with the standard opening. "Thank you both for offering your time for the market research on our latest beer. You've been very helpful."

The two men, dark-haired Lucas and blond Benjamin, eyed him, their anger quickly growing to rage. Benjamin bared his teeth at Jacob and growled. Lucas clenched and unclenched his fists.

The scientists watching through the glass all made notes on their clipboards.

The young men had been best friends since grade school. They had applied to the same Texas college so they could attend together. On a lark, they had stopped at the hotel on their way back to school after a short break in Monterey, Mexico. The front desk provided them with two free coupons for a new brand of beer—plus the offer of a small stipend to share their honest opinions.

The spiked beer Edgars and his team had been perfecting.

Jacob smiled nervously at the two students. "The rage you're feeling is an aftereffect of the beer you just finished. It contained a drug we are working on."

Benjamin growled more loudly this time. Both men looked ready to tear Jacob apart.

The scientists leaned forward, noses nearly touching the one-way glass, clipboards in hand and pens poised for notes. Cameras recorded the whole proceeding, but nothing could take the place of their first-hand impressions.

Both freshmen tensed, desperate for more beer. By now, the euphoria from drinking the bottles had worn off. The rage and hallucinations had started.

But they stayed in their seats. Jacob looked relieved.

The first hurdle had been cleared. Both subjects maintained control despite their rapidly altering mental states. The change to the formula had apparently worked.

Each of the seven scientists made a checkmark on their papers.

Inside the room, Jacob frowned as he looked apologetically at the students. "Unfortunately, we've had a production issue. We have no more beer remaining."

His eyes flicked to the door. It would be opened by the guard on the other side only when given the all-clear by unanimous consent from the seven other scientists.

They all held their breath, waiting for the reaction from the college kids.

Benjamin and Lucas, best friends for twelve of their eighteen years, looked at Jacob with malice beyond words. Their hatred gave the jaded scientists chills.

The coming confrontation would be bloody. The janitorial crew would earn their keep—again.

"But we appreciate the feedback you gave us," Jacob continued. "I'll be back shortly with your cash stipend for your help."

Edgars leaned to the side so he could see. His rapid breathing had fogged the window.

Jacob fidgeted and looked as if he were about to pee his pants. The next moment would be the most dangerous. For Jacob—and the entire team in the basement lab. If the timing was off and the new version of the spiked beer worked more quickly than estimated, Jacob would be gladly sacrificed to keep the rest of them safe.

The two young men could not be allowed to leave the room in their current state. They were twitching and looking around. The psychedelic base of the drug had taken hold. The freshmen would start seeing ghosts, wild animals, aliens, or other scary visions based on their fears and imaginations.

But so far, they hadn't attacked. The timer passed the thirty-minute mark.

Perfect.

Jacob turned to the door. Edgars picked up the phone on the wall of the observation room and instantly connected to the guard outside the subject room. "This is Edgars. Permission to open the door."

One by one, the remaining six quickly gave their names and approval to allow their colleague out of the room.

The door opened and Jacob rushed through. The guard pulled the heavy door shut. It locked automatically.

Later, while watching the replay, the scientists noted what happened as the drug in the beer firmly took hold.

With their first target—Jacob—gone, the two best friends turned on each other.

A blood bath followed.

What goes through their heads?

Edgars longed for a way to speak to the subjects, for them to explain what they saw as the drug took over their minds, but it was impossible. They were not rational.

The scientists made check marks on the papers, watched the clock, and used all their professional detachment to observe the violent scene in the room.

At the two-minute, fifteen-second mark, all agreed Lucas must be dead, laying on the linoleum floor with the leg of Benjamin's chair protruding from his head.

Edgars counted his cash from the pool for having correctly guessed Benjamin as the winner between two minutes and two minutes, thirty seconds. For a moment, the surveillance camera was forgotten. Counting the money helped distract Edgars from the gruesome violence he had witnessed once again.

A battered and bloody Benjamin sat calmly on the remaining chair. His face and blond hair were covered with blood.

What did he see before attacking his best friend? A monster?

The rare wild mushrooms, carefully researched and combined to create a drug that produced first euphoria, then hallucinations, and finally rage, had taken a year and a half to develop. But he had done it. The drug did what was needed—and the beer hid the flavor.

The guard at the door opened the small hatch near the floor and slid a paper cup filled with ice-cold beer into the room.

The student rushed for the cup and downed it in one gulp. He waited, eyes closed, then slowly smiled as the bliss hit him.

Edgars made a final note on his paper. When this dose faded, the student would go through the cycle of violence again. With no one in the room, he would pace and growl, looking for a target. But eventually, it would wear off. The young man would be monitored, but if he was like forty-eight percent of the other test subjects, in six to eight hours he would beg either for more beer—or death.

Or, if the man was lucky, he'd only suffer mild longings like fifty-two percent of the other subjects. The odds were on his side.

The memory of the first test subject's suicide sprang unwelcome to mind. How the man had begged for ten straight hours, his voice growing more and more hoarse from the screaming. How they'd restrained him in a straitjacket so he couldn't harm himself. And finally, how he'd still managed to break his neck against the bed frame to stop the pain of withdrawal.

Edgars shuddered. With a force of will, he turned his mind away from the human side of the project and toward the much less messy and troubling scientific data. He was good at switching off his morals. In his job, he had to be.

Baranov Brands Headquarters
Las Vegas, Nevada

Victor closed the window on the computer, logged off, and moved to the couch in his office. The scientists would have a full report by the time he woke from a nap. The brief rest would keep him going until afternoon when he would sleep for another few hours.

A normal night of sleeping eight hours had become problematic. Shorter periods of sleep kept the regrets—and nightmares—at bay.

Mostly.

As he covered himself with the light afghan blanket knitted by his late wife in the months leading to her death, he wondered whether sleep would come. There was much to do and limited time to handle the details. Strain 31 looked promising enough to develop. The scientists—except for Dr. Edgars, who was the only other person who understood the situation, and deadline—would offer warnings and lists of unanswered questions. They would request time for more research and experiments. But he and Edgars had delayed as long as they could. If he were to accomplish the stated goal —and follow the orders he'd been given—production had to start soon.

Has Edgars been stalling as much as I have? Or is he a true believer?

Victor had been ordered to hire Edgars eighteen months before and set him up with a lab and a team. Progress had been made, so six months later, the entire operation had been moved to Mexico.

If this version of the drug hadn't been effective, I would have a good excuse to not go through with it. But now I have no choice.

He couldn't delay any longer. The operation would go forward. And his life would change. Despite being forced into a position not of his making, his family honor and the desire to keep his son alive gave him no way out.

Victor closed his eyes but didn't sleep. He thought of his father and grandfather from years before they passed, when he was a child. A time the three of them were together, attempting to fish. When they told him about his destiny.

Dad had fumbled, trying to get the worm on the hook. They were far up Lake Mead, surrounded only by the reservoir water. No boats could be seen. They were completely alone. The perfect, sunny day felt wonderful. But though magical, it was also strange.

"Why are we out here?" Victor had asked. "We don't fish."

"Today we do," his father replied absently, still struggling with the worm. After another second, the strait-laced businessman gave up. He threw the worm into the water and hung the fishing pole over the side, the hook bare. "We need to talk."

His father and grandfather had shared a look. Granddad cleared his throat. In his new floppy white fishing hat and colorful t-shirt, he looked ridiculous, not at all like the serious, well-dressed, respected elder businessman he was.

"Family is everything, young Victor. Do you agree?" Granddad asked.

Victor had been raised his whole life—all thirteen years so far—on the premise. But he'd also been frequently tested and knew a trick question when he heard it. "Yes, Granddad. Family and honor."

"Exactly." His grandfather nodded with a smile, acknowledging the successful response. "Now, how do you think our company has had so much success?"

This was a new avenue, but Victor was smart and guessed the answer immediately. "You treat the employees like family?"

"Yes. But there is more. Much more to our history, and it is time you understood it all. Including our obligation. When I was a child, barely older than you, I was given a choice."

Victor had heard this part often. "You could stay in Russia, with your brothers and sisters, or come to America."

"Excellent. You remember well. But there is one part I have never shared with you. Life was not easy at the time in Russia. My family struggled. In our town, most did. I did well in my studies and was recruited to a special school where I learned much more. Business, mostly. Finance, management. English." He paused, lost in his reflections. "Love of country," he added softly.

Victor listened respectfully, as he'd been taught. The old man was a legend to him. Careful, serious, smart. Though the hat made him look ridiculous. A skinny old man, pale and worried about the bright desert sun. His thin nose and narrow face looked suddenly much older to Victor. There was white stubble on the man's neck—he hadn't shaved with his normal care that morning.

Granddad continued to describe his childhood and the years leading up to the trip to America in more detail than the stories he'd told before. The poverty. Lack of food. His large family and their struggles.

"When they asked me to go to America, they saved my life—and the lives of our family members. They gave me money to travel, but they also gave my parents money and food. Without the offer, and my acceptance, many of them would have died. Maybe all of us. Do you understand?"

Victor nodded. He was alive because his grandfather had been given a chance.

"Our family owes its existence to the program that trained me and sent me to America. I founded Baranov Brands with the knowledge the program provided me. The initial money, business plans, and type of company all came from the government program. Since then, periodically, I and your father have received more guidance and assistance." He stared hard at Victor. "We owe everything to Russia. Do you see?"

Victor nodded slowly but felt confused. "Yes, but... we're Americans." He hesitated, hoping he hadn't said the wrong thing. "Right?"

His father nodded to him reassuringly as his grandfather answered.

"Yes. By design. But locked away in our hearts, we are Russian. You must learn this today and never forget. One day, you may be called upon to serve. You will not say no. You will not fail whatever task or mission they give you."

His grandfather continued to tell him the history of his life as the shiny new fishing poles lay forgotten and the rented fishing boat drifted on the lake.

"While you may feel you are American—and should—in your heart and soul you are truly Russian. From today forward, your father and I will teach you all you need to know. You will learn Russian fluently. You will prepare yourself to take over the business—and our family obligation. Will you do this for me, for your father, for your true country?"

Of course he agreed.

That day, he became a man—and a Russian.

On the soft couch of his darkened office, Victor's eyes closed and his breathing changed.

Finally asleep, he dreamed of his late wife coming toward him with a broken wooden chair leg, growling.

Research Facility Alpha
Near the town of China
Nuevo Leon, Mexico

Edgars and the other scientists were tired, but all knew from experience that sleep would elude them. Though the test subject violence bothered them less and less each month, none were ready to sleep. If they went to bed now, the replay of Lucas's head and the chair leg would invade their dreams. They needed the distraction writing the report provided.

Besides, the boss expected a timely update.

Preliminary Report of Live Subject Testing #133

NOTE: Taste-testing conducted in the field. Only Stages 6 (Withdrawal), 7 (Post Effect Timing), and 8 (Aggression) were tested in the laboratory setting.

SUMMARY

Strain 31 [Level 5] performed as expected.

Subjects reacted perfectly to the liquid version of the drug introduced in their beer.

- No flavor issues were noted by either subject.

- The alcohol content of the beer did not adversely affect Strain 31.

- Mild bliss state achieved approximately fifteen minutes after finishing one bottle (each).

- Both subjects remained focused, conversational, and appeared normal.

Subjects were brought to the lab with the promise of more beer fifteen minutes after finishing one beer each. Both appeared to instinctively understand their feelings of bliss had come from the drink.

The subjects were compliant and exhibited only small signs of distress, such as body tension, hyper-focus, and over-politeness to secure the next dose.

In Stage 8, both subjects moved from passivity to aggression at the thirty-one-minute mark. The hyper-aggression exhibited more than made up for a lack of fighting skill from each.

The surviving subject showed no remorse and enjoyed half a dose when offered.

The surviving subject will be held for further testing for the usual 72 hours to test for withdrawal severity. However, as per protocol, the subject will be eliminated, and the body provided to the disposal team in three days.

NOTES:

Strain 31 satisfies all requirements based on initial testing with these two subjects. Bliss state, hallucinations, and level of violence are within requested parameters and time frames.

Further testing with many more subjects is recommended to determine:

- Full effects of dependence as well as duration

- Effects of larger and smaller doses, consumption rate, etc.

- Effects of alcohol on subject's mobility, functionality, and cognition

Testing cannot proceed until more of the product is produced and additional volunteers are recruited.

See detailed report forthcoming for more on this trial and additional recommendations.

~ Research Team Alpha

Edgars added his note to the end. None of the other scientists would see this part.

PS: It is ready. It is time. ~ Edgars.

Baranov Brands Headquarters
Las Vegas, Nevada

Victor startled awake from a nightmare, disoriented. A second before, he had been in Mexico at a run-down resort hotel, accidentally served spiked beer at the pool. Knowing his life was about to change—that he would become addicted to the drug, always desperate for more.

He blinked the sleep out of his eyes and stood. Swallowing hard, he fought the tightly fitted shirt and knotted tie he'd fallen asleep in. Straightening his clothes, he walked to his computer, logged on, and clicked on the waiting report.

Nothing else mattered. He could use the toilet, shower, brush his teeth, and change clothes after the report was read—and a final decision made.

The report showed exactly what he had expected.

They always want more time and resources. Both of which have run out.

He considered the report, the experiment he'd seen a few hours earlier, and—as always—the deadline imposed on him. Reading Dr. Edgars' postscript made his decision easy.

It will have to do. I can't delay this any longer.

The Level 5 product would be enough to appease his handler—barely —and those above him. The scientists wouldn't need to worry about dependence levels or the long-term effects of the drug. They hadn't been told, and didn't realize, that no one cared. The essential criteria were the level of violence associated with the consumption and how long it took to kick in.

He composed an email to his head of production—another of his adopted homeland's countrymen.

Work with Edgars. Use Strain 31 to produce beer in maximum quantities: 24/7 production. Deadline: late December in preparation for New Year's Eve marketing launch.

Mass production hadn't been tested yet, but at this point, it wouldn't matter. Whatever the outcome was would be fine, as long as it was deadly.

Next, he emailed the marketing department. No one there was in on the secret. They thought they worked for a completely legitimate beverage company with a long-planned, often-delayed new product.

Plan a campaign for a New Year's Eve launch of our new beer. Maximum awareness. Free beer gardens in all major Las Vegas hotels.

A full roll-out of the product will begin nationwide in February. Meeting today at 1 p.m. to discuss and plan.

Nine weeks should be just long enough for the advertising, production, and distribution, though the full roll-out would never happen.

It would also have to be enough time to prepare himself for spending the rest of his life in a country he'd never visited, but his family had once called home.

11

DED MOROZ

PRESENT DAY

The Kremlin
Moscow, Russia

Pavel Zimalev, the recently elected President of the Russian Federation, sat at his desk with a pile of reports and maps. The forty-five-year-old had grown up with technology and would have preferred to use his specially adapted, secure tablet. But for this plan, only the highest level of security would do, which left only paper. Easy to track, simple to secure, impossible to hack, unlike a tablet.

Outside the tall, bulletproof windows, the gray sky lay over the Kremlin grounds like a heavy, dingy wool blanket. Fat snowflakes drifted lazily down. Despite the thick glass, he could faintly hear the scrape of a shovel against the ground as the snow was continuously cleared from the courtyard.

In front of Zimalev's large desk stood Joseph Orlov, chief of the foreign intelligence agency. The man looked like an accountant with horn-rimmed glasses and a brown ill-fitting suit doing nothing to flatter his large belly.

Who wears brown suits these days? President Zimalev thought.

There were no chairs for visitors in the office; the President had them removed on his first day. No one was allowed to sit. Sitting promoted relaxing, and in his mind, the country had no time to lose.

The room was uncomfortably cold, the way he preferred. It helped him think.

"Is it enough?" Zimalev asked his top spy, more wondering aloud than asking a direct question. "Using such a small part of the program. Would it not be better to completely decapitate the country with one strike?"

The question served as a good test of the spy. The president had known him for years as they both came up the ranks of the government. But being acquaintances and working together to launch a brazen attack on their country's largest enemy were quite different.

The stocky man's fleshy, dour face didn't look uncomfortable as he answered. "If you planned on invading Alaska, yes. For this campaign, no. The limited strike has a better chance of success. When pushed too far into a corner, the Americans tend to rally. Stand together. That is the last thing we want. It may be counter-intuitive, but here, less is more."

Zimalev gave nothing away to the spy chief, though he agreed completely.

"And the chances of success? How do they look now we are closer to the endgame?"

"Fine," Orlov said, displaying no excitement. His placid, slow demeanor caused many to underestimate him. People meeting the man for the first time often considered him unintelligent, a figurehead installed as chief to allow his assistant to be the power behind the throne, so to speak. "Communication is difficult, as you know, but the report last week indicated all plans were in place."

The American's electronic surveillance surely couldn't be as good as feared. But out of an abundance of caution, all communication with the regional assets in the United States was done the old-fashioned way—in person, and rarely. The sleeper program, designed and implemented over a hundred years ago, continued as originally planned. Low tech, face-to-face, and extremely secret. Currently, only the president, the chief of foreign intelligence, the spy's right-hand man, and the participants themselves knew of it.

Orlov had stopped speaking, but Zimalev knew his mannerisms better after spending so much time together the last two months since he had learned of the long-term operation begun by the former president. The spy had more to say. Zimalev waited patiently. The man could not be rushed, even by him.

"Changing direction at this point would be nearly impossible, Mr. President. It is too late. We are committed—at least to this phase. If the snowstorm doesn't arrive as expected, the chaos in America and the political shakeup will happen, regardless."

"The flaw in the plan," Zimalev muttered. How had his predecessor not created a contingency?

I risk burning irreplaceable assets on a weather prediction.

Not that he didn't desire the same prize the previous president had. No, he'd wholeheartedly embraced the risky move.

If anything, it doesn't go far enough. But I will keep those ambitions to myself. One invasion at a time.

He felt like a child at Christmas who only wanted one toy and had pinned all his hopes on Ded Moroz—the Russian version of Santa Claus—bringing it to him. Nothing else would do.

"The latest predictions for the storm?"

Orlov nodded slowly. "Still solid, Mr. President. The snow will come. By the time it does, the Americans will be in disarray. President Heringten will be disgraced and on his way out of office—or at least powerless," he said in his methodical way. "In less than two weeks, we will have our victory."

Zimalev nodded.

Your victory. Mine will come in the months and years following.

If Zimalev did this right, and the Europeans and Americans didn't respond in full force, he would be unstoppable.

My spy friend jokes about me invading Alaska... but really, what would stop me?

With finesse, he could repeat his predecessor's Crimea land grab easily enough, claiming America's state of Alaska back to Russia where it belonged.

He focused on the present. The laminated map on his desk had markings showing the military units spread along the Ukraine border.

"The troops?"

"Ready, Mr. President. Staged and practicing as in past years. A few key leaders, completely loyal, know the full plan. The others will be informed closer to the blizzard. All rests, of course, on your final order," the spymaster said. The military commanders should have also been here to discuss the situation, but the fewer times they gathered ahead of the launch, the better for security.

Staring at the map, once again Zimalev lost himself in his dreams.

First, this operation. Then I handle Kazakhstan, Uzbekistan, and Turkmenistan.

With the withdrawal of the Americans, he'd already been in contact with the leaders in Afghanistan. They had welcomed his advances. He had no interest in occupying the backward country, but establishing strong ties there would humiliate the Americans.

Soon, Russia will once again be the dominant power in the world. I will return the country to its former glory and be regarded as the greatest leader it has ever had.

Orlov kept his face impassive as he watched the president lose himself in a daydream.

The egotistical idiot will be a useful puppet for years.

The man undoubtedly dreamt of besting America and conquering the world.

This is to be expected—and welcomed. However, he does not need to know about the other plans.

First things first. Once the invasion takes place and he is riding high on "his" success, I will share the rest with him.

He smiled to himself, though his face displayed nothing but the dim, idiotic look he'd perfected as a teenager.

And if anything goes wrong, he will take the blame.

It was the one thing presidents were good for.

12

VENGEANCE

National Guard of Mexico Regional Command Center
Monterey, Nuevo Leon
Mexico

"We lost eighteen men? To get what?" the Chief Inspector asked, his face livid, his voice screeching. "A phone call!"

He paced his modern office in the brand-new building, built at great expense to demonstrate to the citizens of Mexico the government's seriousness at combating crime. The National Guard, under control of the country's Armed Forces, had replaced the Federal Police. At least, in name. Nearly all the people were the same, and with them came the same problems of mismanagement and corruption.

The cartels were too powerful and too rich to beat. Many people felt that if the police—or National Guard—could merely hold back the tide of violence, they'd call it a win.

Captain Hernandez let his boss vent without arguing, concerned for the older man's health if he didn't release the stress and anger.

I feel the rage too but now is not the time. Later, after we have vengeance, I will process the feelings.

To Hernandez, the operation had been fruitful from two standpoints, despite the agony and death he had watched his men suffer. First, it showed attention to detail paid off. They knew the Ruiz cartel had been expanding their production facilities. Using satellite data provided by the Americans, they had pinpointed likely areas for the labs. They had narrowed their focus and asked the U.S. Drug Enforcement Agency for more detailed coverage. The lab raided earlier in the morning had been discovered by noting the comings and goings of a large workforce to an unlikely location for so many people.

Good, old-fashioned police work had produced the result, which the Inspector General should have appreciated. But since it went hand in hand with advanced technology, in addition to thinking several steps ahead, the man didn't like it—or get it. He was an older, simpler man in a younger man's more complex world.

The second and more important takeaway from the raid concerned intel. A classic approach in police work calls for going after small fish to land bigger ones. They knew the Ruiz cartel manufactured and sold higher-end drugs, but couldn't find those labs. But this morning's raid had provided a lead to one. The Sierra De Tamaulipas Mountains lab the men raided was inconsequential in the grand scheme of the so-called War on Drugs. But the cartels were up to something big; it was in the air. Rumors abounded. They were making a move to replace the legitimate government, or they were mobilizing an army to invade the United States, or an expansion into China was the way of the future.

Whatever they were doing involved the production and sale of the high-end drugs. Destroy enough of those labs and their larger plans—whatever they were—would fail.

Along the way, Hernandez hoped, they would discover the true threat from the cartels. All while keeping the country's citizens safe and the American Drug Enforcement Agency off their backs. Both results would keep the politicians happy.

Win—win—win. If I can keep my risk-averse, technophobe boss in line.

Hernandez had enlisted the U.S. DEA, who had turned to the NSA to monitor calls from the surrounding area. One call made shortly after their ill-fated raid from a suspected Ruiz cartel phone line led to a small hotel near China in the state of Nuevo Leon, closer to the USA border.

If the hotel led them to another, better drug lab, the raid would have been worth it, despite the loss of life.

Still, hitting the target by helicopter, before dawn, should have been a surprise. In planning the mission, he and the Inspector General had obviously missed an early warning system—or they had a mole, which would surprise no one. The amount of money dangled by cartels made every one of them consider taking the bribes and switching sides. Even him.

"The men, sir," Hernandez said as his boss paced and mumbled. "A tragedy. I feel the anger too, but we have to focus now on the future. This lead points to a major operation."

"Eighteen men. For a cocaine laboratory," the chief muttered as he slumped into his chair. "One of hundreds. Thousands."

He's gone over the edge. I have to get him to focus on the next step.

"Sir, we cannot let their deaths be in vain." The hold on his own rage slipped and his voice cracked with emotion. He took a long, deep breath to calm down. "We should assault the hotel as soon as possible. Whatever is there won't bring the men back, but if we can put a major dent into the cartel's business, we will avenge them."

The red-faced man stared into the distance. Hernandez waited a full minute, then stood. He would order the preparations, then come back for approval.

Maybe he'll pull himself together by then.

"Attack the hotel as soon as possible," the Chief Inspector said, steel in his voice, sitting up straighter and turning to Hernandez. "And do not tell a soul where you are going. Put the men into vehicles. You drive the lead one, the rest follow. Give no one the chance to provide a warning, understand?"

Hernandez nodded.

"Find out what they are up to, gather evidence, then render it useless to them. The equipment, men, everything. Scorched earth. They must pay for the loss of our brothers this morning."

Hernandez nodded and left to make the preparations, surprised and pleased with his boss's newfound ruthlessness. If they hadn't been at total war with the Ruiz cartel before, they certainly would be soon.

13

THE TEAM

Central Analysis Group Headquarters
Alexandria, Virginia

Haley flipped back through the pages of notes, scrawled on her yellow legal pad in front of her. It all looked good. The debrief of the nurse had gone well. She could feel the thrill of the hunt. Her gut told her that the pages contained a clue pointing to whatever attack was coming.

"That's all we need, Carol. Thank you. Put Axe on the line for me, will you?"

She waited while Carol left the relative quiet of the boat's cabin.

"Did you get what we need?" Axe asked, straight to the point as usual.

"It gets us a step closer. Time to dig and see where it leads. You're close to home?"

"About an hour out."

She almost reminded him not to get stopped by the authorities. Since Carol had no identification, it would be suspicious, which is exactly what they didn't need. But she held back.

He's a pro. He doesn't need me mothering him.

She wished she was in the field with him. At the same time, she was glad she could plan and manage the mission.

I'll do whatever is needed to protect the country. If it means staying in the office, so be it.

"Her brother will pick Carol up. I'll send you the meet details." The noise of the wind and roar of the boat's engines made her want to yell, but she kept her voice low. It would be better to talk more later when they could hear each other better. "Let's do a full after-action at…" She looked at her watch. Out of the corner of her eye, she caught movement. Someone was in the small conference room with her.

She jumped to her feet, her fight-or-flight reflex kicking in.

Gregory Addison, her boss, leaned against the doorframe, arms crossed, eyes narrowed. His long hair, grayer every day he worked with her, was slicked back and perfectly in place. The round frames of his glasses were stylish and modern, making him seem younger than his sixty years. His physically fit body helped with it as well.

I never heard him come in. How long has he been standing there?

"Haley? You there?" Axe asked.

"Gotta go. Talk later." She ended the call and set the phone on her yellow pad, instinctively freeing her hands. An instant later, she had to suppress a smile at her actions. There would be no confrontation with Gregory. At least, not a physical one.

"Good morning, Gregory. You're in early."

"Haley. Early start or late night?" His face was inscrutable. She took a small breath and made herself go blank to match his. Gregory's eyes narrowed. He knew exactly what she was doing.

He had taught her a lot in the past year she had worked at the Central Analysis Group. He'd been an excellent mentor. His respect for her had seemed to grow after seeing her in action on the security camera footage from the St. John mission a few months prior. He'd given her more of a free hand to do the job her way—using her gut instinct and fierce determination to find threats facing the country.

I need to keep in mind he's still my boss. And mentor—there's a lot he can teach me yet.

Instead of denying what he'd undoubtedly guessed, she jumped right in. "I'm working on a potential situation. Nothing much to go on, though. I'll get you a report when I have more."

Gregory nodded but seemed unconvinced. "Are you running an op?"

What's that tone? Judgment? No… Is it… envy?

She hesitated for a split second.

I could lie… I've gotten much better at it.

She decided on the truth—or part of it. "Not so much running it as… supervising."

Is there much difference, really?

He took his glasses off and rubbed his eyes with his free hand. Any envy had been replaced with frustration if she read him right.

"My understanding with retired Admiral Nalen gives you as much leeway as possible to find threats to the United States. But we never agreed you would be actively running unsanctioned operations from this building. As we've discussed before, we aren't an operational unit. Whatever you're doing puts us in legal jeopardy. If Congress found out, or a political enemy of the president, we'd all be in it deep. I don't want to lose you as an analyst, but you can't use the CAG as a cover."

She considered the situation from his perspective. What he said made sense.

Is this my moment? Do I have to choose between being an analyst, fieldwork, and running assets?

"I understand and respect you too much to BS you. The operational aspect has finished. I needed data and the only way to get it involved my asset. But now I have analysis to do. There's a threat out there, and it's big. Bigger than New York City's attack, maybe bigger than the EMPs from the Movement."

Gregory's eyes widened in surprise. Danger didn't get much bigger than the attempt to start World War Three and take over the world that she and Axe had thwarted two months earlier. "Fine. But only analysis onsite. Otherwise, you get to take another vacation, or at least days off. I'm not being called to testify before the Senate about illegal activities, I'm not going down with the ship, and I'm not blowing up my career. I back the president, and you—you've been right every single time so far—but if he wants you to run ops, he needs to get you into the CIA or Homeland Security. Got it?"

"Yes, sir. Thank you."

"Give me a report by the end of the day. If it's important enough to send an asset into the field, I should at least know your suspicions. I should have earned your trust by now." He left the room with barely a sound.

Ouch, that hurt. Doesn't he know I trust him? But he's right. I should have kept him in the loop.

The door to the conference room opened again as she gathered up her legal pad, phone, and pen to return to her desk. Nancy and Dave, fellow analysts Gregory had assigned to work with her, rushed in. They still had their winter coats on. Nancy pulled a hand-knit stocking cap from her head, her long graying hair wild with static electricity.

"Gregory said you needed us," she said in a rush. "What's up?"

Dave calmly unzipped his puffy black parka and slipped it off, then helped Nancy with hers. They were discrete, but the rumors must be true —they were a couple and had been for years.

Haley gestured for them to sit and returned to her chair. Better to talk in here, where the other analysts arriving for the day shift wouldn't overhear about her covert operation. "I have the barest hint of a danger."

It couldn't even be called a hunch. What did she have?

It would be generous to call it an inkling.

"How can we help?" Dave asked. She could see the fire in his eyes, and Nancy's. They were becoming more and more like her as they worked with her. Before, they gathered information and wrote reports warning of what they found.

But the world was changing. Threats to the country came at it faster. They didn't have the luxury of patiently sifting through data and waiting until a threat became clear. Since she had started training them a few months ago, they now hunted for clues to find threats earlier. They were developing killer instincts.

"I'll give you what I have, but as I said, it's slim," she said.

Dave grabbed pens and pads of paper from a supply shelf in the corner of the room and they took notes while she lay it out. "First: something's going on in Mexico."

How much can I tell them?

"A nurse went missing from the villages where she helped out. She exchanged a few emails with her brother, including one with a subtle distress code they had worked out before she left. He got in touch with a cop buddy, who put him in touch with the FBI, who helped him file a missing person report, but couldn't do much more. The intel landed on my desk." She shrugged. "Gregory made sure any oddities or one-off items without an obvious intelligence category get flagged for me."

How to explain the rest of the story? They know about Axe, but we avoid the topic.

"Long story short, she escaped, and I just debriefed her." She held up her notes. "I'm going to sift through these. I need you two to analyze all phone calls the NSA or other entities captured between 2:00 a.m. and 6:00 a.m. local, when her captors found out she had gotten away. We're looking for who held her and why. Soto La Marina, which is a town in the state of

Tamaulipas, Mexico. Three hours south of Brownsville, Texas, along the Gulf coast." She hesitated, trying to put into words what her gut told her. "Also, look for a connection to other disappearances."

Dave, the more skeptical of the two, said, "People vanish in Mexico all the time. They get on the wrong side of a cartel or local criminal gangs."

"Entirely possible, but my gut tells me it's more than the typical criminals or cartel business. I believe a cartel kidnapped her to hush up the number of people missing."

They sat for a moment, considering.

"Also, the CIA has an entry about China being mentioned in connection to the area. Don't obsess over China, but keep it in mind. This isn't the whole puzzle but will give us more clues. Let's get to it."

She felt an energy pass between Nancy and Dave. "What? Spit it out."

There I go, being witchy again. Have to watch that.

"When did you sleep last, Haley?" Nancy asked, a caring look on her face.

I must look like hell.

"I've been here all night. I'll do a few more hours, then—"

"Leave it to us." Dave's voice had a note of finality. Technically, she was his... what? Not his boss. And not senior analyst—he had two decades more experience than her in the business. She led the team, though.

But the way he spoke sounded like he was putting his foot down.

I either trust them or I don't.

She hesitated. They weren't as good as her, but were they good enough, for this part at least?

"Fine. I'll grab a couple of hours. Dig deep."

It sucks to be a manager.

Haley's cold nose woke her up. In the back of the big, boxy SUV she'd purchased, the inflatable bed was quite comfortable. Her winter-rated sleeping bag kept her warm, leaving only her face exposed. She must have tossed and turned—the pillow she kept her head buried under had slid off, allowing the cold to seep in and wake her.

She covered her head with the pillow but knew she wouldn't go back to sleep.

I have to hunt.

She'd worked out a deal with the CAG building security guards, giving them a heads-up about her occasional naps in the SUV.

Only ninety minutes of sleep, but it will have to do.

She checked the blackout curtains on the windows, then stripped while lying on the bed, rolled on fresh deodorant, and put on clean clothes. The pistol went back in its holster—she slept with it under her pillow—and onto her right hip. The ammo carrier went on the left. One of her several black blazers completed her outfit of comfortable shoes she could run in if the situation warranted, khakis she could fight in, and an unrestrictive but feminine blouse.

After making sure she had her toothbrush and toothpaste to use in the office bathroom, she brushed her hair, put it into a ponytail, and headed back inside.

Dave and Nancy shared a double-wide work cubicle. Their excitement was palpable as Haley approached. "What have you found?"

"Listen to this," Nancy told her. "Recorded early this morning, right in the area you had us search." The NSA and other organizations had so much computing power they could vacuum up nearly every phone call made, whether from cell phones or landlines. Especially in areas of interest, like near suspected terror organizations or, in this case, a major drug cartel. Calls were recorded, analyzed by a computer algorithm looking for keywords, phrases, names, or voice patterns on file. Few were ever reviewed by a human. But all were stored for future reference.

Nancy clicked on a small triangle on her computer screen, and a young woman's crying voice filled the cubicle. Haley caught most of it, but Nancy also translated. "She says, 'Mama, the puppy has run away. We cannot find her anywhere.' Who calls at that hour of the morning to tell Mama about the puppy? It's code for the nurse."

Haley agreed, impressed with their find. "What was the response?"

"They hung up, then the woman calls a similar number and repeats the story. An older woman and the younger woman discuss it. The older woman—Mama—says to put out the dog's favorite toy and treats on the patio and she will return by morning. But get this." She gestured to Dave's screen, which showed a map. "Here are the locations of the calls. First, from here to here," she pointed. The receiver of the first call was in an area devoid of any buildings except for one large house—almost a mansion, unusual in that part of Mexico.

"Then, five minutes later, we get lucky." Dave changed his screen to a black-and-white view from miles above. "A surveillance satellite catches this: a car leaving the house. It drives to the nearby town," another click, "then the satellite is out of range. But get this. Hardly any calls at that hour. But there's another call. It goes from here," she pointed at the small city, "to here." A nearby army base. "Could they have called for help from the military to search for the nurse?"

Instead of sleeping, I should have done an after-action with Axe to find out if the military searched for them.

"I can check, but I'd say you've nailed it."

"Tell her the rest," Dave said.

The older woman looked embarrassed and hesitated. "Well…"

"Tell me."

"I channeled my inner Haley," she joked.

"WWHD," Dave added. "What Would Haley Do?"

Haley rolled her eyes and waved her hand for them to get on with it.

"I reviewed the call data in this area over the past year and found a pattern."

"Well, a possible pattern," Dave cautioned.

"A Haley pattern," Nancy said. "Show her."

Dave pulled up another map of a larger area.

"Very few calls to or from this mansion," Nancy said, pointing to the destination of the first call about the lost puppy, where the person had listened, then hung up.

"Lots of calls from this small city. Big town, really," Dave added. "Ten thousand people. Here's a representation of all the calls from the last six months from the town." He displayed an overlay that looked like the route map of a regional airline. Red lines flowed outward in all directions, short and long distances.

"I had a feeling," Nancy whispered. "My stomach. Weird. I don't know if it's what you get or not, but my gut told me to dig deeper." She glanced at Haley for encouragement, then looked away shyly. "Before working with you, I wouldn't have bothered. But something called to me…"

"She's too modest to tell you herself, so I will," Dave said. "She wrote a search algorithm and had the artificial intelligence scan all the calls, looking for anomalies. Then she listened to thousands of them."

"No, only hundreds."

He pressed a few keys. Most of the lines disappeared, except for many leading to one location to the north.

"What's at the end of the line?"

"A hotel," Nancy explained. "Two-star, at best. Next to a big lake. Now, all the calls I scanned are about making reservations, schedules, that sort of thing. But they're slightly off. It's code. Then last night—this morning, rather, a call."

Dave played it, and Nancy translated. "He says, 'Double the number of guests, immediately.' Then hangs up. Hardly a genuine call to book a hotel, or from management to make more rooms available. It was urgent and they skipped most of the subtlety. They're doubling the guard here." Her finger tapped the screen.

With a click, Dave brought up the hotel website showing an attractive white building next to a lake. Just from the photos, Haley could tell they worked hard to put the best face forward, showing palm trees and a sparkling pool. An aerial shot showed the hotel with the expansive lake in the background, surrounded by boring brown desert.

Hardly picturesque.

"And," Dave said, "I found this. A federal police raid on a small farm here," he pointed to the same general part of the country, the long easternmost state bordering the Gulf of Mexico. "It blew up as they raided it. A drug compound, obviously. Several officers dead. It happened ten minutes before the call to the hotel. And the NSA had their own search running for the area. Someone besides us has an interest here, but there's nothing in our database, so it's probably the Mexico federal police."

Dave and Nancy looked at her, excited and expectant.

That raid had nothing to do with Axe or our operation.

Her mind was fuzzy as she tried to put the pieces together in a way that made sense.

I need caffeine.

If she were more awake, she'd probably see the connections and be as excited as them. Instead, it seemed so thin. But to them, it made complete sense. The data connected, she saw that, but didn't share their conviction.

This is what Gregory feels when I tell him about my hunches.

The realization hit her hard.

No wonder he's going gray so fast.

She'd give Nancy and Dave another chance to explain it—or for her mind to shake off the cobwebs and catch up with theirs.

"Big picture—lay it out for me."

Their smiles faltered as they realized they hadn't convinced her.

Dave spoke. "The cartel is running an operation of some sort. That part is still unclear. They kidnap the nurse to keep her quiet but don't kill her. She's too well known. An American citizen dying or vanishing would attract too much attention."

Nancy joined in. "Especially a nurse, not some stupid kid out for drugs or a tourist in the wrong place at the wrong time."

So far, Haley agreed with them. "Continue."

"The nurse gets rescued early this morning. A drug lab gets hit around the same time. Too much of a coincidence," Dave said, quietly making the case.

No, that's exactly what it is, but can I tell them? How much of me running an asset do they need to know?

Dave continued. "A call about the nurse goes to the mansion. Minutes later, a call to the army base from this nearby city. Conclusion: the mansion is the location of a drug cartel leader. The call ordered bribed army members to look for the nurse."

"I agree," Haley said. The other two analysts looked at each other with relief. "But the rest?"

"It's what you're looking for. The raid on the drug lab at the farm and the rescue of the nurse prompt the phone call to add guards at the hotel. It's a front for the cartel. Whatever we're looking for is here." Nancy tapped Dave's screen, showing the hotel website.

It was logical, though it didn't hit her gut the way data usually did.

If I had made the connections, would I feel differently?

Standing back from the process raised doubts, she saw now. It was so much easier to feel confident in a hunch when she had done the work herself.

Yes. If I'd done the research instead of Nancy and Dave, I'd be raring to go. Now I know exactly how Gregory feels. I'll have to do better explaining my process to him—and being patient when he doesn't share my level of conviction.

Nancy bristled. "I'm right, Haley. Before working with you, I never would have dug so deep. And I wouldn't have made the leaps. But this is it. I feel it," she said defensively.

"I believe her, too," Dave said.

I buy it. They've done good work.

"I'm sorry, yes, I believe you," she reassured them. They relaxed with relief. "Do we have satellite coverage for the hotel?"

"No, nothing focused on this area."

"How far is it from the border?"

"About two and a half hours from Brownsville, Texas. Less from McAllen."

Axe and Kelton were in Brownsville by now, having dropped off Carol and returned the rented fishing boat while Haley napped.

Nancy turned toward her computer. "I had just started to dig into the hotel when you came back."

"Too bad we can't get eyes on that hotel..." Dave said slowly, also focused on his screen.

"Yes, too bad," Haley said, not taking the bait she guessed Dave was suggesting—to get her asset in play. "Keep digging. I need to get more sleep, then I can attack it again once I'm fresh."

Or rather, once I get Axe to shake the tree and get me more data.

She went back to her desk to send a note to Gregory, summarizing what Dave and Nancy had found.

They'll be happy to brief you further. I need the rest of the day off to catch up on my sleep.

Would he get it? Would he understand she planned to go off-site for "extracurricular activities," as he called her work with Axe and Nalen?

Yes. He'll read between the lines and know exactly what I'm doing.

14

CHINA

The All-American A+ Diner Parking Lot
Alexandria, Virginia

Haley played by the rules… when she had to.

No operations from CAG HQ? I hope two miles from the parking lot is far enough away.

She sat in the driver's seat of her SUV in the back parking lot of the local diner. Too awake to nap, too tired to function well.

She dialed, and Axe answered on the first ring. "What did you find?"

"How do you feel about a trip to China?" She couldn't resist yanking Axe's chain just a little.

He hesitated. In the background, she heard Kelton. "Did she say China? I don't know about that…"

Kelton wouldn't do well in the country. Kelton's former assistant, Todd Burkley, had convinced a major Chinese firm that Kelton had been behind the attack on its people and business. It had been Todd all along—mostly—but the Chinese company had destroyed Kelton's business, gotten him fired from his own firm, and exacted their revenge. He wouldn't be welcome there—or safe.

"It's far away and I wouldn't exactly blend in, but if that's what you need, I'll go."

"Perfect, but take Kelton. You're going to a town named China, in

Mexico," she said, dropping the hammer. "It's only about two hours south of Brownsville."

"There's a China, Mexico?"

"Yes. And why not? There's a Paris, Texas. They even have a replica of the Eiffel Tower."

"Does China, Mexico have a Great Wall?"

"Not as far as I know. But then, I know virtually nothing. This came from Nancy and Dave, but I trust them. We need to shake the tree there."

"The border crossing will record our details," Axe said, sounding surprisingly cautious.

"A rich guy—well, former rich guy—and his faithful bodyguard. No biggie. I know you've had a long day between rescuing Carol and the boat trip back, but we need this. Rent a car, get to the Hotel Riviera Especial de China. About two and a half hours from you, on a lake."

Axe passed the info along to Kelton. "We got it. Any words of advice?"

"We've connected the hotel to a call from the same cartel holding Carol. But we don't know what's going on. Only the message we intercepted. It ordered a doubling of the guards."

"So we might be expected, or heading into someone else's fight?"

"Unknown. Do what you do best. Set up an overwatch, stealth your way in, or be bold and trust the cover story of two gringo fishermen exploring all Mexico has to offer."

"Safe to return to the scene of the crime, so to speak? The general area, at least."

"The hotel is about four hours northwest from where you were early this morning."

"Same cartel, though, right?"

"Likely, yes. What do you think? Did anyone see you at the compound when you rescued Carol?"

"No. It was dark, and I only encountered one guard, who I zapped instead of killing. He saw Carol, not me, so it's probably not a problem. A different area of operation, no means of visual identification, so I should be fine. The odds of being identified are pretty slim. It's a risk, but I'm willing to take it."

She spoke much quieter, hoping Kelton wouldn't overhear. "How's Kelton working out?"

"Fine. We're good to go."

They discussed details before hanging up. The men would grab coffee, rent a car, and get started.

Haley hung up and leaned back. It would be at least three hours before Axe had intel for her. She could get another nap and be better able to focus. She still had difficulty sleeping more than four or five hours at a time, though the PTSD she experienced after the St. John operation had subsided a great deal. Talking and laughing with Axe and his former Teammates had helped a lot. She had also taken up yoga again and tried her hand at meditation. All of it helped—a little.

I'll head back. I sleep better in the parking lot, anyway.

She put the truck in gear and drove, thinking through the situation. The hotel was the key. The longer she sat with Nancy and Dave's assessment, the more she felt it. An attack on the country was in the works and the hotel held the next piece of the puzzle.

Danger is coming.

She didn't have the data yet. Axe would get it for her. But as she drove the short distance back to the fenced, guarded parking lot of CAG head-quarters, she couldn't shake the feeling she'd missed something important.

PART 2

THURSDAY NIGHT, DECEMBER 29

15

THE DRIVE

"I have questions." Kelton sat in the car—rented with the maximum insurance coverage possible, at Axe's insistence—staring out at the passing Mexico desert. It looked about the same as the Texas side of the border, with low scrub, brown sandy dirt, and the occasional small tree. Plus the usual run-down homes, roadside gas stations, and other small shops.

Questions. Okay, here we go, Axe thought.

Axe knew all the questions. When people found out he'd been a Navy SEAL, they were fascinated. Understandably—there weren't many SEALs, and since they were known as the "quiet professionals," they didn't go around bragging about their exploits. He normally brushed the questions off, saying he'd rather not talk about it. Warriors understood and didn't need to ask. The others… well, how could he explain what he did to people with no concept of the dedication, effort, and drive required? How to communicate his love of the country and its ideals without sounding overly partisan or off his rocker?

And when it came to politics, he had his preferences, but overall, it didn't matter which politicians were in charge. Protecting the country was pretty straightforward. As long as the civilian leadership gathered a top team of smart advisors, listened to the experts, then made informed decisions for the good of the country, he trusted them to lead.

"Let me guess. 'How do you keep from getting scared?'"

Kelton nodded. "You get this all the time, don't you?"

"Yep. But from you—anyone I'm in the field with—I'm happy to answer. Truth is, I get scared occasionally. But I've been doing this for more than fifteen years. Helicopters have hunted me before," he said, referring to their earlier adventure. "We train so often that when it comes to an operation, it feels... normal. Like just another day at the office."

How far do I want to take it with him? It's nice to have a guy to talk to. An outsider. Someone I'm not training, like Haley.

"And... at some point, I just accepted death is part of it. I don't want to get hurt or die, but if it happens, so be it. I'll be gone to whatever comes next. This adventure will be over, but another one will begin. I live each day the best I can, don't put things off, and I'm not waiting until retirement to live. So if I go..."

"No regrets."

"Exactly."

Kelton continued to watch the road for a few moments, then closed his eyes and tilted his seat back. He'd been up all night, handling the boat during the op and all the way back to Brownsville. He looked beat.

"I almost pissed myself on the boat," he admitted quietly. "At first, I was having the time of my life. I hadn't realized we could be in actual danger. It felt like this time I went heli-skiing. There had been avalanches in the area, but I had a world-renowned guide. What could go wrong? We had a great morning. No problem. Later in the day, as the snow melted more, a group on their own got swept. One dead. But since I had chosen the best guide, my odds were good, I thought. Last night, with you there, I figured I was fine." He paused and spoke more quietly. "But it hit me this morning when the helicopters came—we could die."

Axe nodded. "It's about managing risk. And don't worry—you did great. I'd be pissing myself if I had to stand in an office and make decisions affecting thousands of employees' lives and millions of dollars."

Kelton laughed. "I'm not doing any of that these days, either." He squirmed in the seat, getting more comfortable. "If you're good, I'm going to try to sleep."

"I'll wake you when we're close."

Kelton lay silent, but his breathing didn't change. Eventually, he spoke in the same confessional tone as before. "I deserve it all, you know."

Axe drove, not answering, letting the man get it off his chest.

"I complained to Todd," he said, bringing up his former right-hand man who had started the New York City terrorist attacks. "Chang, the CEO of the company Todd hit in New York, had overtaken me on a list of richest men." He shook his head. "So stupid. I gave the go-ahead to take him out. I meant for Todd to hack his company's system. Send a computer virus. Maybe make up some dirt about him and leak it to the press. Nothing violent." He turned his head and looked at Axe. "You've got to believe me."

"I do."

Kelton let out a relieved sigh. "But I started it all. Ordered Todd to hit Chang. Treated Todd like a dog all those years. All because I could. Man, the ego." He slumped in the seat, defeated.

What the hell do I say to him? 'Yeah, you're a jerk and people died because of you'?

Axe said nothing.

"I'm an ass. It finally dawned on me when Todd shot at you on my yacht. My first thought, I'm embarrassed to say, but it's the God's honest truth, was how I'd have to fix the bullet holes if he missed you." After a moment, he wiped tears from his eyes. "What an ass," he repeated.

I have to give him something.

"You've made up for it. Changed your ways this past year. You helped us infiltrate Stefan Conroy's cult. Gave us access to chartered flights, your yacht, financed us while you could. You're along on this op and have handled yourself well. No one is irredeemable."

"I appreciate that, though I know it's less how you feel and more that you have to say something."

Nailed it.

"I'll keep working, trying to right the wrongs. But I deserve the loss of my company, the yacht, the houses, the lifestyle, the money. I'm lucky I have enough money left to live." He sat up, leaving the seat tilted back, and stared at Axe. "I'm just saying... If we're in a situation where it's you or me, don't hesitate. Save yourself. Or innocent bystanders. Whoever. If I get what's coming to me, I'll die happy." He waited a second, then lay back and closed his eyes.

Damn. Now I have a partner with a death wish.

"It's not going to come to that. Listen up, we're going to—"

Kelton's rhythmic snoring filled the car.

As they approached the town of China, Axe pulled off the highway and parked in the gravel lot of a tiny mom-and-pop taco place. The small building had seen better days, but the parking lot had several cars in it. People waited in line at a window to order and sat at the nearby picnic tables. The smell of the food was intoxicating.

Good place to stop. Outside the town, popular with the locals, far enough away from the target.

Kelton's snores had stopped when the car slowed, but he hadn't woken up as they parked. "Kelton, time to eat," Axe said quietly.

"We're here?" He sounded groggy.

"No. We eat now since we might lay in the dirt watching the hotel all night. But we're close. About ten miles away, on the other side of the city."

With the sun setting behind it, the town didn't look like much. A half-mile ahead, the road branched. On the left, the town of China. On the right, the road to Monterey. They would go toward Monterey, past the hotel, and find a place to observe it for a while.

Maybe I can tell Kelton to guard the car while I sneak in. Keep him out of harm's way... and mine.

16

TACOS

Sixteen-year-old Juan looked too young and skinny to be taken seriously or given more responsibilities than that of errand boy. The men guarding the hotel deserved good food, and every day sent Juan to get it.

While Juan had gotten his foot in the door by persistently begging for a job, no one moved up in the Ruiz cartel without proving themselves. Unlike some outfits, where who you knew was key, or how ruthless you were mattered most, Señor Ruiz prioritized intelligence and skill. Guarding a hotel didn't seem important, but it was a choice assignment on the way up. The men took their duty seriously. The hotel—whatever happened there—brought in a lot of money for the cartel.

Juan got along well as the team's most junior member by staying quiet and doing a good job. He had intelligence, dedication, and ambition, despite his age and scrawny appearance. When the bags of delicious-smelling food arrived in the pickup window of the best taco place within thirty miles, he thanked the woman inside, picked them up, and moved to the closest vacant picnic table to compare the items inside to his carefully written order sheet.

Satisfied he had all the food, he turned toward the small pickup truck used to run errands. He stopped in his tracks.

That man...

The rugged face of an American getting out of his car looked familiar.

Something about him...

He was a taller man, two meters at least, and capable. He would fit in well guarding the hotel if he weren't a *gringo*. The big, bushy beard triggered his memory. He almost looked like...

No. It can't be.

Concerned now he would be caught staring, he focused again on the contents of one of the bags of food, then glanced up at the man as he stopped at the back of the line for ordering food.

It's him—the man from the security camera image!

Earlier that morning, when the photograph of the intruder at one of the cartel's other locations circulated, Juan had snagged one. Remembering faces and names had always come easily to him, and the surest way to move up in the organization was to do an extraordinary job, he figured. He dreamed of someday being the right-hand man to the *jefe*. But his near-term goal was to move from being the errand boy to an apprentice guard. A lookout, stationed in a vehicle along the road, or in a small motorboat on the lake. Waiting and watching for police, the DEA, or rival cartels. It would be boring, but a step up—and it paid better, which would help his mother and the rest of his family—whom he loved even more than working for the cartel.

He took a mental snapshot of the man's face, along with the sleepy American standing next to him in line. Also bearded, with longer hair, but with a privileged air about him.

The younger one is an officer. The harder one could be the man in the picture... or am I daydreaming of being a hero again?

Juan detoured past the Americans' car. The small sticker on the window showed it as a rental from America. It was empty.

No woman, unless they have her in the trunk. But it's too warm for that, and they don't seem concerned about the car.

He could be wrong. It would be humiliating to cry wolf. But in the pickup, he had the alert memo folded inside *The Art of War*, a book Señor Ruiz ordered all his men to read.

Carefully setting the food bags inside, he sat in the truck and grabbed the book. The Americans were still in line. He had enough time.

The photo had come from a security camera. Juan didn't know the details. He didn't need to. But if *Jefe* wanted all eyes on the lookout for the man, he took it seriously.

Juan studied the picture and looked up, comparing it carefully to the man in line in front of him.

The night-vision goggles hide the eyes and forehead. But the nose and distinctive beard are the same. The shape of the head seems right. Take away the camouflage paint and it's the man in front of me.

At this moment, he hated the Ruiz cartel's distrust of phones. What he wouldn't give to call this in.

I could follow them.

No. He was an errand boy with no training or experience. They would notice him in moments.

An idea came to him. But how much was he willing to risk? If he made the wrong decision, he would harm the organization... and be punished harshly.

In a second, he left the food sitting in the truck and hurried around the back of the small building. He let himself into the kitchen, staying out of sight of the order window and the waiting Americans.

"Hey—" The grandmother who did the cooking yelled as she looked up from the grill at him.

He held his finger to his lips. Would she recognize him? The guards loved her cooking, so he came here twice a week. Did she understand who she cooked for?

She scowled at him but said nothing more as she turned back to preparing the food.

The phone hung on the wall near the back door. He dialed the guard station off the hotel lobby.

"Hotel Riviera Especial de China," answered a gruff voice in Spanish.

Damn. Lopez.

The man was about to be promoted away from guarding the hotel, onto bigger and better things.

"I have a question about a guest reservation," Juan said, pretending to be a customer.

I took his taco order forty-five minutes ago. Will he recognize my voice?

Lopez hesitated.

He has to know I would never call unless it was an emergency.

"Which guest, please?" Lopez said, confused but playing along.

"Juan Perez," he said, using the common shorthand for a person with no specific identity, like the Americans' John Doe. "From Soto La Marina."

Silence from Lopez. He didn't get it but understood the importance of the call. Juan added, "He left there this morning with his wife."

"Mierda," Lopez swore softly, finally catching on. "I'm sorry to say he has not checked in yet."

"He is running behind schedule—ordering dinner here right now. I just wanted to inform you."

Lopez hesitated only briefly this time. "You're sure?"

This is it. Am I sure?

He had studied the security camera photo and compared it to the American's face as he stood directly in front of him. Juan had a good eye for people. It was the same man.

"Yes."

Lopez asked, "Is his wife with him?"

"No, his... boss. They may need a second room."

"I see. Well, of course we are disappointed our guest has chosen to not dine here at our award-winning restaurant, but that is his prerogative. We appreciate you informing us he is nearby and running late. We will prepare another room for his boss."

What now?

"And if it wouldn't be too much trouble," Lopez continued, "would you mind calling when he finishes dinner and is on his way here? We would like to provide a bottle of our finest champagne, on the house, of course."

Lopez missed his calling. He should have been an actor. He actually sounds hospitable and caring.

"I'm sure he would appreciate it. I will call when they are leaving."

"Thank you again. We appreciate your business."

Juan returned the phone to its cradle after taking a moment to untwist the horribly tangled cord. He took money from his pocket—the change from the earlier dinner order—and set it on the counter near the grandmother, who had ignored him but heard every word of his side of the conversation.

"Señor Ruiz thanks you for the use of your phone."

She nodded once without looking at him.

Juan went out the back and around to his truck. The food smelled amazing. He found his order from one of the large bags, rolled down the windows, and ate while watching the Americans enjoy their tacos.

17

DENIAL

Outside China
Nuevo Leon, Mexico

The tacos were the best Axe had ever tasted, by far.

He finished the last one and resisted licking his fingers, wiping them off on several cheap, thin napkins instead. Kelton had demolished his, too.

"These are incredible. I need seconds—how many more do you want?"

"None. We have to go."

"What? Oh, right." He looked crestfallen. "On the way back, though, let's stop here again, okay?"

"Yes, fine." Axe forced himself to smile to soften his sharp response. "We'll do that. Delicious, right?"

He subtly nudged their empty paper plates and napkins toward Kelton, who unconsciously gathered them up. Axe needed to keep his hands free.

I can't tell Kelton about the kid watching us. He'd look around and give away our advantage.

"Let's get going. I want to get a quick overview before dark."

Kelton threw away the trash, and they were quickly back on the road. Axe briefly debated aborting the mission, but he turned right, toward the hotel. There could be an innocent explanation. The kid could be a lookout for a criminal gang preying on American tourists. It might have nothing at all to do with their op early this morning, four hours to the southeast.

Right, and denial is just a river in Egypt.

They got to the fork in the road, passing the large beige sign in the center median welcoming them to China. On impulse, Axe went left instead of right.

"I thought we were going to the hotel," Kelton said.

"Change of plan. We were being watched back at the restaurant. I need to see if we're being followed."

Kelton turned his body.

"Don't look!"

He stopped and settled back in the seat, chagrined. "Sorry."

For a man so brilliant in the boardroom, he doesn't have street smarts.

"You watch your side, subtly. Look for people sitting in cars at the cross streets, watching for us. You'll know them if you see them. But don't stare and only mention it after we pass by."

"Got it." He adopted a more relaxed posture, staring out his side of the car like a typical tourist.

At least he's trainable.

The run-down town's single-story buildings were painted in sun-faded reds, oranges, greens, and yellows. Vacant lots abound, overgrown with weeds and filled with wind-blown trash. It looked like the poorest Texas or Arizona town, but ten times worse. Except for the road, which was smooth. No doubt well maintained by the federal government, making it easy for tourists to travel to the area—or at least the more popular city of Monterey another ninety minutes along the highway.

"This may sound stupid, but we just passed a kid sitting on his bike. A teenager. He seemed much more interested in us than normal," Kelton whispered.

"Not stupid at all. We've been noticed. But you don't have to whisper."

"What do we do? We're not going to quit, are we?"

"No. We need intel about the hotel. But we can't go marching in there."

"Why not? If they know we're here…"

"I'm still hoping it's not them. It could be a criminal gang targeting tourists."

But that's not what my intuition tells me.

Then again, if the cartel had somehow recognized them, going directly to the hotel would be the last move they expected.

"There's another possibility you're not considering, Axe." Kelton looked embarrassed. "They might be after me. Until a few months ago—and without the beard—I was one of the richest men in North America. Could the person watching us have marked me? I'd be an excellent kidnapping target... if I hadn't let my kidnap and ransom insurance lapse."

Axe appreciated the dark humor and smiled. "That could be it."

He made a few turns, working off the map he'd memorized, taking the road that would follow the lakeshore north to the hotel. If criminals were targeting Kelton, would the hotel be a haven or a trap? And what if the cartel was onto them?

The sun dipped lower. They didn't have much time. Ramming their car or springing a trap would be easier for the enemy in the dark. Fewer witnesses.

I wish I still had the guard's M4 from this morning.

Instead, it lay disassembled on the bottom of the ocean floor, miles off the coast.

The hotel held a piece of the puzzle Haley needed. They'd already been spotted by somebody. The time for stealth had passed.

Fortune favors the bold.

18

MADE

Haley felt much better after her long nap. Nancy and Dave, however, looked worried.

"What's wrong?" Haley asked, taking off her coat while standing outside their cube.

"Thank God you're back," Nancy said. "We may have a problem. First, Dave set up priority search parameters for the Hotel Riviera Especial de China. We get nearly real-time call data courtesy of the NSA. This just came in. It's from eighteen minutes ago." She pressed play on her screen. They heard a youthful male voice, excited and nervous but attempting to play it cool.

Haley could get by in Spanish, which allowed her to decipher much of the call. An AI-generated translation appeared on the screen below the voiceprint waveform. The software had improved greatly in the past few years, thanks to a partnership with a tech company. They listened to the recorded call.

'We may have a problem' is an understatement.

Maybe she was overreacting. "What's your take on it?" she asked Dave and Nancy.

"The young guy sounds like a teenager, but he's good. So is the older man. The algorithm didn't flag it, and neither the DEA nor Mexican police would ever listen to it or care if they did. But knowing what we know…" Nancy looked at Dave for encouragement and got a tiny nod. "Or rather, what we guess…"

There was an awkward moment of silence as they both hesitated to speak.

Finally, Dave asked bluntly, "Your asset is in play there, right?"

Of course they know about Axe. But we've danced around it until now. Plausible deniability and all that.

Haley looked into the nearby cubicles. The other analysts were lost in their work, many wearing noise-canceling headphones to focus better.

To be ultra-cautious, though, she only nodded. Nancy and Dave shared a look.

"Our take is they've recognized him," Nancy said. "They still want the nurse. They risked a call, covered it with an impromptu code, and are on him. Is he going to the hotel?"

"Yes. To shake the tree for us."

"It's a trap," Dave said.

"He can handle himself, but I need to warn him." She pulled out her cell phone and hesitated. She wanted to play by Gregory's rules, but she couldn't run out to her SUV and drive off-property to warn Axe. It had to be right now.

"Grab your laptops and whatever else you need. We're commandeering the small conference room."

She rushed to the room, leaving Dave and Nancy hurrying to gather their gear.

She texted Axe's cell.

You're made. Recognized outside restaurant 15 minutes ago. Proceed with caution.

Haley wouldn't tell him to continue or abort. She didn't want to be that kind of handler. Axe would decide what made the most sense based on the situation on the ground.

19

ADMISSION

Mansion of Arturo Ruiz
Outside Aldama
Tamaulipas, Mexico
Five Hours South of Brownsville, Texas

Arturo's driver floored it. They raced from his fortress-like mansion in the bulletproof SUV, a requirement for the cartel leader. The beast of a vehicle could take a direct hit with an RPG and he'd still be protected. Small arms fire would bounce off it.

Three minutes earlier, a runner from town had arrived in a cloud of dust. The man who had rescued the nurse early that morning had been spotted five hours northwest at a taco stand near the Hotel Riviera Especial de China. Arturo had dropped his fork, left his family sitting at the dinner table, and was in the truck moments later. He normally didn't need to abandon his family to deal with problems himself, but this couldn't be handled by anyone else.

This could be a lucky break—or a disaster.

Despite the urgency, he wouldn't use either a cell phone or a landline from the compound.

The call this morning was bad enough. I won't risk another. The money from guarding the hotel came in handy, but it is becoming riskier than it is worth.

The traffic moved out of their way every time his driver flashed the high beams. No one else in the area had the same type of big black SUV.

On the way, Arturo contemplated the fate of the captain, two hours north, who had allowed the intruder to rescue the nurse from the man's compound.

It will have to be brutal, even by my standards. His screams will serve as a reminder to others to go the extra mile and never let me down.

Twelve minutes later, he rushed into a travel agency in a modern strip mall between a small grocery store and a pharmacy.

"Good afternoon, sir," Arturo whispered into Luisa's ear. She translated the words into English with only the hint of an accent. She was one of many women used by the organization to make calls.

It had been years since Arturo spoke into a phone.

The Americans with their damn NSA, computers, and voiceprints.

The young women spoke for him.

Can't be too careful.

It was an excellent motto to live by.

Arturo continued, and the young woman translated instantly. "We may have a problem with your hotel reservation."

"I'm sorry to hear that," his American contact replied. Arturo knew him only by their agreed-upon code name. He was called the Client. "What seems to be the trouble?"

"Earlier this morning, when your friend checked out of our other property, she left a few items behind. We have been unable to find her in the area to return them."

Arturo's hand clenched on the landline's extension held to his ear. He feared no one, but respected the Client—and the vast organization Arturo sensed in the shadows behind the man.

"Why am I only now hearing this?" The Client's mild, businesslike voice sounded both concerned and cold.

"We had hoped she was merely out enjoying the local riverside and we could find her quickly, but it seems she may have decided to return to her home instead of enjoying our hospitality."

Silence from the other end.

I have to tell him. Get all the bad news out of the way at once and take the hit. Put the responsibility on him for whatever he wants to do next, so he can't blame me—us—for what follows.

"She had a companion. And he may be interested in visiting our sister property, closer to the border."

The Client drew in a sharp breath.

"One man? And my friend is not with him?"

"Another is with him, but a male. His boss, perhaps?"

"That is… unfortunate." A long pause while the Client digested this information. "I will make an email reservation for my friends. Please look for it."

Arturo patted the young woman on the shoulder and thanked her before moving to his tiny office in the back, bolting the door. His driver handed him one of his work laptops, which he connected to the building's ethernet to log on to a shared email account used solely for detailed emergency communication. The Client would compose an email but not send it. Arturo would see it in the Draft folder and continue the email. In this way, he and the client could "chat" with a reasonable assurance of privacy since the email was never sent.

Damn Americans, making all this necessary. Such an inconvenience.

The Client had proposed using a secure communications app for real-time, uncoded voice and text communications. Then came the news reports: the CIA had secretly purchased the company behind the app many years before. They had enjoyed a front-row seat to every supposedly top-secret exchange. Hundreds of spies, criminals, tax evaders, and money launderers were arrested worldwide.

It was only because of Arturo's long-held distrust of communication he hadn't been part of it.

Arturo refreshed his screen every minute, waiting to see the email in the Draft folder.

Surely not all the communications apps are compromised… but using any at this point would be too risky. Better to use the less convenient, old-school ways. Speaking in code over the phone only when necessary, and this cumbersome email system for emergencies.

Finally, his instructions appeared. He read them, sighed, and sat back in his chair.

Disappointing, but not unexpected. After all, I advised him to prepare for this eventuality… and we used it ourselves early this morning.

Arturo typed a brief response, logged out, and returned to the outer office. He needed Luisa to make another important call, but no translating would be required. Only bad news.

Many good men are at the hotel. I want them as far from the lab as possible when it blows.

20

SHORELINE

Southeast of China
Nuevo Leon, Mexico

Axe raced the rental car faster than prudent along the winding shoreline road. He would have to make a choice in a minute. The upcoming fork in the road presented two choices. Going left meant the hotel and possibly the relative safety of Americans and Canadians away from their cold homes for the week between Christmas and New Year.

As long as the cartel values their guests, it's safe. If not, or they care more about capturing me, it's a trap.

Behind him, three vehicles kept pace a quarter mile back. He sped up.

This is my week to be chased.

The right fork would return them to Highway 40. A left there would take them toward Monterey. A right would eventually bring them to the border and home… if they could make it that far.

Kelton had Axe's phone out, looking at the map, trying to be helpful. When it dinged, Axe told him to read the message from Haley.

"She says, 'You're made. Recognized outside restaurant 15 minutes ago. Proceed with caution.'"

We knew that, but nice to have the confirmation.

"You okay?" Axe asked.

"I'm scared shitless," Kelton said in a quiet voice. Any bravado he had on the river eighteen hours ago was long gone.

"Don't worry, it's not bad yet."

"Yet?"

Don't sugarcoat it. He needs to know.

"They're either trying to drive us toward the hotel or keep us from it. I'm not sure which, yet. But when I figure it out, we're doing the opposite."

"If they want us to stay away... maybe we should?"

Axe glanced back again. The train of cars kept pace, neither gaining nor slacking off.

I wish I could drop him off here and come back for him after this is over.

He had to explain the situation in a way Kelton could understand.

"Pretend you're taking over a company," Axe tried.

"I do what's best for me," Kelton said, nodding. "No matter what the other side wants. Ideally, I seize the initiative and do the unexpected. Assuming my competitor isn't bluffing to control me."

"Exactly. But the stakes are too high for them to bluff here."

"Can't we call in the cavalry? Why do we have to handle it ourselves?"

"Kelton, my friend, we are the cavalry."

"Well, shit." He checked the phone. "We're almost at the turn. What are you going to do?"

"Whatever they don't want me to." Axe turned off the headlights. It wasn't fully dark, but the black car against the darkening sky would be harder to see than with the lights on.

No need to make it easy. I wish I had my NVGs right about now. But they would have raised eyebrows at the border if the car got searched.

"Um... Can you see okay?"

"Not really. But neither can they, probably."

The three cars behind him sped up, closing the distance faster than he could outrun them in the rental car.

"Turn in five hundred feet if we're going to the hotel."

Come on... Show me what you don't want me to do.

Axe made out the outline of a truck—no, two trucks on the road to the hotel. One blocked each lane. Their high beams came on as he flew toward the fork.

They don't want us going to the hotel—or they're planning to take us out right now.

"Hold on!"

Not enough imagination. You think because it's a rental car I won't do this?

Axe cranked the wheel hard left, leaving the nicely paved road behind. He drove through the desert, cutting the corner. The car tossed harshly from side to side, then went airborne over a dip.

Branches from bushes screeched as they dragged along Kelton's side of the car, surely leaving deep scratches in the paint.

The undercarriage made a *clunk* as the car landed and the worn shock absorbers couldn't handle the overload. All four hubcaps shot off.

"Glad we got the full insurance coverage," Kelton muttered.

Axe laughed. "Glad it's in your name. I have a terrible history with rentals."

As long as the car could make it another hundred feet, they'd be back on the road and headed where the enemy didn't want them.

Then the shooting started, but nothing hit the car.

Yet.

"Get down!" Axe said. "Into the wheel well."

Kelton complied instantly, sliding his lanky frame from the seat and cramming himself into the floor area.

Axe swerved back onto the road. The firing stopped as the two trucks blocking the road pulled forward, moving out of the way of the cars pursuing Axe.

Well executed, letting the chase cars with momentum through first. These guys are above average.

"Better stay down there. They'll be shooting again if they catch up to us."

"It's only two miles to the hotel."

Two miles is a long way.

Highway 40
Northwest of China
Nuevo Leon, Mexico

In the lead minivan approaching the town of China, Captain Hernandez sighed as his driver couldn't resist trying again.

"How much further?" his driver asked.

Captain Hernandez didn't know, exactly. He guessed only about another ten miles.

It's come to this. For security, I cannot bring a map lest one of my men sees it, guesses our destination, and sends a tip to the cartel.

More than likely, the driver was merely bored... and scared.

Hernandez had picked his most loyal men for the mission. Ordered them to leave their cell phones in lockers at the staging point in Monterey. Had to apologize for the indignity of frisking them to make sure no one had "forgotten" a cell phone in a pocket.

"Patience," he told the driver. "It's the journey, not the destination," he joked.

The man grunted his derision.

A minute later, they approached the intersection where they had to turn south.

"Slow. Turn right ahead, off the highway."

The turn would lead to the shoreline road. A hard right at the fork would lead them to the hotel. They were arriving right on time: full darkness, when their night-vision goggles should give them an edge for the surprise assault.

21

NHA

Nancy and Dave entered the conference room carrying their laptops and notebooks. "We have another feed," Dave announced. "A call from the hotel. Sixteen minutes old."

He spun his laptop toward her. "The last five calls have been routine. Questions about pricing and availability. Inquiries for tickets to the New Year's Eve dinner and party at the hotel. Whether the fishing in the lake has been any good lately." He pressed play on the file.

Haley used her passable Spanish and the translation software to make sense of it. A younger female asked for the manager.

"Mr. Lopez," a gruff voice said.

"Excuse me, Mr. Lopez. This is the corporate office. I have more information about your guest who may arrive soon."

"Of course, how can I help?" The man's voice went from annoyed to helpful instantly.

"Make him comfortable. He is a VIP and corporate would like him to stay awhile. His boss may stay, or not."

The gruff man hesitated. "We already made arrangements to meet him off property."

There was a pause, then the young woman spoke again. "If he doesn't make it for his reservation, we understand, but we'd love to get his opinions about our service and other matters."

"I'll see to it."

"Also, the doctor in the infirmary. Another property needs his services as soon as possible. Escort him to the airport immediately."

"Of course, I will put my best man on it."

"Two."

"Yes, two men."

"The rest of the staff should stay clear of the infirmary for now. It needs a deep cleaning, but we will take care of it if necessary."

Lopez hesitated. "Also understood."

"Excellent. Thank you for your time, Mr. Lopez."

"Always happy to be of—" Lopez stopped because the pleasant female had already hung up.

Haley bit her lip and texted Axe, not bothering to hide it from Nancy and Dave.

Hotel told to intercept you or hold you captive if you make it there. And Kelton is expendable they said. Also, they are evacuating a 'doctor' from 'the infirmary' and escorting him with two men. Advising staff to avoid 'infirmary' b/c it needs a 'deep cleaning.' Time: 17 min. ago. Abort? Or priority… capture Dr?

She hit send.

Should I call? No. Calls are only for when immediate attention is needed. I'm his burner phone's only contact. If he gets a text, he knows how important it is.

She glanced up. Nancy and Dave were staring at their screens, carefully ignoring her texting.

Haley held her phone, hoping for a quick reply from Axe.

Nothing.

Suddenly, she realized what she had missed. The compound holding the nurse might have a surveillance system. They must have a photo of him. He walked right into the area and the guy at the taco stand recognized him because of the stupid bushy beard he'd grown.

How will I live with myself if he gets killed on an operation I sent him into? I should have thought to have him at least shave his beard before going back in, or not go at all.

"Can we upgrade the monitoring of the compound to real-time?" She had no experience with managing an operation like this.

Dave answered. "Maybe, but there will be hoops to jump through. They'll want to know why and have a manager sign off on it. Can we tell them we have an op running, an asset in play?"

"We do not have an asset, nor an op running. I have an asset and an op, not you two."

They paused, looking around at their computers and notepads in a messy group on the table. Dave tried to catch Nancy's eye, but she stared at her screen instead. Haley caught it all.

Uh oh. Relationship trouble.

"How unsanctioned is this, Haley?" Dave asked, concerned. "Are we going to get in trouble?"

Nancy turned to him in a flash. "I don't mind getting in trouble for a good cause. I agree with Haley. There's a danger here. This isn't the usual cartel drug operation."

"I don't want to go to jail," Dave shot back at her. "Do you?"

"No one is going to jail," Haley said.

Go big or go home. I'm already out on a limb. What's a little further?

"As of right now," she said, standing taller, "consider yourselves temporarily assigned to a clandestine group, on loan from the CAG. This room is no longer legally CAG. It's part of the…"

Damn it. We need a name.

Nancy and Dave waited expectantly.

"The NHA."

"The NSA?" Nancy asked.

"No, NHA."

"Never heard of it," Dave said suspiciously.

Nancy glared at him. "She said it's clandestine."

"What does NHA stand for?"

Nalen, Haley, and Axe. But I can't tell them that.

"It's need to know." She gave the man a hard look, letting the killer inside her show through. "Stay or go, Dave, it's up to you."

Dave quickly looked away from her stare, turning to lock eyes with Nancy. They glared at each other across the small table, a silent war of words, arguing without speaking, the way long-term couples can.

Dave finally sighed with a frown. "Fine. We're in."

I hope what I've done is legal.

"Do we have a manager's approval?" Dave asked, tapping on his laptop.

"Give me a minute. For the moment, focus on the hotel. Calls, data, the works. Traffic cams from nearby businesses."

"It's a small town in northern Mexico, Haley. They don't have what you want."

"Satellite?"

Nancy checked. "Not for a while, then only an oblique angle. Nothing great."

"Whatever you can get. Let's not have the asset risk his life for nothing. If he goes in, I want a payoff." She paused as they got to work on their computers. "His name is Axe, by the way."

Please don't let him get hurt. Or Kelton.

She turned away and dialed Admiral Nalen's number using their secure comms app—one she hoped wasn't owned or cracked by her government... or anyone else. Moving to the corner of the room, only a few feet further from Nancy and Dave, she readied her argument.

I hope this works.

Admiral Nalen picked up on the first ring, all business as usual. "What do you have?"

"A situation." Earlier, she'd sent him a text with an update about Axe going back to Mexico. "Axe is walking into a potential trap. I warned him, but want to monitor it—and any apples he shakes from the tree. But the boss already called me out once this morning for running an op here. There's no time to relocate, so I've temporarily assigned my team to the NHA with me."

Nalen paused as he processed it. It took a few seconds, then he laughed. "Nalen, Haley, and Axe? It sounds like a law firm. We need a better name."

"Yes, well..."

"You improvised. Well done. So you need me to run interference with Addison?"

"Yes, and I need his approval for real-time data to flow to us from the NSA."

"Hmm."

Haley held her breath.

"I'll make a call. But this may cost us, down the line."

"It's worth it. My intuition tells me this is big."

"Hang tight. You'll have your answer in a few minutes."

22

EXPENDABLE

Near Hotel Riviera Especial de China
Outside China
Nuevo Leon, Mexico

There were now five vehicles trailing Axe, but at least they had stopped shooting at him.

Why did they change their minds?

His phone dinged quietly with a text. "Read it out loud for me, will you?" he asked Kelton. The poor guy still huddled in the footrest area of his seat.

"Got it." He took Axe's phone from the cup holder and unlocked it as Axe told him the passcode. "Okay. Another one from Haley."

Of course it's from Haley. No one else has the number.

He let it go.

The guy's in over his head. Bringing him was a mistake. He did fine on the river, but I should have come alone for this part. Selfish of me—I miss being part of a team.

"Hotel told to intercept you or hold you captive..." Kelton trailed off.

They were less than a minute away from the hotel. Its lights shone in the distance. "What else?"

In the glow of the phone's screen, Kelton's face had gone whiter, which Axe didn't think was possible.

"'Kelton is expendable, they said.'"

Shit.

"Don't worry about it," Axe said with a smile. "I'm expendable too once they torture me for the information they need!" he chuckled.

Kelton didn't laugh.

Tough crowd.

"I won't let anything happen to you."

"How can you say that? They've already shot at us."

"Not very well, though. And we're still here, right?"

Kelton took a deep breath. "It's fine. I deserve whatever I get. Remember that." He continued reading. "They are evacuating a 'doctor' from 'the infirmary' and escorting him with two men. Advising staff to avoid 'infirmary' b/c it needs a 'deep cleaning.' Time: 17 min. ago. Abort? Or priority… capture Dr?"

Interesting.

"See, shaking this tree is already bearing fruit. What do you want to do?" he asked Kelton.

Welcome to the deep end of the pool, Kelton. Better learn to swim quick.

"Realistically, we can't back out now, can we?"

"Nope."

I hope he can handle the truth.

"Then we keep going." Kelton pulled himself back onto his seat. "I trust you, Axe. Sorry I'm so nervous. I go from wanting my old life back to willing to die to help."

"Let's avoid the dying part."

"Yes, please."

"Great. I figure we can catch up to this doctor Haley mentions. And the infirmary intrigues me. I've never been good at following orders. If I'm told to avoid a place, it's almost a compulsion to go there."

He glanced in the rearview mirror at the train of vehicles following him.

If we even get that far.

"Text back, tell her this. 'Copy. Shaking the tree.'"

23

DENIABILITY

The glass door banged open, startling Haley. Her hand reached for the pistol at her side but stopped in time to merely adjust her black blazer, covering as an angry Gregory stalked in.

Damn, he looks pissed. I wonder what Nalen told him.

"Dave, get the duty officer at NSA for me."

Dave jumped at his command, grabbing the phone and dialing from memory.

Gregory stopped next to Haley, standing at the head of the conference table. "The NHA? Nalen, Haley, Axe?" he whispered. "You need a better name, or at least a way to explain the initials."

He doesn't sound as angry as I thought.

"NSA on line one," Dave called.

He picked up the phone at Haley's end of the table. "Addison, CAG." He rattled off a series of code words. "Give us immediate real-time access to northern Mexico. Grid and location to follow." He nodded at Haley, who scribbled on her yellow pad and handed it to him. "My authorization. We have discovered a high-value U.S. citizen is in danger of being abducted." He paused. "Kelton Kellison. He's part of an active terrorism retaliation alert. Here's the location: the Hotel Riviera Especial de China, outside China, Nuevo Leon, Mexico. Grid 153. All calls, all traffic, all feeds." He rattled off another series of authorization codes. "Thank you."

He hung up and addressed Haley, Nancy, and Dave. "As you know, Kelton Kellison is, despite his recent business misfortune, an important American citizen. He has also been the target of at least one terrorist cell. He is in Mexico, I understand? And you three discovered this and are tracking him for his safety?"

The question hung in the air. Haley picked up on the cover story. "Yes, sir. I discovered data indicating a possible cartel hit against an unknown American target and put my team on it. Kellison is with one bodyguard, on their way to a hotel which we believe is a front for a major drug lab."

"Purpose of his visit?"

Come on, Gregory. Do we have to play this game?

He narrowed his eyes, waiting impatiently.

Yes, apparently we do. Plausible deniability. Everyone wants to protect their asses.

"A quick vacation, but he's since learned an old friend—a doctor—is working at the hotel. He will attempt to make contact."

"This doctor, what do we know about him?"

"Working on that now, sir," Nancy called from behind her laptop. While Dave watched the spectacle of Gregory and Haley doing the deniability waltz, Nancy stuck with her job.

Hearing her speak jolted Dave back to his computer. "The real-time feed is up. Nothing new," Dave added.

"Satellites? Drones?"

"No."

He grunted in disappointment. "You have Kellison's phone number?" Gregory asked Haley.

She eyed Nancy and Dave, wondering if they knew how close she, Axe, and Kelton were. "Well, I have a cell. Often it's his bodyguard who handles Kellison's calls."

"Understood. He's aware of the danger?"

"Yes," she said, playing along.

"And you told him to avoid the vicinity of the hotel... but he's ignoring you... right?"

Ah, I get it. So we're all covered—on the record—if this goes further south.

"I tried, sir. But Kelton Kellison is a headstrong, powerful man—despite his recent troubles."

If you call losing most of his net worth, his job, company, homes, and reputation merely 'troubles.'

"Fine. Looks like I'm caught up." He leaned against the wall and crossed his arms. "Let's get them both out in one piece—and his friend the doctor."

Smooth moves from Nalen to get Gregory on board, and impressive how Gregory covers our asses. I need to learn from this. But I wonder what the cost will be once all is said and done.

Her phone dinged. She read the short text from Axe but didn't share it with the rest of the people in the room. He was still going in.

Good luck, partner.

24

HOTEL RIVIERA

Hotel Riviera Especial de China
Outside China
Nuevo Leon, Mexico

The hotel didn't look like much. White adobe-style walls, two stories high. A large, rectangular box, with the typical glass front doors of a modern hotel, along with a long red welcome carpet under the huge awning, which would keep the sun off the entryway in the daytime.

A circular driveway led to the front of the hotel. A tired fountain sat in the center, water feebly bubbling from the top in the weak glow of a single light shining up at it from the ground.

Axe slowed as they approached the hotel. Two of the vehicles following them crept along behind, keeping their distance as he turned into the entry circle leading to the front doors. The other three drove toward the rear of the building.

In Mexico, the hotel would be ranked three stars. To Axe, it looked rundown and uninviting.

"Probably too much to expect valet parking," he said, hoping to get a laugh out of Kelton.

"We don't have to stay here, do we?" Kelton muttered.

Jokes are good. He's back to a decent headspace, I hope.

"If anyone asks, you're Kelton Kellison, former billionaire on a cheap get-away," Axe said, stopping the car along the curb. "I'm your fishing buddy, not your bodyguard. Play it straight: you're a cocky rich guy. Act like it."

They got out of the car and left it pulled ahead of the red carpet, not bothering with a parking spot.

I doubt we come back to it. But if we do, we'll be in a big damn hurry.

The red carpet had seen better days. Small areas were well worn, enough to see the black rubber backing. The rest was closer to a dull pink than bright red. A sign on the sliding door showed it was broken. An arrow pointed to the single glass door on the right with a large, dull bronze handle to pull.

On instinct, Axe ripped the sign from the door as they walked past.

Are the men following us from the hotel or from town?

He'd know by which door they used. If they followed them in and encountered the broken door, they didn't know the place well.

As they walked inside, the vehicles which had trailed them drove away.

The hotel had a typical lobby with a check-in desk on the right, staffed by a short, pleasant-looking young woman with long black hair and cute dimples. She smiled at them warmly as they let the door swing shut behind them.

"Welcome," she called in English.

Axe waved. "Bar? Restaurant?"

"*Si,* yes. Bar to the left, restaurant straight ahead. Checking in?"

"Perhaps. We haven't decided whether we'll continue on or not. Beer first."

"Of course. Enjoy."

They walked toward the bar, a dim room off the lobby. No one followed them, and there were no guards stationed in the lobby.

Feels less tense than I thought it would. Maybe I played it right. If they don't want to cause a scene, we have some time to recon.

A heavy-set man who looked American strolled past them, leaving the bar toward the restaurant. His sunburned face looked painful.

"Catch anything?" Kelton called out. The fishing in the lake right outside was supposedly excellent.

The man nodded and slowed. "Couple of good ones. And this," he said, pointing to his face and arms, which were bright red. "If you're going out tomorrow, don't be stupid like me. Wear sunscreen! I figured it's

December. How bad can it be?" He looked at Kelton with his head tilted. "You look familiar. Have we met?"

"Oh, no, I've just got one of those faces, you know?"

The man smiled and nodded, not quite convinced. Axe walked forward and Kelton followed with a final word for the man. "Good luck tomorrow."

"You too!"

"Wait!" Axe called to the man as he walked away. "Did you get ointment or anything for the sunburn? At the infirmary, or whatever they have? The doctor?"

The fisherman looked confused. "I don't think they have that here." He took a step closer and whispered, after a glance at the front desk receptionist, who was on the phone. "It's not very fancy. They don't have room service, let alone a doctor on staff!"

Interesting.

Highway 40
Outside China
Nuevo Leon, Mexico

After using the taco stand's phone a second time to report the Americans were leaving, Juan had taken the direct route to the hotel. The men needed dinner, and others were more capable of following the wanted man and his boss—or doing whatever Señor Ruiz wanted done to them.

Lopez had nodded at him when handed his tacos. He hadn't even complained about them being cold. It was the closest thing to praise the young man had received since starting at the hotel.

Then Juan been given a long-range walkie-talkie and sent to relieve the guard on the corner of Highway 40 and the shoreline road leading to the hotel.

A promotion! No longer running errands. I'm now a guard.

He sat in his pickup in the darkness, parked off the road, practically in the desert, and settled in for a long night.

He had been giving thanks for his promotion when the first minivan zipped by, much faster than normal.

Four others followed. He tried to memorize the license plate of the rear van, but the light which should have illuminated the plate wasn't working.

"Alert, alert. Post 4," he called into the radio, attempting to hide his excitement.

"Post 4, go ahead."

"Five minivans just passed me, driving fast, in formation."

"License plates?"

"None visible."

A pause, then the voice said, "Stay in place. Report all other traffic, understand?"

"Yes, I understand."

I'm on a roll. First the wanted American, now this.

Another promotion was assured.

Hotel Riviera Especial de China
Bar Nueva

Axe felt the change in the air as the bartender brought their beers.

He sensed danger.

What is it? What am I missing?

With his back to the wall, he had a view of most of the lobby, including the reception desk. The dimpled young lady had picked up another call, listened for a second, then hung up quickly and ran through a door behind her.

She's panicked. That's not good.

"*Dos cervesas,* my friends. A new brand, very delicious. We hope you enjoy it."

Kelton grabbed a bottle with a shaking hand and took a long, grateful sip. Axe didn't touch his but hoped a beer would calm Kelton's nerves, which were back since they sat in the bar.

"You should try this," Kelton told him. "It's different but good." He looked at the label in appreciation and chugged the rest. He set the bottle on the small table and gestured to Axe's. When Axe shook his head, he picked up the second bottle and drained half of that one, too.

"Get ready to move," Axe whispered to Kelton as he took another deep pull from the bottle.

"What? Where?" He didn't look around, though Axe could tell it took effort.

He's learning.

"I'm not sure. Follow my lead. Something's happening."

"Shit. Okay." He finished his beer and set it next to the first.

***

Hotel Riviera Especial de China
Security Center

Lopez picked up the phone and hit speed dial. He had to inform *Jefe* about the latest development.

Damn it. I was so close to getting out of this place alive.

Despite a complete lack of warning from any of their expensive, highly and lowly placed sources, they were about to be raided by the police.

At least I got Dr. Edgars out safely, and my men are far from the basement laboratory. And Juan has proven himself twice today.

"Riviera Properties. How is our guest?" It was the same young woman he had spoken with earlier. With the caller ID, she knew exactly who was calling.

I pray Jefe is nearby.

"In the bar, drinking beer. But we have another problem. I need to inquire about blackout dates. Five groups of uninvited guests will check in soon. We're unsure about how to properly greet them."

A second passed before the woman spoke again. "We received no reservations."

"Neither did we, except a trusted friend pointed them out to us." *Jefe* would understand about the guards stationed along every road to the hotel during times of high alert. He designed—and paid for—the system.

"All rooms are fully reserved. Turn them away."

"And our two new guests?"

"They must be part of the arriving group. They must go. All rooms are booked."

"Understood."

Hotel Riviera Especial de China
Bar Nueva

"Up! Follow me!" Axe knocked the table over standing up, then ran through the bar toward the reception desk. Kelton followed close behind him.

"What's happening?"

"I don't know, but it's bad." He rounded the reception desk and reached for the handle of the door the receptionist had disappeared behind.

Before he could turn it, the door flew open. Axe assessed the man in an instant. Lean and muscular, a dark and worn face, hard eyes. That alone screamed "warrior" in Axe's mind, and the automatic rifle in his hands sealed the deal.

Taking advantage of the man's momentum through the door, Axe swung and connected his forearm with the fighter's throat, dropping him.

A second fighter tripped over the first one's body as he crowded through the doorway, going down in a heap.

Axe grabbed the head of the man on top and broke his neck without hesitation. He grabbed the man's rifle from his dead hands and used the butt to hammer the first guard's head twice. The two men lay in the doorway, dead in less than ten seconds.

Kelton's eyes were wide as he looked from the men to Axe. His mouth dropped open in shock, and his face went white once again.

"Hold this," Axe said as he handed the rifle to Kelton. "Do not point it at me."

"Wha... You... Those two... Wait, who do I shoot?"

Axe took two magazines from the pockets of the dead guy on top. "Nobody! Keep your finger off the trigger."

The safety is on, but he doesn't need to know that.

Axe rolled the first guard to the side and retrieved his rifle as well, along with more ammunition. And a large keyring clipped to the man's pants.

Keys always come in handy.

"Two minutes," Captain Hernandez called out in his minivan, repeating it over the group's short-range radio network. "Get ready. We are hitting a hotel suspected of being a front for the Ruiz cartel. It could be money laundering, but we think it contains a high-value drug lab. Expect it to be well defended. I will drive straight to the front doors, followed by Team 2. Team 3, you will flank to the left. Team 4, you flank right. Team 5, you will follow the road to the right around the rear of the hotel and gain entry from there. We will meet inside the hotel and clear it room by room, starting where you gain entry."

The team leaders in each of the vans acknowledged.

I hope we have the element of surprise this time.

Using the unarmored minivans had been a risk. But he had a few surprises up his sleeve, too, and the vans would make it easier.

"Prepare the RPGs," he called to his most trusted man. He sat in the middle of the first row of seats, directly under the sunroof. Hernandez repeated the order into his radio for the other vans.

"Weapons hot. We fire if fired upon, and we don't stop until we win, understood?"

The men happily acknowledged his command as they readied their weapons. Finally, they were getting payback for their many dead colleagues.

25

KEEP OUT

Haley clutched her cell phone, willing Axe to answer. She had to tell him about the call they'd intercepted. The men at the hotel had new orders: they were to kill him. And it sure sounded like the place was about to be attacked by a different group, but they didn't know whether it was the Mexican police or a rival drug cartel.

Calm down. He's supremely capable. If he doesn't answer, it's more likely he's kicking ass than dead.

The call went to voicemail again.

"Come on, pick up," she muttered and hit the button to redial.

Axe's Spanish wasn't great, but he could understand the signs on the door. The bold red, black and white meant "Keep Out." The yellow and black one meant the area behind it was dangerous.

Perfect. This is either the most dangerous place to be or the safest.

His phone buzzed for the third time in his pocket. He handed it to Kelton. "Answer this, find out what she wants."

We don't have a lot of time.

He didn't know what was happening, but it would be big. He could feel it.

The keys on the ring he had stolen from the dead guard looked similar, except for one. He selected the larger, thicker key and slid it into the lock.

"No, it's Kelton. Yes, we know... okay, hold on."

"Haley says they've been told to kill us and the building is about to be attacked by five vehicles."

"Good guys or other bad guys?"

"Did you get that?" Kelton listened. "She doesn't know, but suggests we get out while we can."

"It's too late for that. We're in it now, but don't worry, we're going somewhere safe."

"We're going somewhere safe, he says," Kelton told Haley and did a double-take at the door. "Axe, don't those signs say basically, 'Danger, Keep Out'?"

"Yes. Unless she has more actionable intelligence for us, hang up. Let's find this doctor, then figure out what's going on. Hopefully, by the time we're done, the two forces will have taken care of each other for us."

He turned the key and pushed open the heavy steel door.

Central Analysis Group Headquarters
Conference Room C
Alexandria, Virginia

"He won't leave," Haley said, ending the call. "Says they'll figure out what's going on, find the doctor, and wait until the two forces kill each other."

Dave nodded. "That's actually pretty smart."

"As long as he doesn't get in between them," Nancy pointed out.

"This is why I specifically didn't sign on for an operational unit," Gregory muttered in her ear.

Hotel Riviera Especial de China
Employee Area

They stood in a small room, barely five feet square. A simple black plastic chair sat along the wall between the outer and inner doors. Axe touched it. Still warm. The inner door had larger signs with bigger print.

There's usually a guard at this door. Probably one of the guys I killed just now.

Axe tried the outer door key. It didn't fit. He looked through a small window at head height. He could smash the glass, reach through, and unlock the door from inside.

Why not? But first...

Standing so only the back of his head would be seen through the window, he pounded on the door.

"Vámonos!" he yelled. Let's go.

He waited five seconds, then pounded again. A moment later, when he heard faint footsteps from the other side, Axe risked a glance.

A thirty-something, pale man wearing a lab coat pushed his face to the glass. He looked worried. In English, he asked, "What is it?"

"Emergencia. Vámonos!"

The man unlocked the door from his side and opened it all the way.

"What's the emergency? I saw the flashing lights."

Axe pointed the gun at him and moved so he couldn't close the door. "Good evening."

Got him!

"You're the doctor?" Axe asked.

The man raised his hands. "Well, yes, but..." His eyes widened as he saw Kelton. "You're the Americans from the bar."

"How do you know that?" Axe said.

What the hell is going on?

The man pointed at the small black half circle on the ceiling. "Security cameras all over. All visitors are monitored for... never mind. Are you... I mean, is this a rescue?"

He looked hopeful, and there was another expression on his face. Axe couldn't put his finger on it.

Play the odds.

"Yes, this is a rescue. We're here to get you out."

"Oh, thank God. I thought I wouldn't get out of here alive!"

"You ready?"

"Just me?" He glanced back at the room behind him.

"What do you mean? If you're the doctor, yes."

The building rocked with an explosion and the sound of automatic weapon fire came through the heavy door.

"We're under attack?"

"Yep. You ready or not?"

The man hesitated a second, then hurried past Axe into the small room. "Let's get the hell out of here."

Axe let the inner door swing shut and lock with a *clang*. Reaching for the outer door, he saw he would have to use the key to unlock it from the inside as well.

Very security conscious… They didn't want the doctor getting out. Hence the guard at the inner door.

With Axe leading and Kelton bringing up the rear, still holding the rifle, the three slipped into the hallway.

The sounds of a battle were much louder.

That's a fifty-caliber machine gun—on the roof, it sounds like.

A dozen other weapons fired, but none were close.

The building shuddered again, and the fifty cal stopped.

"What was that?" Kelton asked, his eyes wide and voice shaking.

"RPG," Axe said. "Rocket-propelled grenade. Took out the machine gun on the roof. Not bad shooting, only took them two tries."

My guys would have gotten it the first time.

Axe led them down the hallway to the rear door—or what he hoped would be the rear door. They leaned against the wall near it.

"Listen, a halfway competent attacking force will have sent a team to flank on the side or rear. So once we go through the door, we are in the battle. But there's a pool in back. We'll play it by ear, but the tentative plan—"

The building shook hard, throwing them off their feet. Behind them, the heavy metal door they had exited blew off its hinges and slammed against the opposite wall, embedding a corner into the drywall.

Thick black smoke poured out and billowed toward them, filling the hallway.

The doctor backpedaled on the ground, terrified. "Come on!"

He scrambled to his feet, nearly falling again in his haste, and threw himself out the back door, leaving Axe and Kelton to hurry after him.

26

SPOOKY

"If we can't watch or listen, we can be productive in other ways," Haley announced. Gregory leaned against the wall, arms crossed, saying little and staying out of the way.

He's hanging around to make sure we don't cause an international incident. Like dad supervising the kids playing in the pool.

"Let's assume they make it out of the building but don't have access to a car," Haley said. "Dave, figure out a way for them to get across the border undetected."

"Won't it be a problem if they went into the country but aren't logged as returning?"

"We can fix that," Gregory said quietly. "Just get them out."

Dave worked his magic on his laptop.

"Nancy, look at the big picture. What are we missing?" Haley sat down at her laptop. "I'll find the doctor the cartel mentioned."

How hard can it be?

She dove in, starting with a database of practicing medical doctors. She expanded the list to every person in America who had graduated from medical school.

This laptop screen is way too small.

She used the remote to turn on the huge monitor at the end of the room while moving her laptop closer to it. Extending her display, she snapped four windows to the big screen, one per corner. She did the same with her laptop so she could work on all eight at once. The Homeland Security database. Immigration. The CIA and NSA systems. The CAG's proprietary feed next to the FBI information. Census and medical schools data. She opened more tabs for various public search engines, which were often the most helpful.

Then she lost herself in the stream of data, becoming one with it. She let it flow around her, through her. Her eyes flicked from one window to another, changing parameters, writing search strings and macros. Her fingers flew on the keyboard. While a small part of her mind monitored the situation in the conference room, staying situationally alert as Axe had drilled into her, most of her attention consumed data like a black hole consuming a star.

Her time in the zone felt like both seconds and hours. Finally, she had it.

There.

Dr. Edgars. A Ph.D., not a medical doctor. Probability fifty-one percent... but she could feel it—he was the one the people on the phone had discussed.

"I found him," she announced. She looked up from her screens to find Nancy and Dave staring at her, spellbound. On the far side of the room, Gregory looked like he had seen a ghost.

"What?"

Why are they looking at me like that?

"What happened? I got lost in the data—what did I miss?"

No one said a word.

"Speak!" Haley barked. The tone that had made Dave and another coworker nearly pee their pants several weeks before came out unbidden.

"We've never seen you work," Gregory explained, unfazed by her tone. "It was..." He trailed off.

"I know it looks like there's only about a fifty-fifty chance it's the guy, but trust me, it's him."

I hate sounding so defensive. I need to find a confident, dispassionate way of stating my conclusions.

"That's not what he means," Nancy said with a motherly smile.

"We mean you're incredible," Dave added.

"The term 'savant' comes to mind. But in a good way," Nancy added hastily.

It was Haley's turn to look confused. "I don't know what you're talking about. I just do my thing."

"We speed read, of course," Dave said. "But what you did… the speed…"

"No one could do this job without a talent for assimilating information," Nancy said, looking at her funny. "But it would have taken me hours to find the information. You accomplished it in twenty minutes."

"I tried to read half what you were reading. I couldn't keep up," Dave admitted. His tone was a mixture of awe and… fear?

Of me?

"I get an intuition," she started, trying to explain. "I'm not reading the entire material. My mind sees the page and keywords jump out. If nothing pops, I'm on to the next page."

"It's… I don't know the word for it. Impressive," Nancy said.

"Downright spooky," Dave muttered.

Gregory watched her, a look of newfound respect on his face.

Great. Now Dave thinks I'm a witch, too.

"Can we please focus on the problem at hand?" she asked, getting nods all around. "There's a wrinkle," she said. "I found not only Dr. Edgars, but seven other prominent scientists have vacationed to Mexico— and not returned home."

She left the rest unsaid as a test to see if her team—of three now, apparently, with the addition of Gregory into the mix—would pick up on the thread.

Gregory frowned, giving her a look.

He gets it.

Nancy jumped in. "Do I dare ask what their specialties are? Please don't say infectious diseases or sarin gas."

"No. They are all experts in psilocybin's effect on the brain. Magic mushrooms."

Dave looked relieved. "That's not so bad."

Gregory spoke from the end of the room, staring at the windows still open on Haley's screen, but not seeing them. "No, it's worse."

27

RUN

Captain Hernandez fired a three-shot burst from his rifle, hitting a defender who had poked his head up from behind a car sitting by the entrance.

How many more can there be?

He'd brought fifty-five men—eleven crammed into each minivan, the three rows of seats much too small for the officers and their gear.

It wasn't enough.

The decision to not prepare a quick reaction force had seemed prudent at the time. The fewer people who knew about the raid, the less chance of a leak. But what he wouldn't give for a few helicopters filled with men flying to his aid right now.

Moments earlier, an enormous explosion had rocked the right side of the hotel. At first, he thought Team 3 had destroyed an ammunition cache. But he could see Team 3's position—at least, the few of them still alive—and they hadn't moved.

The cartel blew up the laboratory, just like at the raid early this morning. There goes the evidence.

This operation wasn't only for evidence, however. It was for revenge, and to show the cartels they still had a formidable foe.

Hernandez fired again to keep the enemy's heads down. There were defenders alive behind the low wall on each side of the hotel's front door.

Around him, his men lay dead or dying.

His vehicles were destroyed. One had taken the brunt of fire from a powerful machine gun on the roof before they'd taken it out with an RPG.

Eleven men dead in a few seconds.

"All units, report."

"Team 5, rear of hotel. Four men alive. Pinned down but in a secure position, over."

A stalemate.

Firing came from the right side of the hotel, followed by a small *boom* of a grenade.

"Team 4?" He could see the smoking ruin of their position. No need to call, but he tried in hopes his men survived the explosion.

No reply.

Team 2 was dead in their destroyed van.

He hadn't heard from Team 3. Their van had been sprayed with fire as it raced to the left flank, bullets ripping through the thin metal.

That leaves me and four men at the back. Fifty men dead... and we haven't even reached the building.

Could he retreat? Surrender? No. Either choice meant death.

"All surviving units. The vehicles are destroyed. No QRF is coming. Surrender means torture." He took a deep breath, then gave the order. "Prepare to rush the building on my command."

Axe watched the doctor slam the door open and rush out, more afraid of the black smoke from the explosion filling the hallway than the gunfire outside.

"Kelton, let's go!" Axe jumped to his feet, helped Kelton up, and caught the door with his foot before it closed. Kelton's face, surprisingly, looked relaxed, unconcerned by the situation. "This is fun!" he said, smiling at Axe.

Weird. He might be in shock, but whatever gets us out of this.

Axe crouched, brought the rifle up, and pushed the door open with his foot. Then they ran.

Going through a door into an enemy-occupied room or area is dangerous. In a surprise assault, the lead can enter and neutralize the immediate threats with their sudden appearance. Once the initial surprise is lost, however, the second person through the door is in a dangerous position.

Axe expected fire the second he opened the door. But while gunfire came from both ahead and above, none of it was directed at him. The doctor, white lab coat drawing attention like a beacon in the night, ran to the left, toward the lake.

Excellent idea.

Whoever the assaulters were, they had their hands full with men shooting at them from the roof and second-story windows.

Four men ran toward the hotel—a rival cartel, police, or a cartel pretending to be police—firing at the elevated enemy as they came... and were mowed down, dropping in bloody heaps long before they got close to the building.

"Left. To the lake!" Axe hissed at Kelton.

He kept close to the building. Kelton jogged behind.

The men defending the hotel can't see us this close to the wall.

Running to his death, Captain Hernandez took two bullets to his armored chest plate, a graze to his left arm, and a through-and-through to his lower left side. He bled but would live—for now.

He killed three men and gained the front door. He saw many other cartel members dead. His team had done well, though they paid the price with their own lives. The automatic door refused to open, so he had to use the heavy glass door to the side.

I made it. Now what?

He crept through the deserted lobby. Black smoke seeped from under a door behind the reception counter.

Gunfire from the rear had stopped seconds after starting.

Team 5 didn't make it. Where can I do the most good?

The left side of the hotel hadn't been attacked by his men.

Do damage there, or check out the back of the building?

The dark smoke behind the door to his right ruled out that direction.

By myself, I can't change the outcome. I'm still going to die, but I may be able to take more of them with me.

His eyes caught movement ahead of him. At the last instant, he held his fire. A heavy-set, sunburned tourist crouched near the entrance to the hotel's restaurant, his hands raised. "I'm an American," he called in English.

No shit.

"How many?" Hernandez asked.

The American glanced to his left. More raised hands appeared from several tourists as they inched around the wall.

"Don't shoot!" a woman sobbed. She wore a black dress much too elegant for this back-water hotel.

"Federal police," he told them in accented English. "Run south. Along the lake. No roads. Then hide. When helicopters come, wave. Or morning, go to city. China. Understand?"

Still with his hands in the air, the stocky man nodded.

"Bless you," the woman in the black dress whispered. Her heavy makeup had been ruined by tears.

"Go. Now. Fast."

The woman slipped off her high heels, and they all ran—for the first time in decades, he guessed—out the door and into the night.

Ignoring the blood seeping from his side and the wound on his arm, he turned to the left side of the hotel.

Time to do some damage before I join my brothers.

Axe slowed to a stop at the corner of the building, next to the doctor leaning against the wall, gasping for breath. They were safe in the shadows and hidden from any cartel members above them, at least for the moment.

"Haven't... gotten... enough... exercise... lately," the doctor managed.

"It's three hundred yards to the water," Axe said after checking on a still-smiling Kelton, who looked like he was having the adventure of a lifetime. "Are there any boats we could steal?"

"How would I know?" the doctor asked. "This is the first time I've been outside since they brought us here."

Worry about that comment later.

"Take off the lab coat. You'll blend in better. Can you swim?" Axe asked him. He knew Kelton could. The doctor nodded. "Then we'll sprint down the pathway," which unfortunately was lit by ankle-high solar-powered lamps. They would be exposed as they ran. "Don't zigzag. Run as fast as you can. I'll go first to draw fire and shoot back."

"Whee!" Kelton had started dancing.

"What the hell is wrong with you?"

Great, he's lost it.

"He's been dosed," the doctor said as he wadded the white lab coat into a ball and shoved it under a bush. "You must not have drunk your beer."

"I chugged them both!" Kelton said. "Excellent. Best beer ever."

"What's going on?" Axe asked the young doctor.

"You were given beer spiked with a powerful drug. From psychotropic mushrooms. It's fascinating, really. You see, we found—"

"He's high?"

The doctor nodded. "Sky-high for a while. Then…" He whispered in Axe's ear. "Prepare yourself. You're going to need to kill him in less than an hour. Maybe sooner. Not sure how long—we've never tried two beers so quickly."

"Back up, why do I need to kill him?"

"Oh, that doesn't sound like fun," Kelton said, "but whatever. I deserve it. Put me out of my misery. Not having my money sucks," he said, still smiling.

"Most subjects go from a mild buzz to euphoria. After that, if they don't get more of the drug—the beer, in this case—they go into immediate withdrawals and have hallucinations. A very bad trip. They become extremely violent." He straightened, getting set to run. "Afterwards, half have cravings which are mostly controllable. Others…" He stared off into the night, his voice quieting. "Not so much." He shook his head sadly. "Okay, I've caught my breath. I can do this. We should go, right?"

Could we wait here for police to arrive? No. Better to get away now.

"Get ready to run. Kelton, can you handle this?"

"Aye, aye, captain!" He saluted.

———

Hernandez had to make his first shots count. After he lost the element of surprise, he wouldn't get far. Though the acceptance of his coming death might give him a small edge.

At the end of the hotel's main hall for the left wing, room doors were propped open on both sides. He went left, edging into a typical hotel room.

Toilet on the left, short hallway ahead, the bed in front of him with a cheap, flowery comforter. To the right would be the windows—and at least one enemy.

He swung around the corner and fired point-blank into two cartel men, killing them with headshots. Then he spun, dropped to the floor, and lay prone, aiming across the hall and into the other room.

Sure enough, seconds later, two alarmed men ran toward the hallway. He killed them both.

Four down. How many more to go?

Gunfire came from around the corner. Axe switched places with the doctor, looked quickly along the side of the hotel, then pulled his head back. "The firing is coming from inside. Wait for my signal, then follow me."

Axe moved toward the walkway, ready to fire at any sentries. Kelton waited by the hotel as ordered, smiling blissfully.

After Axe had taken only a few steps, aiming the rifle first at the two open windows downstairs, then the ones directly above, the doctor sprinted from the corner of the hotel, running past him.

"No, wait!" Axe yelled, but he was too late.

Muzzle flashes came from the second-floor windows.

Bullets ripped the air near Axe's head. He ran backward, firing as he went, putting rounds into the windows.

His side burned as a bullet grazed him, but then the gunfire stopped.

That was close.

"Kelton, come on!"

His drugged partner sprinted past him excitedly, like a kid on his way to the playground.

28

BOOM

Hotel Riviera Especial de China

Captain Hernandez lay on the worn carpet at the entrance to the hotel room. His rifle pointed down the hallway toward the lobby, ready for whoever came. At some point, the cartel men would check on the gunfire and the lack of response from their buddies. Or they would leave. If his hunch was correct—the earlier explosion on the far side of the hotel had been the drug lab being destroyed—they could clear out.

Either way, laying here for a while made sense.

From the second floor, he had heard more gunfire, aimed outside.

My men—did they survive?

The return gunfire from the parking lot stopped the guns inside.

Certainly not tourists shooting so well. My men. At least one is alive.

Hernandez had to move. Fighting the pain from his wounds, he struggled to his feet. By the time he made it back to the window in the hotel room, all he saw was a shape in the dark, fleeing toward the lake.

My men wouldn't run.

So who were those people? American fishermen could also be hunters, he supposed. But to accurately return fire while being shot at? Doubtful.

To worry about another time. Since I'm up, I might as well finish this.

He stumbled toward the lobby, gun ready.

Lopez stood in his office, dreading making the call. The police had been stopped, but the hotel was a disaster, with bullet holes and dead bodies everywhere.

None of this was my fault. I did well.

Jefe was a smart but hard man. In his organization, success brought rewards. Failure brought punishment… or death.

He pressed the button to dial the main office.

"Riviera Properties." It took only the two words to know *Jefe* stood nearby, and the situation was tense.

Lopez didn't know where to start, how to explain—in hints and guarded language—what had happened. The woman on the end of the line, speaking for Señor Ruiz, saved him.

"Did the arriving guests understand when you explained you had no rooms available?" the woman prompted.

"Yes. They are all gone. I heard the last one… leave… moments ago." The firing from the west side of the building could have been nothing other than mopping up, though he hadn't received a report from either the ground floor or second-story teams.

"And the infirmary?"

"Unfortunately, there was a fire."

"Yes, we were concerned about that. The oxygen containers."

"Yes, of course."

"And the other guests?"

Lopez hesitated. He assumed the warrior and the younger man with him had been killed after being served the spiked beer. He had no doubt their bodies would be found as his remaining men mopped up. "They have left as well. No problem."

"The building may be unstable after the fire in the infirmary. Double-check all tourists are out, then exit. I wouldn't give the old hotel more than fifteen minutes from now before it caught fire."

Lopez looked at his watch, an old wind-up his father had given him.

They are going to blow the place up in fifteen minutes.

He wanted to protest the search for any tourists, but every second counted. *Jefe* had decided. The hotel would be blown up, written off, and the evidence of the laboratory in the basement further buried under rubble, along with proof of the firefight between the police and the cartel. Let the government spend millions excavating in a fruitless search for clues if they chose.

"Understood."

"Then your men should go home. Tomorrow we will need you at another property. Well done."

The line went dead.

Lopez let out a brief sigh of relief. The boss didn't lie. There would be work for him. He had made it out alive, after all.

He joined the remaining men in the lobby. He had lost many in the battle, but there would be enough people to quickly search the bar, lobby, and guest rooms for any tourist stragglers, besides sending home any living employees.

"Listen up. The hotel will be blown up in fourteen minutes." None looked surprised. They understood the boss's scorched earth policy. "We have an important task: to make sure no tourists or staff are left in the building. First, we will—"

His men dropped as full automatic gunfire tore through them. The bullets hit their legs and groins, avoiding their armored chest plates. Men screamed in anguish as they fell. In seconds, all were writhing on the ground. Some had the training to fire their weapons toward the unseen enemy. Others just died as more rounds poured into them.

Lopez drew his pistol and fired toward the western hallway before bullets ripped into his legs. He fell and didn't see, hear, or feel the next bullet pierce his skull.

———

Hernandez scooted back around the corner, rolled on his side, and switched magazines, moving slower than usual and less smoothly than he ever had at the shooting range. Then he aimed the gun around the corner and fired another full mag on auto. He reloaded behind cover again, then dragged himself back to his feet.

I may have caught another bullet or two.

But all the enemy lay dead, or nearly so.

Did he say the hotel would be blown up?

The lobby didn't seem big, but it would take him some time to cross it as injured as he was. He didn't dare risk using the phone at the front desk. There could be more enemy around, and he had to get as far away from the hotel as possible before it blew.

The Chief Inspector will send help when we don't check in.

Hernandez stumbled across the lobby, trailing blood and falling twice before reaching the automatic doors, which still wouldn't move. He barely had enough strength to push the single door on the left open enough for him to stagger through.

A few minutes later, sitting on the fountain to rest, he regretted not checking his watch when he heard the men's leader announce the time remaining.

This isn't far enough away.

With the last of his strength and determination, he limped, then eventually crawled toward the shot-up Team 3 van on the far side of the parking lot.

Central Analysis Group Headquarters
Conference Room C
Alexandria, Virginia

"We have a call from the hotel," Dave announced. "Back to the same number as before. It's from about thirty seconds ago... there was a lag." He played the file.

They listened in silence while reading the AI's translation.

It sounds like Axe is dead and they're going to blow the hotel!

Haley dialed her phone.

Please be alive. And pick up!

Hotel Riviera Especial de China

Axe knelt over the body of the doctor lying face down on the path to the lake. In the feeble glow of the solar-powered lights lining the concrete walkway, Axe saw the four bullet holes that had torn him open.

He was under my care. My protection.

The loss rocked him.

I went first to draw fire, but I wasn't fast enough.

He left the doctor where he lay in the spreading pool of blood.

I'm very sorry, doctor.

Kelton hadn't stopped running and had already made it to the lake where he swam away from shore, heading southwest.

Axe put his feelings of failure in the box to deal with after the mission and ignored the minor wound at his side as he jogged to the water.

What had the doctor said?

The beer had been spiked with a drug. First came euphoria, then uncontrollable violence.

Kelton?

He had a hard time picturing it.

I have to call this in.

He stopped at the edge of the lake after telling Kelton to wait. He'd ignored the phone's vibration as he ran to the water but now called Haley back on the secure communication app.

"Are you okay?" Haley asked immediately.

"Yes, but I don't have much time. We're going to swim across the lake. On the southwestern shore—"

"They are going to blow up the hotel! They're going room to room to check for tourists first. Are you clear?"

"Yes, and we'll be farther by then. Listen. There's another hotel across the lake. Not a far swim, but too far by car to go all the way around if they're looking for us. I'll need a medevac for Kelton. Can you get someone here—maybe from Monterey?"

She didn't waste time with unnecessary questions or chitchat. "Destination?"

"The United States. A friendly hospital with a secure room."

"Description of wounds?"

"Potential drug dose. I got the doctor out, but he got shot as we exfilled. He's dead. I'm sorry." The feelings threatened to escape the box. To keep from choking up at his failure, Axe's voice went flat and monotone. "Poor kid. But before he died, he told me Kelton had been dosed with a powerful drug in the beers he drank at the bar. An all-natural drug— from mushrooms. Euphoria for a while, then rage and violence, along with hallucinations. I may have to knock him out… or worse. The doc said I'd have to kill him. Either way, we'll need to figure out what this drug is."

"There are DEA assets in Monterey. We'll get them rolling your way. But the story is still you're the rich guy's bodyguard and fishing buddy. Nothing more."

"Copy."

"I know you have to go, but when you said, 'poor kid,' who did you mean?"

"The doctor. He was out of shape, but he ran surprisingly fast. I should have been faster, but he took off and drew the fire."

"Tall guy, wild white hair, Caucasian, late sixties?"

"What? No. Thin, five-ten, pale skin, thirties."

"Hold on… That must be Jacob Campbell. What about Edgars—the taller, older one? He's the lead scientist."

Fifty feet in front of him, Kelton floated on his back, relaxed in the dark water, like he didn't have a care in the world.

"There were two doctors?"

Axe turned to stare at the hotel.

Was he in the basement? I could have saved him. I didn't bother checking.

One part of him realized if he had gone further into the room leading to the basement, he would have been blown up seconds later. A bigger part kicked himself for not trying.

"There were eight total, including Campbell and Edgars. An entire team of researchers," Haley said softly.

All dead now, because of my failure.

"I'm sorry," Axe said. "A part of the hotel blew up seconds after I got the doctor—my doctor—out. I didn't check… and a good thing or I would be dead, too. Still…"

"You did what you could. Get going. We'll get you out. Axe—stay sharp."

"Copy," he said without conviction as he hung up.

He secured the phone in his pocket and waded into the cold water.

I failed. I left people behind.

He stuffed the feelings into the box and dove forward. The water welcomed him home. He swam after the man he might have to kill.

Juan parked his truck at the far end of the parking lot and walked, not believing his eyes.

He stared in awe at the smoldering pile that used to be the nicest hotel he had ever seen. His dreams of a promotion were literally up in smoke.

Would they send me to another location? I discovered the wanted American. I warned them about the minivans.

Though young, he knew how the world worked.

They could as easily punish as reward me for the failure here, though none of this was my doing.

His uncle's company in America was desperate for workers to build houses. He wanted Juan to come. He would be helped across the border—legally, if possible. Illegally, if necessary. Either way, he would have work and a different life.

Juan walked through the parking lot, past another bullet-ridden mini-van. Police would be here soon, looking for their comrades. He had to be gone by then. No one would believe—rightly—he had merely come to see what happened. Every smart person in the area not affiliated with the police or cartel would stay away.

In the dim light, he tripped over the man's legs and went to one knee, tearing his jeans. The body sat against the front driver's side tire.

Police.

The man's head drooped, chin to chest. He clutched an automatic rifle, finger along the trigger. Blood oozed from several wounds.

Whether I go to America or stay with the cartel, the rifle has value.

He didn't want to touch a dead body but steeled himself. His mother, aunt, and grandmother were superstitious, but he was no baby. The dead were dead, no more.

He grasped the barrel of the gun and pulled. The dead man grunted and muttered, "No."

He's alive!

With surprising strength, the man kept hold of the gun.

Juan considered how much more valuable a living police officer was than the rifle. Delivering him to *Jefe* for interrogation would guarantee a higher-level position in the cartel.

Or I could save his life.

He had to choose.

On the other side of the van, the rubble shifted with a groan. The movement fueled the fire and flames leapt.

I would rather build up than tear down.

"Keep your gun," he whispered to the man. "I am a friend. I will take you to the hospital."

29

MISSING

"Get the DEA agents rolling in an ambulance, even if they have to steal one," Haley ordered Dave.

"Use my authorization, or give them to me if they need confirmation," Gregory added. "Clear them straight through the nearest border crossing and alert the closest decent hospital. They can get Kellison stabilized, then we'll figure out where to take him. But we're not leaving one of the richest men in the world in a small-town hospital in Mexico. Nor are we answering questions from the Mexican authorities about how and why he managed to get drugged."

Dave coordinated with the Drug Enforcement Agency team while Nancy handled the border crossing plans. Haley sat in her chair, latching onto a memory. Another piece of the puzzle fell into place. Turning to her computer, she dug through databases until she found what she had seen the week before when prepping the mission to rescue the nurse.

ITEM: Cabeza de Rana, near China, Nuevo Leon, Mexico. Population of rural farming village reported missing. 52 men-women-children no longer living in a small enclave in rural northern Mexico.

RUMOR: Massacred by the cartel.

MOTIVE: Unknown.

NOTES: Elderly man living an hour from the village claimed they were not murdered by cartel. "They killed each other. The devil made them do it." Assumption is the cartel paid him to say this. No further details.

What if the old man is telling the truth?

She grabbed her phone and dialed Carol, the nurse. She'd be safe with her brother now.

"It's Haley," she said, not bothering with niceties. "Did you ever visit Casa de Rana?"

"Yes, about once a month. I was scheduled to return but got abducted. Why?"

"I don't know. Did you ever come across reports of people being more violent than usual?"

"No. Why? Have you figured out why they kidnapped me?"

"Not yet, but I may have found a piece of the puzzle. The entire village of Casa de Rana has vanished. Reports are of either a cartel massacre or, possibly, the villagers killing each other. Any ideas?"

"No, they were all farm folk out in the middle of nowhere, southeast of China. Poor but happy. They all knew each other's business but got along well. A real community. They wouldn't turn on each other."

Unless they were experimented on, drugged, and went into a homicidal rage while tripping.

"I'll let you know if we figure it out. Thanks, gotta go."

This is a big piece of the puzzle. Kelton's been drugged and may become so violent he has to be killed. The friendly farmers could have killed each other. It fits. The cartel has been testing a new drug on people.

30

FRIENDS

Central Analysis Group Headquarters
Conference Room C
Alexandria, Virginia

"The DEA is on their way with an ambulance and a friendly doctor," Dave announced. "They say we owe them."

"I've sent them instructions on the border crossing," Nancy added. "They're cleared. No slow down, no inspections. I had to throw some weight around, so don't be surprised if you get a call."

"Understood," Gregory said with a frown for Haley, who shrugged apologetically.

"We're getting another feed," Dave said. "From Aldama, Tamaulipas —the place the hotel called repeatedly. It's going to the United States."

They listened as the call came through in English.

"We're sorry, sir," the same female voice as before spoke. She had the slightest Spanish accent. "Your reservation needs to be canceled. Our hotel suffered severe damage in a fire."

"Oh, I'm sorry to hear that," the American male said, who sounded like an educated, middle-aged professional. "Was it…"

His voice was polite, reserved. Haley pictured him as buttoned up. Suit and tie. Never a hair out of place.

"Yes, sir, the damage was catastrophic, I'm afraid. We will need to discuss a refund... or perhaps we can interest you in another property?"

They're talking about the hotel blowing up... and whether he'll take his business to another of their locations, it sounds like.

"At this time, no. But I may need a place to stay shortly. We shall stay in touch via your online reservation system."

"We understand and thank you for your past business."

"Thank you."

The call ended.

"Are you guys thinking the same as I am?" Haley asked.

"More code. It wouldn't trip the algorithm for live review, but it's definitely a communication between the cartel and their client," Dave said.

Haley nodded. "I agree. The American guy is the key. We need to match his voiceprint."

"On it," Nancy said as she leaned into her computer screen, typing away. The NSA routinely made searchable voice prints of known or suspected criminals, international figures like politicians and businessmen, government employees, and people in potentially sensitive positions like airport workers, pilots, truck drivers, and ship captains. Lately, as computer processing power and storage became less expensive, they had been able to make voiceprints by recording news programs and podcasts, along with the names, titles, and other data associated with each interviewee.

Nancy would isolate the American's voice, similar to taking a fingerprint. Then she would let the computer compare the intonation, accent, words, and dozens of other data points. If the man had been recorded previously, he would be in the system and the computer would find him. It might also find several similar voices. Nancy would then use an even more powerful computer—her mind—to narrow them down or see which voice made sense based on context.

Gregory walked to Dave's laptop and peered at the screen. "This is time-stamped now. How are we getting a live feed from an area hundreds of miles south of our target?"

Nancy kept her head down, focused on her task. Dave clicked on his screen as if he were trying to figure out the strange occurrence. Gregory waited him out.

"Maybe they accidentally added it to your original real-time target request," Dave finally said.

Nancy looked up, nodding, helping him out. "Yes, that makes sense.

They figured with such an important operation to save the billionaire Kelton Kellison, it would be important to monitor the other location, though it was out of your grid."

"They were being helpful, or made a mistake, and we got lucky?" Gregory asked.

"Yes, sir, it certainly looks that way," Dave said evenly.

Gregory turned to glare at Haley. "Haley, a word?"

They stepped outside the small conference room while Dave and Nancy ignored the tension in the air.

There were no other analysts nearby to overhear, though the night shift had come in and were at their cubicles, analyzing data and writing reports.

"This is because of you," Gregory said.

"I didn't tell him to add to the search."

"You didn't have to. You're rubbing off on them."

She fought back a smile, which earned her another of Gregory's glares.

They're learning well.

"The operation is over once Kelton is back in the United States. Right?"

It wasn't really a question.

"I believe the NHA can stand down, yes. But I have a ton of analysis to do. One," she ticked off her first finger. "What drug is the cartel testing, and why? Two, what are their plans? Are we targeted? Three, who is the American on the phone, and what is his role? Moneyman? Technical support? Headhunter for the scientists? Four, where is Doctor Edgars. And—"

Nancy opened the door and stuck her head out. "We found a match to the voiceprint."

Haley and Gregory shared a look, both thinking the same thing.

That was fast.

Back in the conference room, Nancy had commandeered the big screen at the end of the room.

"Victor Baranov," Nancy began, standing next to the screen.

She already has a presentation prepared? How?

"I've heard of him," Gregory said slowly, placing the name. "He's an American businessman. He... oh, no," he muttered.

"Yes, exactly," Nancy continued quietly. The mood in the room had suddenly shifted from the excitement of catching a break to trepidation.

Haley looked from Nancy to Gregory.

What am I missing here?

"Owner and CEO of Baranov Brands," Nancy continued. "Maker of several brands of craft beer and energy drinks."

"They have a great IPA," Dave said.

"He sounds legitimate. It can't be him," Haley said, though her intuition disagreed with her.

Nancy nodded at Dave at his laptop. "Here's him on the phone call tonight."

"Oh, I'm sorry to hear that," came from the big monitor's speakers, piped in from Dave's computer.

"And here's an interview he did with a business program several months ago. He's replying to the host interrupting him to say they were out of time." A video played on the large screen.

"Oh, I'm sorry to hear that," the same voice said, this time from the mouth of a nicely dressed man, mid-fifties, smiling understandingly at the apologetic host.

"Same guy, no doubt," Haley said. "So he's working with the cartel to what—put this drug in his company's beer? Or is he supplying the beer for the cartel to use?" Her mind was off and running. The country loved beer. New Year's Eve was two days away. Lots of drinking and partying. The big college football game on New Year's Day. An entire country run amok. Violence in the streets.

Nancy, Dave, and Gregory looked as shaken as she felt.

"Let's dig deep into this guy. Find out if he's a participant or a pawn. Maybe he's being blackmailed, maybe he's got a joint venture with the cartels."

No one moved. "What's going on? Let's get on this!"

There was an uncomfortable undercurrent in the room. Dave looked at Gregory, who said quietly, "Victor Baranov is a huge supporter of President Heringten."

Dave snorted. "That's putting it mildly. Like saying Russia has cold winters. He donated millions to a super PAC to get Heringten reelected. Explained to his employees why the man would make a better president than his opponent. Had a private, ten-thousand-dollar-a-plate fundraising dinner at his house. To go after him implicates the president."

Nancy nodded to Dave, who clicked his mouse. A photograph of the president smiling with his arm around Baranov filled the screen. Dave kept clicking, cycling through more photos of the two men together, along with headlines from various papers mentioning Baranov's vocal support and the president's grateful appreciation.

"I had no idea," Haley said, her voice hard. "But it changes nothing. I trust the president, but I don't trust Baranov."

They eyed her skeptically.

Gregory spoke up. "If he's innocent, and it gets out that we did a deep dive into him and his company... it's bad for the president, bad for Baranov. And terrible for us."

"It could look political, like we're out for payback against the guy for supporting the president," Nancy explained.

"But we're not," Haley argued. "We're doing our jobs, following up on a potential criminal. Not going after him would be just as bad—we'd be accused of covering it up to protect the president!"

"True. Either way, we're screwed," Gregory told her.

"Look, we're the only ones on this. I'm not telling anyone else."

Dave checked a window on his computer and drew in a sharp breath. "He's scheduled to attend a party at the White House on New Year's Eve. He'll be staying in the Lincoln Bedroom."

A heavy silence hung in the air.

There has to be a mistake. Uncle Jimmy must not understand who this guy is.

"You two," Gregory said to Nancy and Dave. "You're done. Right damn now. Pack it up."

They didn't hesitate. Immediately, they closed their laptops, disconnected cords, and stacked their papers. In seconds, they were at the door, where Gregory stopped them.

"Not a word. To others, or each other. Completely black," his voice was low, verging on threatening. "The last fifteen minutes didn't happen. You know nothing about Baranov or a voiceprint. We'll go over our cover story tomorrow for the events of earlier in the day. But this part," he gestured to the screen where Victor Baranov's face had been seconds earlier. "No. Get your coats and go home. See you in the morning."

Nancy and Dave nodded and hurried out the conference room door.

He made sure the door swung shut behind the other two analysts and adopted a softer tone with Haley. "It's too risky for them. I don't want them hung out to dry if this gets out—whether you find something or not. But you and I..." He shrugged, resigned to fate. "This is big—a political nightmare. It's a potential smoking gun implicating a man close to the president, but I trust you to do the right thing, no matter which direction it goes. The fewer people involved, the better. What I saw earlier... Your analysis abilities are amazing, and you're fast. Can you get to the bottom of this by yourself if you pull an all-nighter?"

"Actually, I prefer it. Nothing against Nancy and Dave, but I have to do this myself. I agree with you—they can't be involved, no matter which way it goes."

"Good. What next—what do you want to do?"

What do I want to do? I want to confront Uncle Jimmy. I want to get Axe on Baranov and make him talk. I want to have one damn day when the world isn't about to crash down on us if I make a wrong move!

Instead, she said, "I want to get busy." She returned to her computer and switched it back over so she could use the big screen. As secure and privacy conscious as the rest of the team was, she couldn't do this research at her cubicle. Anyone could walk by and glance at the computer.

"I've got you covered," Haley reassured Gregory. "You, Nancy, and Dave weren't here for the last part. I found it on my own. Either way it falls, it's on me." She went to the door where he stood, looking as worried as she'd ever seen him. "First, I need to grab some caffeine and use the restroom. Then I will figure this out."

He nodded and held the door for her. As she turned left toward the break room and toilet, he turned right. "Good work today, Haley," he called over his shoulder for the team to hear.

Just an ordinary day of saving the world. Nothing unusual happened...

The stress and lack of sleep were hitting her. She needed a pick-me-up, a bathroom break, and then the data. She would tear Baranov's life apart and find the truth.

Nancy gave her a little wave from behind Dave's back as they stepped through the main doors to the lobby, bundled in their parkas for the trip home.

A few minutes later, she had a two-liter bottle of soda and a tall glass filled with ice. She locked the door to the conference room behind her, double-checked all the blinds, ensuring no one could see in, then sat down and began.

She would be a shark in the ocean of data. She wouldn't stop until she caught her prey—whoever it was.

Time to hunt.

31

BREATHE

Fish Lake
China
Nuevo Leon, Mexico

"How are you feeling, Kelton?" Axe asked. The water temperature didn't bother him—he easily blocked out the discomfort from long practice. If you couldn't handle a cold-water swim, you had no business trying out to be a SEAL. Kelton's chattering teeth, on the other hand, made it clear his body reacted differently.

"A little c-c-cold," he said. He'd handled the swim well. It wasn't all that far, and Kelton had been on the swim team in high school. The variables were the cold water, the stress from the events of the afternoon and evening, and, of course, whatever drug coursed through his blood. "And I feel... weird. Hungover, which can't be. It hasn't been long enough. Unless it's what the doctor said. You think it's the drug in the beer?"

Damn, I hoped he'd forgotten that part.

"Could be, but don't worry," Axe said, taking another side stroke. "I've got your back." They were approaching the shore opposite the hotel, which had blown up spectacularly a while before. Right on schedule from what Haley reported. Even from the middle of the lake, the explosion had been loud. The building had collapsed upon itself and caught fire. The flames lit up the area, but no fire trucks responded. Nor did police or curious people.

The locals know it's a front for the cartel and stay away. And I bet the police came without a QRF in place to maximize security.

In the distance, he heard helicopters.

Finally. Late, but at least the cavalry is coming to help any survivors.

From the smoldering rubble glowing in the distance, though, it didn't look like there would be anyone for them to help.

"Haley's sending an ambulance for us. We'll get an IV in you. Maybe a mild sedative. Then it's straight back home to a good hospital. There will be experts who can fix you up."

In front of him, Kelton slowed his sidestroke.

"Kelton? You okay?"

Kelton offered a quiet growl. Axe stopped swimming and tread water.

That didn't sound right.

"How are you feeling, buddy? It's only another few minutes and we'll be back on land. How about you keep swimming?"

Kelton only growled louder as he turned. In the darkness, his face wasn't clear, but Axe could sense the rage. Axe's shiver came not because of the cold water, but the white of Kelton's bared teeth cutting through the night.

"Keep it together." Axe kicked, moving a few feet further from his friend. A continuous rumble came from Kelton, along with a few snarls.

"Hey, shake it off. You're on a bad trip from the drugs in the beer. Whatever you're seeing or feeling, try to hold it off. I'm a friend. We're going to get you help."

Kelton suddenly splashed toward him, catching Axe in a surprisingly strong grip. The fight was on.

Kelton had no fighting skills, but he made up for it in determination. His sole focus was harming Axe.

Then they went underwater, Kelton clinging to his arm with one hand. He clamped his other hand to Axe's throat.

Once again, Axe flashed back to the second phase of SEAL training, when he had to hold his breath while troubleshooting gear the instructors had tampered with. The problems were always solvable—if he didn't panic... and if the solution presented itself before he ran out of air.

Axe—and all the others who didn't quit after those sessions—learned how to deal with adversity, hold his breath long past the point he thought possible, and stay calm.

He also discovered how to defend himself underwater. While fighting back against the instructors wasn't allowed, Axe learned a few tricks. The students were supposed to take the abuse because of its educational value. But a quick kick of the feet to move out of the way, lessening the impact of a shove, wouldn't be frowned upon unless the instructor considered it an admission of fear. Purposefully sinking worked well for him several times, too, to get out of the instructors' reach.

Axe used every trick now to minimize Kelton's impact. A release of some air caused him to sink, which broke Kelton's grip on his throat.

Unbothered by the cold, black water, Axe sank further, forcing Kelton to decide whether to release his arm or hang on.

How much of Kelton is in there? Does he still have a survival instinct? Is there fear?

No matter how good a high school swimmer, would slowly sinking in a cold, unfamiliar lake trigger feelings inside the man?

Kelton kicked and followed him down.

Interesting. He grew up on lakes—that could be part of it.

Axe could hold his breath longer than Kelton.

He hoped.

I don't want to hurt him. At some point, he'll give up.

The pressure on Axe's ears built to the point he had to hold his nose to release it. Kelton kept kicking downward, holding onto Axe's arm in a death grip. His other hand flailed at Axe's face and chest, felt but unseen in the blackness.

Axe felt the stirrings of concern. His lungs were empty, and his body told him he had to breathe soon. He didn't have long.

Any time now, Kelton.

He had a flashback to BUD/S, laying on the side of the pool, looking up at the supervising instructor leaning over him. Axe had passed out during an underwater swim test, trying to finish the last few yards after running out of air. Instead of giving up, he had pushed on—and drowned.

A safety swimmer got him to the surface. They hauled him out and brought him back to life.

Kelton would quit before Axe would.

Or will he?

Axe's stomach convulsed, which happened when the body panicked and demanded oxygen.

A bad sign.

There were no safety swimmers in the lake, no senior Frogman instructor who hauled out stubborn students who died rather than giving up. Out here, death would be permanent.

Enough. Time to end this.

Axe grabbed Kelton's hand and tried to pry it from his arm, but couldn't.

Nearly superhuman strength.

His mind and body suddenly started working together, screaming at him to surface immediately. Willpower and experience kept him calm.

A little longer. I can do this.

Words from the SEAL Ethos popped into his mind.

'I will never quit.'

He used a tremendous dose of willpower to not take a breath. Despite his mind telling his lungs they couldn't breathe underwater, his body desperately wanted air. Amazingly, Kelton had outlasted him.

Axe pushed down the panic threatening to overtake him. He fought against Kelton's grip, first trying to twist away, then slamming the man's wrist to get him to let go, careful to stay away from Kelton's other hand which sought him in the dark water.

Still they sank. Still Kelton refused to release him.

I can't hold on any longer.

He'd waited too long to defend himself. He had failed for a second time that night.

I'm going to die.

Just as Axe decided to give up, Kelton's hand released its grip on his arm.

Being set free gave Axe a tiny burst of hope and determination.

I can do this.

Axe grabbed his friend's limp, unresisting wrist and kicked to the surface with all his strength, burning the last bit of oxygen remaining. His body screamed at him, more desperate now as they got closer to the surface, unable to wait.

Hold. Hold. Not yet!

He shook and convulsed, wanting to breathe the water. Kelton's body slowed him down.

Leave him behind!

He ignored his mind's panic and his body's desperation. He turned to the tiny part within that he had relied on throughout his SEAL training and in countless battles, scrapes, and close calls.

'The ability to control my emotions and my actions, regardless of circumstance, sets me apart from others.'

Another of his favorite lines from the SEAL Ethos.

During BUD/S, Axe had focused on getting from one rotation to the next. He would tell himself not to quit until he finished the six-mile run—then he would see how he felt. Or to make it to the next meal. Breaking the day, the hour, the minute into smaller segments. Getting to the next minuscule milestone. Pushing on.

He used the skill now.

Two more kicks, then maybe a breath.

After two kicks, his mind and body begged, pleaded, and fought, but the SEAL inside renegotiated.

Good job, but three kicks this time. Then we'll see. Give me three kicks.

Three kicks later, the water seemed darker. It had happened before, in the pool, before he drowned. He was losing consciousness.

Not... yet!

His kicking slowed. He couldn't fight it any longer, but he refused to release Kelton.

Not after losing the doctor—doctors. And whoever else I left to die.

He gave one last kick, then the warrior inside him could no longer compete with his body's needs. He closed his eyes in defeat as his consciousness faded to black.

His body reacted automatically, the mouth opening to breathe... right as his head broke the surface of the lake.

He came to while taking deep, desperate breaths. He choked out a sob. He automatically looked around, embarrassed, to see if his weakness had been heard.

No one's here.

Axe dragged Kelton's lifeless body to the surface. He spun him face up. Then he kicked with all his strength toward the nearby shore, towing him in a lifeguard carry.

———

"Come on, Kelton!" Axe thumped Kelton's back harder than before, then rolled him flat and continued mouth-to-mouth resuscitation.

If the instructors at BUD/S could bring me back, I should be able to do it with Kelton.

But he hadn't been dead as long as Kelton had.

Axe kept performing CPR, willing Kelton alive.

"Kelton! You can do this! Come back!"

With a shudder, Kelton coughed. Lake water spewed from his mouth. Axe gently turned him onto his side as Kelton continued heaving water out of his body. Slowly, Kelton regained control of his breathing. The vomiting stopped as his body finished ridding itself of the lake water he had taken in. After a minute, he calmed, laying spent on the muck of the shore.

Axe sat in the mud next to him, relieved and exhausted.

Then Kelton let out a low, ominous growl.

32

THE ZONE

Haley sat at her computer, stuck in neutral.

She had her target, a plan, and questions needing answers.

But she didn't have the will to begin.

If Baranov is guilty, it could ruin the President of the United States—Uncle Jimmy.

He would be forced to resign in scandal, suffer through a special prosecutor's investigation, or at a minimum lose all political power.

And what if...

No, she couldn't go there. Uncle Jimmy had no motive to work with Baranov to harm the country.

It had to be one of two options. First, maybe Baranov wasn't involved, but people wanted him to look bad to get to the president. Or perhaps Baranov had been coerced.

It could also be exactly as it looks: Baranov is behind a plot to harm innocent civilians.

Where could she start? She steeled herself with one of Axe's Sun Tzu quotes: "Who wishes to fight must first count the cost."

The costs come down to a choice. Which is more important to me? The country, or the president?

The answer was easy.

The country is more important. The president is just one man. But with Nalen and Axe's help, maybe we can save both.

She'd found her motivation.

Haley's fingers flew from database to database. She lost herself and became one with the words, images, and intelligence information. Windows opened and closed. She made notes on paper where necessary. Her yellow pad filled with circled words and lines connecting them.

The zone welcomed her. Nothing intruded. She felt neither joy nor sorrow, concern nor relief. The soda bottle emptied, trips to the bathroom were taken with her eyes glazed, her mind still in the conference room parsing the words she ingested.

After a time, the table filled with her notes. Yellow pages torn from her legal pad lined up next to each other, perfectly arranged. Even in the zone, her core being demanded precision.

Finally, she sat back, stunned by the scope of the problem she found— and frustrated by the one she felt was there, but couldn't find proof of.

If she was right, though, the spiked beer was the least of their worries.

We're in trouble.

PART 3

FRIDAY, DECEMBER 30

33

ALLIES

Central Analysis Group Headquarters
Alexandria, Virginia

Nancy still insisted on driving separate cars to the office. She and Dave had been dating—hell, basically married—for years. Most colleagues suspected their relationship. But keeping up appearances was important to her.

She was grateful to be in her car this morning. It gave them time apart after a tense night together, arguing about their situation. Dave loved working for Haley—or with her, as he insisted on putting it. But the magnitude of their discovery last night had shaken him.

Nancy, on the other hand, felt invigorated. Her passion for intelligence gathering had years before turned from a successful career into a typical job, a way to fill her days while counting the years until retirement.

But working for Haley, a prodigy more than thirty years her junior, she had found a new lease on life. She looked forward to going to the office. The way of looking at data Haley had shown them rejuvenated her. It gave her approaches she wouldn't have tried, not wanting to risk rocking the boat or looking the fool.

Why can't Dave see it? Or at least support me?

She knew, of course. He wanted to play it safe. Run out the clock, make it to full retirement with government pension intact. He played the odds—keeping his head down now in exchange for fun twilight years later.

Living my life can't wait until retirement.

Nancy had already decided to work with Haley in this latest mess. Behind Gregory's back, if necessary. But she'd have to be careful. She didn't want to lose Dave over it and wouldn't drag him down if she got in trouble.

I'll sacrifice myself first. But I believe in what Haley's doing. I want to help her figure this out and save the country. Again.

Helping Haley with the Movement cult in St. John, working all night to discover the location of the shipping containers containing EMPs, knowing what a difference she—they—had made, was the best feeling ever. She'd do nearly anything to replicate it.

Dave's car pulled in next to hers. They usually avoided parking near each other, sticking with the illusion they arrived separately at different times, but today she welcomed it. It was his way of apologizing, or at least supporting her.

She got out as he did. They smiled at each other over the top of the car.

"I love you," Dave mouthed, the white vapor from his breath filling the air.

"I love you too," she returned.

They locked up and moved together toward the door. "We'll figure it out," Dave said quietly to her.

"I'll be careful," she replied.

"I know. I'll help when I can. Run interference the rest of the time. Take on whatever tasks Gregory assigns to you."

"But let me look at it before you send it in," she said, offering an apologetic smile to soften her need to stay on top of any work going out in her name.

"Of course." He held back a smile.

He knows me so well.

She resisted taking his hand in hers. They were at work, after all.

A minute later they were through security, past the lobby, and into their work area, the bullpen where the cheap gray cubicles connected, forming a maze of workstations for the small intelligence service.

Haley emerged from the hallway leading to the restroom and stopped as she saw them. She looked horrible. Her long blond hair had come loose from her normal late-afternoon ponytail and dangled limply around her face. Deep black bags hung under her eyes, which were bloodshot and crazed looking. As she stepped closer, Nancy caught a whiff of the young woman's body odor and noticed Haley's hands shaking.

"I thought Gregory told you to go home?" she growled at them. Next to her, Dave went white, but not as bad as the first time Haley had spoken to them in that tone.

Maybe he's getting used to it.

"Haley, dear," she said, not rising to the bait of the aggressive tone. "We went home. Have you been at it all night?"

The woman is going to burn out before she turns twenty-two. If she lives that long, given what I can guess she's doing in the field.

It wasn't hard to read between the lines. Haley had been out of the office for the New York attack and had probably killed terrorists while helping save the city from unspecified further violence.

I wish I had the clearance—and the guts—to read all the reports from that week. Or better yet, ask Haley what had been kept out of the reports.

Plus, after her so-called vacation months ago—which Nancy bet had been to a tropical island near St. Thomas, where she had likely had a large hand in stopping the Movement cult—she'd returned to the office different. Tougher and sharper.

Dangerous.

Nancy had seen it in her friends after Desert Storm, then in her kid brother after Afghanistan. They had seen action—and killed.

Haley came back from "vacation" looking just like them.

A warrior.

"No, not all night," Haley said absently, checking her watch.

"We left around eight last night," Dave said. He spoke slowly and quietly, as he would to a dangerous, hungry wild animal. "It's eight now. In the morning," he added.

Haley looked at him, confused, before realization hit her. "All night? Guess so," Haley mumbled, before walking to the employee break room.

Nancy shared a look with Dave, who nodded and walked to their shared cubicle to get to work.

I'll give Haley a few minutes, then we'll see what's next.

Haley shoved a frozen entrée dinner into the microwave and leaned against the wall in the tiny kitchen area, closing her eyes with exhaustion.

No wonder I'm starving. I worked all night and didn't notice. Not very good situational awareness. Axe would be disappointed.

She was tired but couldn't have slept if she wanted to. The data filled her mind. The ramifications—and doubts—consumed her. She was finally ready to call Axe and fill him in.

He's not going to be happy. But I hope we can figure out a way to get out of this mess.

Nancy entered the kitchen area and made straight for the coffee machine.

She thinks she's subtle. I may not be as good at reading people as Gregory, but I know where this is headed.

"I know you want to help. But you'd be going against Gregory's direct orders," Haley said as Nancy placed a pod in the machine. "And clearly Dave isn't keen on the idea."

"We worked it out," Nancy told her, not turning around. "Dave's a good man."

If what Haley suspected was true, she'd need all the help she could get.

If she's worked it out with Dave, I can accept her help. We'll deal with Gregory when or if we have to.

"Fine, you can help. Small things that won't get you in too much trouble. I'll be in here in the kitchen at the bottom of every hour, when I can, which will allow us to bump into each other and compare notes."

"Dave will cover my workload, so push as much to me as you want."

"I may have to. First, I need to know where Dr. Edgars went and is now."

When Nancy nodded her understanding, Haley left the room, taking the low-calorie turkey dinner, her fingers burning on the packaging, leaving Nancy adding creamer to her coffee mug.

I've gone from having a team of analysts to managing another unsanctioned asset.

Next, Haley had to talk things through with Axe, then make a hard call to Admiral Nalen. She needed to ask him to trust her, and—more importantly—not mention a word of the situation to his best friend, the president.

I'm too young for this responsibility. And too tired.

She could take a nap in her SUV after convincing Nalen. If she failed with him, she could go home and rest, because it wouldn't matter. Nalen would tell the president, and all hell would break loose.

But first, she had to get Axe to Las Vegas. He had work to do.

Nancy made Dave a cup of his favorite coffee, thrilled to be on the hunt with Haley. When the machine finished, she took both coffees to the double cubicle they shared and handed his to Dave.

"What's on your agenda today?" Dave asked, sipping and nodding his thanks for the coffee.

She already had her cover story prepared. "I found a report on private planes being used to bring potential terrorists into the country. I'll do a feasibility study using actual flights from Mexico. Comparing names, looking at passport controls and security procedures. Are pilots screened, are the planes searched, that sort of thing."

"Smart," he said. She wasn't sure if he meant the cover story, which he had to see through, or the actual idea for the report. "Good luck. Let me know if I can help."

Nancy logged in, planning her search.

This is my job. It's not a bad idea, even if I wasn't helping Haley by looking for a specific person.

First, she checked the overall data. Number of people flying commercially from nearby countries—especially Mexico—to the United States. The most common airports for arrivals.

Looks solid. Since 9-11, we have this nailed down. But what about private planes?

With the War on Drugs, War on Terror, and the security of the southern border, flights were tracked closely. Gone were the days when a small plane could sneak over the Texas or Arizona border by flying at low altitude. But what were the procedures once a flight arrived? There were dozens of small, private airports and hundreds of other places to land. Though the planes are required to stop at an airport of entry for a custom's inspection, did they?

Nancy started there.

An easily defended research topic.

She worked for forty-five minutes, delving into various databases, analyzing the data. Then she "randomly" selected yesterday and today for a real-time look at the procedures. Starting with passenger manifests, she looked at all people entering the United States from south of the border in the past forty-eight hours. It would have saved time to type in Dr. Edgars' name but doing so would have left a hard-to-explain trace. Instead, she scrolled through the list after sorting it alphabetically.

Found you.

He had flown in a private jet, arriving at the Phoenix airport last night. She pulled the custom's report. Three passengers total.

Dr. Edgars and the two escorts. What's in Phoenix? Or is it merely a short flight before disappearing on the way to his actual destination?

Hesitating, she glanced at Dave working hard on his own—legitimate —tasks beside her. She reminded herself of the stakes—a drug possibly in beer, which would make people homicidal—about to be served throughout the country.

This is where it gets hard to justify.

Unless she had a good excuse...

I'm pretending "random" people who flew from Mexico to Phoenix last night are potential terrorists. How easy is it to track them? Where are the holes in our security? This is a realistic, real-world assessment using innocent travelers. That's my story.

Smiling mischievously, she continued. There were security cameras at the private terminal; the feeds were accessible to Immigration, Customs, and Homeland Security, so she could view them, too.

A few clicks brought up the video she needed. She watched as the tall scientist, white hair flying wildly in every direction, walked in a distinctive stooped manner, like someone self-conscious about his height. Two muscular Mexican guards walked on either side of him, nicely dressed in slacks, dress shoes, button-down shirts, and dark sports coats. They looked like competent, highly trained professionals, not like thugs.

They passed out of the small terminal through automatic sliding doors, walking directly to the far corner of the lot where she lost sight of them.

Another camera showing a different angle picked them up. The men, in the top corner of the screen, climbed into a large SUV and drove out of the lot. She stopped the playback and memorized the license plate number.

Now it gets a little harder.

Nancy looked up the license plate in the Arizona Department of Motor Vehicles database. Seconds later, she confirmed her hunch—registered to a shell company. She made a note on her yellow pad to dig into it... or ask Dave, if she could get him on board. He had a knack for sifting through registrations and finding the true owners of companies, often digging down to the level of the law firms who set them up, then back tracing to identify their clients.

The SUV had turned right, west, out of the lot.

Now what? Phoenix is the fifth-largest city in the United States, with thousands of miles of freeways and major thoroughfares.

If it was an actual assignment in real-time, she could issue an All-Point Bulletin with the Highway Patrol. But once again, she had no good excuse why her "terrorist tracking" exercise would need it today.

Stop trying to make it easy. Get on with it.

With a sigh and a sip of the cooling coffee, she used her CAG credentials to gain access to the Arizona Department of Transportation highway and street webcams. By estimating the likely time the SUV would pass each camera on a route, she could track them from camera to camera. If they didn't show on one, she would backtrack and examine the other roads until she found them again. It would be easy if they drove directly to a destination, or extremely trying and barely possible if they took precautions.

With a last sip of her coffee, she settled in for the long haul.

34

VEGAS

Central Analysis Group Headquarters
Alexandria, Virginia

"How's Kelton?" Haley asked Axe, who sounded as groggy as she felt. "Did I wake you?"

"Yeah, no worries. I grabbed a nap. Kelton's fine. I'm right next to his bed. They have him sedated and strapped down. He almost broke a nurse's arm."

"So it's not only you he wants to kill?"

"No. I had hoped the rage would be limited to me since technically I got him into this mess. But the trigger seems to be whoever is closest, especially within reach. We haven't tested what happens if he's let loose when no one is nearby. It seemed better to draw blood and run tests first. We may have to conduct experiments, though, depending on what they discover—and what you think is coming next."

They were speaking on the secure communication app, but Haley still checked around her. The conference room blinds were drawn. She sat as far as possible from the door and windows and spoke quietly using her headset. "Are you alone, aside from Kelton?"

"For the time being. They've got all kinds of machines, and his vitals are stable, so they don't check on him much. Especially with me here. I hope you've sorted this out. What the hell is going on?"

She took a deep breath, preparing herself. Then she began.

"Usually I have only a hunch. We go out on a limb and hope a tree grows under us."

"I'm aware," Axe said, his dry tone hinting at the sense of humor she loved and which he used to manage stress.

"This is the opposite. There's no doubt who's behind it. I have proof. It's not ironclad—you have to read between the lines, but it's there. A prosecutor would have a field day with it."

"What's the problem, then?" Axe asked. "We're golden. Call in the cavalry. Homeland Security will love you."

"It's not quite that simple. The suspect is Victor Baranov. Have you heard of him?"

"No."

"He's a successful businessman. A buttoned-down, upright citizen who owns Baranov Brands."

"I've heard of them. Excellent beer. Now that you mention it, the label on the beer served to us in Mexico looked familiar. It's a version of one of their popular brands. I was on the job, so didn't drink it. Instead of the normal colors of the label, this one was gold."

"Good to know." She added a note to the fresh page of her yellow pad.

"So, what's the problem? We call the FDA or whoever inspects the products. A few tests and, boom, we find the spiked beer. He goes to jail. Case closed. I don't see a problem."

Haley hesitated. Saying it out loud made it sound bad, like her loyalty lay with the president and not the country.

"He's a direct supporter of the president. One of the biggest. He's staying in the Lincoln Bedroom at the White House on New Year's Eve, after a party there."

Haley continued before Axe could question her priorities. "Besides, our present issue, with the spiked beer, is only an opening gambit."

"A feint? A bluff?"

"No, it's an actual attack and we have to deal with it. If I'm right, it's designed to overwhelm and decapitate us, not merely distract. It's possible to survive it, though, if we plan well and get lucky. But we have to keep in mind the other storm following behind this one. We can't get bogged down on the obvious."

She heard him stirring, probably sitting up and getting ready to go. "What do you want me to do?"

"I need to talk it out."

"Okay, what did you find?"

"Eight top United States scientists, researchers, and doctors gave up their lucrative jobs or tenured positions last year. They went on sabbaticals, or vacations—all to Mexico—but never returned."

"The ones I let die."

He's not letting it go.

"You would tell me to put it in a box until after the mission."

Axe took a deep breath, then let it out in a rush of frustration. "You don't think I've been trying?"

I've never seen him like this. Which will he react better to: warrior sister or caring protégée?

Neither. Instead, she said quietly, "I'll have Nalen call you when we're done."

From his silence, she wasn't sure if he was hurt or furious. Then Axe spoke in a quiet voice, his relief palpable. "Thank you. I hadn't thought of it. I bet talking to him would help."

"Okay?"

"Yes, sorry, continue."

"Then there's Dr. Edgars—he's one of the eight. He started working for Baranov eighteen months ago. He's the mastermind. He got rushed out of the hotel before you arrived."

"We need to find him."

"I've got Nancy working on it. Here's the kicker. I'm not positive, but my hunch is the cartel isn't involved in this. Baranov isn't being coerced, but I haven't found a motive yet. His company hired the scientists, and it's pretty clear he sent them to Mexico, where he kept them locked up. Either by agreement or involuntarily. I believe they perfected Dr. Edgars' formula with rare wild mushrooms, manufactured small batches of the beer, like a microbrewery, and tested them on locals and some tourists. Looking at the data, a surprising number of disappearances and homicides occurred in the area of the hotel. Even adjusting for the typical cartel and drug violence in Mexico, it's clear they were using live victims."

"Do you know what he has planned? Because we can't let people become like Kelton. If it means we go out on a limb and destroy the president, so be it. The country can't have millions of homicidal addicts running around killing people."

"It's preliminary, but my best guess is he doesn't have the capacity to dose the entire country. He has facilities all over, but one brewery is the likely base of this scheme. There's an anomaly. In the past year, inspectors came to this plant and were gone soon after. A suicide, one homicide, and two received major inheritances from long-lost family members."

"What are the odds?"

"Astronomically against. Baranov had to have set them up, either with bribes or faking a distant relative's inheritance. However, three months ago a new man started, and he's been there since."

"Bribed or planted?"

"Doesn't matter. They couldn't have started the production of the beer before that."

"How much? And when?"

"Best guess? It takes one to two months to produce it, which means... I don't know. A lot, but not for the entire country. Probably enough for one city. And get this: next year is the company's centennial. They're celebrating starting New Year's Eve in Las Vegas, where they now have their corporate headquarters—and the bottling plant I mentioned. They're throwing tasting parties, free beer bashes, that sort of thing. Going all out. 'Great beer, great times. A New Year's Eve you'll never forget—guaranteed,' is what they're calling it."

"Simple enough solution," Axe said. "The president calls the FBI and Homeland Security who confiscate all the company's beer in Las Vegas. Authorities are warned, bottles tested, proof found. Baranov arrested, crisis averted. Yes, the president takes a hit. But he'll get past it. He's a good man who has nothing to hide."

"We can't alert the authorities or let them have Baranov because of a hunch I have."

"Which is?"

"I'm going way out on the limb here. More so than ever before. But... I think there's more to the plot."

"Okay. What is it?"

Haley hesitated, not wanting to say it out loud. But she had to tell him. "I... I don't know. It's only a feeling."

She'd trusted her gut before, but never to this extent. Would Axe back her up this time?

Is it fair to ask him to?

She continued. "I suspect the operation has two main goals: a spectacularly devastating attack on Las Vegas, but also taking out the president. Weakening him. My sense is by arresting Baranov, it will all come out... which is a less ideal outcome than the original plan, but still acceptable."

"Because Baranov isn't the one driving this bus," Axe said, thinking it through. "There's another hand at work here. Baranov's connection to the president is at least as important as the drugged beer," he said.

"Very good. We'll make an analyst out of you yet."

"No, thanks. The question is, who? Who set this in motion? Why, and what's their entire plan?"

"It would be great to have an answer for you, but I don't know. Which scares me."

"Yeah, I get that. What's next? Do you have any proof? A hint, a report, something to back it up so we don't have to go it all alone again?"

"No. Let me stress this is complete conjecture. I haven't one bit of data pointing to this conclusion. You with me?"

"Gotcha. Total guess. But your guesses have been right on in the past. Though I have to ask…"

Here it comes.

"Not because I don't support you—I do. But what are the chances your feelings for the president have clouded your judgment?" His tone wasn't accusing; it was matter-of-fact, curious, even sympathetic.

She took a breath.

He's not attacking me. He's covering all the bases.

SEALs are trained to look at the holes in their plans, the flaws in their logic, and talk them out.

He's looking out for me. For us, and the mission.

"I've considered it. I love Uncle Jimmy…" She paused as she felt herself harden and suspected her tone reflected it. "But the government is bigger than one person. Look at the former vice president."

She and Axe both suspected the former VP's "suicide" had come at the hands of the president. Because of the report she and Axe had written, the second-highest member of the government had been killed.

"Axe, my focus is on the country first, and always will be."

He was silent for a moment, then he said, "Then we're on the same page. So how does it all fit together?"

"I don't know, which is what has me so worried. I can feel… something. Just like before the New York City attacks. But what if the scheme with Baranov really is set up to weaken the president, embroil him in a scandal, and distract from whatever else is about to happen? Like a magician's sleight of hand—making you look one place when you should be looking elsewhere."

"Then what is it we should be watching instead of falling for it?"

She sighed, letting her frustration show. "I can't figure it out. I could very well be wrong about it entirely."

"I hope to hell you are, but I doubt it. You have incredible instincts. If you think this is a possibility, we have to plan around it. If you end up wrong, fine. But let's take it seriously. So what's next?"

"I'm hoping you can tell me."

Axe had an immediate answer. "We deal with what's in front of us. Las Vegas, New Year's Eve. You coming?"

This is the moment I have to make a choice. Stay in the office, doing what I'm best at? Or go into the field to do what challenges me—and what I enjoy most?

Haley considered it, hesitated, and reconsidered her decision. Though she didn't like it, it made the most sense.

"No. My talents are best used here this time. Like your guy, Sun Tzu said, 'The opportunity of defeating the enemy is provided by the enemy himself.' I haven't found the big picture yet, all the moving parts. Or the enemy's weakness. And I need to."

"You're already reading the book I got you?"

Axe had given her a lovely hardcover copy of Sun Tzu's quotes for Christmas. "Yes, I'm enjoying it."

"You sure about Vegas?" He hesitated. Haley could picture him standing in Kelton's hospital room, maybe looking out the window. She knew him well enough now to have an insight into his thoughts and feelings.

He's thrown by what happened in Mexico with the loss of the scientists. And he's still worried about getting older, slowing down.

"I can't do this by myself," he admitted quietly. "It's too big."

"We'll do the logistics together. And I'll send you help. Nalen will meet you in Vegas—if I can convince him."

"Nalen? In the field?"

"He's who we have. You object?"

"No. Surprised, is all."

"We have to play this close to the vest. If we blow it, we play right into the hands of whoever is behind the whole plot. Nalen will help you on the ground. I'll stay back and keep digging."

"So—New Year's Eve in Las Vegas with thousands of drugged, homicidal civilians? Good times."

She couldn't decide if he was serious or not.

SEALs are crazy.

"Just make sure what happens in Vegas stays in Vegas."

"Deal."

35

GOODBYE

Baranov Home
Henderson, Nevada

Victor Baranov zipped the garment bag closed, careful to not snag the plastic dry-cleaning bag protecting his tuxedo. He patted the exterior pocket, confirming he had added the matching dress shoes, then did the same for the other exterior compartment holding socks and underwear.

What am I forgetting?

He rarely felt this scattered.

It's the stress of knowing my life is about to change dramatically.

Cufflinks. He had forgotten his cufflinks. Retrieving them from his dresser, he placed the padded black box protecting them in the compartment with his socks.

One more look at the small roller bag with pajamas, toiletries, and a casual outfit for New Year's Day. Then he zipped it closed and placed both by the bedroom door.

All I'm taking from a life of fifty-five years.

The pleasantly decorated bedroom looked no different from when his wife died. He didn't have the decorating skill she'd had, nor the will to make changes. Keeping it the same had been one way to hold on to her memory.

In a way, I'm leaving her behind as well, which is also affecting me,

I'm sure.

The grief returned, though he had processed it repeatedly over the years, like an onion being peeled layer by layer. There always seemed to be more—another memory, more sadness at the untimely loss.

Then there was Nicholas.

His lifestyle of drugs, women, and cars will hopefully protect him from the fallout. They have all three in Russia. Or, if it makes more sense, he will be looked after and provided for here in the United States.

Victor had no illusions about what would happen in the next few days. He had been promised a new life, but his analytical businessman side saw not only how easy it would be to offer him as a sacrificial lamb, but the benefits of it.

Conscious of his distractedness, he once again confirmed his tuxedo pants, coat, shirt, and tie, the shoes, socks, and underwear. Telling himself he didn't need to, he felt for the box of cufflinks in the pocket of the garment bag, unable to resist checking. He convinced himself not to open the roller bag and double-check those items; he wasn't that far gone.

Besides, all of this will be confiscated once the truth comes out, or left behind if I'm whisked off to Moscow.

He took a last, lingering look at the room. His wife's decorating handi-work—the duvet cover which matched the curtains, which picked up the eggshell blue of the walls. The bed they shared for so many years. Her three pairs of favorite shoes lined up, toes tucked under her bureau. The dresser itself, the top the same after all these years: her small collection of perfume bottles along the left side, a small metal decorative tree where her jewelry hung on the right, the last birthday card he ever gave her standing in the middle. All of it carefully moved weekly for dusting—done by himself, never the maid—then returned reverently to their places.

Would I be doing this if she were still here? Would she have convinced me to ignore the directive, go to the authorities, fight instead of accepting my destiny? Or would she have honored the generations-old agreement along with me, left it all behind for a life together in Moscow, St. Peters-burg, Sochi, or wherever they have planned for me?

No way to know, but she'd had a strong sense of honor as well.

With two fingers, he lifted the garment bag by its hanger, telescoped the handle of the roller bag with his other hand, and left the room for the last time. Within forty-eight hours—seventy-two at the outside—he would either be dead, incarcerated, or on his way to Russia. A martyr, a criminal, or a hero.

36

UNSANCTIONED

Central Analysis Group Headquarters
Conference Room C
Alexandria, Virginia

"That's correct," Haley said. "Flight 8319. Baranov, Victor. Thank you for your understanding, and sorry for the last-minute notice."

She listened to the scheduler at the car service Baranov had booked to pick him up at the airport. "Yes, of course we understand. Bill the card on file for the cancellation. Sorry again."

Easier than I thought.

It hadn't taken much to cancel Baranov's airport transportation or hotel reservations. Agreeing to pay in full for services not rendered will do that.

She looked around at the small conference room she had basically lived in for the past two-and-a-half days. Leaving for good was going to be difficult. She'd miss it here.

It was fun while it lasted.

There was a lot to prepare and not much time. She hurried to the employee kitchen area. It was 9:30 a.m., time to meet with Nancy, her other unsanctioned asset.

"How's your day going?" Nancy asked as she made yet another cup of coffee. Haley still looked tired, but she moved with more energy, like she had a new purpose.

Nancy had successfully tracked Dr. Edgars. She'd popped into the kitchen at 8:30, but Haley hadn't come in.

I can't wait to see the look on Haley's face when I tell her where the doctor went.

"Busy. Look," Haley said quietly after glancing around to make sure no one could overhear. "You're going to be on your own for a bit."

"What do you mean?" Nancy asked, surprised. "You have a lot of work to do, and I can help."

I don't want to do this on my own—but I don't want off the operation, either.

"You're great, but I've already put you, Dave, and Gregory in a dangerous position," Haley told her, eyes bloodshot and hair a disaster. "You can still help. But we can't meet and have to be very careful about how we talk. I don't think the president is involved, but this will probably hit the fan soon. I don't want you all caught in the crossfire when it does. But before I go, let me guess: is Dr. Edgars in Las Vegas?"

Nancy was shocked.

She is a witch.

"How could you know?"

"I've been working, too. Baranov's base of operations, at least for one part of his plan, is in either Denver or Las Vegas, so I guessed." She smiled and shrugged. "But I don't know the exact address. I'll take it if you have it."

Nancy told her, still impressed by the younger woman's abilities.

Haley leaned closer. "I believe Las Vegas is going to be attacked using the drugged beer. We still have to find out more, though. I have a plan to fix it, but what I have to do will make it much worse for you all if I fail, so we have to keep you out of it."

There was so much to unpack, but Nancy started with her first thought.

"So it's true? Baranov is actually behind it?"

Haley nodded.

"I don't get it," Nancy said. "Why would he plan an attack like this? Why risk it all? And you seem to think it's happening now, but why not wait? Another few months and it will be the big football game. Opening day of baseball season. He could hit the entire United States, not just Las Vegas. Plus, why risk his company and reputation? He has to know he's going to get caught." The questions came out in a flood. "Nothing about this makes sense."

Haley nodded along. "Excellent questions. I don't have the answers. I have suspicions, but…" She shrugged helplessly. "It's a gut feeling."

"What are your suspicions?"

"I don't want to say. But maybe you're curious enough to dive into your questions? Figure them out?" Haley asked her with a desperately hopeful look. "We could keep your role top secret. No one but Dave could know. Though the safe play here—for you and Dave—is to walk away. I might be able to do this on my own."

Nancy considered the proposal. If caught by Gregory, there would be no way to explain away her research. Dave would cover for her, but if she went down, he would, too. It would be obvious he knew and condoned her behavior, or at least did nothing to report or stop it.

He supports me. Besides, this is worth the risk. The country is in danger and no one else is in a position to help.

But if the whole situation deteriorated as Haley predicted, where would she be? There would likely be investigations—what did she know and when? Did she participate in a cover-up? Did she follow proper procedures? Someone was sure to wonder if she was even involved in the plot. Maybe she had a role in the attack. She could be a deep-state traitor.

There would be endless questions combined with lasting suspicions about her loyalty and trustworthiness—and that was the best-case scenario.

Haley has been right time after time. The potential to help her and prevent an attack is worth the risk to my career.

"I'm in. What do you need me to do?"

Haley seemed sad, not happy, at her decision.

Haley looks like she knows I'm going to be sacrificed… but she's willing to let me take the risk.

The realization of how badly Haley thought it might turn out sobered Nancy… but didn't change her mind.

"First thing," Haley said, holding up her phone, "install this secure communication app on your phone. Don't worry—it's not the one run by the CIA. As far as I know, this one is airtight. Next, investigate your questions. My theory is Las Vegas is only a first punch, not the entire fight. We need to understand the big picture. The 'why.'"

Nancy felt overwhelmed suddenly. It all seemed too much. There were too few details, no obvious way to figure out the puzzle.

This isn't how I trained. I'm used to taking my time, looking for holes in our security, or for what other agencies are missing. Big picture, not tiny details.

Nancy pulled herself together, swallowed her pride, and asked the younger woman for help.

"Any suggestions on where or how to start?"

"It's always about vectors," Haley began slowly. She stared off into the distance, almost like she was seeing the data on her computer screens. "Who intersects? Start with all the employees of Baranov Brands. And the FDA and any other government inspectors. A few left their positions under suspicious circumstances. Find out why and how. Later, other people filled in and stayed. Find out what they have in common. No detail is too small."

Nancy made mental notes she could access later.

"Next, look into every person Baranov has had limited, irregular contact with in the past ten years. Forget the usual. We're looking for the unusual. A routine interrupted. He's a guy with no hair out of place, buttoned up. He didn't come up with this on his own. Someone is behind him, running him and this attack. That's my hunch. You need to find out if I'm right. And if I am, who is it... and who or what organization is behind that person?"

"Got it."

I can't read, think, or type as fast as Haley, but I can do this. I'll work non-stop if I have to. Get Dave fully involved. Together, the two of us might add up to one Haley. And I know how much he loved the success of the last operation to find the EMPs.

"Last, your final crash course on analyzing as I do. Look for commonality: the usual, what you'd expect from an important business in a medium-sized city. Most of the employees live relatively near the plant, so their kids go to the same schools, elementary to high school. They shop at the same grocery stores, get their hair cut from the same few salons and barbers, buy their cars from the same dealers. Even Baranov needs groceries, dry cleaning done, meals out. He may have a housekeeper or other hired help, but there will be the usual... and where there is usual, you look for the unusual. For him and his employees. One other trick— look for proportions."

"Proportions? Like..."

"For example, does Baranov work out more often than the average man in his position? Attend more sporting events or fewer? Gamble more or less? Let your gut guide you."

Nancy could see Haley's passion—and her frustration.

She could do this herself so much easier, and more naturally than me. But I've had glimpses of the magic before. I can do it again.

"I'll find out what's happening. But why can't you? What's so important you need me to do it? We both know I'll take twice as long—at least —and that's if I'm lucky. I might not get there at all."

Haley smiled sadly and looked away, toward Gregory's office. She spoke, her tone regretful. "I have to do what I should have done months ago."

37

FAREWELL

Gregory's shoulders sagged as Haley walked into his office.

He has already guessed he's not going to like this, she thought.

"Have a seat," he said, gesturing to the guest chair.

"I better not." She stopped in front of his desk, then changed her mind and collapsed into the chair, holding a piece of paper.

I need to conserve what little energy I have left. I'm going to need it.

"You made progress last night," he said, not asking. "How bad is it?"

She only shook her head tiredly.

"Let me guess. You need another 'vacation,'" Gregory said, leaning back in his chair.

Close, but not quite. Am I really doing this?

"No," she said, shaking her head slowly.

Will he figure it out?

Gregory's eyes widened, and he shook his head as he sat up straight.

He's so smart.

"No. Let me help. You have a perfect record. I believe in you, even if you are a pain in the butt."

She slowly slid the paper, taken moments before from her printer, across his desk. He watched but didn't pick it up.

"It's been a pleasure working for you, Gregory. You've taught me so much. Put that paper into the system. Make it official, but—if you wouldn't mind—make contemporaneous notes saying I'm too good of an asset to lose. File those away. But you have to cover yourself—and the country. This could go bad very quickly."

Gregory reluctantly opened the paper and read portions aloud, his voice disbelieving. "Suffering from PTSD... Having trouble staying grounded in reality... Delusions... Suspicious of rich male Americans... Suspect people who are surely innocent of terrorist activities... Time away to seek professional help... Have misled colleagues and managers, exaggerated claims... Truly sorry..."

His face implored her not to do this.

"Too much?" she asked with a chuckle.

He didn't laugh.

Tough crowd. Maybe too soon.

Gregory folded the paper back into thirds and shoved it angrily toward her. "No. I won't accept this. Go on 'vacation' and fix it your way as you have in the past. I'll cover for you or take the heat if it comes." He held up his hand to cut her off before she could argue. "All this can be said verbally if you get caught doing whatever you have planned. It does not—will not—go into your file."

The staring contest began as they tested each other's resolve. The silence and battle of wills dragged on, uncomfortable to start, agonizing as the seconds wound to a full minute.

Haley caved first. "Fine. But you keep this," she pushed the paper back at him. "And this one." She pulled her backup letter from the pocket in her blazer. "Use the one you need, but one has to go through immediately. Not in an hour, or tomorrow."

He set the first letter—requesting a medical leave of absence due to mental health issues—on his desk and unfolded the second one. "'I hereby tender my resignation from the Central Analysis Group, effective immediately. It has been my pleasure to serve.'" He placed it next to the first one. "Don't do this. You're good at your job. Both the official duties and your..." He trailed off, looking for the term. "Extracurricular, unofficial work. You intuitively think several moves ahead and can somehow predict what our enemies will do. I bet you play a mean game of chess."

She flashed back to New York City's Washington Square Park a few years ago during a rare break from college to tour the city, to be a normal person for a change, not a prodigy. Letting the chess hustlers who called the park home talk her into games—for money. Delighting in kicking their asses as they underestimated her brains because of her breasts.

"We can't risk damaging the president and country with what I have to do next," Haley told Gregory. "It's the best move. I know how smart you are. I know you see it."

For a moment, she wondered if he would argue. But then he nodded, picked up the folded letter detailing her mental health problems—which were only partly exaggerated—and turned to the credenza along the wall behind him, where he had his safe.

A minute later, the letter had been stored safely away, as she had hoped. Gregory handed her a large, plain manilla envelope. "This might come in handy."

A second passport and legend for me?

She opened the clasp on the envelope and spilled the contents onto Gregory's desk. A passport with Axe's picture, but a different name. A driver's license in the same name, along with credit cards in a worn leather wallet. Plus a sheaf of papers with a background and relationships—a full history of a fake life for Axe.

How long has he had this?

The realization hit her.

He knew this day would come. He's been ahead of me all along.

She nodded her thanks, not sure if she could speak without getting emotional.

I have to get it together for what comes next.

"Thank you." She took a deep breath to steady herself. "I expect this goes without saying, but better to get it out, don't you think?"

He squinted at her, suddenly confused.

I've gotten ahead of him, at last! I hope.

She stood, stuffing Axe's legend back in the envelope and methodically closing the small metal clasp to hold it shut while Gregory waited.

"You've been supportive, which I believe is sincere. But you're exceptional at this game too. I might beat you at chess, but not at poker. You've been at this longer than I have." She paused and put steel in her voice. "So if once I'm gone you want to cover your ass, let me say this. If you warn the president, tell him or anyone else what's happening with Baranov... I hate to be so blunt, but it is what it is. I will kill you. Do you understand?" She allowed her inner warrior to show, knowing exactly how it looked: the cold, dead eyes, the energy of a person who had taken lives—many lives.

She saw a quick flash of fear on his face before he expertly hid it. He nodded once.

I hope he is truly a good guy, on my side. If I've been played, I'm going to be pissed.

She held out her hand across his desk, and he rose slowly to shake it. "Thank you for the opportunities."

It took a second, but Gregory found his voice. "It's been my pleasure working with you. The country owes you a debt of gratitude."

"I may come to collect on that debt in a week or two. If my position is still available."

"It will be."

She muttered as she turned and walked from his office. "We'll see."

38

GREETINGS

Central Analysis Group Headquarters
Parking Lot
Alexandria, Virginia

Haley had to hurry. The resignation with Gregory had taken longer than planned.

Standing behind her SUV in the CAG parking lot, she quickly packed her bed and pillows into the huge black plastic storage tub she used to hide that she slept in the SUV half the time. Then she went through the vehicle from front to back, cleaning up and depersonalizing it.

I'll only need a few seconds, so it doesn't have to be perfect, but it can't raise any suspicions.

When she finished, she pulled out of the parking lot, heading to the airport. On the way, she drove through an automatic, self-serve car wash, cleaning off the winter grime as a finishing touch. As the machinery worked its magic, she removed her 9mm and the holster from her right hip, the extra magazines in their carrier from the left, and placed them in the center armrest compartment. Then she unstrapped the small backup 9mm from her ankle, unclipped the folding knife from her right pocket, and horizontal-carry fixed blade knife at the small of her back. All joined the other weapon in the compartment with no room to spare. She locked it, feeling naked.

While waiting for the huge blow dryer at the end of the car wash tunnel, she checked the charge on the small combination stun gun and flashlight from her glove box, prepared the zip ties, and created a simple sign on her tablet. She was as ready as she'd ever be, thanks in large part to Axe's forethought, planning, and insistence on having essential items stocked in her truck.

Now all I have to do is pull this off.

She took in the streets and buildings as she made her way through light traffic to the airport.

This may be the last time I see these sights if today goes badly.

In a dire emergency, she had the passport with a fake name she had used in the Virgin Islands a few months before. It would be tracked, but she could at least get out of the country. If she flew to Europe and arrived before the authorities started looking for her, the open borders would allow her to land in Paris and end up in Portugal relatively easily. A few long bus rides, made enjoyable by the views out the window, would bring her to a lovely coastal village. She had passable Spanish and would fit in there. The weather would be wonderful, and she'd heard great things about both Lisbon and Porto. Money would be a problem, but she could set up an account on a few freelancing sites. People might pay for an analyst with her talents.

Or there's always St. John. Cody and Bec would hide me.

She could have a small house with a garden. Live off the grid, anonymous. Relax.

No, I'd be going crazy within a week.

Maybe she was being too pessimistic. It could all work out.

Or maybe I don't need to worry. I could be dead by the time this operation is over.

Haley pulled into the closest spot she could find in the astronomically priced short-term parking lot. After fixing her ponytail and applying some makeup to cover for her tiredness and look more professional, she grabbed her tablet, hid the stun gun in the back of the SUV, and hurried inside the terminal. According to the app on her phone, Baranov's flight hadn't arrived, but she wanted to be early.

She adopted a neutral look. Not bored, not excited. Customer service focused, but not overdoing it. She joined five other black-clad men and one woman in a group at the passenger exit from the arrival gates. She flipped open the tablet cover, unlocked the screen, then held it up, **Baranov** showing in large letters facing the bored security officer on a tired stool guarding the area where the passengers would exit.

This is all being recorded by security cameras. If it doesn't work out, I have to flee. I can't get caught.

Haley wasn't completely sold on this crazy idea of hers, but it followed a core premise of Axe's—and now hers. 'Shake the tree.' Take action and see what happened. Or, as Axe often quoted from Sun Tzu, "Opportunities multiply as they are seized."

I'm definitely seizing this one.

Her actions today would at least be damage control if there was a reason for the connection between Baranov and the president to come to light.

If Axe and Nalen aren't successful, when it all hits the fan, the culprit won't have recently attended a private party at the White House and stayed overnight in the Lincoln Bedroom as a guest of the president.

Plus, with Baranov under her control, she had options. What those were, though, she hadn't figured out yet.

Haley spotted Baranov before he saw her but waited until he read his name and looked at her before seeming to notice him and putting on an obviously fake but plausibly sincere smile.

"Mr. Baranov? Welcome to D.C. Let me take your bags." She stuffed her tablet into her pants at the small of her back and relieved the man of his garment bag and roller suitcase, which he parted with easily, as any wealthy man used to being picked up by a hired driver did. "Right this way, sir. We're parked very close."

She found the rest of the kidnapping surprisingly easy. After opening the rear passenger door for him, she loaded his bags into the back of the SUV and grabbed the combination stun gun-flashlight from the top of the black storage tub. Zip cuffs went in each pocket of her black pants.

As she closed the hatchback door, she called to Baranov. "I had trouble with that seatbelt earlier. Is it working?"

Checking the parking lot nearby, she didn't notice anyone, so opened the door next to her victim. "Did it click in okay?"

When he turned to double-check, she pressed the zapper against his neck and pulled the trigger. Baranov's body went rigid and twitched. After counting to three, her heart pounding, she released the button. The man went limp, unconscious.

She resisted glancing around, torn between wanting to see if people had noticed and not wanting to appear guilty.

Just helping my client in the backseat. Nothing to see here.

Using the zip cuffs, she bound his hands and ankles. A zip tie connected the two, and a longer one connected him, bent forward at the waist, to the metal under the passenger seat in front of him.

He's not going anywhere and won't be easily seen in that position.

"Great, let's get going then," she called for anyone nearby as she calmly closed his door. Walking around the front of the SUV, she finally surveyed the area. Two people walked by on the sidewalk, too far away to have heard or seen her actions.

She climbed into the big SUV and drove out of the parking lot through the self-pay lane.

I think I pulled it off. Now for the hard part.

Haley sensed when Baranov came to, though he kept quiet.

Faking it? Waiting to see what's going on?

She drove on smaller roads as soon as she could, single lanes where no semis or other SUVs would pass her and possibly see her prisoner.

"You don't have to pretend," she told him. "I know you're awake."

Baranov lifted his head and looked at her in the rearview mirror, but said nothing.

She started her prepared speech, imitating Axe. "We're going someplace quiet. No neighbors for miles. No one to hear you scream or beg me to put an end to it. I've done this before. You will talk. You will tell me what I want to know. The only question is how much you're interested in suffering first."

"What do you want to know?" He sounded curious, not scared.

I don't think this is working. He doesn't believe me.

She laughed. "Everything, of course. I know much of it, but not the full story. Why? Are you ready to talk before I've had my fun? No, hold it in, please. Let me play for an hour. Maybe two. Otherwise, I'm going to be disappointed."

She thought of Pioneer's look, the mad eyes showing his insanity as he stood in his control room on St. John two months before, launching attacks to bring the world to its knees.

Can I make my eyes look like that?

She tried her best, put on a crazy smile to go with it, then looked back to show Baranov.

"You're from Las Vegas?" she asked. "You like the desert heat? We'll get a nice fire going in the fireplace. Leave the poker in the flames—you know, to move the wood around? It's iron. It gets nice and hot." She glanced back again with the same smile and look in her eyes. "But it's a dry heat!" She laughed as maniacally as she could.

Baranov stared at her, unimpressed.

Damn it. He'd be babbling like a baby by now if Axe were here.

It held greater risk, but she needed to turn to Plan B.

Go big or go home. Or, in this case, both.

Bent forward with his hands and feet tied, his suit wrinkled and out of place, Victor didn't know what to do. Escape seemed impossible for now, but the young woman holding him seemed more nervous than dangerous.

Too beautiful to torture me, despite the act she puts on.

Would his handler know he'd been abducted?

No. He wouldn't be monitoring my progress. Too risky.

There would be no one coming to rescue him.

Resigned to his fate, Victor relaxed as best he could in the uncomfortable position. The young lady would either make a mistake, allowing him to escape, or not. At this point, it didn't matter. His life was over anyway. The plan would continue forward without his input, and his connection with the president would play out regardless of whether he attended the New Year's Eve party and stayed at the White House.

Whatever the woman has in mind for me, it's much too late to stop the coming storm. Not that it would matter, but I can't imagine anything she could do to make me talk.

He could tell—she just wasn't the torturing type.

---

155 Laurel Lane
Alexandria, Virginia

Haley pulled into her driveway, the security light on the wall above her door flooding the area with harsh, white light. She had run an extensive surveillance detection route, ensuring no one followed her. The gloomy day had faded to darkness early as winters in the east did.

In the backseat, Baranov slept thanks to the two sleeping pills—courtesy of her primary care physician's concern about her insomnia—she had forced down his throat after pulling over and zapping him again.

She unlocked the house's side door after checking both the security system and her old-school trick of a strand of hair attached to both the door and the frame. Reaching inside, she flipped the switch, killing the bright floodlight. Then she returned to the SUV. After cutting the zip ties, she worked Baranov's limp body out of the back seat, carefully letting him slide to the ground.

He was too heavy to carry, even though he was thin, so she dragged him inside and maneuvered his body onto her spare bed. After locking the doors and setting the alarm, she cut off all of Baranov's clothes and fit a thick towel around him as a diaper. Then she zip-tied him spread eagle on the bed, set her watch alarm to wake her before he would, and grabbed a spare blanket from the bureau. She had to rest. The recent all-nighters and stress had finally caught up with her.

Covering herself, she lay flat on her back on the worn bedroom carpet next to the bed. She fell asleep hoping Axe would pull off his part of the plan—and trying not to worry about what he would say when he learned what she'd done.

39

THE TEAM

As the sun set over the desert city, the taxi dropped Axe off at the address provided by Haley. Less than two miles to the east, under a darkening sky, the lights of casinos on the Las Vegas Strip fought each other for attention. The familiar skyline view felt so close, but the excitement and thrills of Las Vegas Boulevard were far different from the industrial area he found himself in.

The small, white, two-story warehouse sat on a major north-south road. Its front parking lot could fit about 15 cars. Along the side ran a loading ramp for a semi to back into, and a lane leading to a rear parking lot.

Axe pulled the heavily tinted glass front door, expecting it to be locked, but it opened for him. He stepped into the small reception area of the empty building. A single fluorescent light over the beat-up chest-high reception counter dimly lit the room. An open doorway led to the warehouse in the back of the building.

Did I beat Nalen here?

Axe had flown in on the first flight he could catch out of Texas, but someone had to have unlocked the door.

Probably in back.

He walked quietly toward the rear of the building, wishing he had a pistol.

First stop after this: a store to get a gun, depending on how long the background check takes. This whole thing could be over by the time it clears.

"Glad you could make it," Admiral Nalen said from his side, causing Axe to reflexively spin. He had to stop himself from lashing out.

Where the hell did the sneaky bastard come from?

"Jumpy?" Nalen asked with a smile on his long, narrow face.

He's having fun.

His gray hair looked freshly cut, shorter than the last time Axe had seen him at the shooting range in rural Virginia a few weeks before. Regulation short. Going to war short. And as always, his blue jeans were perfectly flat, but not ironed. Folded straight out of the dryer, Axe guessed. His white t-shirt, stretched across his fit body, definitely had been ironed. Shirts don't come out of the dryer looking that nice.

"You have to teach me how you do that, Admiral. I'm good... but not like that."

"We all have our skills. This is one of mine. Come on back, I'll show you what we have so far."

They headed to the warehouse area. A large whiteboard had recently been unboxed—the cardboard lay in a neatly folded pile in a corner, and the board rested against the back wall. A large map of Las Vegas Boulevard was duct-taped on the wall above it. This room was bright, with large overhead fluorescents bathing the area.

They stopped in front of the whiteboard and map. "We have an hour to plan, then you have a ton of phone calls to make," Nalen said.

"How many casinos?" Axe asked, surveying the map.

"From what Haley gathered, several major casinos on the strip will serve the spiked beer. They've been incentivized: Baranov is providing the beer free, along with a marketing push, paying for entertainment—themed to fit each casino, so it seems they all are doing their own thing, not merely pushing his product. He's going all out, as you'd expect with a big new product launch. Twenty casinos total in the city. A few of the higher-end ones won't push it as hard, despite the marketing. They're more exclusive. But we still need to be ready for trouble at them."

Nalen pointed to the downtown area ten miles to the northeast. "Downtown, along Fremont Street, four of the major casinos are going big with the promo. It will be ground zero, I think." He dug into his small backpack, sitting against the wall, and unfolded a close-up map of down-town. Axe grabbed the duct tape and stuck it to the wall.

"An hour ago, I bribed a bartender for one of the special beers being held for release and sent it to Haley. She had an idea that might help us but couldn't talk about it. We'll see. But no matter what, we're going to have our hands full."

They stood shoulder to shoulder, two warriors past their prime, but still in the game. The silence built long past the time it took to contemplate the odds, which were thoroughly stacked against them.

"Say it," Nalen told Axe, turning to him. His shoulders were back, his posture perfect, as always.

He's a squared-away individual… but how does he always know what I'm thinking?

"See, this is why I could never have risen to your level, Admiral. I can't read minds."

"First, from now on, you call me Nalen or Hammer. We have to remove any idea this is a sanctioned op."

"Yes, sir—I mean, you've got it, Hammer."

Nalen stared, waiting patiently for Axe to bring up the subject bothering him.

"Fine," Axe finally said. "Why are you here? You're too close to the president. If your involvement comes out…"

Nalen nodded understandingly. "Normally, yes. Absolutely. My role has been, and should be, light oversight, logistics, big-picture planning. Guidance. This is way outside my normal scope. But in this case, if it goes south, it's over anyway. The president goes down, either through impeachment, resignation, or playing out his term with zero political clout, because of his connection to Baranov. Me being here has little risk of impact."

Axe nodded.

Makes sense. If he still has what it takes.

Nalen laughed and subtly shifted his stance, sliding his left foot back and lowering his center of gravity a few inches. "You want to try me, Axe? See if I've still got it?"

Standing within striking distance of the admiral, Axe could feel his strength and power. Axe slowly raised his hands in surrender. "That won't be necessary."

He's still got it.

"So how many men do you think we need?" Axe asked, turning back to the map and hoping Nalen dropped his challenge.

"All of them."

Axe glanced at him to see if he was kidding. He wasn't.

"Or as many as we can convince," Nalen muttered. "Haley put together a list," he said, pulling a tablet from his backpack and handing it to Axe along with a stylus. "There's an office behind the reception counter. Start calling. SEALs first, then other top-tier units. Basically, anyone retired, competent, and willing. Sample script, also courtesy Haley, with a few changes from me. Also, a voicemail script—don't leave the full info on voicemail. We don't want it coming back to bite us in the ass. Get going. I'll start on the mission brief."

Axe rubbed his eyes and squinted at the tablet, then made a check mark next to the last name.

All the retired SEALs on the list had offered an enthusiastic "Yes!" They either knew Axe personally or by reputation. For the old-timers, he'd used Nalen's name.

Most of the other veterans had said yes, too. Only a few had turned him down, out of family commitments or being unable to travel to Vegas in the required time frame. All had sounded heartbroken at having to decline.

Axe had a last name on the list. He had left a message earlier for Doug "Mad Dog" McBellin but knew the man was notorious for ignoring voice mails.

One more try.

This time, Mad Dog answered, sounding at least half drunk. "Yo! Who's this?"

"A voice from your past."

"Oh, shit! Axe?"

"Yes, how you doing, Mad Dog?"

"Living the dream, of course. The unemployed, single with no prospects dream. But it beats the one where I'm in my tighty-whities taking the college entrance test in high school, I guess." He laughed and belched. "Whatcha got for me? Work, I hope."

"Yes. How would you like to come to Las Vegas and give me a hand? Can't say much on the phone, you understand, but I could use your help."

"Pays good?"

"No. None, actually."

"Hmm. Okay. Is it at least easy?"

"Probably not."

"Safe?"

"Doubt it."

"Fun?"

"Depends on your idea of fun."

Mad Dog was cracking up, holding the phone away from his mouth as he laughed. "Sounds great—I'm in!"

Axe smiled. The man was crazy, even for a SEAL. "Las Vegas. I'll text you an address. Come as soon as you can. Are you sober enough to drive right now?"

The laughter died. "Well, no. Shit. It's the week between Christmas and New Year's Eve. Party time," he explained defensively.

"Eat a big meal, drink a lot of water, then gear up. Sleep for a few hours, then leave when you're safe. Better a few hours late than leaving a trail of destruction in your path and you dead in a ditch."

Axe heard liquid poured into a sink—the beer, he guessed.

"On it. I'm only a few hours away, between San Diego and LA. Okay if I leave in the morning?" He lowered his voice to a conspiratorial whisper. "I'm kind of drunk."

"Morning is fine. Shoot to be at the address I send you by noon."

"Got it. Vegas, baby!" he shouted into the phone before hanging up.

Axe closed the cover on the tablet and slid the pencil in the holder along the side. He wandered through the building, looking for Nalen, finally finding him sitting outside the propped-open backdoor. Lawn chairs sat against the block wall of the building. They had been angled to face east toward the bright lights of Las Vegas Boulevard.

I doubt the people who work in this neighborhood experience the action on the Strip very often.

Nalen gestured for Axe to join him and reached into a small cooler between the chairs. "Beer?" he asked, pulling out a bottle and handing it to Axe.

Axe's eyes widened.

"Relax. Imported. Completely different brand and bottler. I checked."

Axe accepted it and drank.

"This going to work?" Axe asked after a moment.

"Depends on your definition of success. Yes, we're going to save many people. Prevent a lot of death and destruction. But we won't contain it all."

Axe had been thinking. "What about calling in a bomb threat? Or assaulting a few casinos, shooting up the slot machines, scaring the crap out of people? Get the casinos shut down, people evacuated."

"Not bad. But the beer is still out there. We'd be delaying the inevitable. No matter what we do, they've got us boxed in. It doesn't feel like checkmate, but it's close."

The late December nighttime desert air was far warmer than Virginia but still cooled quickly. Axe and the Admiral ignored the temperature, sitting in companionable silence, lost in thought.

Axe debated bringing up his feelings around losing the doctor in Mexico, along with not rescuing the other scientists.

For all my conversations with Haley about talking out what's troubling her, I guess I'm not so good at doing it myself.

Nalen finished his beer, reached for the cooler, then stopped and put the bottle down next to it without getting another. He returned to staring at the lights of the casinos a few miles in the distance, visible over the low roofs of the surrounding buildings. "Feelings won't stay in the box?"

Damn it. I have to learn his mind-reading trick.

Then he realized, at least when it came to helping Haley, he already had.

The master knows the student.

He could learn from Nalen's experience.

"You got it. I'm getting old. I failed. Maybe I should get out of the field. Recruit one of the younger guys... maybe add a level of management between you and the front-line team. Keep you safely out of the mix. I could help Haley manage the assets."

Nalen stretched his legs out and crossed an ankle over the other. "My level—or one level below, as you suggest—is about the big picture. You've always struck me as more of a hands-on type of guy, not management. Otherwise, you could have stayed on the Team, accepted the promotions offered."

"True." Axe considered it... being with the men, but not going on the missions. Being a liaison with the brass. Mission planning. On one hand, he'd be a valued member of an elite force. A teammate. On the other, he'd be effectively out of the fun. In the rear with the gear.

"On second thought, no thanks," Axe said in the darkness of the back lot.

"Then first, you get the pep talk. Here it is. The mission at the hotel was never rescuing hostages. It was shaking the tree, which you did successfully. You got Haley the next piece of the puzzle so we can work the big picture. We're about to save hundreds, maybe thousands of lives, not a handful. Next, you didn't have intel. Haley didn't know exactly how many scientists there were, or their location, when you arrived at the hotel. Had you been given a mission to rescue people held hostage, in a super-secret basement lab, I know you would have taken care of it. But if we had solid intel, we would have called it in. Your entire old Team would have assaulted the place, not one guy undercover with Kelton—an amateur—tagging along. Got it?"

"Yes, sir. It makes sense, but…"

"Have you ever lost a Team member under your command?"

"You know the answer. No, because I've avoided command. We've lost a few Teammates, and it sucked every time. But never because of what I did or didn't do. Bad luck. It could have been me or any of the other men. Wrong place, wrong time, lucky shots."

Nalen sat quietly for a long moment. He was lost in thought.

Remembering.

"In some ways, losing a man—or a protectee, I imagine—is like your first kill." He spoke so softly, Axe had to lean to the side to hear. "It's overwhelming if you think about it much." Nalen adjusted his legs, sitting up straighter, and his voice returned to full volume. "But right now, we're starting a mission. Put what you can in the box. You know how to do it. Any thoughts or feelings that claw their way out, you use them as motivation. 'It won't happen again,' type of attitude. Gain strength from it."

He stopped talking. Axe eventually looked over, and Nalen caught his eye. "Process it fully once the mission is done. First things first. The country is at risk and our precious feelings can wait until the time is right to deal with them. I need your head in the game, Axe."

"Aye, aye, sir."

Axe detached from his feelings of pain and failure, making a conscious decision to deal with them later, putting them in the box. He took a slow, deep breath, feeling his power return. Talking with Nalen had helped tremendously.

"Good man," Nalen said. "Come on, I got us some rooms for the night at a decent hotel nearby. Then tomorrow, we get some."

It made Axe smile to hear the older man talk like that.

Nalen noticed. "Don't count me out, Axe. I can hold my own."

I have no doubt.

40

PLANS

The Kremlin
Moscow, Russia

President Pavel Zimalev poured over maps in his chilly office late into the night, reviewing the invasion timeline. He reluctantly had to admit his predecessor had done a fine job with the attack plans. The deceit and distractions were works of art.

The west won't see it coming until it's much too late.

Units were staged in perfect positions, in the right amounts to represent a bluff they wanted to look like preparations for an actual invasion.

The audacity impressed him.

Letting the West's military commanders and politicians think they have us figured out, when it's a bluff that's not a bluff.

Like every winter, the Russian units would rush the border, threatening to attack. They would begin when he gave the order during the early part of the snowstorm. After a few charges toward the border, only to turn away or stop at the last minute, the defenses would grow complacent and cocky, figuring the moves were the same as previous years.

And that is when I will order the real strike.

The final border assault wouldn't stop, but continue through, overwhelming defenders and rushing to the interior of the countries.

Pavel smiled, wishing he could be among the men as they invaded.

At least I'll be able to visit and build their morale before the storm hits.

His trip to the units would be excellent propaganda and seal his position as a visionary leader for his beloved country.

This mission will be looked back on by history as the start of the next chapter in Russia's success.

Additionally, the secret sleeper assets in place throughout the American government and major businesses moved up the ladder of success each year. It wouldn't be long before he had sources in the highest levels. He would have access to the secrets of the United States. With a word, he'd be able to cripple industries, wreck the country's economy, and disrupt the government.

Or he could play it close to the vest, using the assets sparingly to bring down the country slowly but surely from within. It wouldn't be as spectacular as some of his dreams but would achieve the goal.

Soon, Russia will take the place of America as the world's biggest, most capable superpower.

41

DREAMS

Erik had been Senator Jonesley's personal assistant for two years and hated every minute of it. Doing exceptional work for her while covering his revulsion for the woman's viewpoints had been much harder than switching out the normal sleeping pill she took with the one provided by his father.

He stood over her bed and watched the despicable woman breathe in the dim glow of the bedside lamp. There was one more step, and he hesitated. The senator would be the first person he murdered.

But I'd gladly do it even if I hadn't been ordered to.

Finally, he stopped savoring the moment and withdrew the hypodermic needle and small vial his father had given him to use.

Carefully moving the sheet and the blanket, he uncovered the woman's old, ugly feet.

His father had suffered through Erik's early stumbles, enduring jab after jab with the needle filled with saline solution until Erik's skill increased and he could perform the injection perfectly.

He filled the syringe from the vial with practiced efficiency, his hands steady because of all the practice.

Thank you, Dad. I'd be a mess right now if not for your tolerance.

The empty vial went into his sport coat pocket—as during all the dress rehearsals.

The extra-fine needle went into the vein in the senator's foot, but she didn't stir. The doubled dose in the sleeping pill he'd slipped her did its job.

He pushed the plunger on the syringe very slowly, careful to not stress the vein.

The concoction entered her body.

Erik didn't know the contents of the vial—only that his father had told him it would make the senator's death appear to be from natural causes and would be undetectable should there be an autopsy.

I'm going to get away with murder.

The thought made him smile. He had been raised to loathe the politics of the West, and specifically the drivel Senator Jonesley had passionately fought for her entire life.

A life that had gone on much too long, in the eyes of his father and whoever he reported to.

It would take some time for the drug to circulate in the senator's body, starting at the foot and traveling to her evil, black heart. Time for him to leave her home and join up with her other employees—whom he also hated for believing in the senator's toxic ideology—but they would provide him the perfect alibi as they worked into the night preparing for the next year.

Which, thankfully, the vile woman would never see.

Erik slipped the cap back on the syringe. It, too, went into his pocket to be dumped in a public trash can far from the senator's home.

Rearranging the covers over the woman, he turned off the light and gave her one last look. Her security team wouldn't think twice about him being in the room—she'd grown more and more dependent on him over the last year. He would be questioned in the morning when they found her dead, but he'd handle it easily. After all this time living a lie, he was a natural.

Poshyel k chyertu.

Go to hell, senator.

PART 4

SATURDAY, DECEMBER 31

42

CHOICES

155 Laurel Lane
Alexandria, Virginia

Haley stared at the beer on her old kitchen countertop. A bottle had been delivered minutes before, special overnight express. The gold label glinted in the overhead light.

Can I do this? Haley asked herself.

She retrieved a small white funnel from the third drawer down, then looked for tubing. A few straws were all she could find, but they wouldn't do the job.

I can use the funnel by itself. I'll hold him down or zap him, tilt his head back, and pour it down his throat.

While she prepared all she needed, her mind fought her, reminded of what she'd learned in school, and believed with all her heart. The United States is a nation of rules. Prisoners—even despicable terrorists—have rights. Due process.

Aren't some rules meant to be broken? What about, 'The end justifies the means'?

But if everyone broke the rules, if more people did what she contemplated, what happened? What about the American values the country's forefathers fought and died for a few hundred years ago?

I don't know where the line is. For the country, or myself.

She wasn't going to truly torture Baranov. He would be drinking his own beer. It would be his fault, not hers.

Does it serve him right? Or am I becoming a monster, splitting hairs to justify my actions?

The joke Nancy and Dave used from time to time flashed into her mind. They asked themselves, "What would Haley do?" Could she turn it around?

What would Axe do?

Nalen wouldn't have overnighted her the bottle if he didn't agree with the tactic, right?

Maybe he thought I would get it analyzed, not use it. Or knowing Nalen, he left it up to me to follow my gut.

In the living room, she started streaming an action movie—car crashes, gunfights, and most importantly, a lot of innocent people screaming. Setting the volume loud enough to cover Baranov's inevitable noise, but not so loud the neighbors would complain, she returned to the kitchen. She started her phone's voice recorder and slid it into her pants pocket to capture the next step.

Standing in the kitchen once more, she decided how to start, and made last-minute preparations. Then, still not knowing how far she would be willing to take it, she gathered up the bottle, the funnel, and a roll of duct tape. Carefully carrying her implements of torture, she went to the spare bedroom to wake up Baranov.

He looked ridiculous. A thin grown man, face pale, eyes sad, his hair messy from the night spent tied spread eagle on her spare bed, wearing a towel as a diaper. His eyes were open, and he looked well-rested.

"Rise and shine," she said, using her hip to close the door behind her.

Baranov reacted instantly when he saw what she carried. The bed shook as he flailed, his eyes wide with terror, focused on the bottle in her hand.

She could make out the words despite his gag. "No. Please," he mumbled, quiet, polite, and desperate.

"Yes, breakfast of champions."

This time, the less said, the better.

She was grateful for the noise of the TV as he screamed and pleaded through the duct tape covering his mouth. She couldn't hear the movie very well, so she doubted the muffled sounds from Baranov could be heard, but if anyone came to the door, the noise from the TV would buy her a few minutes… and be a good excuse.

"What are you saying? You'll talk? Why yes, I believe you will," she said, more to herself than Baranov.

After setting the beer safely out of range of the bed and the man's constant thrashing, she took the knife from her pocket. It had a razor-sharp point, perfect for cutting a hole in the duct tape for the end of the funnel. Baranov fought her, making it impossible to slit the tape without cutting him.

If he moves like this when I'm pouring…

"Stay right there," she joked, then hurried to the kitchen, grabbed a disposable red cup from the cupboard, and returned. Half of the beer went from the bottle to the cup.

"Just in case you make me spill. This came directly from Las Vegas, as you've already guessed. Special delivery first thing this morning. It cost my partner a fortune in bribe money to a casino bartender to get a sneak peek at it."

Baranov hadn't stopped bucking and tugging. Blood flowed from his wrists and ankles where the zip ties rubbed his skin raw.

The professional, button-down, reserved businessman was long gone. In its place, her prisoner babbled behind the duct tape, pleading with her while trying to destroy her bed or break the plastic ties holding him to it.

"Stop for a second," she said with a sigh. "You want to talk? Fine. I'll give you one chance."

He held still, tense, breathing heavily through his nose, nodding his agreement.

"Using your fingers, tell me how many ounces it takes to get addicted."

Baranov thought for a second, then shrugged.

"You don't know?"

He nodded, but he said something which sounded remarkably like, "I'll talk."

"I know you'll talk. I have time. You can get drunk, go crazy with rage, then we'll see what's on the other side. According to doctors working with a friend of mine from the hotel in Mexico…" Baranov's eyes showed surprise. "Yes, we know about the hotel. They're saying the rage disappears at some point, often replaced with desperate pleading for another dose—or death. Has your research shown this?"

Her captive nodded briskly, then repeated his mumbled, "I'll talk," before adding a longer phrase she couldn't catch.

"Say again?"

He said it again, slowly, trying to enunciate under the duct tape.

"What do I have to lose? Is that what you're asking?"

His eyes pleaded with her.

He certainly looks defeated.

What did she have to lose? The spiked beer reportedly took time for the victims to cycle through the stages. And there was a fifty-fifty chance he wouldn't get addicted. If he were willing to spare her the risk and wasted hours, why not?

They locked eyes—his begging, hers skeptical.

Listening to him could save me from making the choice—and a huge, personal mistake.

Haley took the stun gun from the bureau and moved next to Baranov. Pressing the freshly charged device against his neck, she flipped off the safety and held her finger near the button to release the voltage. "One chance," she whispered to her captive. "Lie, or delay, and I zap you and force the beer down your throat."

He nodded his understanding. She ripped off the duct tape.

Victor flinched as the strong duct tape tore at his skin.

I didn't believe the hot poker threat. But this I believe.

He felt he understood this woman. Dedicated, beautiful, capable, and certainly a threat. He couldn't see her physically hurting him. But in her mind, he suspected, making him drink his own tainted beer to make him talk would save her from crossing a line.

She'd be making me take my own medicine, so to speak. It would be my fault, not hers.

He could tell from her demeanor she meant business. She would shock him and pour the beer down his throat, then wait until he begged for more of the drug… or death. He'd talk in the hopes of getting one or the other from her. The woman had found the one button to push to make him give up his secrets. He couldn't risk being addicted and desperate.

I won't go through what I've watched some of the test subjects endure. Not for Russia. Not for my father, grandfather, or our family commitment.

Shame hit him. He wouldn't go through it even for his son. Not when the plan couldn't be stopped. Talking now would give her, and whoever she worked for, nothing useful.

I'll talk.

43

SECRETS

As soon as Haley removed the duct tape covering his mouth, Baranov started talking, the words flying from his mouth. "I'll tell you everything, but please, don't give me the beer. I've seen what it can do. Please?" he begged her again.

"We'll see. Talk."

"It started when I was thirteen. My father took me fishing. We never went fishing. He said his father, my grandfather, had taken him when he was ready to know the truth." Baranov took a quick breath and continued immediately when he saw her impatience. "I thought it would be about the birds and the bees. I knew all about sex, or as much as one can without experience."

He hesitated. Haley moved the stun gun an inch away from his neck and pressed the button. A loud crackling came from the zapper as electricity flashed between the two prongs.

He started to speak, stopped, started again, then closed his eyes and took a deep breath.

Haley waited, silent, not wanting to do the wrong thing and break the spell. The man was wrestling with his conscience, torn between the promise of the beer being forced down his throat and his enormous secret.

Finally, after a full thirty seconds, Baranov let out a defeated sigh. He opened his eyes to look at her sadly. "My father told me I was to be a third-generation spy for Russia." Behind the regret at the admission, Haley detected something else.

He's relieved to finally reveal the secret.

He continued quietly. "One day, I would be called on to serve, he said. Perhaps I would be ordered to sacrifice it all: my life, wealth, the company my father would groom me to lead and leave to me. Or maybe I would only need to provide other assistance requiring less sacrifice. But whatever the call, I would comply, no matter the cost."

His eyes stayed locked on hers, searching for understanding. "My grandfather had been recruited, trained, and entered into an agreement which would span decades and generations. In return, our family in Russia—my grandfather's brothers and sisters—would be allowed to not only live, but prosper. Thrive. He was trained, given money, and sent to America to build a successful business. Once he was on his feet, after a few years in America, ties were mostly severed. Few communications with Russia. He was on his own. A sleeper, I believe the term is. Waiting for a call which never came for him, or my father. But did for me."

He continued, telling her the full story his grandfather had told him about how the program started.

Eventually, Baranov wound down, spent. He relaxed onto the bed and closed his eyes in defeat or relief. Haley couldn't decide which. Through the entire confession, she'd forced herself to be blank, giving away nothing. But inside, she couldn't contain her shock.

I didn't see that coming. I have to get this information to Nancy.

She traded the zapper for duct tape over his mouth, meeting no resistance from Baranov.

"I'll be back in a few minutes." She picked up the beer and waited for him to open his eyes to look at her. "Will we be needing this for the rest of the answers I want?"

He shook his head.

"I'll put it in the fridge, just in case."

She headed to the kitchen where she put the bottle and half cup of beer in the refrigerator, careful to not disturb the contents of the large mason jar filled with beer on the top shelf, the lid excessively duct-taped on. A band of tape around the front had a warning written in red permanent marker: DANGER! POISON. DO NOT DRINK!

It was there if she needed it. She closed the door of the refrigerator and leaned back against it, relieved.

My bluff worked.

She thought about the spiked beer in the mason jar. Would she have used it in the end?

I'm glad I didn't have to find out.

Haley threw away the empty bottle of regular beer she had poured into the bottle sent to her by Nalen and considered her options.

How much can I tell Nancy?

The recording of the interrogation would freak her out, so Haley would have to summarize. Opening the secure messaging app, she sent a quick text.

I suspect Baranov is a third-generation Russian sleeper asset. Assess your findings with this in mind.

She also sent the details of the program's beginnings to help Nancy search.

If there's one sleeper spy, there might be more. Maybe Nancy can find out.

Back in her bedroom, Baranov looked resigned to his fate. With the stun gun ready, she once again removed the duct tape.

"You reported to someone?" he asked softly. "Your government, I assume? I'm at your mercy. I've confessed my greatest secret. My life as I know it was over yesterday morning when I left Las Vegas. Would your country consider granting me asylum?"

"Once you and I are done here? Perhaps. It's not my department. But play your cards right, and we'll work it out. For now, I need more details. How can we stop what is about to happen in Las Vegas?"

Baranov looked at her in confusion. "It can't be stopped. Even if I were to call all the casinos, they still would go through with it. Too much money has been spent, the marketing is in place." He shrugged as much as he could, bound spread eagle.

Haley didn't let her disappointment and frustration show. "Then what are the next steps? After the beer in Las Vegas?"

Baranov held her eye, and she thought he told the truth. "I don't know. I assumed I would be exposed as the culprit, harming the president and his reputation. Then, if possible, they would get me out of the country—to

Russia, where I would be shown off... proof I was a Russian spy." He glanced away, ashamed. "I guessed they would interview me on television after feeding me the lies they wanted me to say. 'The President of the United States knew all about it ahead of time,' or, 'The president is a Russian spy,'... that type of propaganda. Making up all sorts of stories—whatever would do the most harm."

That's brilliant—and worse than I figured.

Some people would see the interview on Russian television for the bullshit it was. Others would at least wonder. The president would be out of office within the day, though, no matter what.

"Next, who is behind this, and why?"

"Russia, of course. I don't know the motivation. I followed orders."

"Your handler or local contact?"

"I don't know his name. I can describe him to you. He reminds me of a former football quarterback. All American."

"Yes, we'll get to that before we're done. Along with how he gets in contact with you and all that. But what about Dr. Edgars?"

Baranov looked at her in surprise. "How...?"

"I'm good at my job. Answer the question."

"I was told to form a new division in my company seeking to create the next great beer. I would place ads for a brewmaster. Edgars would apply. I would conduct the interview process as usual but hire him in the end. I did as instructed. He started the department and developed the drug over the last year and a half. Lately, we had to hurry the testing. The formula didn't work, or the beer tasted horrible. One problem after another." Baranov spoke quieter. "I don't expect you to believe me, but I stalled the process as much as I could. Withheld direction. Delayed shipping supplies to the lab. Perhaps Dr. Edgars stalled as well, which is why it took so long. But I imagine one of your questions is why we didn't wait longer. I don't know the exact answer, but my handler provided a deadline. Some type of product had to be ready in whatever limited amounts we could produce by the end of the year. They suggested New Year's Eve, which we were able to handle, albeit without the amount and type of testing I would prefer."

"Why the deadline?"

"I don't know."

I've gotten all I can out of him for the moment. He seems truly remorseful—and resigned to his fate. Now, all we have to do is take his pieces of the puzzle, combine them with what we already have, and figure out what the hell is actually going on.

The Russians wouldn't burn a rich, successful, integrated sleeper agent on a relatively minor attack on Las Vegas. How could it benefit Russia?

They would only implement this plan if they had a much larger, more important target. One which would benefit from America being distracted by violence and upheaval.

What are they up to?

Victor heaved a sigh of relief when he saw the woman's focus change from dosing him to figuring out the angles of what he'd confessed. He finally relaxed and closed his eyes.

Because of an agreement his grandfather made many years before, Victor had done terrible things.

How did I let it go so far? I'm an American, not a Russian.

If his wife had still been alive, with her strength, could he have refused the instructions and risked their deaths as payback?

Could they have taken Nicholas and gone into hiding? Confessed the entire operation to the FBI and trusted them for protection, knowing there must be others like him occupying prominent positions in the government?

Or would he have made the same choice, taken the coward's way out, and hoped for the best?

He could never be forgiven for what he'd already done. But admitting his long-held secret to this young lady was a start.

I'm sorry, Dad and Granddad. I did what you should have done: turned to America, our true country.

44

THE BIG PICTURE

Central Analysis Group Headquarters
Alexandria, Virginia

Nancy stood outside Haley's cubicle, debating.

She wouldn't mind. She'd encourage me to do whatever it takes, Nancy thought.

Her biggest worry was Gregory. Working Saturday wouldn't normally raise an eyebrow, but with the events of the week, combined with taking over Haley's desk, the boss would know she was working on Haley's operation against his explicit orders.

But she needed a change. She sat down and unplugged Haley's laptop, moving it to the side. In its place, she hooked up her computer. The solitude of Haley's cube would be better than her own space. Dave, sitting next to her in their shared cubicle, had been an unintentional distraction all morning.

If I'm going to pull this off, I need to do better the rest of the day than I've done so far. Haley's desk might help. Maybe her magic will rub off on me.

A few people, like Haley, had much larger monitors than the rest. Haley had huge dual displays which dwarfed the ones she and Dave used. They could help Nancy with the puzzle she had to figure out.

Haley's expensive noise-canceling headphones hung on their charging station.

I'm going to need these, too.

Nancy quickly paired them with her phone, started a classical music mix, and got to work.

At first, she struggled to get into the flow, the way she had all morning. When working under Haley's direction a few months before, looking for the EMPs missiles, she had briefly gotten into the zone, similar to what Haley described happened to her when she worked.

So far today, however, it wouldn't come. Nancy had done the basics already, but she had no spark, no intuition.

She sat back, adjusted the chair to better suit her, and started again.

According to Haley's secure text, Baranov's grandfather may have been recruited as a sleeper agent as a teenager. She added a page in her spreadsheet for his data.

Present day: Baranov had to be directed and given orders. So he had a person who managed him. And his handler had a handler, up the line to a person in power, probably in Russia. She added columns to the spreadsheet.

Who's to say the handler doesn't work at the company? An executive, a janitor... it doesn't matter, as long as they could easily communicate with Baranov—ideally in person, for security reasons—without raising suspicion.

In fits and starts, she added to her worksheet, getting closer to being in the zone.

The IRS database went on one large screen, her spreadsheet on the other. Names, social security numbers, job titles, salaries, addresses, phone numbers, and more, all courtesy of the IRS.

On her laptop screen, she accessed other databases: NSA, CIA, FBI, Homeland Security, ICE. A few clicks and they all went to work on the names and social security numbers she'd harvested, churning away in the background. If any of the employees were using legends, fake documentation, or were already suspects for a variety of offenses, she'd find out soon enough.

The data sprawled in front of her. She split windows on the big screens, first displaying two windows per, then clicking to make each screen show four windows, one per corner.

Nancy dove into the data the way Haley had done, letting it wash over her. Making notes on the legal pad on the desk when necessary, but letting her mind absorb both the big picture and the tiniest details, gelling together. Her brain switched back and forth from the analytical to the creative, making connections and leaps she would never have before working with Haley.

After a time, she noticed a plastic spoon and cup of yogurt on her yellow pad.

Did I get up and get it?

No, Dave must have placed it where she would see it—all without her noticing. She tore off the foil top and ate, famished, then drank from her freshly filled coffee mug, lukewarm now. Her eyes barely left the screens.

Incoming alerts flashed, responses to her search queries, which provided more information for her growing spreadsheet.

Suddenly, an overwhelming need for the restroom hit her.

Uh oh. Getting older—especially for women—is not for wimps.

She ran, both out of physical necessity and a deep need to stay in the zone she'd finally found. Whether people looked up to see the spectacle of a mid-fifties woman dashing to the bathroom, lost in thought, she didn't know or care.

Returning to her desk, crisis averted, she slipped gratefully back into the flow. It felt like swimming deep in a lake, feeling the water surrounding her but only noticing if she thought about it.

Her mind became one with the data.

At some point, a hot slice of pizza magically appeared before her on the desk, so she ate it, and drank again. Then she had to repeat the run to the bathroom a while later.

While jogging back to her desk, her body not used to running and regretting every step, she felt the puzzle coming together.

I'm almost there.

The picture had become progressively clearer, but she held off a full examination until she had the last few pieces.

One part of her didn't want the exquisite feeling of being in the flow to end.

Another part was afraid to see—and be forced to admit—what she sensed.

This is deeper and worse than I could have imagined.

The playlist must have gotten stuck because she started hearing the same classical pieces as earlier. So when the headphone battery died, it came as a relief. Nancy's ears ached from wearing them, and the music had started to annoy her. Hanging the headphones on the charging stand, she stretched briefly before diving back in.

With a few clicks, she enlarged her spreadsheet, color coded, and filled with hundreds of rows, dozens of columns, and tabbed pages that scrolled off the right side of the window.

She marveled at the brilliance, the sheer audacity, and commitment of the plot she had uncovered. Exhaustion hit her suddenly and she could barely keep her eyes open. Letting them close for an instant, her chin slumped to her chest.

"Nancy?" A whisper in her ear, heard as if from a great distance, an echo in a vast canyon. A warm feeling filled her—drowsiness mixed with love.

Dave.

"Drink." A hot mug in her hand. The smell of coffee and creamer. She sipped automatically, a forty-year habit.

By the third sip, she felt like herself again.

"Can you talk, or do you need time?" Dave asked, squatting beside her chair in the tight confines of Haley's cube.

"I can talk." Nodding at the spreadsheet with its highlighted boxes, she asked, "Can you see it? It's incredible."

"No, I don't see it. Walk me through it?"

"Not here." She chugged the last of the coffee, ignoring the heat, and disconnected the laptop. She grabbed her yellow legal pad. "Conference room," she whispered and led the way.

Nancy connected the laptop to the large screen on the wall. They had spent so much time here lately, the conference room felt more like their office than their shared cube. She had Dave wait until she used the coms app to reach Haley. "Can you talk?" Nancy asked her.

"One second."

They waited, Haley on speaker, hearing running water in the background.

"Thanks. Okay, go."

"Haley, it's bad. The drug in the beer is the tip of the iceberg. Do you know about the other sleeper agents?"

"No," Haley admitted. Nancy could hear the tiredness and strain in her voice. "But I wondered. It makes total sense. Tell me what you found."

"I'll send you the spreadsheet if I can figure out how to get it from my laptop to my phone." There were protocols in place to prevent transferring data from their computers. "But for now, here's my big picture view. Then we can dive into the details. Using what you gave me earlier, I found hints and subtle references to the operation, mostly rumors over the years from human sources. Without the tip you provided, no one would have noticed —or given it much attention if they did. I've pieced together that in the early 1920s, the then-Soviet Union launched a major intelligence plan. They trained agents, funded them, and sent them to America—at least. I haven't had time yet to delve into other countries. Or, for that matter, much into the United States; I've focused on our immediate problem. Our government has been infiltrated. How deeply, I'm not sure yet. I eventually narrowed my search to third or fourth-generation Americans with grandparents or great-grandparents from the former Soviet Union. There are many in the government, and I'm not finished searching yet. Finding others in the business world is too big of a job for us to do alone."

"Can we judge people and assign guilt based on someone's heritage?" Dave asked. "Where their grandparents or great-grandparents came from? All three of us have families from other countries. I'm a third-generation German. America was built by immigrants—notwithstanding the Native Americans, I mean. It feels wrong to focus on them like this. It's a bit like McCarthyism."

"You nailed it," Haley said over the phone. "We can only judge these people by their actions. But we can suspect them. Look for signs they are compromised. We can, and do, research everyone's background if they want to work in the government. We presume innocence... but, 'Plan for the best, prepare for the worst.'"

"I'll send the list of... let's not call them suspects," Nancy told Haley. "How about..."

"Persons of interest?" Dave suggested.

"Yes. Assuming it will be useful to you?"

"I'll put it to good use. Well done, Nancy, and thank you. Let's talk again shortly."

Nancy ended the call and regarded Dave. "I'm sorry to get you involved. I didn't mean to. I just got lost in the data. Thanks for the food and drinks. They kept me going."

He smiled at her and the handsome, bearded face she had fallen in love with years before lit up. "We're a team. Aren't we?"

"Always."

Haley waited impatiently for the list and other data Nancy had compiled to arrive. By the time the phone's *ding* finished ringing, she had the message open.

Dr. Edgars. No real surprise there.

A few people in key positions at the bottling plant. Again, unsurprising.

Next came a long list of names with job titles and locations. With her speed-reading ability, she had taken in the first several before forcing herself to slow down. She thought the list would be in alphabetical order, but Nancy had sorted it as she would have—by priority and concern.

Erik Zorkin: Assistant to Senator Jonesley—California

Tabatha Rogov: Chief of Staff to Senator Greenlich—Wyoming

Leo Porter: Chief of private security for Senator Barbara Woodran—Utah

Three long-term, influential legislators. Surrounded by potential sleeper agents of Russia.

What about the president?

Nancy would have looked there first. He's safe—I hope.

Haley read the list again. There were suspects—no. "Persons of interest" in the Food and Drug Administration. The Environmental Protection Agency. The Internal Revenue Service. And several other lesser government agencies. None in the intelligence agencies, which was a tremendous relief.

There were thirty-four people on the list. But Nancy said she hadn't finished yet, either.

What the hell do I do with this?

Could she sit on the information? Shouldn't it be shared? They had only conjecture, a suspicion that some people's ancestors might have been Russian sleeper agents. Did the risk to the politicians, government agencies, and the country justify potentially ruining the careers of apparently loyal people? Many of the people on the list had been in their jobs for years without incident.

Haley tried to wrap her head around the information, unsure of her next action.

This is a big problem. But there are so many other important questions. What is the endgame? Why has Russia finally activated this long-term plan? What do they want? How many are involved?

And what could she do about it, with a tied-up criminal—a spy, really —in her spare bedroom, and no access to her precious databases containing the river of data she needed?

I can work the problem the way Axe taught me. Follow the steps.

First, the mission. One—protect the country from immediate attack. Two—understand the overall operation.

Next, assets and resources. Nalen and Axe in Las Vegas. Tied up tonight, but ready and able to move after New Year's Eve.

Nancy—and Dave, too. He was in deep now.

She felt self-conscious, but she had to include herself in the list of assets.

But can I solve this and plan the overall operation without my usual access?

She had her laptop, a fast internet connection, and nowhere to go... unless she was prepared to leave Baranov alone, dump him on someone else... or eliminate him.

I can't do any of those, but especially not the last one.

Third, planning. She considered her options.

I can get Axe and Nalen on the sleeper agent situation.

Three of the most alarming potential sleeper agents—the ones close to the senators—were likely with their politicians in their home states for the holiday recess.

They're within driving distance of Las Vegas.

Fourth, contingencies. Her mind raced with potential problems, but she would have to rely on her teams to handle the ones on the ground.

Big picture. If Axe and Nalen succeed in Las Vegas, the Russians won't be happy. They'll have their own contingencies. I need to plan for them.

She contemplated the problem for a minute but came up short.

It comes back to motivation. With no idea what the Russians want, why they're doing this now, I won't be able to do much to stop it.

Fifth, minimize risk. She had resigned from the CAG, which went a long way to reducing their exposure in case she got caught abducting

Baranov. But with this explosive of a situation, getting caught should be the least of their worries... unless the president was also a sleeper agent.

No, he's not Russian. Uncle Jimmy isn't a spy.

Nancy had done an amazing job carrying the ball to the one yard line; it was up to the rest of them to carry it across. She and Dave could be told to stay back off of it now, to keep them out of the spotlight when this all came out.

Last, delegate. She'd done all she could.

Finally, it was time for her to step up and do what else she could.

Hunt.

Haley moved to her home computer in the living room after checking on Baranov, snoring softly after reluctantly accepting another sleeping pill. She connected it to the large TV so she could do her work with more windows than her small computer screen would allow.

She triple-checked her virtual private network connection. She didn't need her internet service provider—or the NSA—watching over her shoulder as she worked.

Then she brought up a map of Russia, zooming out until she had it centered, showing the surrounding countries.

Okay, big picture first. What does Russia want?

The country had a new leader, more hardcore than the last, long-term president, which no one had thought possible. When the cyber-attacks and a few EMPs from Stefan "Pioneer" Conroy had hit the country, the anger and blame had fallen squarely on the shoulders of the man in power.

That's what you get for taking credit for every tiny success. When something goes wrong, no one believes you weren't in charge of that, too—and messed it up.

After decades in charge, he'd been forced to resign, booted from office by his right-hand man and protégée.

A better question would be: what does Pavel Zimalev, the new president, want?

He needed to rapidly repair his country's damaged reputation and the perception of its vulnerability introduced because of Stefan Conroy's attacks.

More importantly, he had to prove his power and cement his control over the people—both civilians and the government.

Haley dove into the man's history. The aristocratic childhood filled with sporting success as a teenager. Biathlon—winter cross-country skiing combined with rifle marksmanship. A silver medal in skeleton, sliding headfirst down a bobsled track.

The man even excelled at table tennis.

Using only the resources available to the public, she vacuumed up data about the man's life. Grandmaster in chess at age twenty-three. His time in the army. Likes and dislikes. Favorite food. Family tree. Everything she could find.

Finally, Haley relaxed and rested her hands on her lap. Instead of staring at the screens in front of her, she closed her eyes.

She became Pavel Zimalev.

Breathing in, she pictured herself sitting in an office in the Kremlin. After much maneuvering, she was finally in charge. There were forces against her within the country and without. She had to protect her new position as president. There would be others looking to stab her in the back and take control, the way she had with her mentor.

The world would be watching. The United States, a thorn in the country's side for decades, had won the Cold War. They kept introducing sanctions against Russia, interfering in her beloved country's affairs.

NATO knocked at the door of her borders, expanding its influence and making the country look weak.

Haley fell deeper into a trance, similar to when she analyzed information. In the zone, swimming like a shark, hunting in the sea of data. She let herself go deeper into the mind of Pavel Zimalev.

I have tools. Power. Leverage.

The long-hidden sleeper asset program. Military might, though not as strong as in years past. Natural gas resources the countries of the area desperately needed and were willing to pay virtually any price to receive, especially during this unusually cold winter.

And I have the guts to reclaim what is mine.

Haley had an inkling of the plan as she opened her eyes to look at the map of Russia on her large TV screen.

The pieces fell into place.

I will injure the annoying, bothersome United States with a crisis.

With Russia's primary opponent—and the world's enforcer—sidelined, the way would be clear to expand.

She would invade, occupy, and reclaim Ukraine back into the fold of Russia.

If any of the other countries in the region objected, she would threaten to cut off their essential natural gas—or simply jack up the prices until they realized their lack of power over her.

The action will prove my strength. Give the people a reason to back me and my agenda.

It hit home, ringing true as Haley came back to herself, the feeling of being Zimalev fading.

If her gut instincts were right, Zimalev wanted greater influence in the region. Controlling Ukraine would expand the Eurasian Union—the group of states, formerly part of the Soviet Union, serving as a counterpoint to the European Union, both economically and politically.

There are also Ukraine's natural gas pipelines.

With even more control of the flow of natural gas, he'd be able to command higher prices.

More money. More power. More land. The many Russian speakers in Ukraine would welcome him.

And it would put an end to all talk of Ukraine joining NATO.

Haley sat back, having only used her computer to look up the map of the area and research the man's life.

I guess I don't need all those top-secret databases, after all.

Haley changed her mind about keeping Nancy and Dave out of this.

This is too big for me to handle on my own. I need them.

In the past operation against Conroy, they had proven especially good at what they did. She needed that expertise. They might be able to confirm what she felt in her gut: Russia was destabilizing America and about to invade—or otherwise take control of—Ukraine.

While it wouldn't directly threaten the United States, it would cause problems. For one, the president had drawn a line in the sand around Russian intervention in the area. He would look weak and lose credibility at home and on the world stage if he didn't act. The country's other enemies, and many terrorist organizations, would be emboldened.

Besides, an aggressive, expansionistic Russia had to be stopped immediately, but without starting World War Three.

Axe, Nalen, and I have to stop him before he can invade. But how?

The plot had to revolve around the senators. If Russia placed sleeper assets close to them, they were important for a reason—and in danger.

Haley had to turn to the computer. She didn't have a working knowledge of every legislator's vulnerabilities, beliefs, and agendas.

She searched for Senator Jonesley from California. News articles from overnight filled her screen.

Senator Jonesley Pronounced Dead at Home in San Francisco

San Francisco, CA — In the early morning hours of the last day of the year, Senator Jonesley was found dead by her security team.

While authorities are investigating, one source, who spoke on condition of anonymity, said the senator appeared to have died of natural causes, slipping away peacefully in her sleep.

Haley scanned the rest of the article quickly, suspecting foul play despite the news reports.

Next, she searched for Senator Greenlich from Wyoming.

There was no recent news, which was a relief.

At least he's not dead yet.

The most recent story, from a few days before Christmas, reported him leaving Washington, D.C. to spend the holidays with his family at their ranch in Wyoming.

Next, Haley ran a search on Senator Woodran from Utah, a close friend and supporter of the president.

Please don't let her be dead.

No bad news, only a similar story about celebrating the holidays at home in rural Utah, east of Provo, with her family.

What do these three have in common?

Two were from the president's party, one wasn't. Senator Greenlich fiercely supported the president, but the other two supported or opposed him depending on the issue, especially Senator Woodran, an old-school independent.

If she had access to the FBI or NSA databases or the extensive files at the CAG, she would have an answer quickly. And while she could turn to Nancy, it was worth a shot to try it on her own.

Let's see how smart search engines have become.

She opened a new search window.

What do Senators Jonesley, Greenlich, and Woodran have in common?

The screen filled instantly with the answer.

Score one for big data. Too bad we don't have this technology for our intelligence analysis searches. Or maybe not—anyone could do my job if it's this easy to find information.

All three leaders strongly supported the president in his hardline opposition to Russian interference in Ukraine. With their leadership, power, and the respect they commanded, the president could sway Congress and the public to block the Russians. Without them, the president was greatly weakened… especially so if he were to be implicated in the coming Las Vegas incident.

Jonesley is already dead. Greenlich's Chief of Staff may be a Russian spy. And Woodran's head of personal security when she's at home puts him in the perfect position to kill her or let others do it.

There was one way to thwart Russia's plan. She had to keep the two surviving legislators safe, stop the drugged beer from causing a disaster in Las Vegas, and keep the president insulated from any fallout. He'd then be able to mount a successful campaign of sanctions and rally world leaders against any Russian military actions.

As long as I'm not missing another component we haven't discovered yet.

She had to put the possibility out of her mind for now. Nancy and Dave would look into it all and find the truth.

What should I do about Gregory?

He had earned her trust, but could she risk telling him what they'd found? So far, they had no real proof.

Would he believe and support us in pursuing the big picture, or hold us back until we have more solid evidence?

There wasn't time. They had to act. As unlikely as it was, she couldn't risk Gregory slowing them down. Or worse: getting others involved and losing their advantage if the wrong ears heard about their suspicions.

There could be other sleeper spies we don't know about yet.

The safe play was to keep it under the radar. Only the NHA—plus Nancy and Dave—for now.

What Gregory doesn't know can't hurt him… or us.

45

THE BRIEF

Axe marveled as at exactly noon, Admiral Nalen walked through the assembled men, his ramrod-straight posture contrasting with his casual blue jeans, running shoes, and today's tight black t-shirt. The men parted respectfully before him as he made his way to the back wall of the warehouse where Axe stood, next to the whiteboard, which had been hung on the wall next to the maps.

He has such command presence, Axe thought. *It's impressive.*

A part of him wanted it. Another part hated the idea.

I've been running from being a leader too long. It's going to catch up to me soon.

"Listen up," Nalen called. The tone, honed over decades of commanding troops, caused all conversation to stop instantly. The men squared themselves up. While not exactly coming to attention, their mood and focus changed.

Impressive. Was he born for leadership, or did he learn it?

"I know some of you on sight, the rest by name and reputation. For any who don't know me, I'm William Nalen. Not Bill, not 'Admiral.' 'Sir,' but only if you must."

"What about 'Hammer?'" one older SEAL, from Nalen's generation, called from the side.

Nalen's lips twitched into a tiny smile. "I'll answer to it, Doom," he said to the man. They shared a nod of mutual respect, then Nalen continued.

"Before we begin—we have all branches of the services here. There will be no rivalry, no bullshit. You're all highly trained and experienced warriors, or you wouldn't have gotten the call. So leave the egos out of it. You hear me?"

"Yes, sir!" the men shouted in unison.

"Excellent. Another item to get out of the way. This is a completely volunteer situation. It is not only unofficial, they wouldn't approve of it if they knew. I do not speak or act on behalf of the Navy or any other individual in the government, no matter what rumors you may have heard about me or who I may have as friends."

The men nodded. They took it as a source of pride that one of their own, President Heringten, a fellow warrior, had risen to the rank of Commander in Chief. And while no one broadcast it, they all knew Nalen and the president went way back.

"If this goes tits up, it's on each of us individuals. We are civilians in this beautiful city for a few days of sightseeing, gambling, and raising hell. Understood?"

The collection of warriors nodded.

"Next, the why behind our little adventure. We have intel there may be a terrorist attack in the city. Probably tonight. But as often is the case, the intel is sketchy. In this case, extremely so. More of an educated guess—or a hunch—than actionable intelligence. We have no proof whatsoever. The people we think—believe—could be behind it make it difficult to go to the authorities, even to investigate further. It's a sticky, convoluted mess with no clear fix. Hence, our role as standby saviors of the city."

Nalen nodded at Axe, standing to his right. "However, Axe has first-hand experience with what we're looking at. Axe?"

"This goes no further than the room," Axe began. "Seriously. Top Secret and all that. Our educated guess is that beer may be spiked with a 'magic mushroom' type substance. It causes euphoria in small doses—think a sip or two—but in larger doses is devastating. I've seen what it does. A subject drank two dosed beers quickly. He acted drunk and happy after a few minutes. Around the thirty-minute mark, he became uncontrollably violent. Homicidal to the point he had no self-preservation instinct. He died trying to kill me, when he could have easily saved himself instead or pulled back to restart the fight a minute later without risking his own life."

"Did you make it?" Mad Dog quipped from the back, causing ripples of laughter.

Axe had to smile. "I did, believe it or not. But let me tell you—it was close. And I had to kill the subject to live. The struggle took place in the water and he drowned. I brought him back, as several of us experienced during BUD/S."

A few men from the SEAL group shook their heads, surely recalling their failure, death, revival, and later success in completing the swimming rotations required to graduate.

"Pay attention here. After I brought him back, he growled and, still coughing up water, resumed his attack on me."

"Geez," Mad Dog muttered.

"I restrained him. He's under observation in a hospital. People smarter than us are at work figuring out both what caused his homicidal rage and the cravings that followed."

Mad Dog raised his hand partway. "And you're saying people here in Vegas are going to turn into these zombies tonight?"

Damn it, Mad Dog.

"Dude," one of the nearby men muttered with a shiver.

"We should avoid that word. They aren't undead. They're hopped up on a drug that causes psychotic rage and loss of self-control. My guy experienced rapid withdrawal symptoms and a bad psychedelic trip. In his mind, I might have been a tiger, or alien, or had just kicked his puppy."

"Technically, though," Mad Dog said quietly in the back, "zombies aren't really undead either, right? I mean, they—"

Various discussions about zombies broke out. A few men suggested Kelton's homicidal actions sounded a lot like some of their former instructors and drill sergeants.

"Men," Nalen called, and the discussions stopped. "I realize it's been a while since you were on active duty, but let's stay focused here. The lives you save may be your own."

"Sorry, sir," a few men muttered.

"Is it contagious? They can't bite and turn you into a zom— One of them, right?" a soldier from the far side of the room asked.

"Good question. Unknown, but not that I've heard. My advice, though, don't let it come to that."

"Good call," Mad Dog said.

Axe added one last thought. "One issue that could help or hurt us: how does the alcohol affect people? If they're falling down drunk, are the effects of the drug magnified or reduced? We won't know until tonight, but my hope is the alcohol will at least partly cancel out the drug. If not... we're in for a world of hurt." He let his final hope—and concern—hang in the air for a moment, then nodded to Hammer.

Nalen took over. "Thanks, Axe. The spiked beer will be served as part of a promotion only in specific beer garden areas at each of the participating casinos. They're using it as a draw to bring people in, get them drunk, then keep them around losing their money. Good news is they don't start serving the beer until 22:00 hours—10 PM. We won't have to worry about the problem until then. While the effects of the drug take hold immediately, our best intelligence guess is the euphoria stays as long as they keep drinking. The rage and bad trip don't start—at least the worst of it, as far as we know—until people stop drinking the beer."

He paused to let it sink in. "But intel indicates there may be a limited supply, so it may run out after a few hours, or people may celebrate until after midnight and head home afterward. Be on alert from 22:00. Whenever people stop drinking the beer, it's on. We're warning security at each casino. They should be able to handle the few that drink, stop, and go to the next stage of the effects. Our job is the main event."

Nalen pointed at the map. "You'll pair up and receive specific casino assignments," he continued, "then join into standard four-man fire teams. Designate one person as fire team leader. Fireteams into squads, squads into platoons. Each platoon will receive a designated area so you can back each other up. With luck, each pair will be within sight of another. Set up in parking lots or on streets to start. You'll use your personal vehicles. Organize yourselves as you see fit. There's limited command and control, so use your best judgment."

He gestured to the stack of boxes along the back wall. Axe and he had received the shipment and unloaded it from the semi earlier in the morning.

"Those boxes contain both zip cuffs and long, straight zip ties. Stuff all you can into your pants pockets, jackets, small backpacks, whatever looks nonthreatening. Security will be tight on the Strip and downtown tonight, and we don't want to draw attention. Stay in or near your vehicles as much as you can before it starts going down. One, we may need you mobile.

Two, it's good protection. Three, easier to hide in plain sight, as long as you don't look too suspicious sitting in a particular location. Last, we're going to cram your cars and trucks with extra zip ties."

Nalen looked hard at each man. "These are innocent civilians, drugged without their knowledge or consent. Rules of Engagement: subdue. Do as little harm as possible but put them out of commission. Use the zip ties. You may have to connect them to a telephone pole, parking meter, sign... whatever is around so they don't come after you or the next guy."

"A lot of people in the city tonight. Doubt we have enough zip ties," a retired Delta man said, not appearing worried, merely stating a fact.

Nalen nodded, looking at Axe.

It's exactly what I told him an hour ago.

"R.O.E. if the zip ties run out: I hope you remember your hand-to-hand combat. Break arms and legs. Avoid damage to heads. In a pinch, lure them into an enclosed area and lock them in. They may go after each other, they may not. But at least we don't have non-drugged innocent civilians being attacked."

"Exfil?"

"Back here in your personal vehicles. We're two miles from the Strip, ten from downtown. If the roads are closed, march. If you're under surveillance or in trouble with the law, escape and evade. If you're caught, deny everything. Stay silent or, for those of you who find that nearly impossible," he craned his neck to see Mad Dog in back, who had the decency to look chagrined, "you tell them the God's honest truth. You came to Vegas for fun and to see a few friends—your swim buddy and fire team, not all of us. When you saw the chaos, you were prepared—as always—and did your best to non-violently help. You're patriots. You live to serve."

There were calls of "Hooyah!", "Oorah!", and "Hooah!" from the men.

"And whatever you do, don't drink any beer while you're in Vegas unless we clear it first."

Nalen glanced at Axe to see if he had anything to add, but Axe shook his head. "Break open the zip ties, load your vehicles, and gear up."

They got to work. Seventy-seven warriors who had been there, done that, and gotten the scars, the PTSD, and the stories.

Seventy-seven men. Sevens are lucky but it's an odd number. It won't work for platoons. Maybe Nalen will stay back.

They needed a man on the radios and the maps, running logistics.

I can't ask him to stay behind. He'd be insulted. Should I volunteer?

The idea of holding himself back from the operation made Axe's soul ache.

'We before me.' It's a great slogan, but can I live up to it?

He'd do it if he had to.

The SEAL from Nalen's era, who had spoken earlier, strode up with arms spread and a huge grin on his face. He and Nalen embraced, crushing each other in a long bear hug.

"Holy shit, Willy. It's been years."

'Willy'? From 'William'? I have to remember that.

"Doom," Nalen said with genuine pleasure. "Man, so good to see you."

"You heard about Gloom?" Doom said, his voice cracking with sadness.

"Yes, so sorry." Nalen turned to Axe. "Axe, meet 'Doom.' Dominic, actually. He and 'Gloom'—Glen—were swim buddies in my BUD/S class and looked out for each other their entire careers. Saved each other's asses over and over. Mine too, a few times." His voice lowered. "Gloom died last summer. Cancer. Too young."

The three men shared a moment of silence. Axe felt the loss, though he'd never met the man. A brother warrior, gone in a way no warrior should have to.

"How's Jimbo?" Doom asked Nalen.

'Jimbo'? He can't mean James Heringten, President of the United States, can he?

"Haven't spoken with him in a while," Nalen said with a shake of his head. Both Axe and Doom saw through the lie.

"Ahh, too bad. Next time you run into him, you tell him from me: 'Keep your head down!'"

The two old-timers cracked up at the inside joke.

Doom turned to Axe. "You've got one too many men. I'll stay behind and run comms if it's okay with you? My grandchildren would murder me if I got myself killed. I hate to miss the fun—and I wouldn't be volunteering if the numbers had worked out—but this makes sense. Unless," he glanced at Nalen with a sly smile, "old Hammer is staying in the rear with the gear?"

"Not a chance!" Nalen replied with a firm shake of his head.

"Then it's settled. Bring me up to speed on the comms plan, then let's get this done. We've got a city to save."

46

ACT OF WAR

"Go ahead, Haley, you're on speaker with both of us." Axe held his phone so Nalen could hear.

He and Nalen shared a concerned look as Haley hesitated, taking a deep breath.

"Just start at the beginning," Nalen said.

"I resigned from the CAG, abducted Victor Baranov from the airport, interrogated him, and I've figured out the plan," Haley said in a rush.

Axe took it in, remembered rescuing her outside her apartment building nearly a year before, and couldn't resist. "So, you got tired of being kidnapped and decided to see how it felt from the other side? And otherwise, just a typical Saturday?"

Haley let out a small chuckle, relieving some of the tension.

"Where is Baranov now... and what is his status?" Nalen asked her, all business, apparently taking in stride their teammate's risky, unilateral actions.

In other words, did she torture and kill him?

"I have him zip tied in my spare bedroom. I gave him another sleeping pill. Overall, he's fine. Regretful. The Russians funded and trained his grandfather. A sleeper agent assignment has been passed down like a family heirloom. Honor, tradition, commitment, that sort of thing. Plus, he has an unknown number of relatives he's never met whose lives are on the line if he didn't cooperate."

Axe and Nalen considered this surprising turn of events.

It's an audacious long-term operation. Amazing—and potentially devastating for America.

But the practical outweighed the big picture, at least for the moment. "Back to the abduction part. Did you get away clean?" Axe asked.

"Yes. He was supposed to go to the White House party tonight and stay over. I called pretending to be his assistant and cancelled with his regrets, so he won't be expected. Yesterday, I cancelled his airport pickup and hotel reservation. He gave his assistant the week off, so there's no problem. We only have to worry about whether the Russians are watching or not. He claims his handler rarely contacts him and won't know he's not around."

"What else?" Nalen asked.

"The spiked beer in Las Vegas tonight is only the opening salvo. The new Russian president is counting on the United States being forced to contend with a high-casualty event."

"We're going to take care of that," Axe threw in.

"I have no doubt. But part two of their plan has already started. Senator Jonesley died last night, supposedly of natural causes. But one of her assistants is like Baranov—an American with a great grandfather from the same part of Russia Baranov's grandfather was from. It's likely he's a sleeper agent."

"You think he's responsible for her death and Russia is assassinating our leaders? That's an act of war," Axe said.

"Only if there's proof," Nalen said. He stared out the window at the parking garage, getting busier as evening approached. "So, how do we prove it?"

Haley continued. "I have my hunch, and we have Baranov's story. But after tonight, what is his word going to be worth? Don't worry, though. I have a plan." She sounded confident and excited.

He and Nalen shared a look, both smiling with pride.

We've taught her well.

"I'll explain it to you, but first I need you to arrange a few things for me, Admiral. I need a private plane with only my name on the passenger list, even though I'll be bringing Baranov with me to Las Vegas."

"I can take care of it."

"Great. Get ready, gentlemen. Your night is going to be interesting, but I know you'll handle yourselves well. Save some energy, though, because to save our country, we have to stop the assassination of two more American leaders."

Axe felt a surge of excitement as they hung up.

Nalen, Haley, and me together in the field? We'll be an unstoppable team of three.

47

BELIZE

Tabatha Rogov, Chief of Staff to Senator Greenlich from Wyoming, was thirty-five and nearly done with the rat race. The senator's Washington, D.C. office in the Capitol Building was dark except for Tabatha's tiny cubicle, though others worked in the building. In her sweatshirt, blue jeans, and baseball cap covering her short, dark hair, she looked like any of the other overworked, underpaid staffers dedicated to keeping the country running—even on a weekend, during the Senate's recess, on New Year's Eve.

The last of the emails transferred to the small flash drive on her laptop.

Ten years of secrets, lies, and backstabbing. All idiotically committed to email, she thought.

Of course, this wasn't the senator's official email account. Like many of the members of Congress, the senator "overlooked" the rules about using only the government-provided email accounts in favor of his own, more secure—and completely private—ones.

When will politicians ever learn? Nothing is ever completely secure.

Tabatha used her phone to log into the bank account in Belize set up by her grandfather.

Two-hundred-fifty thousand dollars. Not a bad start for an hours' work.

Plus, she had to acknowledge, a complete betrayal of her long-time employer. But he was a jerk, anyway. He would finally get what he'd had coming for a long time.

With what I already have saved, plus the second payment, the amount will be more than enough for the minimalist beach life I have planned.

When her beloved grandfather had taken her aside the week before and given her the story about being a Russian sleeper spy, she'd laughed in his face.

When he'd gravely explained the threats facing their family, she'd laughed harder at the old man's idiocy.

What do I care about long-lost relatives in Russia?

Nor did she particularly worry about her asshole parents being in danger by her unwillingness to follow the directive Pawpaw claimed was her duty. They were self-absorbed and busy with their careers—and always had been.

Now if my nannies had been threatened—the caring women who actually raised me—I would have gone along.

But apparently neither Pawpaw nor his oh-so-secret Russian spy handler had realized who she truly cared for.

Her laptop beeped at her. The files were done. She double checked the flash drive—twice—ensuring the transfer had worked and all the emails were there.

Time to get the hell out of this miserable place.

Tabatha had been an idealistic intern when she'd started working for the senator. Ten years later, she was jaded, cynical, and desperate for a new start.

Belize will be a great place to begin my new life of leisure.

"What will it take for you to do this for me?" Pawpaw had finally asked her, beside himself at her refusal to go along with his plan.

She'd been waiting for the moment when he would realize the threats against her family—even herself—meant nothing to her. She didn't believe for an instant his childish scare tactics.

"Five-hundred-thousand dollars," she replied matter-of-factly. "Half up front, in a numbered offshore account. Half when I turn over the material."

If he was serious—and the entire notion wasn't an old man's desperate bid for relevancy, or a figment of his imagination—she'd know by his reaction.

Pawpaw looked at her like she was an alien from a distant galaxy, but she also saw a glint in his eye.

He's proud of me.

He'd raised her bitch of a mother.

So basically, he created her, she created me... We are what we are, the entire family.

"I'll see to it," he'd told her after only a second, surprising her. "Now, here's what you need to do."

In the dark office, she pulled the flash drive from her laptop and shut it down.

It was only a short metro ride to the bar where her friends were celebrating New Year's Eve.

They don't realize it's the last time they'll see me.

Pawpaw claimed no one would trace the emails to her, that she'd be able to resign with everyone else as soon as the shit hit the fan. But despite being family, she didn't trust him. After the party, she planned to drive to Texas, cross the border, and make her way to Belize.

I'll start the rest of my life with a long, relaxing road trip.

But first, the exchange. As she neared the bar, she saw a tall, thin woman leaning in the darkness against a closed shop, one booted foot up against the wall behind her, texting.

I think that's my contact.

"Cold night," Tabatha said as she approached.

"Not so bad, all things considered," the woman replied. She was older than Tabatha, and harder. Her eyes, face, and body all radiated menace. Her contact would make a formidable opponent, mentally and physically.

I'm glad she's on my side.

"I have what you need," Tabatha said quietly.

"And I have what you want," her contact replied, completing the silly code exchange. Swinging her large leather purse around, the hard woman pulled out a sleek laptop, opened it, and held out her hand impatiently to Tabatha.

"What, you don't trust me?" Tabatha joked to break the ice, but the woman didn't smile.

"No." The woman's dead eyes spooked her, but Tabatha handed over the flash drive. A few seconds later, the woman's face relaxed as she looked at its contents on the laptop screen.

"Well done," she said with an approving smile at Tabatha. "I'll transfer the rest of your money." She closed the laptop and slid it into her purse, but the flash drive went into the pocket of her black cargo pants. "I have it pulled up already—all I have to do is hit send. Want to watch?" she asked, reaching into another pocket.

It's happening. I'm destroying that asshole senator and finally escaping this damn city for good.

"Hell, yes!"

The woman removed her hand from the pocket and lashed out.

Tabatha gasped at the pain in her stomach. It took a second, but her mind processed the reality.

The bitch stabbed me.

She opened her mouth to cry for help, but couldn't. The blackness closed in on her as she fell forward into the woman's waiting arms.

PART 5

SUNDAY, JANUARY 1

48

MIDNIGHT

Near Fremont Street
Las Vegas, Nevada

Axe wrapped up his call with a former SEAL in charge of security for the biggest casino on the Strip. "Okay, stay safe. We'll catch up on the other side."

It made sense that many of the top casinos hired SEALs. If you need the best security, the most robust planning, the most highly trained and motivated men, you turn to SEALs.

Most of the casinos serving Baranov's beer had SEALs in high-level security positions. They had all responded favorably to Axe's calls warning them about the situation with drunk, out-of-control patrons headed their way.

Axe looked at Nalen, sitting in the rented minivan next to him. They were still waiting on the ground floor of a downtown casino's parking garage. "That's the last of them. Between the calls yesterday and these conversations tonight, I've never spoken with so many SEALs in twenty-four hours," he sighed. "I'd rather be fighting zombies, or whatever Mad Dog called them."

Nalen chuckled. "See, you're already getting the hang of being a desk jockey!"

Axe offered him a glare reserved only for people who truly pissed him off. It only made Nalen laugh harder.

He loves being back in the field... and giving me a hard time.

"They say they've got it covered, no matter what happens," Axe continued over Nalen's quieting laughter. "They thought I was nuts when I described what to look out for. I wish we could tell them about the beer."

He, Nalen, and Haley had decided the best they could do was offer a warning about intelligence chatter of a potential threat: tainted or dosed drinks, possibly alcohol. Be on the lookout for people turning more violent than usual. Difficult to contain. They offered suggestions, and mentioned a contingent of retired veterans in town for a meetup, available to help if needed.

"Ready?" Axe asked Nalen needlessly. The man was itching to get into the thick of it.

Nalen checked his watch. "23:45. Might as well be out there for the countdown. But in case things get crazy before midnight, happy New Year, Axe." He stuck out his hand.

"You too, Hammer. Stay frosty."

They slung their backpacks stuffed with zip cuffs and ties, and each picked up a large box full of them from the back of the van. Then they were off, walking through the garage, along the narrow entrance lane, and to their assigned corner of Fremont Street.

After pushing through the mass of humanity, they set their boxes down against a building. Ahead, the gaudy neon slammed Axe's senses.

I've never been on such a well-lit operation.

Tourists of all shapes, sizes, colors, and types surrounded them. Few were sober. Axe's trained eye picked out the people who were—the hustlers, thieves, and workers for whom New Year's Eve was merely another night of opportunity.

Some street performers had called it a night, but many remained, including those who stood around in outrageous outfits. Tourists paid to take photos with the half-dressed women—and men—to show friends back home the craziness of Sin City. Basket weavers sold hats made from palm fronds. Drummers, one to their northeast and another to the south-west using drumsticks and a upside-down five-gallon buckets, made time and provided rhythms hundreds in the crowd danced to.

The streets were mobbed; wall-to-wall humanity enjoyed the atmosphere combining a block party, carnival, and freak show. It looked like half the people were there to watch, with the other half dressed in ways they never would back home, happy to go wild in the promise that what they did here would stay here.

Axe and Nalen pressed against the side of the casino, protecting their boxes crammed full of zip cuffs.

"Hammer to Doom, over?" Nalen spoke into the long-range walkie-talkie picked up from an outdoor store that morning for every member of the team.

"Doom to Hammer: go."

"In position. Normal activity. How copy?"

"Solid copy. Other teams report the same."

"Copy. Happy New Year."

"You, too, Hammer. Stay safe."

The plan called for all teams to recon their sectors in the afternoon, get their vehicles into position, then wait. Axe and Hammer had enjoyed a casual walk up and down the length of Fremont Street, old Las Vegas' first strip of casinos and hotels. The street was permanently closed to vehicles and was in effect a covered outdoor shopping mall. Tourist trap shops lined each side of the street, anchored by bars, restaurants, and large casinos. It ran for five blocks and drew crowds twenty-four hours a day with its spectacular light show, outdoor stages, and areas for mimes, living statues, and other street performers.

They passed the other teams assigned to the area, including Mad Dog and his partner, two Rangers, and another team. They were all doing the same thing: checking out the area and getting ready for the chaos.

They chatted up bartenders and the street performers, getting a feel for the area, choke points, and casino exits. Nalen pulled aside a few security guards and police officers, many patrolling on bicycles, and flashed a Homeland Security badge. He mentioned being off duty but around if anything went down they needed help with. They treated him with respect, but Axe could tell they thought the older man was desperate to feel important and get back in the game.

If the shoe fits... but they don't know what kind of man Nalen is—or how much help they will need tonight.

"Five, four, three," the crowd chanted around them. "Two. One. Happy New Year!"

Nalen and Axe, surrounded by happy partiers, nodded to each other, ready for anything. Haley thought the action wouldn't start until the beer ran out, or people headed back to their hotels. 00:15 to 01:00 was Nalen's guess.

The bright neon lights of the casinos flashed and pulsed. On Fremont Street, the ceiling high above the walkway showed an underwater scene, with digital fishes swimming by overhead. Drunk tourists flew by them on zip lines, face first on their stomachs.

I wouldn't want to be under them tonight. If there's a drunk who can't hold his liquor—what a mess!

———

Kim had turned twenty-one the week before. Her boyfriend Milo had given her a cheesy coupon instead of an actual present. But when she untied the bright red ribbon and unrolled the paper, she'd been thrilled. New Year's Eve in Las Vegas!

Yes, they checked into a dodgy motel behind the cheapest downtown casino, but it was Las Vegas, it was the last night of the year, and she was here to party.

The trip had only gotten better when they lucked into a beer garden with live entertainment and all you could drink beer starting at 10 pm— some new brand with a cool gold label on the bottles.

Kim was having the night of her life. She'd drank before, of course, but it had never felt this good. Even their matching "I'm with stupid" shirts—with arrows pointing at each other—had gone from silly to hilarious.

Swaying to the live band, she felt a sense of bliss.

I think we should move here. I could get a job as a waitress. Milo can tend bar.

"I hope this night never ends," she yelled shortly after the countdown ended, when she and Milo had kissed long and hard, a promise for what else the night held later, once they got back to the low-rent motel.

Her bliss faded only a tiny bit when the bartender wouldn't give her another beer.

"We're out!" he yelled over the music and gave her a red label beer instead. "On the house, but the next one you have to buy—or go sit at a slot machine, they'll serve you free," he explained before turning to do the same with the next person, and the next, all lined up at the bar clamoring for more of the liquid gold, as she thought of it.

Fifteen minutes later, she wasn't feeling so great. Milo's constant pawing at her was annoying.

Geez, it hasn't even been twenty-four hours since we did it last.

She pushed his hand away, harder than she meant.

He growled at her. An honest-to-goodness growl, loud enough to hear over the music.

Asshole. He never could hold his liquor. I'm one up on him and he's growling at me?

They stared at each other, all the affection gone.

Wait, what's happening?

"Sorry," she yelled and took his hand to put it back on her waist.

He pushed her hand away and growled again.

A man next to her stepped in to save her.

He snarled at Milo, and then it was on.

Milo launched himself at the guy. They went down in a heap, bumping into others along the way, who used the disruption as an excuse to join in the fight.

Great. Just great. A bar fight.

She felt weird. The men and women fighting around her looked strange. Like aliens, with long arms and greenish skin. Straight out of one of her nightmares of being abducted.

Kim ran. Out the indoor "Biergarten" area, through the casino, colliding with others who looked at her like she was the alien.

One guy stood in her way, so she punched him in the gut, then continued to run. She got lost in the maze of slot machines and blackjack tables.

I have to get outside. I need fresh air, that's all.

She found the crowded main aisle. Growing angrier by the moment at all the slow-moving people in her way, she finally saw a sign for the exit.

With a burst of speed, she was outside, under the huge canopy covering the street. It was just as crowded here, but at least she had escaped the casino.

She stood, taking in the light show above her, trying desperately to get back the feeling of bliss she'd had earlier.

A man bumped into her, his green skin and long alien arms moving threateningly toward her face.

She growled at him and attacked, knowing she had to kill him if she hoped to survive.

49

00:25

Fremont Street
Las Vegas, Nevada

One minute, the corner where Axe waited with Hammer was filled with fun, drunken revelry. Men and women danced to the beat of the drummers, or the music in their heads.

The next moment, the energy changed, rippling from the nearby entrance of one of the lower-end casinos. A woman screamed, different from the excited sounds of the previous forty-five minutes. This had an edge to it.

The sound of terror.

Axe felt the mood change as people, drunk as most of them were, reacted with their lizard brains to the panic near them.

In front of Axe, a burly man with a full beard and bald head, who looked like he could handle himself, stopped dancing. His gorgeous wife or girlfriend had her hands in the air, one holding a drink in a plastic glass, eyes closed, lost in the joy of the evening. The man made eye contact with Axe, who nodded confirmation to the man's unasked question.

Yes. What you sense is real.

"Take her and go now," he called out. "That way," he pointed away from Fremont Street.

"Come on, babe. Time to go." He took her hand and led her through the crowd. Several others, either experienced with violence, not as drunk, or lucky, were also moving away.

"Hammer to Doom. It's on."

"Copy, Hammer. It's on. Keep your head down."

"Copy."

Axe ripped open the top box and grabbed a fistful of zip cuffs. Nalen did the same. Their pockets and backpacks were already full.

"Let some of them clear out first. We'll never make it against the tide," Nalen yelled.

There were more screams and shouts. Glass shattered.

"Run!" someone yelled from the front of the nearby casino. It caused a surge as people reacted. Some tried to go up or down crowded Fremont Street, but most chose the path of least resistance: the less empty cross street.

People hurried past Axe and Nalen, jostling them and each other.

"Stay calm!" Axe repeated every few seconds. "Keep moving."

The screams came more frequently now. More glass broke, and the sounds of fighting could be heard from around the corner.

It could be a normal, drunken scuffle.

Then he heard the growling.

Okay, not now—that's the bad trip talking.

As people staggered and ran past them, an opening appeared. He and Nalen both moved forward, their warrior instincts telling them it was time to intervene.

As they came around the corner, the scene shocked them.

Whatever I had thought would happen, this is worse.

Already, people lay on the ground, bloody and not moving. Dozens of men and women fought, toe to toe or rolling on the ground, trading vicious blows, or tearing at each other. They cared only for hurting their opponent, not at all for self-preservation. The violence was horrific, even to Axe's experienced eye.

"Axe!" Nalen broke into a run, fighting against the remaining crowd containing drunk people who didn't realize how dangerous the street had suddenly become.

Ahead, pressed against the wall of a casino, a police officer used his patrol bike to hold back three crazed men trying to kill him.

"Right behind you!"

By the time Axe caught up with him, Nalen had already pulled one man off, flinging him away. Axe took the second down with a leg sweep.

Unfortunately, this gave the officer a chance. With his eyes white with fear, he pushed the bike hard, propelling his last attacker back. The officer reached for his gun and in his haste, pulled the trigger as he drew. A shot ricocheted past Axe, close enough to feel. Then the officer brought the gun up.

"No!" Nalen shoved the man's arm into the air as the gun fired again.

"Homeland Security!" Nalen yelled to the overwhelmed officer. "They're drunk and very dangerous, but they're innocent."

The attacker Nalen had spun away returned, but Axe tackled him to the ground. While down, with the man wiggling like a fish on the bank of a river, Axe slipped the flex cuffs around the man's wrists, securing them behind his back.

"Holster that weapon, son, and use these," Nalen commanded, the authority in his voice making the officer hesitate for only a second before following orders and taking the handful of offered zip cuffs.

Nalen kicked the second attacker between the legs as he approached, dropping him long enough for Axe to cuff him.

By the time Axe finished, the officer and Nalen were handling the third attacker.

That wasn't so bad—

Before Axe could finish his thought, a massive force slammed into him from his blind side. He crashed to the ground, stunned for an instant. Then the first attacker Axe had cuffed landed on top of him, hands still locked behind his back, using his body as a battering ram to seek revenge on his captor.

"Hammer!"

In a second, the officer was there, not Nalen, pulling the man off Axe.

"Hold him down!" Axe yelled and grabbed a regular, long zip tie from his back pocket. He used it to secure the man's kicking legs together. Then both Axe and the officer rolled off the enraged man, whose mouth was a bloody snarl of missing teeth. He twisted on the ground, trying to get up.

"Thanks!" Axe said to the officer.

There was no time for more talking, or even for the officer to call for help on his radio—not that it would have done any good. Police throughout the city would be overwhelmed by now as well.

Enraged, drugged men and women spilled out of the casino which had the biggest free beer launch celebration.

Axe, the officer, and Nalen were immediately overwhelmed. The attackers—even Axe was having a hard time not thinking of them as Mad

Dog's zombies—fought ferociously, forcing the three of them to continually retreat.

"Back up to the food truck!" Axe yelled. "We need a choke point or we're going to be overrun."

They angled sideways. Each fought off attackers, pushing them back more than handling them, waiting until the right moment.

Finally, they were between a barbecue food truck and the wall of one of the casinos. The opening, only six feet wide, allowed them to stand shoulder to shoulder, narrowing the attack vectors from the crazed men and women.

A chubby grandmother with blue hair and a fanny pack barreled at Axe, snarling. He punched her in the stomach, which took her breath away for a few seconds and caused her attack to falter. He used the time to spin her around and zip tie one wrist. With her still bent forward, trying to breathe, he zip-tied her right wrist to her left ankle, effectively limiting her mobility. He pushed her behind him, toward the back of the food truck, and she tripped, landing hard on her right side, unable to rise.

"Great idea!" Nalen called, using the same technique on his attacker.

"The key is to take the fight out of them for a second," Axe called to both Hammer and the officer. "A punch to the stomach, the sternum, or between the legs," he said, using the groin kick again with the twenty-something male attacker who had appeared in front of him, taking the place of the woman.

They had their hands full, but they got into a rhythm. Once incapacitated for a second, or taken to the ground, the zip ties came out. If Axe moved fast enough, he found he could connect a wrist to the opposite ankle, which hobbled and distracted the zombies, rendering them less harmful.

These people are difficult and dangerous, but they're easier to handle than Kelton had been.

It had to be the alcohol. They'd all been drinking free spiked beer for a few hours, and who knew what else in the time before the beer gardens were open. They had a great deal of the drug in their systems, true, but an equal amount of alcohol inhibited their bodies.

If they'd only given out one or two bottles per person, this would be a much different ballgame.

A major tactical error from their enemy—but he wasn't complaining.

For a short while, they operated smoothly. The "zombies" exiting the casinos seemed instinctively drawn to Axe, Nalen, and Rankin, the officer.

Some got away to rampage up or down the street, attacking whoever they came to first, which often meant two zombies going after each other. The larger one usually won, but not always. Either way, they mostly canceled each other out, leaving both injured on the ground, out of commission. Axe didn't have time to worry about them.

The other teams to either side picked up zombies that broke away, as Axe's team did for the ones slipping into their sector.

The situation grew more tense when a group surged toward their location, drawn by the growling of the bound men and women behind the truck and the commotion in the choke point. Men and women of all shapes and sizes snarled, snapped, and lunged at them.

"Fall back!" Hammer yelled. Axe and Rankin took three steps back with him, further limiting the reach of the crowd to the few people in front.

A melee ensued. The attackers were stronger and faster than earlier, forcing Axe, Rankin, and Hammer to work as a team. Axe would push back the crowd, fending them off, while the other two took down the nearest attacker, zip-tied their hands and feet, and flung them back, toward the back of the truck.

Thankfully, the zombies haven't figured out how to attack us from behind.

The three brothers acted as one, without conscious thought. They'd always been close. Born ten months apart each, they were practically triplets.

The eldest saw the three monsters by the food truck and knew without a doubt, deep in his core, they were the ones to blame. He didn't know what they were to blame for. But it was up to them to stop the monsters responsible for... whatever.

With a grunt to his brothers, he nodded at the beasts hurting the innocent tourists, tying them up to be eaten later, no doubt. He let out a deep roar and led the charge.

Three huge men with bulging muscles, brothers from the looks of them, roared and pushed their way through the next wave of attackers. Their eyes blazed and spittle flew from their mouths as inhuman sounds came from them.

Axe flung himself at the men, tackling the closest one, pushing him into his brothers as he fell. For a second, they were mashed together against the wall.

This is bad.

But Nalen was right there with a zip tie, slipping it first around the ankle of the nearest standing man, then around the wrist of the one Axe struggled to contain on the ground.

"Rankin—block the one on the right," Hammer said to the police officer, who looked like he was about to collapse with exhaustion.

But the man followed orders, finding the strength which enabled him to stand in front of the third bodybuilder, trapping him against the wall.

Nalen stayed low. Axe crawled past the first man, who yanked his arm, trying to get free. It pulled the second guy's foot, toppling him, and they turned to fight each other.

Not ideal, but better them than us.

Axe grabbed the second man's arm and held it, preventing him from hitting his brother, but taking a blow to his head in the process. He was dazed for a moment but held on as Hammer slipped a tie around the man's wrist.

Together, they pulled the huge arm toward the last brother, still grappling with Rankin, who had taken blows in the meantime.

Inch by inch, they forced the arm close to the right leg of Rankin's attacker. Nalen slipped a cuff around the leg, then used another tie to connect number two's wrist to number three's ankle.

"Fall back again," Nalen said.

They did, leaving the three huge guys tied together awkwardly. They fought with each other as best they could, blocking the opening between the food truck and the wall, giving Axe, Hammer, and Rankin a few seconds to rest.

A few feet behind them, though, one of the dozens of bound attackers rolling on the ground, ankles and hands zip-tied, had figured out how to get to her feet. The others noticed, and within seconds, all were hopping around, growling and slamming into each other.

Between the muscle heads in front of them, and the hopping tourists behind, it looked like a demented fight club.

This would be downright humorous if they weren't so dangerous.

"We need to do more, faster," Hammer said, breathing hard. He had a cut on his chin and his always perfect t-shirt—black tonight—was wrinkled. The neck had been pulled, stretching it, making it look like it was twenty years old and worn out. Axe already had a sore arm from a punch he didn't see coming. His nose hurt from another attack, but it wasn't broken. His clothes were torn, and his body ached all over from tackling zombies.

"A lightning strike?" Axe offered. "We run out into the middle of Fremont Street—hit and run. One of us knocks 'em down, the other cuffs their ankles. It won't stop them from hitting, but it will slow them down."

"I can tackle the next one as you two finish up," Rankin suggested. "It'll go faster."

Watching the brothers attempt to harm each other and largely fail because of their bindings, he had another idea.

"Let's zip them together. Ankles and wrists."

Hammer got the image right away, shaking his head and chuckling. "Only you, Axe," he said.

Rankin looked at them like they were both crazy, then smiled as the realization dawned. "I get it. Yes, that's great. But the first and last ones have to be anchored, or they will bend around."

Axe could see it in his mind and agreed. "Great. Let's do it." He told Rankin, "Hammer and I will drop 'em, you cuff them together. It'll be more efficient if all of us aren't fumbling for the cuffs. But first, let's get these under control," he said, pointing to the hopping attackers behind and near the back of the truck.

He quickly removed the paracord bracelet his girlfriend Connie had given him as a Christmas present.

If she had meant it to be only a piece of fashion, she would have given me a different bracelet.

He unraveled it and secured one end to the trucks' door handle.

Overhead, the brightly lit canopy now showed a scene of fireworks exploding.

What a way to start the year.

"Knock 'em down!" he called to Nalen and Rankin. With relative ease, they swept the feet from the tied, attacking zombies, who fell to the ground. Before they could rise, Axe threaded the twelve feet of cord through their cuffs. When he had all those nearby secured, he yanked the line tight and tied the free end to a pillar. The zombies were stuck, unable to go far or cause much damage to each other.

"Nice one!" Officer Rankin called before taking down a beautiful dark-haired woman with a shirt proclaiming she was with stupid. Stupid, however, was nowhere to be seen.

Wonder what happened to him.

Axe ran over and cuffed her right wrist, then pulled her to his home-made catchline, where he slid the other cuff around her left ankle, effectively securing her to the cord in a way too awkward to allow her to do any damage.

They moved from behind the food truck and enacted their plan. Axe dropped the nearest zombie, a grandfather type who was assaulting another older man. Rankin zipped his wrists around a bike rack bolted to the ground near the wall of the casino while Hammer pushed back against the other grandpa. Then, with Axe holding the first elder's legs, he zipped the man's ankles together.

"Ready," he said to Nalen. Axe stood watch while Rankin cuffed the second old man's wrists through the zip tie holding the first one's ankles together.

The first links in our human chain.

It went quickly after that. Since most of the drugged people were already engaged with others, they merely pulled one away, zipped wrists to the previous zombie's ankles, then added the next person.

"Hammer to Doom, how copy?" Nalen called on his walkie-talkie while Rankin and Axe worked.

"Solid copy. What's up?"

Hammer described their process to Doom, who said he would relay it to the others.

"But from the reports, you've all stumbled on a similar design. Cuff one to an immobile object, then one to another in a way to at least minimize the damage they can do. Hang in there. Stay safe."

They got into a rhythm. Axe and Hammer alternated tackling the most dangerous-looking zombies, the ones doing the most damage to their fellow victims. Rankin swept in and zipped them up.

At last, after hours of fighting—and a run back to the boxes for more zip ties—Axe surveyed the scene. Around him lay dozens of zombies attached to each other. He looked closer and counted clumps of people.

Not dozens. Hundreds.

The human chain stretched down the block, curved around a pillar, and came back—Hammer had wanted to keep to their assigned zone. Some people rolled from side to side, seeking escape. Others lay on the ground, staring up at the ever-changing spectacle displayed on the roof of the street, mesmerized and exhausted. They growled from time to time but were out of the fight.

Up and down the pedestrian street, as far as he could see, hundreds of men and women, old and young, lay on the ground. Many were injured, though some were simply exhausted. All were secured to each other or a bike rack, pole, or whatever immovable object had been nearby when they had gotten zip-tied by one of the teams.

It looked like a scene from a horror movie.

Another thirty hopped around, ankles and wrists bound, ineffectively attacking each other. With every fall, fewer had the strength to rise.

Police, fire, and ambulance sirens wailed a few blocks away.

How many innocent people die tonight because of this?

With few people standing, the nearest other teams were visible: Mad Dog and his partner to the northwest, and two Army Rangers Axe didn't know well to the southeast. He gave an exhausted thumbs up to each and received the same back.

Axe waited next to the large open area of the casino where the most zombies had emerged from and took out another as he staggered from inside, growling.

"Is it me, or is this getting easier?" Rankin called from a few feet away as he wrestled another zombie to the ground like a rancher with a calf. He expertly zipped one ankle and one wrist together.

"These are survivors of fights or drunker than the first ones. Either way, easier for us, though I hate to think of what it looks like inside the beer garden."

After several more minutes of lethargic attackers, the night appeared over. Inside the nearest casino, gambling tables lay upended or on their sides. Gaming chips were scattered across the dingy carpet like coins in a fountain. Injured workers lay where they had fallen defending their casino's money and property.

"It's on the Strip, too," Rankin said, listening to his radio, then approaching Axe. "What the hell happened?"

Axe ignored the question. "You did well tonight, Rankin. But there's more to be done."

Nalen joined them, nodding. "Triage. Look for badly injured. I'll get the van. We'll transport them to the nearest hospital."

"They're overwhelmed," Rankin pointed out.

"Yes, but better there than letting people die out here," he said, turning toward the van.

"I'm coming with you," Axe told him. SEALs stuck together.

Never leave your swim buddy.

"Guys," Rankin said, stopping them. "Thanks for being here. Reports on the radio said there were a bunch of you. What's really going on?"

"Just here for a quick vacation is all. Lucky break for you, I guess!" Axe said with a charming, though tired, grin.

Rankin smiled and nodded, but his eyes were hard. "And the zip ties?" He nodded at the hundreds of people restrained around them.

"Another lucky break," Axe said, more seriously.

Is he going to push this?

Rankin stared at them. Seconds ticked by. Finally, he nodded. "I guess. Lucky the casino had all those extra zip ties sitting by their door, just in case."

"Yes, exactly," Nalen said. "Without the forethought of the casino security staff, this would have been even worse. Make sure you add that to your report, son." He stuck out his hand. The officer took it and held back a wince.

I know how strong Nalen's grip is. I doubt I could keep my face so composed if he let me have it.

"Maybe you could mention to your fellow officers how the casinos' security teams provided the zip ties. See if the same situation played out all over." He stared the man down.

After a second, Rankin nodded. "Yes, sir. I'm sure they were thinking the same thing."

"Good man."

The Warehouse
Las Vegas, Nevada

Axe and Nalen spent the rest of the night ferrying the bound, injured zombies to the hospital, gently laying them on huge tarps set up in the parking lot as triage areas. The other teams did the same.

As the sky lightened, they had done all they could. A drive through deserted streets took them back to the warehouse. The smell of hot pizza greeted them. Some teams had already returned, while others followed soon after Axe and Hammer started chowing down.

One man had a speaker paired to his cell phone with the local news radio station streaming.

"At the tone, the time is seven AM. *Beep.* Good morning. Our top story: a horrible tragedy last night to ring in the new year. Shortly after midnight, as people celebrated in our casinos on both the Strip and downtown, rioting broke out. Hundreds of people were injured, many seriously. So far, we have reports of at least five people dead. Authorities say the death toll may go up as recovery efforts continue throughout the city and overwhelmed area hospitals report. We are joined by reporter Franklin Smith, reporting live from Fremont Street. Franklin?"

"Thanks, Keith. From what I've learned, the rioting was worst along this downtown street as people spilled out of many of the casinos around 12:30 this morning. Police are still looking into the situation and caution it will be several days before all the facts are gathered. But my sources say the mayhem appeared to start because of drunken revelers fighting, which caused others to fight back, both inside and outside many casinos. An anonymous source at a hospital told me she had counted over five hundred people injured and another several hundred with horrible hangovers causing them to be virtually immobile. As terrible as it is, the situation would have been much worse if not for several dozen—perhaps as many as one hundred—off-duty police and former military members who are in town for a reunion."

"Veterans?"

"Yes, Keith. I've confirmed with two sources, who requested anonymity because they did not have permission to speak on the record, who said both off-duty Homeland Security officers and retired members of our armed services joined in to assist security guards and LVPD. Many of the casinos had pre-placed plastic zip cuffs and zip ties as a precaution. They accessed those caches to secure hundreds of rioters."

"Amazing reporting, Franklin."

"Without the forethought of the casino personnel and the assistance of the men in town for a reunion, our brave police would have easily been overrun. If you see a veteran today—or any day, for that matter—thank them for their service."

"Well said, Franklin."

"For more coverage, we turn to—" The stream stopped at a motion from Nalen. The warehouse area was filled with tired, beat-up, sweaty men, covered with scrapes, bruises, and cuts. Their clothes were torn, and many were stained with blood.

"Doom—headcount," Nalen called.

The older man stood proudly at the front of the room next to Nalen. "77, Hammer. All present and accounted for."

"Casualties?"

"None. Minor injuries."

"Outstanding." He turned to the men who were stuffing themselves with pizza. "Men, last night you saved this city. I cannot imagine how many would be dead if not for you and your willingness to serve. To drop everything and show up with little notice. I'm proud of you." He met the eyes of the men. "Now, grab a drink. I have a toast."

Many already had sodas from ice-filled coolers Doom brought in along with the pizzas. Others fished around for one.

"What, no beer?" Mad Dog joked to groans. "Sorry. Too soon?" he asked with a huge grin.

Nalen ignored the black humor. "Since we come from different backgrounds and have several mottos, let me use this one instead. I've always found it inspirational." He raised his soda toward the men. "'Who Dares, Wins.' To you, men, the ones who dare."

"Who Dares, Wins," the men repeated.

"Finish your pizza, then get the hell out of here. No sense being around when the police start digging into this. Well done, and thank you."

Hammer walked into the crowd, shaking hands, expressing his thanks, and saying a few words to each. Axe followed behind, doing the same, learning from the best.

About halfway through saying thank you and goodbye, his phone buzzed. He excused himself to check the text from Haley.

Just landed. Well done saving the city! We need to guard Baranov for a few days. Any of the men need work? And—we have another problem.

50

BLONDIE

Haley led a staggering, zip-tied Baranov into the warehouse, leaving her rental car parked right next to the front door. "Don't worry about him," she told Axe, seeing the look on his face. "More sleeping pills. He'll come around in a bit. Do you have somewhere we can stash him?"

She felt like hell, and from Axe's glance at her after checking out Baranov, she must look it.

Not getting much sleep for days on end will do it, she thought. *First thing is getting us on the road. Second is making sure we all get some rest... ideally starting with me.*

"Mad Dog?" Axe called.

The short, muscular, dark-haired man with the physique of a rugby player emerged from the back warehouse space. "Hey, Haley! Long time, no see. Why is it," he asked with exaggerated exasperation, "every time you're around I have to fight off a horde of crazy villagers?"

She had to smile. All SEALs, in her experience, were a little crazy—in a good way. They made the most of every moment, at work or play. They also had thick skin and didn't take the world too seriously... except for the important issues. Country, honor, duty, Team. Protecting the innocent and wreaking havoc on their enemies. Then—watch out. They had no match.

But Mad Dog took their 'Moderation is for cowards' motto to the extreme. Hector, or "Thor," from Axe's old Team, was truly funny, always ready with a quick quip or funny line. Mad Dog made him seem as light-hearted as a funeral director. If ever there was a class clown of the SEALs, Mad Dog was it.

"Let me point out, Mad Dog, that you were there, too. And I bet you've been on many ops back in the day, long before I was around, with your back against the wall. Maybe it's on you, not me. Ever think of that?"

"Excellent point, Blondie," he said, pulling out her rarely used call sign. "I will give some serious thought to cleaning up my karma. So, Axe said you could use some gifted and talented individuals to save the world and my name was at the top of your list?"

She laughed. It was good to be back with the men. "That's exactly how it happened."

How did I ever think I could sit in an office and stare at a computer all the time? Or manage assets like Axe and Mad Dog without being with them?

A few other men wandered in, but she didn't recognize them. They nodded respectfully to her and didn't check her out.

Either I look worse than ever, or Axe had a word with them. Maybe both.

"Can you take this guy and find him a place to sleep it off?" she asked Mad Dog, handing over Baranov. "Incommunicado."

"Hold on there, Blondie. Slow down when you use the big words. I'm just a dumb SEAL..." he trailed off as he escorted Baranov to a room behind the reception counter. The other three men chosen to guard Baranov nodded at her, smiling at Mad Dog's antics, and followed him.

"Axe said we have another problem?" Nalen asked her as they walked to the back of the warehouse. Three beat-up lawn chairs sat along the back wall under a clean whiteboard and maps of the Las Vegas area.

"First, it's Christmas again," she said, setting down a large backpack on the chair and unzipping it. "I know we already exchanged presents, but..." she told Axe, pulling out her short barrel M4 and passing it to him, followed by several magazines of ammunition.

"Haley, you shouldn't have... but I'm very glad you did," Axe said, slamming home a magazine and loading a round after checking the safety.

"I want it back when we're done."

"Absolutely."

"Admiral—"

"'Hammer,' please. 'Nalen' if you must. But while I'm in the field, unsanctioned, let's keep in mind I'm acting on my own."

"Of course, Hammer." She pulled out her larger 9mm and plenty of mags. "For the man who has everything. Merry Christmas."

He removed the weapon from its holster, loaded it as Axe had done, and secured it on his hip. The extra magazines in their holder went on his other hip. His black t-shirt had dirt and dried blood on it. His blue jeans were rumpled, too.

But he's standing even taller now that he's armed.

She removed her small backup pistol and placed it on her hip. "Now that we're all prepared, I'll give you the update, grab some pizza, then we have to get on the road." She looked back at the last few slices, growing cold in their boxes... and two of the men on Mad Dog's guard detail hovering over them. "On second thought, let me grab a few bites, then we'll begin." She jogged to the pizza, snagged three slices from under the noses of the men, and jogged back, stacking the slices together and biting the ends off all three.

"The president has three major allies against Russia," she said, trying to make the words clear around the food. "Senator Jonesley from California died yesterday. This morning, as we landed, I read a news flash. Senator Greenlich of Wyoming had his email compromised. Ten years' worth of personal and official emails came out late last night."

The pizza was hitting the spot, so she paused for another bite, putting off the impatient men in front of her. She moved her backpack and collapsed into the old lawn chair, nearly breaking it.

"The email archive was sent directly to national newspapers and well-regarded reporters. This isn't a hit job—it seems like the real deal. The initial reports were pretty vague but hinted at 'alleged improprieties and felonies.'"

"Senator Greenlich from Wyoming?" Nalen asked, sitting carefully in another one of the rickety chairs. "I can understand the improprieties—there have long been rumors. But not felonies. He's a straight shooter with the law, from what I understand."

Axe sat down also, looking only slightly less tired than Nalen.

"I'll have Nancy look into it if she's not already," Haley said around the pizza.

It's New Year's Day. I wouldn't normally expect them in the office but given the current situation with Senator Jonesley and now Senator Green-lich, I wouldn't be surprised if Gregory called in several extra people.

"I wonder about classic Russian psychological operations—PSYOPs. Release the damaging, real emails, but also include fake ones which are more incriminating," Nalen said.

I should have thought of that.

"Makes sense," she said, swallowing and pausing before taking another enormous bite. "It would be hard to say, 'Yes, I certainly did those bad things, but not those other, worse things—those are made up.'"

Nalen nodded. "No one would believe it."

"The report I read speculated he would be forced to resign. Even if he doesn't, if he's in the middle of a huge scandal, he won't be much good to the president."

She explained her theory of the Russians using the destruction in Las Vegas, Baranov's friendship with the president, and the attacks on the senators to give them the freedom to invade Ukraine, weaken NATO, and mess with Europe.

Axe and Nalen stared at her, stunned.

"No proof of this, aside from Baranov's interrogation?" Axe asked.

"No. And his confession only confirms Russian backing for the Las Vegas attack, nothing else," she admitted.

Do I still have their trust?

Axe didn't seem concerned with her lack of evidence.

Actually, he looks happy to have another mission.

"So we have to stop it ourselves? The three of us against the world?" Axe turned to Nalen. "Or could we tell the president, now that Baranov is out of the picture?"

Hammer paused for several seconds, thinking it through, but eventually shook his head. "No. If the Russians have a contingency plan in place to blame the president for the events last night in Las Vegas and tie him to Baranov, I don't want him informed. He needs to be truly shocked when he hears the accusation. Besides, if you're right about the sleeper spies," he said to Haley, "we may have to keep them in place until we can sweep them all up at once." He nodded decisively. "We're on our own."

"Exactly," she said, stuffing the last of the pizza into her mouth. "So let's get going. We have a lot of prep work to do—and a senator to save."

51

HUNCHES

Central Analysis Group Headquarters
Alexandria, Virginia

Dave looked at his screen, trying to find a different explanation than the one in front of him.

I will not make the leaps of logic Haley—and now Nancy—love so much, he thought.

His screen displayed a map of the Russia-Ukraine border. To the north, Belarus, then Latvia, and finally Estonia. All countries of the former Soviet Union, which modern-day Russia would love to have back in the fold.

Overlaying the map was the latest real-time plotting and analysis of the Russian armed forces. Every winter they conducted war games designed to train the troops and, those in the West suspected, cause endless headaches and stress to NATO. Estonia, Latvia, and Lithuania, the three area NATO members, were especially vulnerable. It was a dangerous geopolitical boiling pot of potential conflict and disaster.

Dave clicked on the map to zoom in. A few small units over the past several days had gone one direction, stopped cold, and reversed to go to a different spot.

Mistakes happen. Orders get confused. Men without proper rest or training turn the wrong direction.

He hated admitting it to himself, but he had a funny feeling. An intuition.

A hunch.

What if the mistakes revealed their true intentions?

He delved into the various databases at his disposal, looking specifically for rumors and reports from human assets, along with electronic intercepts from the area. It was all there, an incredible volume of information, whatever the United States and its allies could collect, shoved into a variety of different systems. Just waiting for people like him to make sense of it for the politicians and military commanders.

But these days, just like Haley, the men and women in charge often wanted to go with their gut instincts instead of relying on what the data showed.

Isn't that what I want to do now?

The data showed yet another winter exercise. His hunch painted a far worse picture.

When in doubt, write it out.

He opened a new window, pulled up a plain spreadsheet program, and started listing the reasons his gut could be right, along with the many more reasons it was probably wrong.

Expanding his scope, he read raw Human Intelligence (HUMINT) reports from the entire area.

He had to enter multiple passwords to access more information from their sister agencies in other countries. Further credential checks—the highest he had—were required to read intel about America's allies and their leaders.

A pattern emerged. One he didn't want to see and had a hard time believing.

It's so terribly thin. Is it there, or could it be confirmation bias?

Was it true because he already believed it to be, or because the facts were there?

The day slipped away, another in a long line of lost days off, missed holidays, and time spent at a desk under fluorescent lights instead of on a ski slope or snuggled with Nancy in front of a cozy fire, reading a novel and sharing good wine.

At least we're in it together. Sort of.

Nancy had given up their shared cubicle for the time being, moving first to Haley's desk for the huge dual-screen setup, then to the conference room because of the sensitive nature of what she had on the displays.

So while not sitting side by side, which was their preference, at least one of them wasn't sitting home, bitter about the other's work habits and excessive hours.

Dave continued to methodically list reasons supporting and opposing his—what?

I hate to keep calling it a hunch.

Theory.

Yes, a much more scientific word and approach.

He had a theory that he would either prove, disprove, or neither.

Then I'll pass it to Haley, no matter which direction it goes.

If his theory proved correct or leaned that way, he shuddered to think what she'd do with it.

It's been a fine career. Maybe, if we don't end up unemployed or in prison because of this, Nancy and I can open a bed and breakfast in the mountains somewhere. Leave the city, the long work hours, and the stress behind. Start fresh.

A smile flickered across his face, thinking of him and Nancy trying to run a B&B.

That'll be the day.

52

NIGHTMARES

Central Analysis Group Headquarters
Alexandria, Virginia

The normal weekend day shift analysts got their coats and went home while Dave worked. His spreadsheet had rows upon rows of facts supporting the commonly held thesis of just another Russian winter war game exercise.

On the left of his screen, a few meager listings supported his theory of a more dangerous plot.

One of the biggest arguments against his theory came from Russia itself. Six months before, it had sent notice to NATO, Ukraine, the USA, and all area governments warning of readiness drills it planned for early January.

As the time approached, Ukraine, NATO, and its allies went on high alert. They watched like hawks but expected no surprises. Russia played the same games every winter. It rushed the Ukrainian border with tanks and armored vehicles, bluffing an attack, testing the response while hoping for an overreaction they could use to sway public sentiment toward them. If the overreaction were large enough, with vehicles destroyed or men killed, it might get the West to relax some sanctions as a sign of goodwill.

But the pesky feeling nagged at him. The short but significant left-side list seemed to taunt him as he kept searching for more indications his gut was right and his intellect was wrong.

Gregory stalked through the office, getting surprised glances from the night shift intelligence analysts.

Earlier, he'd been trying to enjoy a quiet New Year's Day away from the office. He had been antsy, not enjoying the football game on TV, even kicked back in his comfortable leather lounge chair with his feet up and beer nearby. Instead, he had worried about Victor Baranov, the President of the United States, drug-spiked beer in Las Vegas, and his unpredictable —yet supremely capable—former analyst Haley, who was off handling the problem on her own.

He'd had enough contact with Admiral Nalen to understand he didn't need to save Haley, nor handle the situation in Las Vegas. Somehow, Nalen, Haley, and her former Navy SEAL asset Axe would take care of it with their secret resources. While he hadn't been told in so many words, he understood they had a semi-off-the-books organization that handled issues too sketchy for the other security groups. Nalen's call to him requesting assistance for Haley with the hotel in Mexico had been yet more proof.

Gregory had decided on Friday, when Haley resigned, the best thing he could do was keep his mouth shut and stay out of their way.

As long as she doesn't mess with or harm my Central Analysis Group, that is.

The CAG had been formed with a specific, limited mandate. What Haley did was way outside its scope. If found out, they would be shut down and lose their jobs—at least. Given Haley's willingness to bend— and break—rules, prison wasn't out of the question, either.

His wife had sat on the couch, headphones on to block out the game, reading a book. Later, they'd have some wine and stream a movie—her choice, since he'd commandeered the TV for football.

At some point, though worried, he'd dozed off—a rare occurrence.

Then he had dreamed—an even rarer event.

In the dream, Haley sat in his office, at his desk, talking on his phone, commanding people around the world to do her bidding.

He'd awoken with a gasp. A glance at his wife showed she hadn't noticed.

He didn't like to work from his intuition, but it didn't take much imagination to wonder if Haley's resignation had removed her from his office.

Five will get you twenty she has Nancy funneling her information. Am I risking the CAG by not putting a stop to this?

Would the president back him if he allowed his team to help out the NHA, as Haley called it?

Or will we be caught up in whatever scandal is about to hit him—and also hung out to dry?

Maybe the best way to address his concerns was to show up at the office unexpectedly after dinner on New Year's Day. He'd apologized to his wife, bundled up, and come into the office to assess the true situation.

Maybe I'm worried for no good reason.

Gregory stopped behind the shared work area of Nancy and Dave. Nancy wasn't there, so he watched Dave work. His senior analyst was nearly the opposite of Haley. Methodical instead of impulsive. Driven by proof and logic instead of feelings and guesswork. Experienced instead of new.

Haley isn't so new these days. And credit where credit is due—she's as exceptional as she is unorthodox.

As solid as Dave was, as many times as he'd contributed intelligence analysis which had helped protect America, Haley had done more single-handedly to save the country in the past year than Dave had in his entire career.

Dave's right-hand screen had two spreadsheet columns, but Gregory couldn't read the small type from outside the cube. He cleared his throat quietly, not wanting to startle the man lost in his work.

It backfired. Dave's head whipped around, surprised, but he covered well. "Good evening, Gregory. What brings you in?"

He ignored the question. "What are you working on this late on the first day of the year?"

Dave closed his eyes and sighed, then turned back to his computer. "I'm trying to convince myself I'm crazy," he said, gesturing at his screen and moving out of the way. Gregory moved closer to read the words. He recognized the system as a simple pros and cons list, one he'd used extensively himself in his younger days as an analyst when he had been a maverick—much like Haley.

See? This is a legitimate CAG analysis. Maybe I was worried about nothing.

On the left of the page were a mere three rows under the heading, *Theory*. On the right were several rows under, ***Expectation.***

"What am I looking at?" he asked, the uneasy feeling he'd had at home returning.

"The annual Russian war game exercises along the Ukraine border."

"Seems like Expectation is in the lead."

Dave hesitated. "Yes, it looks that way."

Gregory waited, but the man didn't continue. He only stared at the screen. "But?" Gregory finally asked.

With a sigh, Dave spun his chair to face him. "This feels different," he said, shaking his head at his own words. "Maybe Haley's approach is rubbing off on me, but there is more going on than meets the eye. A few tiny things were off about the Russians' deployments. They fixed them quickly, but I noted them over the last few days." He hesitated, struggling. Finally, after several seconds of seeming to fight with himself, he blurted out, "I have a bad feeling about this."

Gregory worked to keep his face blank, showing neither the doubt he felt—nor the frustration.

Damn Haley.

He could barely handle one genius analyst. If the way she approached analysis took hold, he'd have a whole team of people telling him, "My gut tells me," and "I have a hunch that…"

But the sooner she handles this latest situation and gets back to work here, the better. For all her gut feelings, she has a stellar track record.

Dave was a solid analyst. Careful, methodical, precise.

Now he's guessing, going with his instincts instead of facts and proof.

"Let me understand," Gregory began. He was well informed about the Russian exercises. They were at the top of the list for analysis by his team. Gregory had read several other analysts' reports on the war games from multiple different angles. "The CIA, NSA, and all our considerable military resources point to a standard Russian military exercise like they've done the last several years. One they gave us six months' advance notice about. Where our satellites are watching every move. You're saying they've all missed something. You've found a thread indicating…" He sighed, letting the situation get the best of him. "What are you saying?"

Dave looked frustrated himself. "I understand how it sounds—I do. But I believe…" Again he hesitated.

He doesn't want to say it out loud.

Gregory knew the feeling. Saying it would make it real, an issue they had to deal with. They'd have to work to either prove or disprove it. Once it was out in the open, they wouldn't be able to pretend it didn't exist.

Gregory and Dave stared at each other. "Go on, say it," Gregory told him. "Let the chips fall where they may."

"I believe Russia is going to attack—in force—not only Ukraine but also Estonia, and Latvia." He must have caught a look on Gregory's face because he hurried on. "Wait, it gets worse, believe it or not. The past few years, Russia has taken over Belarus economically and politically. I also believe Belarus will invade Lithuania on their behalf. Taken together, a lightning strike will overwhelm the relatively small militaries of all the countries."

"Latvia and Lithuania are in NATO. Russia would be crazy to do this and provoke us."

In a rare sign of dissent, Dave shook his head before Gregory finished speaking, holding up his fingers and listing his arguments. "One, President Heringten is a hardliner against Russia, but he's not as powerful as he thinks he is. Two, Europe has no stomach for fighting. They won't go to war with Russia over Latvia, Lithuania, and Ukraine. Not after what we all did letting Russia just take Crimea. Three, the European politicians will bog down in debate, their people won't support it, and none of them want to risk losing the supply of natural gas provided by Russia. It's been a harsh winter already," he added, "and another huge storm is coming. Four, war with Russia would shut off the natural gas. More Europeans would freeze to death than be lost in the fighting, especially with all the snow on the way."

Gregory had to assess this report as he would any other. It came from an experienced, reliable analyst who rarely went out on a limb.

Could Dave be right?

If Haley reported this, he might believe her because of her past successes. But Dave—solid, careful Dave? Why would he be thinking so far out of the box?

Is there a chance he's trying to keep up with Haley? Worried the next generation is pushing him out?

In his position as head of the CAG, Gregory had to look at all the angles.

What is the most probable explanation here? The entire Western world's intelligence agencies are wrong, or one of my senior analysts is jealous and worried about being put out to pasture?

Dave turned toward his monitors and pointed at the map on the left.

"Look—they gain Black Sea ports, show their might, and knock on the door of Poland and Romania, making those countries much more malleable and compliant. NATO debates and finally doesn't come to the defense of Latvia and Lithuania, which destroys NATO. Why have a mutual defense treaty if no one will honor it when the need comes?"

Dave zoomed out on the map, showing the vast distance between the USA and the area. "The United States is forced to decide—do we go to war with Russia, by ourselves, whether limited or full-scale—over Ukraine? Come on." Dave shook his head and rolled his eyes. "No way. It throws the president's second-term agenda out the window. Our politicians bicker. The uncertainty upsets our economy. With one move, Russia gains big without much risk. They take the hit of our retaliatory economic sanctions easily by raising the price of natural gas. We're impotent, they're powerful. It's a masterstroke."

Gregory followed the man's thinking. It made sense—if Russia had the guts to risk it. Would their new president need to hold on to power after forcing the previous one out? The plan would have been in place for months, started by the previous president, who had definitely been daring and expansionistic.

Still, there was more Dave wasn't telling him.

He's holding something back. I can feel it.

The thought made him pause.

Great, now I'm going with my gut, just like Haley.

He took a shot in the dark and gestured for Dave to stand up. When he did, Gregory stepped close to him, invading his space.

One way to find out.

Their faces were only a few inches apart. Gregory stared at him, letting the seconds stretch by and the tension build. "What aren't you telling me?"

Dave had been in the game almost as long as Gregory. He was good—but not good enough. Not only did Gregory see the tiniest flicker on Dave's face, he could sense the man's energy or his aura, whatever mumbo jumbo people called it these days.

"What do you mean?" Dave asked, looking confused.

Gregory wasn't one to use physicality to get results. While in good shape, especially for his age, he looked at the use of force as the realm of the military branches. Here, they used their minds, the power of their intellect, to get results.

There's a time and place for everything.

He stepped forward, his nose almost touching Dave's, projecting the force of his will onto the man.

"Tell me," he said, his voice as dead as his eyes.

Instead of replying, Dave shut down. His eyes went blank, and his energy dropped. But he kept staring at Gregory, not flinching away. Both were tells.

A confused or innocent man would act differently. This is Haley's doing—again.

Gregory took a step back, his decision made. "Where's Nancy?"

The same flicker from Dave showed more information he wanted to keep to himself.

"I'll meet you both in conference room C in two minutes," he said and caught another of Dave's micro-expressions.

Damn. I knew it.

"Get your laptop and notes and come with me right now."

Dave reluctantly did as ordered, following Gregory as he marched to the conference room.

The door was locked. Gregory got the key from his pocket and unlocked the door, stepping inside as Nancy stood from the table, a look of surprise on her face.

He held the door open and sensed the communication between his two senior analysts as Dave stepped into the room.

I guess the rumors are true—they're definitely a couple.

He locked the door behind him. "We're not leaving here until you tell me exactly what the hell else Haley has gotten us into."

53

FLYING

10,000 Feet over Utah

Axe jerked awake when the pilot loudly cleared his throat over the engine noise. "We're about twenty minutes out," Martini called from the cockpit of the small single prop plane.

Time flies when you're having fun—or trying to catch up on sleep, Axe thought.

Outside the plane's dim interior, the sky was black. Lights of a small city glowed far in the distance. Provo, Utah.

Tightly packed next to him in the open area behind the cockpit, Nalen rubbed his eyes and cracked his neck on each side. They gave each other a nod, then turned to look at Haley sprawled and snoring quietly on the floor behind them.

"You sure she's ready for this?" Nalen asked, just loud enough to be heard over the engine.

"She'll be fine," Axe said. Years before, a buddy had tandem jumped with a civilian engineer into a combat operation, and that guy had been afraid of heights. Haley would be a dream in comparison.

"I'll be fine," she mumbled, wiggling to get more comfortable. Then she started snoring again, louder this time.

"Give her another few minutes," Axe said. "You need more time?"

"No, I'm good."

He's hardcore. We've gotten about the same amount of sleep, done the same fighting against the zombies. He has to be feeling it as much as I am. More, given he's twenty years my senior.

Another line from the SEAL Ethos sprang to mind. "My Nation expects me to be physically harder and mentally stronger than my enemies."

That's Nalen. And me, I hope, when I'm his age.

Nalen and Axe already had their parachutes strapped on. They double-checked their weapons.

I wish we had more firepower than one M4 and two 9mm pistols, but guns are hard to come by on a moment's notice, even out west.

That morning, after hearing Haley's plan, Axe had called his helicopter pilot friend Robert Tucci, who had saved his life during the New York operation. Axe asked Tucci for a crazy airplane pilot willing to help protect the country on the down-low. He'd come through with a friend based in Vegas—a fellow veteran—who owned a skydiving business. Martini—they weren't sure if it was his last name or a call sign—had gladly agreed to fly them wherever they wanted to go, no questions asked. Martini had only raised his eyebrows in surprise—and escorted them to his storeroom to pick what they needed—when they'd requested parachutes.

"Haley, wake up," Axe called after another minute. "It's time."

"Two minutes," Martini yelled over the wind noise from the door on the right side of the plane, wide open, the cold air rushing in.

"A review," Nalen yelled. "We treat this as a hostage rescue. Rules of engagement: non-lethal force against any security or police. The personal security guard, Porter, is fair game if he threatens the senator. Any assaulters are enemy combatants. We capture the guard or the bad guys if possible, but kill them if necessary. I'd love to interrogate one, to get more intel and proof of what's going on, but not at the risk of our lives or the senator's. Clear?"

"Clear," Axe and Haley repeated.

The one-minute call came from the cockpit. Axe had worked out the location for the drop with Martini earlier in the day while they were planning the mission. They were far enough east of Senator Woodran's sprawling ranch to not draw attention. They would jump, then freefall, traveling west as far as possible before pulling their chutes and drifting silently into the compound.

After successfully landing undetected, all they had to do was sneak in, avoiding any legitimate, non-traitorous security they couldn't shoot, get face-to-face with Woodran, and convince her of the threat from her long-time security guard.

No problem. Another day at the office.

The plan was sound, though a little desperate. They had debated several options. Admiral Nalen could come partially clean to the president, who could call the senator. A western, old-school woman who went into politics the day her youngest son went to college, she was no stranger to guns and could handle herself. She'd believe the president when he warned her of the danger. But they decided involving the president, even in a limited way, presented too much risk. So far, Haley and Nancy only had Baranov's story and their intuition as proof of the other potential Russian sleeper agents.

As they prepped the mission, they also debated Nalen reaching out to the senator. They could get her direct number from Nancy at the CAG. Woodran would recognize his name and likely accept the call. But again, it left her alone with one or more compromised security personnel—if she even believed Nalen's warning.

This will work if we're right about everything.

Were the Russians actually behind it all? The death of the first senator, the release of the second senator's emails, and the dosing of the beer for New Year's Eve? Were they targeting a third member of the government to further weaken the country and the president?

A thought haunted Axe from time to time. Like now.

One of these days, Haley might be wrong.

He flashed back to the marina in Isla Mujeres, Mexico. Taking her picture while she unexpectedly fired the speargun past him, impaling a person against the side of a yacht. The worry he'd felt, believing she had made a huge mistake and killed an innocent man instead of the terrorist they were after. Then discovering later she had been right all along—the man's appearance had changed enough for Axe to doubt Haley's judgment... but she had known.

Someday she might make a mistake, but not today... I hope.

Axe double-checked his equipment, then the attachments holding Haley's harness to his own. He could feel her tension as they sat in the doorway of the plane. They had to do a nighttime jump perfectly—Haley's first time skydiving—without getting caught, injured, or killing themselves.

"We do it exactly as we discussed," he said in her ear.

Haley nodded and gave him a thumbs-up, but didn't turn her head to meet his eye.

"Thirty seconds!" Martini yelled. "Get some!"

Axe gave him a thumbs up and tapped Haley's shoulder. "Climb onto the strut."

The plane had a small place to stand over the right landing gear. Together, they scooted out the door and placed their feet on the rough patch of non-slip coating.

The darkness surrounded them as they stepped into the black void. The cold wind cut through their jumpsuits and clothing underneath. Against him, Haley started shaking.

Once this operation is done, we have to start her jump training. This is no way to experience the fun of skydiving for the first time.

Axe reached around and confirmed she had her arms crossed in front of her. Touching them must have reminded her of his other instruction, because she arched her back and dropped her shoulders in preparation for the jump. "You're going to love this!" he yelled in her ear. Her body shuddered.

"Jump, jump, jump!" Martini yelled from the cockpit.

Axe launched them into the night, knowing Nalen would be right behind him.

Haley floated through the darkness, feeling Axe inches behind her. Intellectually, she understood they were falling, but her senses told her she was floating. Through the borrowed, geeky eye goggles, a few tiny pinpoints of light moved below her. In the far distance, the city of Provo glowed.

My God! This is better than sex—almost.

Her face would hurt tomorrow because she couldn't stop grinning.

She focused on maintaining the body position dictated by Axe so he could control their descent and direction.

Arms crossed, back arched. Enjoy the ride, as he said.

The fall went on forever, it seemed, as she watched the dim, regularly spaced lights in a huge rectangle grow slowly closer.

The fence around Senator Woodran's ranch.

They were right on target. The security lights of the perimeter fence showed the extent of the large grounds.

Axe tapped on her shoulder—the signal he would deploy the parachute. She relaxed and seconds later felt yanked into the air. Thankfully, Axe's harness bore the brunt of the force. All she felt was a strong tug as the feeling of gravity returned and they dangled beneath the canopy.

The most dangerous part of the mission—until we get on the ground and have to assault a high-ranking senator's private compound without being able to shoot back at anyone who catches us. Well, except for the one potential bad guy inside and any other assaulters outside.

Brainstorming with Axe and Nalen, they'd red team planned possible Russian moves against Woodran. The OPFOR—opposing force—would want to preserve their undercover asset's career. If Axe and Nalen were the Russians, they would stage an assault on the compound disguised as some sort of American extremists—there were plenty to choose from. Axe would have the third-generation sleeper agent get the senator alone and eliminate her, or put her in a pre-planned location for the assaulters to do it.

To preserve the asset's identity, he would be non-fatally injured in his supposed heroic but unsuccessful attempt to save the senator's life.

Were they right? And if so, would it happen tonight, or would the Russians wait a few days? How tight was the overall timeline?

The natural death of the first senator, the release of a second senator's emails and his coming resignation, plus the attack on Woodran, all in a few days, would raise red flags in the intelligence community and the media. But—if she were right—America would have much bigger problems soon. President Heringten might be under scrutiny for his connection to Victor Baranov. And Russia would invade Ukraine.

Unless we can put a stop to it all... which I'm not sure is possible.

The task seemed insurmountable. Surely the Russians had plans she hadn't thought of yet. Other sleeper agents existed in the government, and how many more like Baranov were there in large, important companies? What if computer programmers had already sabotaged the operating systems of the nation's personal computers, or were even now preparing to take out the country's electrical grid? Or shut down the air traffic control network? Or how hard would it be to use the IRS's powers to freeze the assets of millions of individuals and businesses?

I can't ascertain how vulnerable we are out in the field. Should I be back at my desk, checking on how easy or difficult it is for a few strategi-cally place individuals to sabotage the country?

There was so much to look into, she didn't even know what she didn't know.

Regret and doubt flooded her, taking away the wonder of floating gently under the canopy as the ground grew closer with every second.

Instead of being at my desk, I'm out here playing super-spy, assaulting a compound like I can hold my own next to two retired SEALs who can out-shoot, out-move, and outfight me with their hands tied behind their backs.

Her night vision had finally fully kicked in. She could see how fast they were moving as they zipped over the fence line, its decorative lights effectively illuminating the area below them. At the last second, she brought herself back to the moment, remembering Axe's instructions to raise her knees to her chest as they came in for a landing.

54

THE KIDS

Senator Barbara Woodran's Family Ranch
East of Provo, Utah

Her sister didn't know it yet, but Catherine had already decided to kill the senator herself.

She lay in a deep wash in the high desert, a natural ditch formed by erosion over thousands of years. Her sister was behind her and to the side, where a smaller ditch joined the wash. It was unlikely there would be any guards or roving patrols—her brother had seen to it—but it paid to be careful.

They were out of their element. They were both city girls. While they had skied and hiked during college, these days the kids took up all their time when they weren't working.

I wish we could have hit the senator in Provo, Catherine thought. *Roll up on her SUV, let loose with a shotgun, and peel away.*

It would be blamed on gang violence or a political nut.

Then we could shoot a shithead drug dealer, plant the weapon, and get a commendation.

Instead, the plan called for the assassination to take place out in the damn desert.

I can't let her or Leo take the shot. I'm the eldest. It's my responsibility.

Catherine hated the situation with a passion, but with all their kids' lives at stake, she'd do what had to be done.

As she lay in the darkness, watching the rear of the senator's house, waiting for the top of the hour, she hardened her resolve. Despite her commitment "To Protect and to Serve," family came first.

Even if her family included an insane, decades-old commitment to Russia none of them had known about until a week before—and still couldn't fathom.

I'm not doing this for Russia. I'm doing it for the kids.

Fulfilling her duty would buy her time to figure a way out of the situation by going to the FBI… or by taking out the handler her father so badly feared.

Kill him, gather up the kids, and we all flee the country together.

Catherine would not allow any of them to be put in a position like this again.

And their long-lost relatives in Russia would just have to fend for themselves.

The details could be worked out later, but as long as they were together, she'd be happy.

But first, the senator has to be sacrificed so the rest of us can live.

One life in exchange for thirteen—or fourteen, if she forgave her father and didn't leave him behind to deal with the inevitable fallout from their disappearance.

55

ASSASSINATION

Senator Barbara Woodran's Family Ranch
East of Provo, Utah

Axe pulled the toggles to flare the parachute, bringing them in for a silent landing on a flat, dark patch of dirt on the far side of a barn to shield them from view of the house.

I wonder if either the good guys, the bad guys, or both saw us.

He unclipped Haley's harness from his and watched as she moved forward, drew her compact pistol, and took a knee, covering one-hundred-eight degrees in front of them along with frequent glances to their rear.

We better have chosen correctly. If we come under fire now, she's not hitting much at a distance with that tiny thing, no matter how good of a shot she's gotten to be.

Axe gathered his parachute quickly while Nalen did the same nearby, stuffing them into large backpacks brought for the purpose. They'd take them along if possible, to avoid them being traced back to Martini if the mission went south.

Their other gear went into the packs as well, including the jump-suits. Then Axe and Nalen covered three-hundred-sixty degrees while Haley stripped off her gear, revealing the all-black tactical outfit matching his.

He slung the pack on his back, readied his M4, and signaled Nalen and

Haley. They had figured any assault from Russian agents—whether actual Russians or American sleeper agents with combat training—would come from the rear of the sprawling ranch house. A meandering, rocky wash ended at a small bunch of trees two hundred yards from the back porch. Landing to the side, hidden by the long, wide barn far from the house, they had hopefully remained hidden.

If tonight is even the night and people are out there waiting to strike.

Before planning the op, Haley had risked drawing her coworkers further into danger, contacting them to find out whether Senator Woodran's schedule was publicly or privately available. They had used their magic analysis abilities to report a high conviction of the entire family being at a concert in Provo—except for Woodran, who would be home.

Tonight's the night. I don't know how Haley's team discovered the data, but if they could do it, so could the opposition.

Much of the senator's small security detail would be with the extended family, he guessed. Woodran wouldn't want them unprotected in this dangerous day and age. A large gathering of her family would be too juicy of a target for those wishing to protest some of her stances. She was one of the last true independents, holding firm beliefs which didn't conform to either side's specific policy or agenda. Many of her constituents loved her for it, but some on both sides of the aisle hated her with a passion bordering on pathological.

As planned, Axe silently moved toward the rear of the property, angling to approach the wash from the side in a flanking maneuver.

Nalen and Haley angled off to the right. The CAG team had predicted the senator would be in her study on the southwest corner of the house, near the front. That room's window was lit, attesting to their accuracy. Nalen and Haley would either get Woodran's attention through the window or access the house from the front door while Axe took out any assaulters in back.

With luck and timing, the suspected security guard—Leo Porter— would be near the back to let in the assaulters, not in or near the senator's office.

Axe moved silently through the semi-arid landscape dotted with large bushes. A narrow wash, more a small ditch, ran west to east. He stepped

carefully down the crumbly dirt slope. The large backpack with the parachute and gear hindered him. A few pebbles trickled down, causing him to
go stock still.

Damn it. Did anyone hear?

Nothing moved. After thirty seconds, Axe edged forward more slowly,
trading speed for stealth. He crouched to stay below the lip of the ditch
and moved forward at quarter speed.

I wish I had my night-vision goggles.

The waning moon provided only enough light to see a few feet in front
of him while in the open, but less here in the ditch, surrounded by small
trees.

*A plate carrier and armor would be nice going into a potential
gunfight, as well.*

Without them and their protection, he felt naked. Vulnerable.

After several more steps, he neared the wider north-south wash where
he suspected the enemy would stage until given the go sign by the sleeper
agent.

Two men? Four? How many would Russia risk on this assignment?

His senses tingled with danger. Instinctively, he pivoted, turning back
the way he'd come.

A dark figure stood right in front of him, its knife coming at his throat.
He leaned left without thinking, the point of the blade nicking the side of
his neck instead of plunging into his larynx.

Axe shoved the M4 at the face of his attacker, landing a lucky,
glancing blow on their face, causing them to take a step back. A follow-up
with the butt of the rifle sent the person to the ground and gave Axe a
second to let the rifle drop on its sling. He reached behind him, drawing
his fixed blade knife from its horizontally mounted sheath.

Axe thrust the knife at the man's throat as he scrambled to his feet.
The man deflected the blade to the side with his arm. Then Axe had to
draw his stomach in and lean back to avoid a return stab at his midsection.

Slashing at the attacker, Axe connected with the man's shoulder,
causing him to gasp, a soft, surprised sound in the dark.

That's not a man—it's a woman.

Axe hesitated.

Women can be warriors. Look at Haley.

The instant of thought cost him. The woman was undertrained but
lightning fast. Her speed enabled her to lash out with her left fist,
connecting with his cheek. The punch came unseen in the darkness, not

sensed until the last second when he angled his head to soften the blow. If he hadn't, the punch may have knocked him out, making him easy to finish off.

He fell back a step, then another, leading his opponent. Letting her think she had the upper hand.

Axe could only see well enough to make out her slim shape in the dark.

One more step.

He moved backward, then gasped and let his rear leg lower as if he had twisted his ankle.

The woman fell for his trap, believing he was suddenly vulnerable, and sprang forward faster than Axe expected. He barely had time to raise the knife, which plunged into her stomach instead of upward into her heart as he intended.

She gasped again and swung her knife arm at him, but Axe caught her wrist and overpowered her. They stood frozen, face to face, the woman's eyes close enough now to see the white of fear and pain.

"It's not fatal," he whispered in her ear. "Surrender. Confess. Help us get the other sleeper agents. We'll get you fixed up and protect you."

She didn't fight him, but didn't give in, either.

Axe's instincts saved him again. One instant, he waited for her answer. The next, he spun their bodies, controlling the woman with his arm and knife. Something made him do it, a sense far from conscious thought.

The woman cried out and sagged against him. Behind her, Axe saw the dim outline of another attacker as they removed the knife from the woman's back with a wet, sucking sound.

He shoved the woman back into the second assailant, who reacted as expected by catching their comrade and lowering her to the ground instead of letting the body drop on its own, which would have been the smarter tactical move.

Taking a risk, Axe grabbed the rifle hanging from its sling and swung it up, stepping backward to create distance between him and the attackers. He got his finger on the trigger and sent two bullets into the chest of the rising second attacker. He stopped, avoiding the kill shot to the head as they staggered backward.

The unmistakable sound of the rifle rang through the night.

If it's a team of four, instead of two, I just gave away my position—and all surprise.

Keeping the gun up, Axe stepped forward and kicked the attacker in the chest, right where they had taken two shots in what he guessed was an armor plate.

He—or she—grunted in pain and fell over, landing hard on their back. Axe fell on them, flipped her—he realized—over, and took a zip tie from his cargo pants pocket, securing her wrists.

Yes, she's wearing a plate carrier, so she's not badly injured. Couple of broken ribs, maybe.

He put a knee on her back and put his weight on it, getting a moan of pain from the woman.

"How many attackers?"

"Stop!" she gasped. "My ribs."

He leaned with more of his weight, slowly adding pressure.

"Okay!" she cried. "Just the two of us." Axe eased off. "Is she okay?" the woman asked.

The first attacker lay flat on her back, hard to make out in the dark, but unmoving, his knife still sticking out of her stomach. "I don't know. She's not moving."

"Did you kill her or did I?" Her voice was filled with anguish. "You spun so fast," she said, holding back a sob.

"Doesn't matter. Why are you here?"

"I want my lawyer."

All Axe had to do was lean forward, starting slowly, putting more and more weight on his knee in the middle of the woman's back. "Do you see any lawyers out here?"

"You can't—" she gasped. "I'm a cop!"

What?

He immediately shifted his weight off her.

Have I made a terrible mistake?

Senator Barbara Woodran knew the sound of gunfire when she heard it. Growing up in the west, her entire family, boys and girls, learned to safely handle firearms at an early age. She was already an expert shot by her tenth birthday when she received a hunting rifle and a cleaning kit.

She sat in her study, working on priorities for her next term in the Senate, putting in the long hours she was famous for while her extended family enjoyed a classical music concert in Provo, an hour away.

Calmly setting down her pen, she opened the bottom right desk drawer and punched her code into the small gun safe. The gas strut feature allowed her to slide her hand in and quickly pull out the gun as she watched the knob on her office door slowly turn.

Leo Porter hesitated at the senator's door, his hand on the knob.

What the hell happened to the plan, and why was there shooting out back, twenty minutes before go time?

His nerves were frayed. They had been for a week, since Christmas morning when his dad pulled him aside after breakfast and opening presents with the kids.

"Son," he said, his face grave and pained. "We have to talk."

Fun conversations never started with those words, and the following chat was anything but enjoyable. It had been devastating, in fact.

Over the course of the thirty-minute story, he learned his father and grandfather were Russian sleeper agents—and he was expected to be, too.

"We were told not to tell you, until now, for your protection. With all the background checks and lie detector tests, the decision was made to keep the truth from you. But now is the time, and it is your duty, your honor, to do what must be done."

Leo had reasoned with the man who, until that morning, he had thought he knew. Then he argued. Finally, he flatly refused but said he wouldn't report his father to the authorities as long as they never discussed it again, and nothing further was ever asked of him.

With tears rolling down his cheeks, his father informed him of the devastating threat hanging over their heads. They stood in the doorway between the kitchen and the family room, watching the kids—both his and those of his two sisters—play with their recently opened presents, their dream-come-true Christmas.

"They will kill the children if you don't agree," his father whispered.

First one sister looked up, then the other—both patrol officers for the Salt Lake City Police Department. They, like him, had been strongly encouraged, and even, he could see now, pushed toward careers in law enforcement. They met his eyes. He could see their mixed feelings. Fear. Rage. And, ultimately, resignation.

The seven kids—five his, one each so far for the sisters—laughed and played near the Christmas tree, their fathers on the floor with them, along with Leo's wife, all playing happily together. The dream of Christmas, realized.

"What do I have to do?" he had asked his father.

Standing with his hand on the doorknob to the senator's office, ready to finish turning it, opening the door, and shooting her, he fought with himself, weighing the lives of the children versus the senator's.

I don't know if I can go through with this.

His sisters were supposed to do the actual killing, out of his sight. They would sneak in through the door in the back he unlocked for them. One of them—he hadn't been told which—would burst into the room, surprising Woodran, and shoot her.

Before leaving, one of them would shoot him in his bullet-proof vest and his shoulder or arm, which he wasn't looking forward to.

He'd be a wounded hero, shot while defending the senator from an overwhelming force.

The senator would be dead.

And they'd all get away with it.

The children would be safe.

At least until the next time he was ordered to do Russia's bidding.

Now, the unmistakable sound of rifle fire from his sisters' position meant the plan had gone horribly wrong. The ladies carried only knives and pistols, confiscated from criminals and not logged into evidence. No rifles.

His hand trembled, wondering how to get out of the trap he found himself in, set up a hundred years before by his long-dead grandfather.

As soon as Haley and Nalen heard the M4 from behind the house, they gave up on stealth. Their fear had been the timing of the operation. When would the sleeper agents attack? Or would the guard on security detail act beforehand, killing Senator Woodran before their arrival?

"Back door!" she whispered to Nalen, leaving him behind as she sprinted toward the back of the house. He would continue with the original plan of trying the front approach.

She wanted to run to assist Axe but held back. Axe could handle himself.

Bounding up wooden steps, she flew across the large wrap-around porch, small 9mm pistol drawn and ready to face whatever army awaited her.

I hope the gunshots gave Woodran a warning.

Leo finished turning the knob and opened the door, bringing up his gun. He had to kill her. The lives of his children depended on it.

The senator sat at her desk, directly in front of the door, facing him, her eyes catching his as the door swung open.

"I'm sorry," he said as he lined up the shot.

Barbara had earned her vaulted position of power by being both smart and intuitive. She'd kept her seat in the Senate for so many years by being ruthless and fast. Once she reached a decision, she took action.

Porter had been acting strangely since his brief Christmas vacation. Usually focused yet easygoing, he seemed stressed and distracted. Between the gunfire outside and the knob turning—without even a knock, she put the pieces together.

Someone is coming to kill me, and it's probably Leo Porter.

She didn't know why, nor did she particularly care. Her state had its share of crazies from across the political spectrum. As a fiercely independent senator who voted with the other side as often as she voted with her own party, plenty of people protested her campaign events, public speeches, and recently had harassed her family. She supported free speech —the First Amendment to the Constitution. Hell, she occasionally paused her events and brought the protesters on stage with her for impromptu debates. She wasn't afraid of dissension or frank discussion and usually kicked butt, making a mockery of those who wished to argue with her in front of a crowd.

She believed just as strongly in the Second Amendment. Sure, there were good reasons for gun control, and she'd crossed the lines to vote some of them into law. However, so long as the law allowed her to have one, she'd carry a gun wherever legal to do so.

Like in her home, swinging the barrel up at her formerly trusted security guard.

She put three bullets into him, starting at center mass and walking them up, well aware of the bulletproof vest he wore under his shirt and suit coat.

The last bullet hit him in the mouth, rocking his head back, but not before one of his slammed into her.

56

FAIL SAFE

Senator Barbara Woodran's Family Ranch
East of Provo, Utah

The handler—Constantine—heard four shots from the house. From his vantage point on the hill, he had a clear view of the house and garage.

He aimed the night vision scope on the hunting rifle at the senator's office window but couldn't see in because of the closed curtains.

Why shoot her four times? Constantine wondered.

Something was wrong.

He scanned the area in front of him through the scope's narrow field of vision.

It's a good thing I'm here. I guess the higher-ups know what they're doing after all.

He wasn't happy with his role as fail-safe—the backup plan in case it all went wrong. But his boss had a point. The brother and two sisters could easily decide to back out of their duty. Or fail. Either way, he had to be here, laying in place all day, since the early morning darkness, to make sure the family killed the senator—or he would do it if they didn't.

A glorified babysitter—and I don't relish having to kill the kids if the parents rebel.

Constantine would have no trouble killing the senator if he had to. The things she'd said about his family's home country made his blood boil.

But it would be better if the assassination happened as planned. Leo would place the blame on an extremist group and maintain his cover. He would be useful again in the future.

Continuing his scan of the area around the house, he tried to put aside his annoyance and focus on the task at hand. He had much more essential duties to attend to. Another senator's death wouldn't change the fate of the operation as much as the Las Vegas attack's big reveal. He should be back there, ready to leak the story about Baranov Brand beer's role in the previous night's death and destruction, timing it perfectly for the biggest impact. Then he'd spin conspiracy theories to his many blogging contacts: the president knew and approved of Victor Baranov's plan; the president was a Russian spy himself; Russia had warned the president ahead of time but was ignored; the same drug was in the nation's water supply. He had a notebook filled with conspiracy theories to get the bloggers started.

I can't imagine how awkward it will be for President Heringten to realize the man responsible for the mayhem spent last night in the Lincoln Bedroom.

His east-coast counterpart would handle the extraction of Baranov to Russia, but it would be up to Constantine to decide what to do with Nicholas Baranov.

Victor will play along and I won't have to do a thing. I can leave Victor's son in place as leverage.

When Constantine heard the shots from the wash moments before, he'd been pleased. One sister, he guessed, had gotten cold feet. But the other must have shot her.

The family that kills together, stays together.

Then he'd seen the older man with the perfect posture hammering on the front door, trying to force his way in.

Where had he come from… and is he alone?

Constantine had graduated from third-generation sleeper spy to managing the entire western United States, proving himself over the years with his complete lack of morals. So while he'd rather be in a comped hotel suite at a casino, enjoying champagne while watching Las Vegas burn out the windows, he'd do as ordered and make sure the rest of the family didn't have a change of heart as, apparently, the one sister had.

In a few moments, all will be revealed. Either I'll get the all-clear signal from Leo, or I'll go in there and clean up myself.

Axe had heard four shots as he moved carefully up the hill.

The senator must have been hit. Or, God forbid, Hammer or Blondie.

He moved quietly, but not silently. He had too much ground to cover and not enough time to do it. Hopefully, flanking the position kept him out of the line of sight of his enemy.

He'd slow and move more quietly on the final approach.

The female officer he'd shot, hogtied in the gulley far behind him, had admitted her sister and she were the only two outside attackers. Inside, her brother—Leo Porter, the guard—would grab the senator. The sisters would kill her, then injure him so he could be a hero despite failing to protect Woodran.

Exactly as we figured, and not a bad plan.

Except for the three attackers being relatives. What if they wanted to rebel, tried to turn themselves in and confess?

I would have an extra person here as backup.

Axe started up the slight rise in elevation, which could barely be called a hill, stepping more carefully now.

Always trust your gut.

There were two good overwatch positions with views of the approach to the rear of the house, the side where they guessed the senator's office was, and the front. With complete surprise likely, there would be no reason to choose the lesser position. He'd go for the best view and angle, so it's the one he stalked.

He wanted to hurry, but he couldn't risk it. Near the top of the rise, he dropped to his stomach. He wouldn't be as quiet approaching at a crawl, but it afforded better protection in case there were two people on overwatch—a sniper and a spotter who doubled as security.

With infinite patience, Axe raised his head bit by bit until he could see the flat area of the hilltop.

Nothing. Scrub brush, two bushes, and several medium-sized rocks.

He'd guessed wrong.

Are they on the other rise?

While his eyes had finally adjusted to the night, he couldn't see the other hill well, but it looked the same as this one. No one lay exposed and ready to shoot up the house.

Next time, I don't leave for a mission without NVGs.

Did he have time to approach the other rise to be sure? From this higher elevation, he'd be fully exposed if he did.

I'd have to crawl the whole way.

He didn't have time.

Where else could they be?

Axe examined the front of the hill he lay on. Maybe he, or they, had set up closer to the house.

Not a damn thing.

Except... his intuition tingled.

What did I miss?

He looked closer, starting lower down the hill, taking more time to examine the ground. In the dark, it was nearly impossible, but he took the extra seconds, tracking up the hill.

Finally, he had it. The tiniest movement from a chunky, low-profile rock.

Rocks don't wiggle.

57

CONFRONTATION

Senator Barbara Woodran's Family Ranch
East of Provo, Utah

Disregarding her own safety, Haley sprinted through the huge country kitchen, past a granite island larger than her spare bedroom. The pistol fire had come from the front of the house. Two guns, four shots.

Are we too late?

A loud noise came from the front door.

Hammer trying to gain entry.

Luckily for her, the back door had been unlocked.

Haley slowed as she came around the corner, seeing a man lying on the ground with his face a bloody mess, in a white dress shirt, simple black tie, and black suit coat. The door to the room in front of him was open. She advanced, quietly now, gun up, aware of how stupid it was to rush into the house without clearing it first.

Is there more than one?

The other gunshots had come from somebody.

To assess the situation, all she had to do was stick her head around the doorframe. Haley had watched Axe do it enough.

Whoever is in there might have heard me tearing through the house.

Movement drew the eye, so she crouched low and slowly eased around the edge of the door.

Immediately, the frame exploded an inch above her head. She flopped backward, landing ungracefully on her rear.

Another shot from within the room sent a bullet through the drywall four inches in front of her face, making her scamper backward, crab walking faster than she thought possible.

The pounding continued from the front door. Hammer was having trouble getting in.

To clear the senator's office without getting killed, I need Hammer's help.

No other shots came her way, but she kept low until she reached the kitchen. She stood, veered left through the family room, and took a second hallway to the front door.

Now, as long as Hammer doesn't shoot me, too...

Haley stood as far to the side of the door as she could and reached her long arm to the frame. Using her knuckles, she delivered four quiet, fast raps. *Knock Knock Knock Knock.*

Will he get that it's Morse Code for 'H'?

A second later, soft knocks answered her.

A... M...

Hammer.

She unlocked the deadbolt and the lock on the knob, opening the door to Nalen. He stood with his pistol ready, not exactly pointing at her, but close enough to shoot if it had been a trap.

Haley pointed to the left hallway and signed, holding up one finger, then drawing it across her throat, signaling one person dead. Holding up a second finger, she shrugged, then made a pistol shape with her left hand and pulled the imaginary trigger.

Nalen pointed at her hair with raised eyebrows, communicating Senator Woodran's famous white hair bleached bright blond. Haley shrugged. Turning, she led the way, with Nalen right behind her.

Several silent steps brought them to the side of the open door to the Senator's office. Haley went low, pointing at the bullet hole in the drywall on the other side of the door. Nalen nodded and stepped back several paces, then went low himself.

"Senator Woodran, friendlies out here, don't shoot!" Hammer called in his command voice.

"You come anywhere near the door, and you'll die like your buddy, whoever you are," Woodran called from inside the room.

From her position on the hardwood floor, Haley caught the strain in the woman's voice.

She sounds like she's hurt—but trying to cover it up.

"Senator, it's retired Admiral William Nalen. We met once at a gala several years ago. Do you remember me?"

"Of course I remember Admiral Nalen. I'm old, not senile. But how do I know you're him, and what would you be doing here, anyway?"

"We had intel from Haley Albright you were in danger. You know the name?"

"I know the young woman by name and reputation only. But again, how am I to know you're not a follow-on force to take me out? Names are easy to come by."

Haley looked over her shoulder at Hammer, who nodded at her. "Um, hello senator. Nice to meet you. I'm Haley Albright. Uncle J—I mean, the president speaks highly of you."

I wonder if she knows about my relationship to the president.

"Hmph. Well, let me think about this for a second." The woman paused for a few seconds, an eternity to Haley laying on the floor, wondering if Axe was safe, or if more assaulters were on their way to kill them all.

"Okay, here's what we're going to do. Nalen, if it is you, I'll know your face. Lead with your hands through the doorway, slowly, then the rest of you. But if you're not Nalen, better think of a different approach. I've already reloaded and have plenty more treats for any tricks you try."

"Yes, senator. I have a pistol but I'm holstering it." The gun went to his waist, and he walked slowly the few steps to the door. "Hands coming into view now." He eased his hands into the open space. "Okay so far?"

"Keep coming."

Definitely pain in her voice, and she's weakening, too.

"I'm going to push this guy a little so I can step forward." Hammer used his leg to nudge the dead guard a few inches to the side, careful to not stand in the spreading pool of blood, then stepped into the doorway.

The pain made it hard for Barbara to hold the gun steady, but she wouldn't let her guard down now. She tracked the body of the man as he came into view.

Well, I'll be. It is the admiral.

A few years older, but just as fit and serious looking. Black jeans and a long-sleeve black t-shirt instead of his dress uniform, but she recognized him easily.

"You truly here to save me?" she asked, the gun wavering slightly, but on target.

"I am, ma'am. A little late, it looks like. Haley is here, in the hallway, and we have one man outside. It sounded like he fired upon whoever else this guy had coming for you."

Barbara had a decision to make. Trust him, shoot him, or hold out for help from someone she knew better, which might be a few hours.

I'm not going to make it that long.

The lucky gunshot from Porter had hit her chest on the left side.

Missed my heart. Or where my heart should have been, if I had one, as my critics would say.

Nalen had a stellar reputation from decades of service.

But then again, so had Porter. Not as many years, but still, never a hint of betrayal.

Until he tried to kill me.

She made up her mind.

"Fine," she said, lowering the gun. "If you're here to save me, let's get a move on. I'm in trouble here."

58

MANAGERS

From the side of the house, one of the three garage doors opened. Axe watched the big SUV back out fast, angling hard left, knocking down a wooden trellis as it slammed to a stop at the front porch.

Has to be Hammer or Blondie driving. Looks like they're evacuating the wounded.

The sniper laying disguised in front of Axe would shoot whoever came out.

The unmistakable figure of Haley got out of the truck and ran toward the front door. Axe only had a few more seconds.

The house phone line was down—disabled by the guard, Hammer guessed —and he had no cellular reception out here in the boonies. So he carried Senator Woodran in his arms, carefully edging into the hallway, stepping over the dead guard. The woman was a big-boned Western woman, through and through. While not overweight, she was heavy enough that Nalen gave thanks for all the predawn workouts.

The last few years he'd felt like a fraud, getting up at 04:15, grabbing a mug of coffee, and hitting his home gym in the basement by 04:30 every morning. No exceptions. A man his age, in his sixties, eating salads for dinner with skinless grilled chicken. Avoiding pasta, rice, and other carbs except on special occasions. Working out as if he had asses to kick like back in the good old days. When he was, at most, a handler of Haley and Axe. He provided logistics, advice, and support, not operational assistance.

He was a manager. Not an asset—not even close. So why the zero-dark-thirty weight sessions? The five-mile runs outside, whether it was ten degrees or ninety?

Hammer cradled the injured woman, hurrying toward the front door but being careful not to bump her head against the hallway wall.

This is why I do it, Hammer thought. *Because you never know when the training will pay off. Maybe never, true. But tonight makes it all worth it.*

"You said it would hurt, Admiral, but not this much," Senator Woodran gasped in his arms. The small first aid kit in the bathroom off the senator's office had supplies, which he'd used to dress the wound, but no morphine or other decent pain killers. She'd have to endure until they got her to a hospital.

"Please, senator, call me William," he said, as Haley came through the front door to help.

"If I call you William, you have to call me Barbara. Deal?"

"Deal."

"And William?"

"Yes, Barbara?"

"You get me through this alive and I'm buying you the best steak you've ever eaten. No, wait. I'm making you the best steak you ever had. Understand?"

He had to smile.

I'd like that.

"It's a date."

Constantine slowed his breathing, preparing to take the shots. He had an excellent position, was well within range, and wouldn't hesitate to kill.

I don't know what's gone wrong, he thought. *I don't know who the hell the man at the front door or the woman in the senator's SUV are. But whoever comes out of the house is going to die.*

He could salvage this.

I have to.

Somewhere, there might be a man like himself, doing the same job. Ready to kill Constantine's family if he should fail.

Axe prepared to launch himself, silently drawing his knife.

I'd like to take him alive. A dead Russian asset with a rifle outside the senator's house is one thing. A live one with operational intelligence would be even better.

Out of the corner of his eye, a shadow appeared in the open front door of the house as a person neared the opening.

No time. I can't risk anyone getting shot—including me.

Axe dropped his knife and rose, swinging the rifle from his back, where he'd had it while he crawled.

The noise drew the attention of the lump pretending to be a rock, which rolled, revealing a man with a long barrel rifle.

Constantine was so focused on the front porch of the house, he'd let his situational awareness slip. But when he heard the crunch of rock behind him, he knew instantly what it was.

I've been outflanked. The people in the house have to wait. I can't kill anyone there if I'm dead.

He rolled to his side, desperately swinging the long gun around at the man in black bringing his rifle to bear.

It was going to be close.

Axe's finger found the trigger and he fired first, the short barrel M4 on target faster than the enemy's longer rifle. Two to the chest, one to the head, as he'd been taught.

He scrambled to the still figure, dressed from head to toe in a desert camouflage sniper ghillie suit.

Dead. Not ideal, but I couldn't take any chances. Not with a gun swinging toward me.

Down at the house, the truck doors slammed. The SUV accelerated, its tires churning up the desert landscaping as it flew across the yard and onto the long driveway.

59

TIME

Haley drove, expertly handling the large SUV.

Hammer had the senator in the backseat, half on his lap. "Turn east onto the highway," the senator told Haley.

Haley glanced back. Hammer was putting pressure on Woodran's wound, doing what he could to reduce the bleeding. "Go straight thirty minutes," the senator added. "You'll see the red cross for the emergency room." Her voice sounded fainter with every word.

"Haley," Hammer said, catching her eye in the rear-view mirror. "We don't have thirty minutes."

"On it," she told him.

The SUV was the same make and model as hers, only a few years older.

The road ahead was straight. She couldn't see the town—there were small rolling hills in the way—but a glow of light far in the distance had to be it.

Let's see what this thing can do.

"Buckle up, Hammer. We're going to make it or die trying."

The powerful engine growled as she quickly pushed past sixty, seventy, and eighty. On the dark, deserted road, it felt like they were standing still.

Thirty miles at sixty miles per hour is thirty minutes. At one-twenty, that's fifteen minutes. Plus time to accelerate and decelerate…

"How's she doing?" Haley asked.

"She's lost a lot of blood. I stopped it as best I could, but…" Hammer trailed off, his voice tight with concern.

Haley gripped the steering wheel tighter and pushed the big vehicle to one-thirty.

How fast can we go—safely?

At one forty, she started sweating despite the cold of the truck.

If there's a deer or coyote on the road, we're dead.

The SUV shook at one-fifty. Haley eased off. One-forty-five felt reasonable in comparison.

The lights of the town brightened as they sped toward them. After a few minutes, she could see a large glowing red cross far in the distance.

Hammer's hand was covered in the senator's blood.

"Just in case I don't make it, William," Barbara whispered to him, briefly conscious again. "Thank you for coming to my rescue. My knight in shining armor. I used to think it was all bullshit, but tonight… It felt good." She smiled at him. "Don't you dare repeat that, though."

"You got it. Hang in there. We're getting close."

He pulled his phone from his pocket. The screen showed it still searching for a signal. They weren't close enough for cell coverage yet.

Come on, come on.

After several more seconds, it locked on and was ready. He dialed.

"9-1-1, what is your emergency?"

"This is Admiral William Nalen, US Navy. I have Senator Barbara Woodran. She has been shot and is in critical condition. We are approaching the hospital in Roosevelt, Utah. They need to meet us at the door with a full crash cart. She's lost a lot of blood and I believe the bullet is still in her left upper chest. How copy?" he added, falling back to his days in the field.

The operator must have been a veteran herself or had seen movies. "Solid copy. Hold the line, Admiral, I'm alerting the hospital now." She paused but didn't put him on hold.

Must have some type of written alert system.

"What's your location, Admiral?"

He held the phone against his chest. "How long?" he asked Haley.

"We're doing one-forty-five and it's eight miles. You do the math. I'm busy," Haley said, focused on the road.

"We're coming fast on the highway from the west," he said into the phone. "Less than four minutes."

"I've scrambled the emergency room. They'll be ready for you at the ambulance entrance. Do you know where that is?"

"No. Send traffic."

"You can't miss it. Second left into the hospital. There's a sign."

"Copy second left."

"Wait one," he said, then held the phone against his chest again.

"You'll drop us off, then pull forward," he told Haley. "Not fast, not slow. It'll be natural to get the truck out of the ambulance area. Then you keep going. Normal speed."

"I'm coming in with you," Haley said.

"Blondie," he said in his command tone, "you'll do as I say without giving me any shit."

He waited for a long few seconds.

She's headstrong and has never served in the military. Will she follow orders? Can she?

"Yes, Hammer," she answered finally. "Pull forward, keep going. Where?"

"Back to the ranch. Pick up Axe. Leave the dead guard in place. Then get the hell out of there. Provo or Salt Lake. Wipe down the truck, leave it in long-term parking in a garage or the airport. Text me its location when you can. Then disappear."

"What about you?"

"If she pulls through, I'm fine. She'll vouch for me, but I'll need to run cover on the investigation."

"If she doesn't make it?"

"Then there will be a hell of a lot of questions. We can't all get bogged down. You and Axe figure this out and finish it."

"We have no idea—"

"Finish it. And Blondie—the gloves are off. We have proof someone tried to kill a United States senator tonight. I don't care who's behind it. You find them, and the rest of the plot, and you put an end to it. By any means necessary. Are we clear, young lady?"

He'd never spoken like that to her. Hell, he hadn't spoken that way to anyone in years. Decades. But he still had the edge, could still project his authority. And if there was time to use what he'd learned over those long years of service, it was now.

Someone is going to pay for this.

Haley couldn't risk taking her eyes off the road, but she desperately wanted to catch Hammer's eyes in the mirror and make sure she understood what he meant.

Any means necessary, she thought.

The phrase stirred her resolve.

No matter how difficult or dangerous, Axe and I will get it done.

"Copy that, Hammer," she said.

A mile ahead, red and blue lights lit up the night as a police cruiser pulled in front of them and accelerated, its siren wailing. An escort, trying to help, but Haley wouldn't slow down for them.

She felt foolish following the rules of the road while driving so fast, but she signaled left and moved into the oncoming lane. They passed the police cruiser like it was standing still.

A few miles later, she let her foot off the gas but didn't brake.

When this is over, besides skydiving, I have to take a tactical driving course. But for now, I hope this works.

The hospital entrance loomed. Haley took the corner too fast. For a second, the heavy SUV tipped onto two wheels. She didn't know whether to fight it or hold on, but it felt better to do something, anything, so she coaxed the steering wheel to the side.

The truck landed heavily back on its left tires and sped, much too fast, toward the doors of the covered ambulance entrance.

"Hold on," she called as she slammed on the brakes.

The truck's anti-lock system kicked in, bringing them to a shuddering halt perfectly in line with the entrance doors.

Doctors and nurses swarmed the backseat. Hammer gently handed the limp body of Senator Woodran to them and slid out the back. They set her on a gurney and sprinted inside.

"Nalen, United States Navy," Nalen called to a heavyset local police officer standing near the door, looking dumbstruck and frozen. "I need security set up around the hospital. Right now. Police, guards, whatever you have. Do it. The senator's protection is your responsibility."

It was the last she heard as he closed the SUV's door.

Haley pulled forward. No one thought to tell her to stay put.

She swung around the drop-off area, turned left onto a side street, then right when she reached the highway. The police escort finally pulled into the ambulance area to her left, not noticing her as she turned.

Instead of pushing the truck, she sped up normally, settling on sixty-five miles per hour. The great speed difference from before made it feel like she was moving in slow motion.

She thought through Hammer's orders and started making plans.

Pick up Axe. Dump the truck. Go… somewhere. Rent a car and drive back to Vegas? Hole up in a hotel?

They needed to be invisible, off the grid, in case Woodran didn't pull through. Either way, Hammer faced tough questions about what happened, but with her dead, it would be much worse. How had he ended up at the senator's ranch without a vehicle—and why? Had he shot her along with the dead guard? And the third question—did he do it alone, or with accomplices?

More importantly, though, we have to get ahead of this. The Russians are behind it. I have no doubt, but others would surely question the intel, especially such an explosive accusation.

If she had more proof, or could convince people about what she believed true, assassinating senators would require more than mere economic sanctions.

Uncle Jimmy would start a war, and Congress would be right behind him declaring one.

But what if the Russians wanted a war? Did they think they could win?

This could be bigger than we know.

There was no way to predict or prevent what else the Russians had planned.

We've been behind the curve the entire time. Reacting to their moves, not making our own.

A Sun Tzu quote came to mind from the book Axe had given her. "One mark of a great soldier is that he fights on his own terms or fights not at all."

And another. "He who is prudent and lies in wait for an enemy who is not, will be victorious."

On his own terms… Lies in wait…

Her mind sped through scenarios as if she were playing chess against a Grandmaster, which, in a way, she was. Thirty minutes later, as she turned from the highway onto the senator's meandering gravel driveway, she had her answer.

We're going to take the fight to them.

The way to stop this wasn't to pick off the sleeper agents in the government and private industry one by one.

They had to take care of the problem at the source.

60

CAUGHT

"Just so I'm clear," Gregory began, resisting the urge to pace. Instead, he walked to the conference room's large monitor. Nancy's impressive spreadsheet occupied one half of the screen. Dave's list of reasons his theory made sense versus reasons to discount it took up the right side. "You two believe—"

"And Haley," Nancy threw in, interrupting him.

She knows I've grown to trust Haley's wild hunches, Gregory thought.

"The three of you believe," he tried again. "Wait. Let's start with the big picture first. One, our government and essential private industries have been infiltrated by Russian sleeper agents. They are second-, third-, and possibly fourth-generation Russian Americans who are indebted to Russia via family ties and duty."

He looked at them for confirmation. They both nodded.

"Two, Victor Baranov, owner of Baranov Brands, is one of these sleeper agents. He orchestrated the riots in Las Vegas last night. Which, in fact, weren't riots, but innocent people drugged against their knowledge after drinking spiked beer courtesy Baranov Brands."

Once again, Dave and Nancy nodded.

If this is true, the entire country is in trouble.

Gregory's logical, practical side kicked in, willing—for a moment—to accept the possibility the information his two senior analysts had provided him was true.

The search for the sleeper agents alone will cause chaos.

Suspicion of a person because of their family origins would cause an uproar.

It's not what America is about.

It would be extremely damaging to the country.

Countless innocent people would undoubtedly be wrongly accused. Who had done what? How many were true sleepers, as yet unactivated? How many had already helped the Russians?

They would have to pursue the search, no matter the costs.

What about my department—can I trust all my people?

"Sir?" Nancy said, taking him away from considering that awful question.

"Sorry, I got sidetracked. Three, Haley is off-grid? You haven't heard from her in…"

"Since last night. New Year's Eve—no, wait," Nancy said, stopping. "It was this morning, sorry. I've been here nearly non-stop for days and they run together."

She pulled out her phone and clicked on it.

"Please tell me you have a secure way of communicating—that the NSA isn't tracking all this."

Nancy held up the phone. "Secure comms app." Another click brought her to where she wanted. "Late this morning our time, she wanted to know Utah Senator Barbara Woodran's schedule for today and tonight."

Gregory stared at her, unsure what to ask, or whether he wanted to know.

She shrugged. "Of course I gave it to her. She's Haley!"

Dave clicked on his laptop. He gasped, his eyes shooting to Gregory before quickly returning to his screen.

"According to Homeland Security, Senator Woodran has just been admitted to a small hospital near her home in Utah." He gulped, glanced at Gregory again, and said, "She's been shot in the chest."

Dave and Nancy shared a look.

Are they thinking what I am? It couldn't be Haley's doing… right?

"Find out more," he told Dave. To Nancy, he said, "Where is Baranov tonight? Right now?"

She searched much longer than he'd expected.

"He's gone, sir. He flew first-class from Las Vegas to Washington D.C. Friday. His name was on the guest list for the White House New Year's Eve party, but he didn't attend. I find no record of a hotel reservation or a flight back to Vegas—or any other destination."

People as rich as him can disappear much easier than the average Joe.

"Access TSA footage from the airport. Track his movement from deplaning to leaving the airport grounds."

"Senator Woodran is in surgery," Dave announced. "Critical condition, but an initial assessment looked cautiously optimistic. She lost a lot of blood, and they have to remove the bullet. Local police have locked down the hospital."

On the outside, Gregory kept his face neutral out of long habit. No need for Nancy and Dave to see how he truly felt.

Inside, his pulse raced with a dizzying mix of emotions. One second, he feared for his career. He didn't know the exact brief of Haley's super-secret NHA, as she called it. But he wondered about the legality of her and Axe, her retired SEAL teammate, doing whatever they were up to.

Haley wouldn't harm a United States senator.

He caught himself. The thought wasn't completely accurate.

If Haley wanted to harm the senator, the woman wouldn't be in the hospital with a gunshot wound. She'd be dead. No question.

Another feeling surfaced, stronger than the fear of losing his job and pension.

I believe in her.

When she first started working for him, he'd doubted her, to his detriment. She'd been right at every turn. In her time at the CAG, she'd correctly called the ambush a team of SEALs walked into, then prevented New York City from becoming a radioactive wasteland. She'd also figured out Stefan Conroy's plot to destroy the world.

While he had helped last time, had he done enough?

"Oh, no," Nancy whispered.

"What?"

She shook her head and refused to look at him.

"Put it on the main screen, please," Gregory said, speaking gently to his distraught analyst. He would do everything in his power to help Haley this time. No holding back. If it cost him, so be it.

"No," Nancy said.

"Excuse me?"

"I... She...." Nancy said. "Sir, there has to be a reasonable explanation."

He walked behind her to view the laptop screen. Dave joined him.

She childishly tried to cover the computer with her hands.

"Nancy, come on," Gregory coaxed. "We can help her. Let me see."

She reluctantly dropped her hands. On the screen, she'd stopped a video on the scene of Haley at the airport—looking like a hired car driver—carrying Baranov's garment bag, pulling his roller case, while he followed along behind her.

Once more, Gregory's feelings bounced from a desire to kill Haley himself to agreeing with Nancy—there must be a good reason for what he saw.

His analytic abilities kicked in. There had to be an explanation.

I bet she abducted Baranov to keep him from going to the White House. It makes complete sense. She's not crazy—well, she is, but also clever. Devious.

It was time to take charge and lead his team. "We have to assume she's acting in the best interests of the country, as she repeatedly has," he began.

Nancy and Dave still looked shaken by Haley with Baranov and the revelation from the hospital in Utah.

"Next, we figure out how we can prove what we suspect about Russia's plans, both the sleeper agents and the invasion of Ukraine. Get to it. Find us the proof we need."

They both returned to their screens, looking for information that likely didn't exist. Gregory gave up and started pacing, turning it all over in his mind.

The big question is, when do I tell the president?

61

DEAL

Senator Barbara Woodran's Family Ranch
East of Provo, Utah

Axe held the would-be female assassin's cuffed wrists as they stood in front of the SUV. Haley had returned a few minutes before. Once Axe saw she was alone, he'd brought out his prisoner—Catherine. She looked defeated and shocked at the deaths of her brother and sister. But she'd been relieved when Axe told her he'd killed a sniper on the hill. "That's Constantine, our handler," she'd said after he described what remained of his features, happy to hear he was no longer an immediate threat to her children.

Haley checked her watch every few seconds. "We've got to go," she told him.

Axe nodded and continued explaining his plan to the police officer. "The Russians will be convinced you're dead, all three of you killed in the failed effort to assassinate Senator Woodran," Axe explained. "Your families will be safe."

Catherine nodded. "But I'll never see them again."

"True. But at least they live. Any other way, they die, right?"

Once again, she nodded reluctantly.

"It's time," Haley said, stress in her voice. "They'll be on their way already. If they use a helicopter... We can't be caught here. And we'll need to get to cell coverage so I can make arrangements."

"Time for your answer," Axe told the prisoner. "Help us against the people who put you in this horrible mess. Or stay and face the music. We have people who can fudge a report if you come with us now but leaving you alive here we can't keep quiet."

"Could you..." The question hung in the air as she looked at Axe, one warrior to another.

"No," he said immediately. "I'm not going to murder you. This is it. Right now—what's your answer?"

Haley had already locked the front and back doors of the house and wiped down any surfaces she may have touched. It would help keep their role here limited to a few carefully selected people.

"I'll come with you."

"And confirm the entire plot."

"Yes. In exchange, you get my family—nieces and nephews, in-laws, all of us—out."

"Not happening. But they'll be safe with you supposedly dead."

She reluctantly nodded and stuck her cuffed hand out as much as she could behind her. "Deal."

They shook, then Axe put her into the car, belted her into the backseat, and ran a daisy chain of zip ties from one ankle to the metal underneath the front passenger seat.

She's not going anywhere.

"Can we please go now?" Haley asked, checking her watch again.

"Yes," he said, detouring around to the back of the truck. He used the fancy multipurpose tool Haley had given him for Christmas, much smaller and lighter than his old one, to remove the license plate. Then he did the same to the front before jumping into the truck and driving them away.

Catherine slumped against the window in the back.

But she's going along with the plan. That's something.

Sun Tzu said, "Build your opponent a golden bridge to retreat across." He'd offered her a way out—though it surely didn't look like a golden bridge to the woman.

Her children's lives in exchange for her full cooperation.

Basically, the same shitty deal the Russians had given her.

Too bad. 'To the victor goes the spoils.'

Axe had been inspired by Haley's abduction of Baranov. Whether the rest of the operation went well or not, they now had two people who would testify to Russia's sleeper agent plan.

Once back on the highway, Haley worked her phone the instant they had cell coverage while Axe drove. She informed Hammer of their deal with Catherine.

His reply came immediately. *Copy. Going offline soon in case phone is confiscated. Do your thing. Making tough call next. No choice. Fingers crossed. Hammer out.*

She stared at her phone, wondering.

What tough call?

Did he mean a difficult decision or a literal phone call?

I hope he's not calling the president.

Nalen stood in the hospital's tiny waiting room for family of people in surgery. Through the window in the door, he saw the young policewoman who had arrived moments earlier, her short, stocky body guarding the room.

He wasn't sure whether she kept him safe or prevented him from leaving.

Scrolling through his phone, he found the contact Haley had shared with him before leaving Las Vegas—just in case. He needed it now.

Nalen considered sending a text message through the comms app, but another look at the officer helped make up his mind.

She's guarding me—the suspect—not protecting the rescuer.

Nalen hit the call button on the app, wondering if she'd answer.

"Hello?" Nancy, Haley's coworker at the CAG, sounded surprised.

"Nancy, we don't know each other, but I work with Haley."

"Okay…" She sounded more spooked now.

"Sorry to drag you into this, but I needed a secure way to speak with your boss. How quickly can you get to Gregory Addison?"

She hesitated a second before saying, "He's right here."

62

PLANS

Haley continued working her phone while Axe drove the senator's big SUV at two miles per hour over the speed limit southwest toward Las Vegas. Holding the phone close to her chest to make sure Catherine, sitting behind her, had no chance of seeing, she typed out a message. Her only hope was help from Bec Dodgeson, the hacker on St. John who had helped stop Stefan Conroy's cult and now led it along with Cody, her fiancé and new Pioneer, or leader of the Movement.

Bec—You're probably sleeping, but I'll be very busy soon, so I'll write out what I need and hope you're both willing and able to help. This is an emergency or I wouldn't ask. Please trust me. But also know if you can't help, I will understand.

Do you and Pioneer have a super loyal follower in Georgia (the country), Armenia, or Turkey who is dedicated to peace in the region (and world)?

Someone from Russia would be fine if necessary, but only if he or she is more loyal to Pioneer, the Movement, and democracy than their country.

Here's what I need: a no-questions-asked ride from Tbilisi

International Airport to Sochi, Russia. Date and time TBD, but soon. Probably thirty hours from now. And one other very specific item.

The truck ate up the miles. Axe relaxed into the driving, alert but taking advantage of the downtime to rest his body. The pace would speed up again in no time. Whatever Haley had planned, it had to be big. She'd only had time to tell him Hammer was fine, and the senator had lost a lot of blood. It was still touch and go. She tapped away on her phone, composing an email or text. After hitting send, she let out a sigh and whispered, "I hope this works."

Seconds later, her phone buzzed. "Uh oh," she said before answering.

"Go ahead," Haley said to Nancy on the comms app, not wanting to give their prisoner any additional operational information, even a first name.

"Can you talk?"

Oh, shit, Haley thought.

Instead of Nancy, Gregory spoke to her on Nancy's phone.

"No, but I can listen," she said, using the button on the side of the phone to decrease the volume to make sure his voice couldn't be overheard.

"That's not going to do it. How long do you need until you can talk? And don't say tomorrow," Gregory said. "I'm thinking a single digit number is best, followed by 'minutes.'"

"Yes. Less than ten." She hung up before he could continue. She turned to Axe. "We need to stop. Bathroom break, and I have to make a call."

Axe nodded. He'd know it wasn't Nalen.

They pulled off at the next freeway exit, out in the boonies, and turned down a side road. The night was dark, the sky filled with stars.

After they all took care of their business and Catherine was secured back in the SUV, Haley walked down the road until out of earshot before calling Nancy's phone.

"Where are you?" Gregory asked immediately.

How much does he know? Can I bluff him?

"Let me stop you before you start," he said, interrupting her planning.

"Dave and Nancy covered for you, but it's all out now. And I just got off the phone with Admiral Nalen. I'm in the loop, and we're on your side. Plus, Dave has uncovered intel you need to hear."

She bit her lip, deciding which way to go.

If Hammer brought him in, we're desperate.

A terrifying thought occurred to her.

Could he be lying?

Nalen had spoken with him at least twice in the past.

He might suspect we're on an op. Maybe Dave and Nancy aren't actually talking.

When had she become so paranoid?

How can I figure out the truth?

"While you're thinking through the angles, here's where we are on our side. I have a trusted ally from Homeland Security handling the senator's ranch. He'll control the FBI. The report will say what we need it to. They'll report four dead bodies. The security guard was obviously shot in the face by Senator Woodran. One woman will be reported killed by a sniper round. A second female will be listed as shot and killed by the same rifle at point-blank range. The second woman stalked the sniper on overwatch. She shot him, only to be killed herself as he died. And Nalen's name and involvement will be kept out of it."

Gregory paused. "How am I doing so far, boss?"

Haley chuckled in the dark.

I'm going to take his joking as a good sign.

"Excellent."

He wouldn't have the full story without Nalen. I can trust him... I hope.

"We're on our way to Las Vegas," she explained. "We have the second female, who Axe captured. She admitted she's a Russian sleeper agent, along with the dead guard and the other woman at the scene—her brother and sister. Put up to the scheme by her father. Her whole family, adults and all the kids, were threatened with death if they didn't comply."

"She'll testify to all of this?"

"As long as her family is unharmed."

"And Baranov? We saw the security footage. We know you must have abducted him."

That was fast. They're very good at what they do.

"Yes, he's locked up safe. If his involvement comes out, the cover story for now is he suspects his beer to be the culprit behind the rioting.

We're scapegoating a sleeper agent named Dr. Edgars, who came up with the formula. He's the true bad guy in this."

"Baranov is not an angel."

"No, but he's not the devil, either. His father indoctrinated him very young and prepared him to do his duty. The Russians also threatened his son. Plus, he's willing to spill all his father told him about the sleeper program, and how it worked at Baranov Brands."

"So we have two witnesses. Is it enough to go to the president?"

He's not asking for my approval. He's thinking out loud.

Haley had to trust him with the reason behind the operation.

"I don't think so. The big issue is Ukraine. I believe the Russians are going to invade Ukraine and—"

Gregory cut her off. "Did you talk to Dave?"

"What? No. Listen, I understand how much you hate my hunches, but my gut tells me—"

"Stop. You figured out Ukraine on your own? How?"

What the hell is going on?

"I put myself in Zimalev's shoes. It's the logical move. What are you talking about—what did Dave find?"

"He thinks Russia will invade Ukraine, Estonia, and Latvia, destroy NATO, and force our weakened president to choose between backing down and going to war with Russia. Probably without the support of Congress—or much of the American public."

Estonia and Latvia, too?

She didn't know what to say. Her mind examined the possibilities.

"Speechless is unusual for you, and I don't like it."

Haley found her voice. "Dave found proof? It's not just my gut?"

"It's slim. He found enough for us to suspect, but not enough for the president or a formal report. That's the problem. What do we do with this? I'm open to suggestions."

Here's where I have to draw the line. I can't tell him what I have planned. It's for his protection.

"Can you handle the Homeland-FBI investigation? It's essential. If word gets out Catherine—the second attacker—is alive, she'll refuse to help."

"I told you, we're on it."

"What about holding, protecting, and debriefing Baranov and Catherine? Right now, I have trusted former SEALs on it, but they're unofficial. The sooner we get formal confessions, the better I'll feel. But it has to be completely secure and off the grid. Minimal personnel, absolutely trustworthy."

Gregory thought for a minute. "I can do it, but it will take time."

"I'll put you in touch with Mad Dog." She held back a laugh but couldn't resist a smile. "He's going to drive you crazy—better have Nancy handle him."

"Fine, whatever. What about informing the president?"

She could tell he didn't want to do it any more than she did.

"Not unless you have more than conjecture about Ukraine. Besides, the search for sleepers will have to be done carefully and quietly or it may destroy the country—not to mention the lives and careers of some innocent people."

"My sentiments exactly. And all we have, besides Baranov and this Catherine woman, is…"

He hates having to say it.

"A hunch," Haley said for him.

"Yes, thank you. But something has to be done. Backchannel communication to our allies? An anonymous tip? Or," he sounded like an excited kid with a crazy idea, "what if we make up a human source in Russia? A defector," he said, warming to it. Haley had never heard him like this. "He knows about the true plan to invade. We create a report, put it in a database, and raise the alarm with it?"

Do I need to say it, or will he get there?

Gregory sighed. "And then we all lose our jobs for faking intel."

"Yes, but it might stop the war."

"No, with the logging protocols, other analysts would see through it quickly. We'd need an exceptional hacker."

Does he know about Bec? Could we use her? No. Our systems are likely too secure.

"It's a great idea," she said. "Years ago, we could have pulled it off. Or if we had an operator in Russia and more time, we could stage it. But I don't think it can work before it's too late."

"I agree." Once more, Gregory was himself, in charge and based in reality, not spinning fairy tales. "Dave has more details for you—I'll put him on in a minute, but he thinks Russia will attack in forty-eight hours. A huge blizzard is coming. He predicts they will invade then."

Do I have enough time?

Suddenly Gregory's idea of making up a Russian defector didn't sound as farfetched.

"What are you and Axe going to do, and how can I support you? Nancy, Dave, and I are all in. Consider us your team of three very capable unsanctioned assets."

There are things you cannot know, Gregory. It's for your own good.

"Axe and I are going to look for Dr. Edgars. Nancy said he drove to Las Vegas."

There was silence from Gregory's end of the line. The seconds crept on long enough for her to hold the phone away from her face, confirming she still had a connection.

Finally, it dawned on her.

He knows I'm lying.

"I'm trying to protect all of you," she whispered as if it would help avoid trouble should anyone be able to monitor the call. They were in deep enough with what had already been said.

"It's too late for that, isn't it?"

"I don't think so."

"Damn it, Haley, what are you into?"

He sounds pissed—no, wait. He's frustrated because he's offered to help. Put himself, Nancy, and Dave on the line, and I'm holding back.

She couldn't do it. They couldn't know.

"I can't tell you what's next."

"Is it part of your medical leave recovery plan?" he joked.

Funny, but charm isn't going to work any better than his annoyance.

"Gregory, you really don't want to know. Even on secure comms, I can't comment. Dave and Nancy should just go home right now. You, too, once you arrange for Baranov and Natalie's debrief. Go to bed and forget about me for a week or two."

"If I only could. Are you truly not going to tell me what you're into?"

"Truly. But... I'd take Dave's intel if you're still offering."

"Shouldn't this be a two-way street?"

"No. We play this wrong and it's a one-way street to hell for all of us. At least this way, you can admit you helped but didn't know what I had planned. That I went completely off the script and acted without permission or oversight. I'm going to handle this. But if I don't by the time the blizzard hits Ukraine, go to the president directly and brief him on our intel, the hunches, everything."

She waited again, not sure which she'd prefer—for him to hang up and go home, leaving her out in the cold, or offer her the help she needed.

Finally, she heard the noise of the connection change. "You're on speaker with Dave and Nancy. They have intel you need to hear."

"Sit tight," Axe told Catherine as he removed the keys from the ignition and hopped out to join Haley in front of the truck. The night was perfect—clear sky, crisp air.

There's something to be said for living out west, Axe thought. *I could get used to this.*

He'd traveled all over the world on active duty but had lived his childhood and the time since retiring within fifty miles of where he was born.

"How much trouble are you in?" he asked Haley, who paced back and forth in front of him in the lights of the SUV. Five steps, then turn. Five steps, and turn.

"I'm in as much trouble as usual. The bigger concern is my office team. If my plan doesn't work, they'll bear the brunt of it."

"Why won't it fall on us?" It took a second, but it finally hit him. "Oh."

She hadn't yet told him the plan, but he got it.

We'll be dead.

"So what's next?"

"As I dropped him off at the hospital, Hammer said the gloves were off."

"You have a plan? Am I going to like it?"

"Honestly, I'm not sure," she said.

That doesn't sound good.

"Let me fill you in. My team thinks the Russians are going to invade three countries: Ukraine, Estonia, and Latvia."

Yep, it's bad.

He thought it through. Wars, or, technically, conflicts, were a hard sell to the people of America in the best of times. With three of the president's hardline allies unable to help—one dead senator, one about to resign in scandal, and one near death—he wouldn't have the backing to convince the public of Ukraine's strategic importance. Russia invading it and the other countries wouldn't resonate with people. Without oil wells being threatened, gas prices rising in the USA, or the homeland being invaded, no one would care. America was sick of war.

Russia would gain more influence over Europe and hold it hostage with natural gas supplies. The country would also be emboldened. Zimalev would push the envelope again, whether in a few months or years. At best, a new Cold War would be at hand.

And America would have missed her opportunity to stop it.

"That's it? We can't do anything? Let's tell the president what's going on." Axe hated the idea, but it seemed the only solution. The man had to know. It would put him in a bind, but better he know the situation now than later.

Haley shook her head in the glow of the SUV's headlights. "We only have conjecture. 'What if's' from my team. Catherine and Baranov's testimony proves Russia's sleeper asset plan, but not the reason behind it. Gregory and Dave both admitted the intelligence is thin about the invasion. No one would believe it, especially coming from one analyst. If the president bought in, people would say he's a retired trigger-puller who misses his glory days. He wants to start a war to prove how tough he is or improve his favorability numbers."

"But if we go to the president now, he could preempt it. Send in troops, warn the allies. Go on TV, draw a line in the sand. Freeze assets, impose more sanctions."

"My guess is Russia has a plan for if he tries any of those. Or maybe it's what they want. They take his ultimatum and go forward, anyway. He can't go to war over those countries without NATO backing him."

"And Europe is overly dependent on Russia's natural gas."

"Exactly."

"So that's it? All we've done, what we know, means nothing?"

"Sometimes, maybe all we can do is hold on and hope for the best," Haley mumbled with a shrug. "Face it, Axe. We've done good work. You, Hammer, and the men in Las Vegas. Tonight, we saved a senator. We discovered a Russian sleeper spy program and took out Baranov, the two sisters, their brother, and their handler." She threw up her hands. "But we're stuck. We're two people in the middle of Utah, far from any place we could make a difference." She shook her head in frustration. "Axe, it's over. We've won all the battles we've fought, but finishing the war isn't up to us."

Her words hung between them in the cold air.

Is she right? Is it the end of the road?

They could take their wins and call it, leaving the rest up to Nalen to decide if it should go to the president or not. They were grunts. Their jobs were finished.

Axe let the thought simmer for a moment, then shook his head.

No. I can't believe she's giving up. She may be done, but I'm not.

"It's not the Navy SEAL way," he told Haley. "All we need is a mission. SEALs take aggressive action and think way outside the box. So —what could stop this? You said you had a plan. Let's hear it."

A tiny smile crept onto Haley's face.

I've been had! Damn, she's good. This entire conversation has been to get me worked up, so I'll go along with her plan.

"If you went to this much trouble..." He trailed off, looking at her suspiciously.

"It's aggressive as hell," she said, nodding. "Illegal, too—technically. I don't think you're going to like it."

I don't think I am, either.

"You may be right, but at the very least, it's a start. And I bet it makes a great story someday."

She shook her head slowly. "Only you and I will know."

Whoa.

He gestured impatiently for her to spill the details.

"Fine." With a last glance at the SUV, Haley turned her back to it and pulled a passport out of her pocket. It had the heft and feel of authenticity and his picture, but a different name.

Nathan Lillington? Not my first choice of fake names, but whatever.

Axe slid the passport into his pocket. "Tell me."

Once again, the thin smile appeared. "We're going to assassinate the President of Russia."

He chuckled.

Now that's funny. My sense of humor has rubbed off on her.

He waited for her to laugh and explain the actual plan, but she held his eye.

She's serious.

He thought it through.

It makes sense, in a hyper-aggressive, 'take no shit' way. Best of all, they'll never see it coming.

Axe nodded, decision made. "Let's go," he said, leading the way back to the SUV.

This is going to be the best story I can never tell.

PART 6

MONDAY, JANUARY 2

63

IMPOSSIBLE

The Warehouse
Las Vegas, Nevada

Haley stood in front of Mad Dog, nearly eye to eye.

I'd tower over him in heels, she realized.

"I'm counting on you, Mad Dog. This is more important than you know. Keep Catherine and Baranov safe until relieved by... I don't know who, yet, but here's the passphrase." She told him and he grinned.

He's the epitome of 'Moderation is for cowards.'

"Got it, Blondie, leave it all to me," he said. With his dark hair, beard, and brawny physique, he looked solid. Reliable, but with a sparkle of either humor or madness in his eyes which worried her.

And when he opens his mouth, he makes me wonder about his trustworthiness... and sanity.

Mad Dog leaned forward to whisper to her. She pulled away. "It's okay, I've got a secret for you."

Haley wasn't sure she wanted his breath in her ear but held still as he leaned in again.

"The wild man schtick—it's all an act," he whispered. "Don't worry, I'm as solid as Axe—and a hell of a lot more fun," he added as he pulled away with a wink and a charming smile.

Eww.

He laughed harder at her expression. "Not that way! You're much too young for me. Besides, you're not my type. 'No more blonds' has been my motto since my ex and I split."

Thank goodness. The last thing I need is to fend off advances from half-crazy former SEALs—or feel like I have to play them to get what I, and the country, need done.

"Good to know. Now, give me your phone."

He handed it over, unlocked, and she went to work. She had to delete a few apps to make space for the comms app.

Mad Dog moved to her side, watching over her shoulder. "Hey, I like those games!"

"When the op is finished, I'll buy you a new phone with more space and reinstall them. For now, we may need to be in touch. Here's the contact of a person—you don't need her name. She'll provide intel. But if you're caught, you destroy your phone and say nothing."

With the app installed, and Nancy's contact information saved as well as hers and Axe's, she handed it back. "I need you to come through for me, Mad Dog, just like on St. John. You saved our asses and we need you to do it again."

Finally, he looked serious. "Don't worry, Blondie. I've got you. My boys and I will do whatever you need."

She gave him a page of notes. "Details are here, and your intel officer will give you more if needed. Find a guy named Dr. Edgars. He's likely lying low in Las Vegas. Maybe with guards, maybe not. I need you to capture and hold him."

"Not capture or kill? Capture is harder."

"You're a Navy SEAL. Get it done."

"Well, technically I'm retired, so..." His serious expression changed after a second as he laughed again at the look on her face.

"You're going to have to learn to lighten up, Blondie, or the stress will kill you before the enemy," he said with all seriousness.

Her eyes and tone went ice cold as she stepped close, invading his personal space. "At least I'll die at the hands of my enemies and not my teammate."

His lips moved, at a loss for words, then he shut his mouth and swallowed hard.

"Yes, ma'am," he answered finally.

With her face still set in stone, she slowly winked at him.

Gotcha.

Mad Dog grabbed at his chest and staggered back. "Haley, seriously, I almost had a heart attack."

"You've got to learn to lighten up, Mad Dog. Now, can you and your guys handle this or not?"

He snapped to attention. "Capture him, aye-aye, sir. Ma'am. Ma'am-sir."

Heaven help me. Out of all the men Axe had here helping, I get stuck with this nut job?

She hid her exasperation—and a smile.

"The doctor is untouchable. Got it?"

"What if he's already dead when we find him?"

Where does he come up with this stuff?

"Truly already dead," she asked, "or 'Yes, sure, he was dead when we got here, I promise!'"

"No," Mad Dog said, turning serious again in an instant. "Dead-dead. Not by us."

She had to think.

"It would be much better if we had him alive, but I won't cry if it works out the other way. The important thing is to find him. And better dead than in the hands of the enemy."

"Who are?"

"Need to know. But trust me, you'll know when you see them. They'll be the ones trying to kill you."

Axe flipped Haley's tablet face down as Mad Dog entered the rear warehouse room and headed straight toward him.

No one gets even a hint at what we're doing.

"Where did you get her, Axe?" Mad Dog asked quietly. "She's hard-core. I mean, we knew that from St. John, right, but that woman is going places. She's got her shit together. Do me a favor and don't get her killed, okay?"

Mad Dog walked away without waiting for a response.

A real warning disguised as Team banter.

He suspects how dangerous this next part is for us—and wants me to remember that as good as Haley is, she's still new to this.

Axe returned to examining the pictures Haley had downloaded.

I hate to say it, but the mission is impossible.

They'd have to find another way. Call the president and come clean. Heringten would trust Haley's word. Turn the whole mess over to the grownups and let them figure it out.

Haley joined him by their pile of gear. One of Mad Dog's fellow SEALs, who Axe knew only in passing from the New Year's Eve operation, had done an impressive job of procuring the needed items.

Haley surveyed the parkas, gloves, hats, mittens, high-tech sleeping bags, suitcases, and photography equipment. "They say New York is the city that never sleeps. Obviously, they never heard of Las Vegas."

"Amazing what you can find at pawn shops in the middle of the night."

"And how easily doors open when you throw money at people," she said. They'd both maxed out their credit cards, using the ATMs at several casinos to withdraw all the cash allowed.

After so much time together, Haley knew Axe's mannerisms, and she could tell he wasn't happy. "I know how you feel about 'spy shit,'" she told him. "This time, we don't have to raid a compound and fight to the death. Success isn't us shooting it out with dozens of bad guys. Winning means killing one man and getting away clean. Are you okay with this?"

"I'm fine with that part," Axe said. "Really. But I've looked at the photos. I don't see how the plan can work. I'm sorry."

He handed her the tablet, expecting an argument—and getting one. But with a smile.

"Which is exactly why it will work. If we get lucky. The shot isn't the problem."

"Easy for you to say. You're not the one taking it," he pointed out. "I can't hit a target moving at ninety miles per hour. It's not possible, especially from the distance we're looking at. And if you thought I could shoot through this window," he said, showing her the photo of the take-off area, "I can't. And with whatever untested rifle we're likely to get? Accuracy can't be counted on. I can't guarantee hitting a small target—like a man— moving across my field of vision." He glanced around, confirming none of the remaining men were in the room.

A little paranoia never hurt anyone.

"You don't have to go through the window or hit a moving target." She zoomed in on the photo. The low-resolution picture blurred, but Haley pointed at the one open-air section of the track where the target wouldn't be moving fast. "I know exactly when Zimalev will be at this spot. If I give you a 4.1-second warning, can you put a bullet in this area?"

Axe stared at Haley, the partner he'd been through so much within a relatively short time. He hated questioning her judgment, but he had to. "How can you possibly—" Suddenly, it clicked.

Brilliant—if the timing is accurate.

"I get it. Yes, I can put a shot there. But a four-second travel time means we're too far away for me to be accurate. What about a one or two-second warning?"

Haley squinted at the photo. "It will depend on the angle. But yes, as long as I can see when he takes off, and you can take the shot when I tell you, it will work."

He thought of the many other details needed to go their way to make the operation a success. "Are you sure this is the best approach?"

"Yes. But if it doesn't work, there's a fallback plan. Gregory will call the president if we fail."

He'll have to because we'll likely be dead or captured.

Then there will be a war whether the Russians intended one or not.

And we will have caused it.

Haley hesitated, looking suddenly unsure. "My real worry is, what if I'm wrong? What if the invasion is an elaborate bluff that Dave and I have fallen for? If we do this, and Zimalev never meant to attack…"

Axe shook his head. "Doesn't matter. We already know Russia— presumably Zimalev—ordered the drugging of innocent people in Las Vegas. And likely ordered the killing of one senator and the release of a second senator's confidential emails. We know for a fact he's behind the attempted assassination of Senator Woodran. Any one of those is enough for payback. The possible Ukraine invasion just adds a deadline, that's all." He thought of what had already been done to his country and shook his head. "Nobody gets away with harming the USA on my watch."

Haley smiled tightly. "Our watch."

He stuck out his fist for a bump from her. "Even better."

Haley took one last look back at the warehouse as she slipped into the taxi after Axe. They hadn't said goodbye to Mad Dog and the other SEALs, but she could feel their eyes on her as she closed the car door.

This is it. We have to succeed, for the country, the president, and our European allies.

In the backseat next to her, Axe put his head back and closed his eyes.

He'd done all the driving from Utah while she worked the phone, setting up the op.

We can sleep on the plane.

The business class tickets had cost a fortune. She wondered where the money came from when she used the credit card with her fake name Gregory had given her months ago when she first went undercover.

It's a link to the government. I hate to use it, but I had no choice.

She tried resting for the short trip to the airport, but her mind spun.

Could she trust Mad Dog to find Dr. Edgars with no adult supervision? Was he rock solid or a loose cannon? Were the jokes and banter truly an act?

He saved us in St. John. He'll get it done.

She and Axe, on the other hand, might not.

The plan is overly complex. Too much has to go right.

Haley gave them a twenty percent chance of completing the mission successfully. And a five percent chance of getting out of Russia alive.

64

DECISIONS

President Pavel Zimalev read the national security briefing report over his second cup of coffee in his high-ceiling office. The sky outside was gray again, though no snow fell.

Next, he turned to a single sheet of paper prepared for him more secretly than any other. He sipped his coffee while he read the update about the activated sleeper assets with annoyance.

The first senator had "died in her sleep of a heart attacke" as planned. The American authorities suspected nothing.

A success, he thought.

The second would resign in the next twenty-four hours. Aides were writing a farewell speech, and others were already scrambling for new jobs.

Another remarkable achievement. It's the type of operation I'll be able to do more of as needed.

The third senator lay in a hospital in stable condition.

Not dead, unfortunately. Frustrating, but not insurmountable.

The Las Vegas incident had not produced the death and destruction predicted. Nor had one of the long-term sleepers been linked to American President Heringten, as promised.

I'll speak with Orlov after the invasion about ramifications—and punishments.

More troubling, the managing asset supervising the sleepers in the region—Constantine, he recalled—had vanished.

Concerning, but not every plan succeeds.

An unconfirmed intelligence report had four dead at the third senator's home. Presumably, the asset had been on site to manage his sleeper agents and had been killed.

Better killed than captured. He knew little and had no obvious ties to Russia, but still.

Now, Pavel had an important decision to make. He poured more coffee from the carafe into the bone china cup on its saucer. He'd prefer a larger mug, so he could enjoy a decent size cup of coffee, instead of this unnecessarily fancy china. But the china was tradition, and he could accept minor inconveniences while remaking the country into the powerhouse he imagined.

He had to face facts.

The operation in America hasn't done the job needed. It is not a complete failure, but enough of one to be troubling.

Should he abort the planned invasion of the three countries because the United States was not as weak as expected? Or proceed despite the danger?

The snowstorm of the decade approached the area. It would be devastating, sweeping through quickly, but leaving feet of snow falling so heavily, in such a short amount of time, it would incapacitate the region.

His superior equipment and more experienced men would have a distinct advantage in such weather. NATO, should the maniac American president somehow convince the allies to fight back—would be hamstrung. They relied too heavily on airpower, which wouldn't function during the intense storm. They'd be grounded while he rolled on.

Once well inside the countries, NATO wouldn't dare attack him for fear of collateral damage and the destruction of critical infrastructure.

They will have no way to stop me—if I give the order.

The troops were on standby. Select, trusted commanders had the plans and were prepared pending his final decision.

How much face will I lose in their eyes if I hold back?

That question alone made him lean heavily toward action.

Without the invasion, it would take years to achieve his goal of a reunified, powerful Russia. Time would pass while the diplomats negotiated and spies schemed.

Besides taking too long, negotiations and diplomacy bored him to tears.

The sleepers were incredibly valuable to control America, but he had Europe to worry about as well.

No. He would inspect and inspire the troops, as planned, then travel back to Moscow to manage the invasion. No sense tempting fate by staying in the region. The Americans could be unpredictable, and as much as he loathed the man, he needed to remember not to underestimate President Heringten.

Even though he's a has-been warrior, he still needs to be watched, especially since the planned operations to clip his wings have failed.

Once the worst of the storm started, Zimalev would send word to attack. Then Russia's new era will begin.

65

TRUST

The White House
Washington, D.C.

President Heringten left the Oval Office at five o'clock on the dot. Aside from one senator dying from a heart attack, another with hacked emails revealing scandalous behavior, and Senator Woodran's attempted assassination over the weekend, it had been a light day. The economy hummed along decently. With the two parties evenly split in Congress, next to nothing would be accomplished.

The world recovered quickly from the EMP and cyberattack strikes from a few months ago, with countries throwing vast sums of money at cybersecurity.

As usual, about half the people in the United States thought him a magnificent leader.

The other half wished him dead—or at least out of office.

The same held for the world at large. Many countries sang his praise for playing fair with the ransomware keys from the mad genius Stefan Conroy's attempt to rule the world.

Other countries, including many allies, considered James a fool for not remaking the world while he held near-total power over his enemies.

The most powerful man in the world? James thought. *What a joke. More like the most hated man in the world.*

He walked through the door to his private residence area—basically a sprawling apartment ornately decorated in a style he still, after four years, was uncomfortable with.

When I'm out of office, will I miss the constant attention, the dozens of staff cleaning up after us? Doing all in their power to make my life easy so I can focus my energy on running the country?

At least he had four more years to find out. He'd won by a slim margin, squeaking out a win despite the horrible attack on New York City in the spring.

The Movement cult's actions two and a half months ago had come too late to affect the outcome.

If Stefan Conroy's destruction had occurred a few days before the election, instead of a few days after, I'd be packing up instead of heading to the fridge for a beer before whatever wonderful dinner Chef has prepared for us.

He nearly bumped into his wife, Brenda, as she hung up her coat. Her face looked pale and serious.

"Darling, where are you back from?" he asked with a quick kiss as he set his briefcase near the door. He had reading to do, as always. Intelligence analysis, economic predictions, and more. Reports upon reports. It never ended. "I didn't realize you were going out today."

She silently took his hand and led him away from the door and the Secret Service agents stationed outside in the hallway.

"Sarah called and invited me to an impromptu lunch. The agents picked a location they were comfortable with, and we went."

"What a nice treat. How—"

Then it hit him. Sarah, his wife's best friend since childhood—and Haley's mother.

The last time they got together on the spur of the moment, Brenda brought a letter from Haley to me.

Brenda nodded at the look on his face and took a piece of notebook paper, folded into a small square, from her purse. "For you. Haley set up her mom's phone with a secure way to communicate. Sarah said she transcribed it exactly. Good luck."

We've never spoken about it, but how could she not know the chaos Haley's last letter brought?

"Let me know if I need to reschedule dinner," she said.

James held the tightly folded paper as she headed toward the bedroom, leaving him standing in the living room.

Oh, Haley, what now?

The last letter from her ended with him murdering his vice president in the man's office.

He took the note to the kitchen, grabbed the beer he'd been looking forward to, but sat down without opening it. Then he unfolded the paper. The short note was in Sarah's handwriting, but Haley's voice. He read it slowly.

Dear Uncle Jimmy,

Time is short, so I can't explain as much as you might prefer.

I ask you to recall the previous letter I wrote and trust me again.

A snowstorm is approaching the Washington, D.C. area. Please do this for me. At the first possible moment, arrange to go sledding on a toboggan down a small hill with children—local kids, children of aides or reporters—it doesn't matter who.

But make it a huge media event: the President of the United States, playing in the snow with children. Down a hill, on a toboggan—those are the essential elements.

Don't ask why. Don't look for or ask about me. Don't try to contact Nalen.

Do it for me, your favorite niece.

If it works out as expected, I may be able to explain one day.

If not, I beg your forgiveness.

Much love,

Haley

James could practically feel his hair turning gray from the stress.

'Trust me again.'

Haley had saved the country from a traitorous vice president and kept New York City from becoming a radioactive wasteland. How could he not trust her?

But what she's asking is ridiculous.

How could sledding down a hill help her? And what the hell was she up to?

66

LEVEL 10

The Warehouse
Las Vegas, Nevada

Mad Dog regarded Victor Baranov, seated on the floor of the warehouse's empty small office. "People are on their way to take you into custody. Before they do, I was hoping you'd help us out. I'm going to collect Dr. Edgars. Any advice?"

Baranov stood and straightened his wrinkled suit as best he could.

He's trying to look like a successful businessman and not my prisoner. But the guy could use a shower.

"I'm happy to help. In exchange, I ask a favor."

Mad Dog exaggerated his inspection of the tiny, bare office Victor occupied. The window, high on the wall, had steel security bars. The thin, gray industrial carpet glued to the cement floor couldn't be comfortable to sleep on under the blanket Haley had provided.

"Dude, you don't even have a pillow!" After looking around to make sure no one else could hear—in the empty room—Mad Dog whispered, "I hate to break it to you, but you're not in the best position to negotiate."

The man's lips twitched in a brief smile. "True. Which is why I'll help you get him with no conditions. Only afterward will I make my request."

Mad Dog rubbed his hands together excitedly. "Come on, I've never been good at waiting. When I was a kid, I'd sneak downstairs a few days before Christmas, unwrap all the presents—not just the ones for me—then spend hours re-wrapping them. Tell me what you want."

"I want my son."

Well, damn, doesn't that pull at the old heartstrings?

"You're incommunicado. Can't talk to him."

"I want him safe. Here, or a place of your choosing. But..." Baranov hesitated, embarrassed. "When the woman abducted me, I was unable to process the wire transfer for his allowance on the first of the month."

"Wait, how old's your kid?"

"Thirty-one," he admitted.

"Must be nice!"

"Yes. Well, by now he's in trouble with the people he surely thought were his friends, but actually are his drug dealers. Enablers. And they've likely cut him off." Baranov looked worried. "He'll be hurting now."

Mad Dog understood. "The love of a parent, right?"

Baranov nodded.

"Dr. Edgars first. Then we'll see."

"Thank you," Baranov said. "You'll need my key card—the woman took it."

"Yes, we've got your stuff."

"But, as she may have guessed, you need several codes for various doors. If you have a pen, I'll write them down for you."

"No need," Mad Dog said with a smile, tapping his head. "Let me have 'em."

Baranov Brands Corporate Headquarters
Dr. Edgar's Lab
Las Vegas, Nevada

Edgars sat in the lab—his happy place. It made no difference where the lab was. He had been equally happy at the one in Mexico where he'd imprisoned himself a year ago with the others.

May they rest in peace.

They had been good men, doing good work.

Sure, people might one day compare them all to Josef Mengele, who also performed medical experiments on people.

They'll only compare us to that evil hack if people find out.

It looked like Las Vegas' Lady Luck was on his side. The TV above his lab table had shown footage from New Year's Eve—what the press continued to refer to as "rioting." No authorities had seized the bottling plant or come knocking on his secure lab door. They hadn't made the connection between his beer and the actions of hundreds of people on New Year's Eve.

And for some inexplicable reason, Constantine, his friend and Russian handler who directed the operation, hadn't tipped off the press to Baranov Brands beer being behind the deaths and injuries. By now, the blame should have fallen on Victor—and the American president by extension.

Edgars shook off his worry and speculation. The politics and spy games were fascinating, but he couldn't focus on them. He only truly cared for his experiments.

Preferably on people again. Soon.

He would keep perfecting his concoction. If it was safe to do so, they would reestablish a lab for him in Mexico. Or Honduras, where people would be even more desperate for money, welcoming it gladly in exchange for taste-testing an ice-cold beer.

Or whatever will hide the disgusting flavor of the mixture.

On the laboratory table in front of him, he had finished a new version of the drug. He estimated it would be twice as powerful as the one they'd perfected in Mexico, so he called it Level 10. With his deadline over for a specific product—Level 5, which could be easily hidden in beer—he'd been free to spend the last few days on a more interesting mixture. The clear liquid looked harmless enough, but it would be the fastest acting, most potent version yet.

If we can get past the taste issue.

In Mexico, they'd been forced to settle on the Level 5 formula because the hops successfully disguised the taste. Above that level, people wouldn't take a single sip.

Plus, beer is easy to manufacture and distribute.

Edgars bet they might find success hiding more potent versions in flavored vodka. He smiled at the thought. His father and grandfather—old school Russians to the core—would roll over in their graves at the idea of vodka flavored with strawberries or pineapple. He missed them both, but his grandfather most of all.

They had encouraged his youthful science experiments, found the money to send him to college, and sat attentively around the dinner table listening to him speak about every lab experiment as a student.

They had even overlooked his occasional experiments with the neighborhood's stray dogs and cats.

His beloved grandfather helped him with his homework while his father cooked. After dinner, Grandpa told him stories of his childhood in Russia and the extended family he had left behind.

As college graduation neared, they dropped the bomb. They were a family of Russian sleeper spies. His schooling and their entire lives were owed to his grandfather's homeland.

Edgars had been understandably stunned. His father had smoothed the way and eased his mind.

"Son, you will apply at a top pharmaceutical company. After several interviews, you will be hired, guaranteed. There, you will start at the bottom and work your way up. Your natural abilities will be welcome. In exchange, at some point, you may be called on to help Russia. It is a good fit, and you will have a wonderful life doing exceptional work."

That had been decades ago. The plan had gone exactly as his father predicted. After a few years at the company, he'd been approached by a man who used the correct code words. Edgars was to provide secret, proprietary information on the drugs being developed at the company.

Which, of course, he did. It seemed harmless to him. The science should be shared with the world. In his mind, giving secrets to Russia was a good first start.

Finally, two years ago, a man with broad shoulders, a square jaw, and a typical American accent stood behind him at the grocery store. A code phrase was muttered into his ear. After loading the groceries into his car, Edgars had walked to the coffee shop in the shopping area, had an herbal tea with Constantine, his new handler, and learned about the position soon available at Baranov Brands.

It had been the beginning of the real payback.

His gaze lingered on the test tubes lined up in the stand.

If we had perfected Level 10 in Mexico, New Year's Eve would have ended much differently.

He theorized Level 10 was faster acting, much more potent, and even more addictive than any other version.

We'll fix the taste problem. Prepare millions of doses. No one will stop us.

Edgars frowned and adjusted the black stopper on one test tube.

I keep thinking in terms of my team. 'We. Us.'

He'd do it alone if he had to, but he hoped Constantine would recruit new people to replace his former team, blown up in the basement lab in Mexico.

This time, I need flavor specialists. I have the drug—now we need an undetectable delivery system.

He heard a noise in the room outside his lab.

Finally. Victor.

It could only be him. No one else had the code to the outer door.

He'll have the statistics. Number of people dosed. Their reactions, survivability rates, initial reports of how addictive Level 5 is on a larger population.

Edgars had been looking forward to the data from New Year's Eve. Information from the police and the hospitals. Eyewitness accounts.

And further instructions from Constantine.

The sooner I get more staff, the sooner I can perfect Level 10.

He nearly opened the door without going through the security procedures drilled into their heads by their handler. "Never open the door without checking."

Looking through the peephole, ready to turn the handle, Edgars stopped, shocked.

A bear of a man stood smiling politely outside the door. His dark beard was well-groomed, and he looked strong and clean-cut in his white shirt and black blazer, which struggled to contain his muscles. He wasn't tall but made up for it with his physique.

"Dr. Edgars? I'm Doug, Mr. Baranov's new chief of security," the man called through the door. "He sent me to bring you these documents you wanted." He held up a packet of papers.

My data.

Again, his hand pushed the sturdy silver handle of the door down but stopped before the latch disengaged.

Wouldn't Victor have called first?

He stepped away from the door, dread filling him. Somehow, they had been discovered.

Could I be mistaken? Perhaps Constantine assigned a security detail to Victor and me?

The sound of metal on metal—a crowbar of some sort, prying at the door near the handle, confirmed his worst fear. He would be caught and then... his mind swirled. Whatever they did to him would pale compared to the torture of not being able to conduct his research every day. To be a scientist.

He frantically looked around the room for a solution. The sole entrance was being violated with a vengeance by the muscular man. There was no escape.

Think! I'm a scientist. I can figure this out.

His eyes landed on the tray of test tubes. He ran the calculations in his mind.

Level 10 minus my advanced age against that... monster.

They wouldn't send an untrained man. The door held, for the moment, but eventually would give way.

If I were younger, I would fight.

There were scissors in a sleek black desk organizer on the corner of the lab table.

I can't be locked in a cell. Deprived of my research. Reduced to an animal.

He picked up the scissors and opened them wide before setting them on the edge of the table. Then he removed the stopper from one of the test tubes.

The noxious smell hit him, and he fought to not gag.

I have to time it perfectly.

He would use the euphoria stage of the drug to take his own life. From the experiments on the test subjects, he guessed he wouldn't feel the pain.

It's the only logical solution.

The door proved harder to open than Mad Dog thought it would.

Am I out of practice? he wondered.

No. He was as strong as ever, but he'd been limited in the length of the crowbar he could smuggle into the facility. He only had his pant legs—as short and stubby as ever—or under his arm, hidden by the jacket. Also relatively compact. SEALs came in all sizes and colors. He was on the shorter side of average, but also more muscular than most.

Pity I couldn't bring a longer crowbar. Still, only one way in means one way out. I'll get to you when I get to you, Doc.

Mad Dog set the bar again and yanked. This time the whole frame shook, but the door held strong.

This is pissing me off.

He dug the bar's tip in as deep between the door and the frame as he could and put his body into it.

The door stayed locked, but the frame popped free of the wall.
That'll do.

The clear liquid burned Dr. Edgars' throat as it went down. He heaved, his whole body shaking as it immediately tried to reject the horrible concoction. With a force of will he didn't know he possessed, he kept himself from vomiting.

We will never be able to cover the disgusting flavor. It tastes like a combination of—

He forced his analytical mind to stop before the contemplation of the taste made him heave again.

Suddenly, as if a switch had been flicked, he relaxed, his cares fading.

It works so fast.

He found it fascinating to be on this side of the experiment.

I should make notes.

He reached for his pen and notebook on the table and noticed the scissors.

They are important for some reason...

The door frame separated from the wall in a cloud of dust. A chunk of drywall fell to the floor. In a moment of clarity, he remembered.

I have to kill myself before it's too late.

He picked up the scissors, then closed his eyes with a small smile.

This feels so good. I don't want it to ever end.

He fought himself and the original plan.

If I live, I can document this experience. Perfect it.

But if he lived, they would take away his lab. Lock him in a cage. His mind would waste away.

With what felt like another switch being flipped, the euphoria stopped and the rage hit.

They did this to me. Took me from a world of helping people and turned me into this monster.

In the distant background, his inner scientist noted the wounded animal sounds coming from his mouth.

The door drew his attention. The frame was wrenched further from the wall, revealing a savage beast. Edgars backed away, shocked. It stood ten feet tall, its mangy hair brushing the ceiling after it stooped to walk through the opening where the door had been. From its mouth came angry growls. White foam bubbled from six-inch-long fangs. Red, glowing eyes bore into him.

"Ta-da!" Mad Dog announced with a grin as he pulled the entire door frame out of the way and stepped through the opening with a flourish.

The smell hit him first, a horrible mixture of decomposing flesh, days-old fish, and filthy socks.

"Dr. Edgars, I presume?" He choked out the line he'd come up with on the drive to the facility.

The scientist cowered against the back wall of the small lab, his eyes wide.

"Hey, buddy, calm down." The man was sweating profusely and shaking.

"You okay, doc? Ready to come with me?"

Dr. Edgars stopped shaking and stood tall. Then he growled, low and threatening.

This isn't going the way I expected. He sounds like the zombies from New Year's Eve... only much worse.

Edgars made himself big. Isn't that what one did to scare off a bear? Maybe a show of strength would deter the animal. A growl came unbidden from his throat.

The towering, dark creature didn't come closer but didn't back away.

Edgars didn't stand a chance against the wild thing. But he would go out fighting. With a snarl, he launched himself at the towering bear, knowing it would be the end.

I'll be home soon, Grandpa.

Mad Dog got his hands up just in time to protect himself—at the expense of his hand getting cut with the scissors the scientist carried.

He was immediately on the defensive. The doctor moved faster than his sixty-some years and had the strength of two men.

Disarm him and take him to the ground.

Easier said than done.

He backpedaled, moving through the doorway as the doctor kept coming at him. He trapped the man's hand, tried to wrench it far enough to make Edgars drop the scissors, but it didn't work. As the older man clawed at his face with his free hand, Mad Dog snapped the wrist.

Captured alive doesn't necessarily mean unharmed.

The scissors clattered to the floor as the doc screamed like an animal in pain, not a human. Then the crazed man slammed into him, taking him heavily to the ground.

Yes, the ground was the plan, but not exactly like this.

Mad Dog had received the finest hand-to-hand fighting instruction the SEALs could provide. Countless hours had been spent training with his Teammates during downtime on deployment. With his technique and strength, he should have been able to easily subdue a man more than twenty-five years older.

But Mad Dog was merely holding his own. The man fought with a fury triple the zombies on New Year's.

He must have dosed himself—with something a lot stronger than he put in the beer.

He wrestled with the man, using every mixed martial art move he could.

These work on humans, but I'm wrestling with an animal.

The doctor pinned him for a second. Mad Dog only broke free when the man bent forward, trying to bite his face. He rolled, managing to switch places, ending up on top for the first time in the fight. Grabbing a handful of the man's white lab coat, he used it to pull the doctor's arm behind his back, forcing Edgars onto his stomach.

"There, now let's play nice."

With a howl, the doctor fought him as he slipped flex cuffs over one wrist, then caught the other and did the same. Flopping like a fish, Edgars kept struggling, making capturing the ankles harder than it should have been.

Finally, Mad Dog could take a breath. He sat on the floor, marveling as Dr. Edgars, eyes wide, mouth snarling, wiggled inch by inch toward him.

"I guess this means we can't be friends?" he asked as he scooted back a foot, out of reach of the man's snapping mouth.

Mad Dog tipped the hand cart back onto its large black wheels, slung Dr. Edgar's book bag on his shoulder, and picked up the crowbar in his free hand.

This should be fun.

He'd gotten a few looks as he waltzed in earlier, using Baranov's pass card and the memorized codes on the door locks. But with every door opening before him, people soon ignored his presence and did their jobs.

The way out, with a snarling, growling Dr. Edgars zip-tied to the hand truck, would be interesting.

A few people looked like they were about to stop him as he made his way to the parking lot, but the noises coming from Edgars kept everyone away.

"Off his meds," Mad Dog said as if that explained everything. He nodded politely to people and kept walking.

Captured, not killed, as ordered, ma'am.

PART 7

TUESDAY, JANUARY 3

67

SLEDDING

Tuesday, January 3

The White House
South Lawn
Washington, D.C.

James Heringten stood in snow boots, jeans, and a black parka. He had a red scarf draped loosely around his neck, more for decoration and a display of patriotism than warmth.

It was a beautiful day. The fresh snow sparkled like diamonds in the morning sun. Along the south lawn of the White House, four of his aides' kids made snow angels. Others, a few years older, had an impromptu snowball fight. Three sat on a toboggan and slid down a small hill.

The press ate it up, filming and taking pictures while the president smiled and waved, his parka not hiding his muscular frame.

This is great optics. It's a perfect feel-good photo op on a snow day.

Besides helping with his approval rating, James was genuinely having fun.

"Mr. President," one of the television producers called from behind her cameraman. "Why don't you take a ride with the kids?"

Nicely done, Chad.

The president's Chief of Staff had arranged for her to make the suggestion.

He laughed and waved her off. "They're doing fine without me!"

One of the kids, the daughter of a close aide, clomped over to him, her snow boots too big on her feet. She looked up at him from under her stocking cap and brushed her bangs out of her eyes. "Please?" she asked, taking his hand.

Exactly as planned.

"Okay, Olivia, let's go."

Holding hands, they walked a few steps to where the kids had been sledding. The snow had gotten packed down, allowing for an easy takeoff and fast ride. Or as fast as it could be, given the size of the tiny hill.

James sat on the back of the five-foot sled, his legs stretched out. The little kids piled on in front of him excitedly.

"Ready?" he called out.

"Let's go!" they yelled.

He dug his hands into the snow and pushed them forward.

Everyone screamed with excitement, including him, as they slid ten feet before slowing to a gentle stop.

Laughing with the kids, he stood and helped pull the sled up the hill. Chad nodded at him with a smile. The cameras had captured the scene perfectly.

After a few more waves, James left the kids and staff to play for a while longer. He had work to do.

I hope this is what you needed, Haley.

68

GEORGIA

Tbilisi International Airport
Tbilisi, Georgia

Axe and Haley collected their suitcases from the baggage carousel. Axe knew little about the country of Georgia—or the region in general, but it seemed more modern than he thought it would be.

Too much time in the Middle East. Heaven help us if we go to war in this area.

For the last decade or two, all the combat experience of the SEALS—and the other armed forces—had been in a desert environment.

I hope the Teams are training more in cold and snow since I retired.

If he and Haley didn't succeed, they might need it sooner than expected.

Wearing no makeup, and with her gorgeous long blond hair in a bun under a plain baseball cap, Haley attracted less attention than expected. Men and women glanced her way from time to time, but the busy tiredness of airport travel kept most people in their own little worlds. And, as always, no one gave him a second glance, despite his rugged handsomeness and bushy beard.

Their fake passports passed inspection at customs without a problem, as they had on every leg of their trip.

The passports are real—only the names aren't.

Their luggage received a cursory inspection at a metal table, more for the two young men to practice their English on the attractive American woman than out of security. They didn't care about his only questionable item—high-power binoculars with built-in rangefinder.

The expensive camera gear caught their eye, and they pantomimed Axe taking pictures of Haley—or Holly, as her passport called her. Axe nodded, and they smiled happily.

Going undercover as photographer and model definitely works.

Haley quickly exchanged cash for both Georgian lari and Russian rubles, in case they needed to bribe their way out of trouble, then headed outside.

At the curb, it looked like any other modern airport, busy despite being 10:00 p.m. They'd only taken a few steps when a newer white hybrid car pulled forward from its idling spot twenty yards to their left.

It can't be this easy.

Then again, after all the difficult, dangerous, uncomfortable missions where everything that could go wrong did, shouldn't there be operations where things go as planned? Where not everything goes to hell?

A thin man of indeterminable age waved at them. He had on a dark hat, pulled low, covering his hair. A black scarf wrapped around his face, and large, black-rimmed glasses drew the eye, instead of his features.

Good disguise.

The man rolled down the passenger window but held up a finger when Haley reached for the door. He put his gloved hands together three times —*clap clap clap*—and looked expectantly at them.

Axe and Haley had sat through enough of Stefan Conroy's speeches a few months before to respond correctly to the improvised code. "Pi-o-neer" they said together quietly.

The man nodded, satisfied, and unlocked the doors. They loaded their gear quickly into the hatchback area. Then Haley—the more social of the two, and better with people—climbed into the front, as planned.

"Thank you," she started in English, though she had memorized words in both Georgian and Russian on the flight.

Pulling away from the curb, the man shook his head, holding up his finger to his scarf-covered lips.

This is going to be a long drive if we can't talk.

Once out of the airport, the driver reached under his seat. Axe tensed, prepared for a pistol, expecting a double-cross. Instead, the man handed

them a large silver cloth bag. He used the universal hand signal for a cell phone and mimed putting it in the bag.

Very security conscious. I like it.

They each dug out their cell phones, already enclosed in their signal-blocking Faraday bags, which would prevent the phones from being detected and tracked.

With a nod, the man spoke in heavily accented but perfect English. "My friends," he began, exactly as Conroy had as Pioneer Prime, and Cody continued as the current Pioneer of the now much less radical Movement. "Welcome."

PART 8

WEDNESDAY, JANUARY 4

69

SOCHI

Tbilisi - Senaki - Leselidze Highway
The Border of Georgian and Russia

A mile ahead, the border crossing was lit up by enormous lights on tall poles.

Five hours into their drive, Axe was looking for just the right vehicle to trail through the border inspection.

"There. Follow that car," Axe told the driver, pointing at the car they had started to pass. Haley and he weren't sure how much English he spoke —he hadn't said a word since greeting them at the airport—but he complied, slowing down and signaling to change lanes.

The cheaper-model car ahead of them, dark blue or black, was clean and in good shape, but looked like it had a lot of miles on it. A perfectly nondescript car driven just under the speed limit in the right lane by a younger man—mid-twenties—with a large mustache and a beat-up ball cap.

My gut tells me he's shady—or at least worth another look.

Maybe the border patrol guards would feel the same way.

They stayed behind the dark car as they neared the busy southern Russian border crossing. Axe eyed the cars ahead of them as they slowly made their way forward.

It looks like they are spot-checking cars.

Semi-tractor-trailers had their own inspection lanes and checkpoint to the right, separated by a large concrete barrier. One plan for dealing with the border had been to sneak out of the car and slip across attached to the undercarriage of a trailer. They would drop off as the eighteen-wheeler accelerated and wait for their driver to pick them up along the road.

That plan went out the window as the trucks were directed to the side.

No plan survives first contact with the enemy.

Now they had to place their trust in the fake passports, along with their driver's nerves and ability to cover for them.

And Haley's beauty, if it comes to that.

The car moved forward a few more feet as the border guard waved the latest car through with barely a glance.

Two more cars, then us. We're in position to be stopped and searched. It's us or the car in front or behind.

"Are they going by a pattern—every third or fourth car—or are there criteria?" he asked Haley in a low tone. The driver glanced at him in the rearview mirror but said nothing.

"A little of both is my guess," she said, taking off her ball cap and shaking out her hair. In the glare of the floodlights turning the area into daytime, her blond hair glowed.

The driver glanced at her, looked away, then turned to look again before returning to gaze straight ahead, obviously resisting the urge to stare.

"Don't overdo it," Axe cautioned in a quiet voice as she put on lip gloss. "We don't want to get detained because they want to hit on you."

"But if we get stopped, looking like the model I'm pretending to be is essential."

"Good point."

Axe debated pulling out his camera from the backpack on the seat next to him but decided against it. Every country gets touchy about photos taken at the border. He could show the camera off if they were questioned.

At least Haley's boss put together a good legend for me.

Before leaving Las Vegas, Axe had familiarized himself with the online portfolio prepared for him. Axe's actual photos from his photography website had been put on a different site with his fake name. Featured prominently were artistic ones of Haley in a bikini from their time hunting "The Assistant" in Mexico a few months before.

If I can get them to pull up the website, we win. Haley is a natural model and the pictures of her prove my abilities. They'll buy the cover story of us taking winter photos in exotic locations for my summer art show.

The car at the head of the line received a more thorough check. One guard looked at the passport of the driver while another guard shone a flashlight through all the windows. Then the trunk popped open, and the second guard dug through it, but with little enthusiasm.

The rifle I requested is hidden somewhere in this car. If they find it, we're screwed.

He and Haley could plead ignorance and blame the gun on the driver... but would their Movement contact take the fall or give them up?

Guard number two slammed the trunk much harder than needed, making the entire car shake.

A petty display of power.

The first guard handed the driver's passport back, and the car drove through the border crossing.

Their driver pulled forward a car length.

One more, then us. Come on, sketchy-looking guy!

The guards looked tired, but they took their boring jobs seriously. Once again, guard number two used his flashlight to check the interior of the older car through the windows while the other inspected sketchy guy's identification.

How much will they care about Americans crossing the border in the middle of the night? I wish we had passports from a different country.

The trunk of the car in front of them rose. The second guard inspected it. After a few seconds, he called to his partner. He didn't sound concerned, but something had caught his attention and demanded a closer look.

Excellent. They have the same feeling I did.

This mission was all about stealth, intelligence, and planning instead of brute force and firepower. From Haley setting the trap for Zimalev to their undercover border crossing, it could work.

SEALs are more than just trigger pullers. We can be subtle—when necessary.

Guard number one directed the car to pull to the side. A third guard—tall, mid-thirties—came out of a small, sturdy guard shack and took his place as the first two followed the car selected for inspection.

Our turn.

The new guard impatiently gestured them ahead.

The Movement man turned on the interior dome light as he pulled forward. He greeted the guard in what sounded like Russian and handed over his passport, along with Axe's and Haley's.

The guard flicked them open, holding them up one by one to compare their faces with the pictures. He asked a question.

I don't speak Russian, but that sounded like 'Americans?'

Their driver said something that sounded reassuring—and pointed at Haley.

That has to be, 'She's a model.'

The man spoke again and gestured at Axe.

And I'm a photographer.

Their driver continued, apparently explaining the cover story Haley had emailed Bec, which must have been passed on. The guard glanced at Axe, but his eyes kept returning to Haley as she smiled at him.

Careful... don't overdo it.

Finally, the guard glanced at the long line of cars behind theirs, made up his mind, and handed the passports back. Then he said something and gestured them forward.

We made it.

An hour after the border crossing, they pulled off the highway, stopping along a deserted side road. Their driver guided them to the back of the car, where he squatted and reached under the rear bumper. He tugged, pulling out a rifle protected by old bubble wrap. The weapon looked well maintained, had the 4x scope common to the model, and a magazine of ten bullets.

If I need more than one bullet, we're in trouble.

Still, the extras felt good.

They'll be nice to have for the worst-case scenario.

Axe hadn't mentioned it to Haley, and hoped she wouldn't think of it herself, but they couldn't be captured alive. Being discovered dead would be bad enough. Taken and interrogated, tortured until they agreed to provide an all-too-real videotaped confession, would be devastating.

Dead, he would be a former Navy SEAL who went off the deep end and took matters into his own crazy hands. Haley would be an office worker from Washington D.C. who had fallen in with him, not the president's adopted niece.

Axe's world revolved around contingencies. He hated the idea, but he already had a plan if they were discovered. First, he had to kill Haley. It would be horrible, but he would break her neck.

He wasn't sure about breaking his own, though. And without any of the three knives he normally carried, however, he had planned on it.

The gun eliminates that concern, at least.

The model wasn't ideal for a long-range sniper shot, but it's what he expected. It had been in production for decades in the region and was easy to find… and to buy on the black market.

It will do… if Haley's trap works.

Axe nodded his approval. They re-wrapped the gun and used duct tape to attach it to its hiding place.

Their odd, nameless driver, who continued to avoid all communication, went where they pointed on the map Axe had provided. On the outskirts of Rzhanaya Polyana, Russia, sixty kilometers northeast of Sochi, Haley stopped him at the remote spot they had identified before leaving the warehouse in Las Vegas over thirty hours earlier.

He left the car in gear but turned off the lights, along with the overhead dome light.

Axe and Haley slipped out, gathered essential gear in their backpacks —and the Russian sniper rifle—and left the rest of their luggage behind. Axe slammed the hatchback, and the car took off immediately, driving several seconds before its headlights came on.

From here on out, carrying a sniper rifle like this, we cannot be seen. Even a glimpse compromises the mission.

They set off up a hiking trail. The night wasn't as cold as Axe had expected from Sochi, Russia—well above freezing. But he remembered the controversy around having winter sporting events in the area where it rarely snowed. It had also been a mild winter so far this year, with less snow than usual. The ground looked more like southern Virginia in fall than Russia in winter. There wasn't even a dusting of snow, and the temperature felt like it was in the upper thirties.

With any luck, and the gear we brought, we won't die… from the cold, at least.

Axe set a brisk pace, but Haley kept up easily. Ideally, they would have arrived hours earlier, in the middle of the night instead of six in the morning. But the plane schedules didn't allow for it, and the long ride from the airport took time.

If the Russian president had already taken Haley's bait, security would be tight.

How far out will they extend the security zone, though, for a last-minute addition to the schedule?

They hiked through the dark, dawn two hours away, finding a compromise between speed and stealth.

The luge, bobsled, and skeleton track sat in a valley on the other side of the mountain.

Axe stopped where the trail leveled off, branching left and right, circling the mountain. They were sweaty. Both had removed their warm beanie hats and unzipped their parkas. The mild temperature was a blessing, as was the lack of snow.

But here's where it gets tricky.

The sky now had light enough to see better. Axe edged forward on the hiking trail, going left, much slower than before. Haley moved behind him, not as quietly, but acceptable.

For now, when no one is near us, she's quiet enough.

On the flight, he'd coached her on moving more stealthily. She'd walked the plane's aisle as people slept, practicing.

There's a big difference between an airplane and the woods, especially when they are filled with soldiers.

Haley followed Axe, carefully stepping where he had, remembering what he had taught her.

'Slow is smooth and smooth is fast.'

Whatever that meant.

Vadim and the dog were making good time today, and it was light enough for him to turn off the headlamp. They both loved running this trail, the one circling the mountain halfway up its side. The climb from the resort wasn't difficult, and the trail was the perfect length for an early morning workout before his shift at the hotel.

It also got the dog exercise, so he'd sleep in the apartment all day and not bark at every sound, annoying the neighbors.

Vadim picked up the pace, pushing it. He'd gained a few pounds over the previous weeks—and so had the dog. But now it was the new year. Time to get back in shape before the surge of tourists starting next week and continuing through spring. He had to look good for any lonely women from Moscow hoping for a vacation fling.

In front of her, Axe froze at the sound ahead of them on the worn hiking trail.

It's the jangle of a dog collar.

It could be a guard, but it would be the first they'd seen or heard. Could it be a local out for a hike?

Axe stepped off the trail and moved up the steep side of the mountain. She followed close.

We can hide behind those trees.

Twenty feet up the slope, they stopped behind the group of trees and froze. She heard a dog panting, along with the pounding of a man's feet. A trail runner, perhaps?

If the dog's off the leash, we're screwed.

They could pull out the camera Axe brought along, but anyone seeing the sniper rifle would have to die.

I don't want to kill innocent civilians.

But did they have a choice?

What is one life when we are trying to stop a war?

The pounding feet and jangling collar drew closer.

Please keep running. I don't want to have to kill you.

And what about the dog? They would have to kill the dog, too, right?

Don't stop. Please, don't stop!

Seconds later, the person ran by on the trail below, the dog leading the way, never slowing down to investigate their scent.

Haley relaxed with relief, grateful she didn't have to kill either the person or the dog.

They waited another few minutes, then returned to the trail and continued their journey. Axe led the way, even more cautiously than he had before.

Physically, the hike was well within her ability. It wasn't too cold, they moved relatively slowly to avoid making noise, and she was in excellent shape.

Mentally, however, she struggled.

So much is riding on this.

A lot had to go right for her trap to work.

Did Mom give Brenda—the First Lady of the United States—my message? Did Aunt Brenda pass it along? Finally, did Uncle Jimmy trust me and do the sledding stunt?

And as much as Haley had poured herself into learning about Zimalev, and felt she knew him, could she truly predict his actions? Or was she deluding herself?

If he's putting the finishing touches on an invasion plan, will he care about one-upping President Heringten?

Could the man's ego be that large?

So far, they had no sign he'd taken the bait. There was no security on the roads. No patrols in the woods. Nothing but a sleepy tourist area in the mountains a week after the holidays. Who goes on vacation during the first week of the new year? No one.

Which is why I thought Zimalev would be willing to visit on the spur of the moment.

Security would be simple. He already had a trip on his public schedule —a plan to visit Rostov-on-Don, a port city only an hour's flight north. He would inspect the troops stationed in the area prior to the invasion—which the world didn't know was imminent.

He won't be able to pass up a chance to show off.

Haley couldn't decide if she was hopeful or delusional.

With her mind swinging from doubt to certainty and back, they walked through the woods as the sky lightened.

Are we lucky there are no patrols? Or is it proof we're wasting our time?

At least if the plan failed, Gregory, Nancy, and Dave would back them up and get word of the coming attack to the president.

70

REPORT

Central Analysis Group Headquarters
Alexandria, Virginia

"Mr. President," Gregory began, "it's our conclusion the Russians are about to invade Ukraine in an effort to destroy NATO as a first step to exerting more influence over Europe. Additionally, your niece Haley has disappeared."

He paused, took a deep breath, and sighed.

No. I have to leave Haley out of it until he asks.

Gregory sat in his office, strategizing what he might say to his boss, the President of the United States, if Haley's plan—whatever it was—went to hell.

Which could be happening right now, for all I know.

He couldn't guess where she was or what she was doing, but he tried to put himself in her shoes.

What is the most logical—but completely insane—approach in this situation?

He drew a blank.

He'd once been like her. Young and brilliant. Brash. Chafing at the rules. Rebellious.

What happened?

He'd been ground down. Starting out, by the conservative culture of the CIA, where covering your ass came before exceptional analysis.

Later, by his desire for comfort. After several years of consistent paychecks for the car payment, mortgage, money for investing, and fun vacations, risking it all for a principal no longer made sense.

Lifestyle creep is the problem.

With each small raise, his spending went up accordingly. Instead of camping, he splurged on a hotel. Another year, a higher salary, and suddenly the two-star hotel wasn't good enough. First a two-and-a-half star made sense, then three-, then a four-star, all in nicer, more expensive locations. Once, a vacation for a week in Sarasota made him feel like a millionaire. A few years later, not even Miami would do. The Caribbean and Hawaii emerged as his go-to vacation spots.

'Pick your battles' became his motto. Gregory stood his ground and fought to be heard on the big ones, but let the rest go. He'd had more than his share of spectacular successes because of it. But if he didn't have a high conviction, along with an actionable plan to take to his bosses, he let it go.

He wrote detailed reports, including his analysis—properly couched in hedges such as, "potentially," and "may be possible that…" Right more often than most other analysts, he'd gotten a reputation for being smart and perceptive—and a team player who didn't rock the boat.

In other words, he didn't go out of a limb making crazy predictions he couldn't back up with facts—even when he felt he was correct, and later proven right.

I learned to play it safe.

For the last few months, Gregory had tried to change his ways by supporting Haley and her unorthodox methods—many of which he'd used years ago, before abandoning them for the straight and narrow road of caution and personal security.

But as much as he struggled to not fall back into his old ways, he'd found it exceedingly difficult—especially when first Nancy, then Dave, started to rely on their hunches and gut feelings.

"Mr. President," he began again, trying another approach. "Your niece is remarkable. She and two of my other analysts have uncovered a plot to destroy NATO and weaken Europe, along with the USA, of course. The data is slim, but it's there. Haley is off doing… something. She wouldn't tell me. I don't have any recommendations for what you should do, or concrete proof, but here's what we suspect."

How would the honest approach be received?

I'll be the laughingstock of the intelligence community unless I tell only the president.

And where the hell was Haley?

She has every right to not trust me with her secret plan. She doesn't understand how much I believe in her, Nancy, and Dave—and want to support them.

"Mr. President," Gregory started, practicing yet another approach. He hoped Haley and Axe succeeded, but if they didn't, he had to be prepared for the most critical presentation of his career.

This was one battle, and analysis, he'd risk it all for.

71

COMPETITION

The Kremlin
Moscow, Russia

President Pavel Zimalev stalked through the outer offices on his way to the helicopter. He would fly to Rostov-on-Don, inspect and inspire the troops, then return well before the storm—and the invasion. If he could return before dinner, all the better.

I had enough horrible army food during my active-duty days.

He stopped in front of a small television showing the international news channel. The President of the United States sat behind children on a toboggan, pushed off, and slid down a small hill. The children yelled with delight. In the background, the White House loomed.

The scene cut to two news reporters in a studio, smiling and remarking what a wonderful winter scene it was.

Pavel grudgingly admired the propaganda. The clip would play all day around the world—until the snowstorm hitting Europe replaced it.

After which, the news would report on his invasion.

But for a while, the world would smile along with the American president and the children.

Let it go. Sledding down a small slope with toddlers is pitiful for the leader of a country.

Pavel had competed at the highest level, sliding down steep bobsled courses on a tiny piece of plastic at one-hundred-forty-five kilometers per hour. The silver medal hung in his office.

And yet the American president got accolades for playing with children.

He took a step, then stopped. Behind him, Timor, his Chief of Staff, nearly bumped into him. A thin, tall, bookish man with a sharp, devious mind, he stood ready to do his president's bidding around the clock.

"I will go to the bobsled track outside Sochi first," the president said, "ride the skeleton, and show the world how a true leader goes sledding. Then I will fly to Rostov-on-Don and inspect the troops. I will share their evening meal in the mess hall with them. See to it."

I'll gladly suffer one more army meal to show up the American idiot.

Timor nodded, then hesitated.

"What now?" Pavel glared at the man.

"Mr. President, of course I can make this happen. But may I suggest another day? We need more time to set up adequate security."

His Chief of Staff was aware of the invasion plans, of course, but they were so secret even he didn't know the full details.

There will be no other time. After today, the blizzard, then the invasion. I will have no time for sledding—and will have missed my chance.

"No, I will do it today. The area will be deserted this week. No one is aware I am coming. There will be no time for anyone wishing me harm to prepare for my arrival. You will gather a crowd of locals—and television crews—and we will show our people their leader in action."

"Yes, sir," the man said, spun on his heel, and rushed to make the arrangements.

The world press would show the clips side by side, making Pavel's point for him.

Domestically, he would ensure the news programs ran footage of him sledding, but also eating with his troops later. He would be seen as a young, athletic president loved by his comrades.

"Bring me my old helmet and racing jumpsuit," he said to another aide. It had been a few years, but the outfit would still fit. He kept himself in excellent shape.

Pavel spun and returned to his office. It would take the staff time to make the changes to his schedule and gather the rest of his gear.

72

RISK

Axe led them to the location they'd picked from online satellite maps.

They had still not encountered any patrols. Even with the sun up, the sleepy sports complex in the valley below them looked deserted.

From the trail, Axe used the binoculars to check the angle and range to the track. It would work—barely. They were directly in front of the bobsled track start area, a half-mile away. The starting line was covered, like much of the track. But from this position, they could see into the darkened building with the open front at top of the run. There was seating for spectators on the left, with the right side reserved for coaches, competitors, and officials. The track ran flat for ten feet, then came a steep slope before the twists, turns, and more drops of the rest of the course. This top part was where competitors sprinted to launch their bobsleds, luges, or, in this case, skeleton sled.

The Russian president had excelled at the event in his youth, earning medal after medal before aging out. According to Haley's plan, this is where he would be at some point today.

Where I'll shoot him.

Axe passed the binoculars to Haley, who surveyed the area, then nodded to him.

They inspected the immediate area and found a nearby spot above the trail where several large trees grew close together. Axe eased up the steep slope, stepping on rocks to avoid leaving footprints. With no snow to worry about, seeing the best places to step was simple.

Several feet up, behind the big trees, was a small, flat area. Bushes and smaller trees shielded it from view of anyone on the trail.

This is perfect.

While Axe lay down, he gestured for Haley to join him. They needed to double-check the angle before starting the camouflage process which their lives would depend on. He took the rifle and looked through the 4x scope.

I wish I had more powerful optics, but what are you going to do, deep behind enemy lines, completely unsupported on an unsanctioned mission?

He lined up the shot.

The president runs from the starting line, pushing the sled, preparing to drop onto it... Damn.

He couldn't see the launch area. The roof blocked it.

Through the scope, he aimed again. The angle was off. They were too high by a few feet. The only shot he'd have was targeting lower on the track than they'd planned, after the first steep drop.

Not only would Haley's carefully calculated timing be off, the target would be moving faster, magnifying the chance of missing—and failure.

It's one thing to die for a successful mission. It's another to die for nothing.

"Don't run to your death." The SEAL saying certainly fit here, despite them not physically running. It also meant don't hurry to do stupid stuff which could get you killed.

He wiggled left and right, looking for a solution. Haley joined him on the ground, watching with concern.

Could we excavate deep enough for it to work?

Their camouflage plan already called for digging "graves" to hide from the inevitable searches once they took the shot. Axe scooted forward more, down the slope, doing his best to not leave traces of his movements, before checking again.

No. This position won't work. Not for the shot we planned.

He whispered in Haley's ear. "Too high."

She whispered back. "I can't see the start line, either. Without it, I can't calculate the timing to tell you when to take the shot. What about lower, down the mountain?"

Axe shook his head. They'd be much less likely to be discovered several feet above a trail than below it. No matter how dedicated the soldiers were, they would use the trail system to search, branching off from it in likely shooting places. And the men would see much more looking down than up.

"Position two?" Axe suggested.

She nodded.

I wonder if we came all this way for nothing. But if so, we can chalk it up to paid training for the next time.

Haley scattered leaves carefully over the position they had just ruled out. They scrambled back to the trail, then hiked toward the second position they'd considered back in Vegas.

Haley looked through the binoculars at the deserted starting area at the top of the track, covered by an ornate roof. The day was bright and cloudless, letting in light through the thick glass windows behind the spectator seating. She could see where Zimalev would start his run.

Factoring the timing for the shot won't be a problem. It's actually easier from here.

She'd watched video of the Russian president's medal-winning events from when he was a teenager. She had compared his old start times with dozens of other young athletes from the past few years. Then she'd done calculations based on Zimalev's age, fitness level, and expected abilities. No matter how she calculated the variables, the answers were within one second of each other. All he was doing was running along the track, pushing his sled, then laying down on it. From this position, those seconds of pushing the sled were blocked. But an instant after falling to the sled, he'd be exposed, still traveling no faster than his sprint had propelled him. Four seconds from when he started running, give or take a few hundredths.

Unless he slips or trips and falls. Or takes it easy. Or has been practicing without our knowledge.

Or any of a dozen other variables.

The shot was too risky. Those few hundredths of a second meant the difference between success and failure.

No, this position is worse.

The expected frontal shot at the previous position would have been perfect. With the president running straight toward him for ten seconds, before falling onto the sled, Axe could have hit him easily without worrying much about the timing. Any semi-accurate shot within that ten-second window would have succeeded.

We should abort. No sense dying over a lost cause.

The memory of when she first shot Todd "The Assistant" Burkley hit her. She felt the same now—like she'd made a mistake of epic proportions.

I've risked our lives and put the United States in danger by coming here. If we were to be caught…

She didn't want to think of how bad it would be for the country, Uncle Jimmy, or her and Axe.

With Burkley, her instincts had been accurate after all. But this was different.

Besides, no security is here. Having no shot doesn't matter without a target. I'm calling it.

She scooted closer to Axe to whisper in his ear, which now seemed foolish. No one else walked these trails. They were alone, except for a few workers and guests in the resort in the valley.

He held up his finger, asking her to wait.

I recognize that expression.

He had an idea.

Axe took the binoculars back from Haley, looked at the scene below them, and worked the problem.

Three-quarters of a mile. Far out of the standard range of the gun.

Haley had asked for a sniper rifle, and one had been provided. Unfortunately, the Russians had developed and mass-produced this type of gun more for a well-trained marksman to use in support of a squad of soldiers, not as a true long-range weapon. But with thousands of them manufactured over the past decades, he had guessed this was what he'd end up with. A true, high-end rifle would have been much harder to acquire.

At least it's a good design and looks well maintained.

He had his concerns, however. Was it zeroed in? Had the ride in the car thrown off the scope? Were the bullets military grade? How clean was it?

They'd had no time or opportunity to test the weapon. He had to take it as it came.

Position three?

Their last-ditch location was the closest to the building. It had a good angle, straight on—similar to their first location, not off to the side like this second one.

I can guarantee a hit from there, with this weapon, the angle, everything.

But they were extremely likely to get caught.

Which we'd both rather avoid.

He sighed, frustrated.

Wait. What if...

The construction of these big sports venues, under deadline for a major world event, always went over budget and were finished only at the last minute.

If corners were cut in the construction, combined with the years passing, and the elements...

Axe looked at the decorative awning above the main viewing area at the top of the track. It looked like metal.

A planned ricochet?

No. The bullet would go right through it.

But below it, supporting the wavy roof, was a concrete pillar. Further down the track, other pillars held up smaller canopies, sheltering the track from the elements. They had extensive padding, in case of a disaster where an athlete lost control and came off the ice. Near the start, however, at the slow speeds along the straight portion of the track, the gray concrete sat bare.

How much damage would a bullet do to the concrete? Would the pillar absorb it? Or would chips of concrete—or chunks—go flying upon impact?

Landing right on the track.

The track's first steep slope started immediately below where he surveyed. The competitors picked up a lot of speed before a sharp turn.

Is it worth the risk?

He wouldn't make the call on his own. Haley would have to agree.

From their hide, Haley and Axe heard, then saw, troop transports arrive. They hunkered down, not using the binoculars—avoiding the risk of light glinting off them and giving away their position.

Haley felt elated.

Zimalev fell for it!

The plan could work. There were still many things that had to go right, but they were on track. She hadn't wanted to mention her concerns to Axe earlier, that the whole thing was a colossal waste of time, and didn't have to. He felt it too, she could tell.

When they discussed Axe's plan for the shot, she went along with it in part because she'd given up hope. Zimalev wasn't coming.

But not long after, the patrols started. They were undisciplined, casual. The first two-man team eventually passed on the trail below them, smoking and chatting.

They're out for a pleasant walk in the woods with the officers back in the valley.

She suppressed a satisfied smile, understanding their lack of concern.

The decision wasn't made to come here until this morning. There would be no time for an enemy to arrive. In their minds, the patrols are pointless.

Still, what they lacked in discipline or attentiveness, they made up for in numbers. Every fifteen minutes, a group passed below them. Some took their jobs more seriously, walking slowly, looking around.

Or maybe they're lazy, strolling instead of covering more ground.

She and Axe kept their heads down, not watching the soldiers. They lay in shallow trenches they'd dug in the unfrozen ground. She knew Axe well enough now to hear him call them graves, merely from the look he shot her when they were done digging. The crazy smile reminded her of Mad Dog.

They're all cut from the same cloth.

Whether it was the training, the experiences, or the type of men the SEAL Teams attracted, they all had a similar black humor.

I wonder if I'll end up with it eventually, as well.

As Axe had camouflaged her, face down and pointed toward the valley below, it had felt like a day at the beach as a kid when her friends had buried her in the sand. She lay tucked in her sleeping bag, covered in dirt, leaves, and dead moss. Only her head and arms were exposed. They were well disguised, too, with branches and leaves attached to hide her outline in the unlikely event the soldiers ventured several feet up the steep slope toward them.

Axe lay next to her, similarly hidden, and whenever patrols

approached, they practiced his black hole disappearing technique, which he'd taught her in the airplane on the flight over.

Axe froze. Beside him, Haley did the same.

Someone is out there again. Better than the others—much more disciplined.

Sensing an opponent wasn't a skill they'd been shown in BUD/S. As far as he knew, it couldn't be taught—but it could be learned. Place yourself in enough dangerous situations and eventually, you either pick it up or die trying.

People were coming toward them. Soldiers who knew how to move stealthily.

These Russians are different. They are pros.

Axe had his face turned toward Haley. He nodded slowly and shut down, hoping the lessons taught on the plane worked in the field. It was one thing to attempt to disappear with the regular soldiers who had passed below them so far. Against the men approaching now, it would be essential. While they couldn't be seen from below, an experienced warrior might sense Haley, or at least know a danger lay nearby.

Axe had never before tried teaching his innate ability. During sniper training, he'd discovered a talent for turning invisible. He could go dark and somehow limit his energy or aura. As long as he was even partly hidden, no one could see or sense him. It worked amazingly well during training, to the frustration of many instructors who prided themselves on being able to detect their newbie students and teach them important lessons.

"First, I guess I calm my mind. No thought," he'd told Haley as the people in business class on the plane around them slept. "I let it all go. No worry, no fear, hope... nothing."

"That alone is much harder than you make it sound," she'd replied.

"True. Think of it like being asleep, but conscious. Try it."

Axe turned away in his spacious seat, giving her a few seconds. He could still easily feel her. "Are you trying to force your energy inward?" He turned back to see her frowning.

"How do you know?"

He shrugged. "I've done this a very long time. Try again. Don't direct the energy. Let it go completely. You're not the dark side of the moon. You're a black hole."

They practiced for an hour before agreeing they needed to rest. By the time Axe returned from using the restroom, Haley was asleep under the blankets provided with their seats.

He sat near her for several minutes before she walked up with a huge grin on her face, picked up the blanket covering her carry-on bag, and got ready for a nap. "You walked right past me on your way back from the bathroom," she explained. "The black hole trick worked."

Laying in their graves, they both went dark.

A few minutes later, the men stopped on the trail directly below them.

They're good.

Did they sense him or Haley? Had they left an errant footprint to be discovered?

If I had my knife, we'd have a fighting chance. I could kill at least one silently, put them in our graves, and we could climb up and over the mountain. We might make it out.

Without the knife, he couldn't risk it. If the guards overpowered him, they'd be captured. And gunshots would bring more of the enemy.

After a few minutes, the men moved down the trail.

He cracked his eyes to stare into Haley's, only a foot away. With the tiniest of movements, he tried to communicate what he sensed.

One of them is still there.

Her eyes closed slowly.

The wait seemed like forever but was probably only five minutes. Axe sensed more than heard the second man finally continue walking.

He's an experienced professional. From now on, we're dark, just in case he comes back.

Small assault helicopters patrolled overhead a while later, but the thick forest on the slope of the mountain shielded them from view. The tall trees surrounding them provided plenty of cover from the air.

Zimalev is on the way.

Haley felt exhausted from remaining invisible.

Having no energy signature takes a lot of effort.

Dozens of vehicles entered the parking area nearly a mile ahead and below them.

Busses of spectators and press. He needs the audience to feed his ego. Simply staging it for TV won't give him what he wants.

She lay still and waited.

The fighter jets circling overhead signaled Zimalev's impending arrival.

The pounding sound from a huge helicopter confirmed it.

Axe opened his eyes and breathed out heavier than he had for the past four hours they'd been dark, waiting.

Haley's eyes cracked open and met his.

It's time.

In slow motion, they both moved, adjusting stiff muscles. He wondered if Haley's more youthful body felt the effects of holding still so long as much as he did.

Probably not. But she will someday, assuming we live through this afternoon.

While she looked through the binoculars, he used the underpowered scope.

If a shot presents itself as Zimalev leaves the chopper, do I take it?

He got ready, just in case. He centered on the likely landing spot of the helicopter, checked the wind, calculated the drop, and adjusted the scope.

A deep breath in and out, relaxing. He calmed his body and mind and slowed his heartbeat.

The helicopter came in from the north, circled once, then landed.

A crowd of about one hundred people cheered and waved from behind a barricade. Axe had no shot. The helicopter blocked his view. President Zimalev must have stepped out of the helicopter once its rotors had stopped spinning, though, because the crowd went wild.

Seconds later, they calmed down.

He's in the building.

Axe continued preparing himself to assassinate the lawfully elected leader of a foreign country.

He banished any doubts about whether it was the best choice. They'd been over it again and again as they planned in Las Vegas. Zimalev was responsible at least for the death of one United States senator and the attempted assassination of another. Plus the spiked beer served to innocent Americans.

The threat facing the country from the man warranted it.

Axe put his desire for revenge in a box.

If we fail, it will cause more harm than good.

That concern joined the others in the box to deal with after the mission.

He thought through his contingency plan once more before putting it away with his feelings. If they were about to be captured, Axe would have to kill Haley first, then himself.

My life doesn't matter.

He'd lived when he should have died, too many times to count. He was ready for the darkness, the light, Valhalla, or whatever came next.

But what about Haley? She's at the beginning of her life and career. She's too young to die. Can I kill her?

The thought of shooting Haley point-blank or breaking her neck proved too difficult to stuff away.

What did Nalen say when he gave me the pep talk on New Year's Eve Day?

Any feelings that clawed out of the box could be used as motivation.

Fine. I won't have to kill Haley because I'm going to make the shot. Then we go dark and lay here until they give up looking for us.

Axe focused on the pillar next to the icy sledding track, putting aside all the feelings churning within.

The crowd roared. They'd either brought whistles, horns, and cowbells, or they had been provided. The noise reached Haley, loud even at this distance. She watched through the building's windows as they waved Russian flags.

It must be deafening inside the starting area.

The powerful binoculars made her feel like she was in the stands, close to the action.

Zimalev entered wearing a skin-tight jumpsuit in white, blue, and red, the colors of the Russian flag.

"Soon," she whispered to Axe.

Next to her, his breathing slowed further. Otherwise, he didn't speak or move.

The Russian president accepted a skeleton sled. It looked like a futuristic black tray, four feet long, with runners on the bottom and handles along the top. He hoisted it in the air and shook it, playing to the crowd, a huge grin on his face. The spectators cheered louder.

Haley recalculated.

The energy from the audience will inspire him. He'll go faster than he otherwise would.

With the shot Axe had planned, it wouldn't make much difference, but it mattered to her.

I want the debris to land right in front of him. Early enough so he's distracted and panics, late enough so he'll act instinctively and jerk to the side.

Any fear or sudden movements while on the sled, going face-first down a bobsled track, chin inches above the ice, would prove catastrophic.

We hope.

They were betting a lot on a tricky gunshot, guesstimated timing, and the concrete pillar.

Zimalev accepted a black helmet from an aide.

"Helmet is on."

Pavel relished the cheering spectators almost as much as being back on the icy track. He'd changed into his form-fitting jumpsuit, proud of his fitness level. He felt confident and focused, two essential qualities for sliding face-first down the track at high speed.

He waved to the crowd, which went crazy with enthusiasm.

I have to commend my staff. Wherever they recruited these "volunteers" from, they did a great job.

Holding the black skeleton sled, he readied himself, tuning out the noise from his fans and preparing for his run.

Time to show the American president how a real man sleds.

The crowd kept the noise up while the president composed himself. He held the sled and stared down the track.

"Ready," Haley whispered, keeping her voice as quiet as possible, but needing to make sure Axe heard.

He let out a long, audible breath, the signal he was ready to fire.

This is it.

The Russian pushed off and started sprinting down the track.

One-one thousand, two-one thousand.

"Now!"

Axe fired. She absently heard the crack of the gun. She adjusted the binoculars.

Chunks of gray concrete flew onto the ice. An instant later, a white, blue, and red blur went by before disappearing under the awning covering the track.

Did it work?

73

FLIGHT

Pavel Zimalev reacted with the instincts of the soldier he had become, not the world-class skeleton slider he had been in his youth. When the gray material peppered the track a half meter in front of him, he slid off the sled, convinced he was being targeted.

For a brief moment, he thought he would be fine. The sled continued without him, bumping over what looked like rocks as he slid safely by, off to the side of the track. The sled picked up speed as both it and he dropped down the first steep section of the track and entered the banked curve.

He underestimated how fast he was going and overestimated how much control he had.

Digging in his toes and hands, he tried to slow himself, but his efforts made no difference.

He swung up the side of the steep curve, picking up more speed, sliding on stomach, chest, legs, and arms.

Never before had he been in a situation like this.

Can I drive my body like a sled?

It was his only hope, but he had trouble getting his head around it.

One false move...

An instant later, Pavel reprimanded himself. Any fear on the track, at these speeds, only made matters worse.

In the brief moment his nerves faltered and his mind considered the danger, his body moved the wrong way at the wrong time.

He lost control and was still gaining speed. His body bounced on the ice and careened wildly from one side of the track to the other.

The next drop caused him to go even faster. He fought the fear growing by the second, trying to get his body under control along with his mind.

At the next curve, he swung higher up the ice, then higher…

He left the track, flying through the air.

No! Oh, no!

The blue padding covering the concrete pillar filled his vision.

He crashed into it headfirst, blacking out instantly.

Haley had tracked the president sliding out of control—off his sled—as he went in and out of sight on the winding course. Suddenly, he came back into view, sailing higher and higher as the bobsled track seemed to spit him off.

He flew through the air and slammed headfirst into the concrete pillar.

Was there enough padding to protect him?

Axe watched through the scope as people rushed to Zimalev's body lying at the base of one of the concrete pillars.

Is he dead, or at least injured badly enough to prevent the invasion?

A man carrying a small medical bag, who appeared to be a personal physician—the same as an American president always had his doctor along—dropped to his knees next to Zimalev, who had landed on his back at the base of the pillar.

Axe considered what he and Haley were about to go through—dozens, if not hundreds, of soldiers combing the area looking for them. Even if it had been too noisy because of the cheering crowd to hear the gunshot down in the valley nearly a mile away, surely the soldiers who had been patrolling would wonder about it.

What are the odds our concealment, as good as it is, holds up against the determined efforts of men whose president we just killed?

Axe didn't like their chances.

But it had to be done. Aside from stopping the invasion and threat to world peace, the man responsible for the attacks on our senators had to be punished.

A last look at Haley, laying a foot away, confirmed she was perfectly camouflaged. Someone would have to be standing right on top of them to notice. But he rehearsed again the moves he would make if their hide was approached by soldiers. If they were about to be captured, it had to be done, no matter how much he loathed the idea.

Quickly reach over with both hands as the guards come up the slope. Break her neck before she realizes what I'm doing—I don't want her to know what's coming and be afraid. Then put the rifle to my forehead and pull the trigger.

Killing Haley and himself was the last thing he wanted to do. But he'd gladly sacrifice them both for the United States of America.

If it comes to that, killing ourselves is the only way to be sure we don't get captured and cause a bigger problem than we solved.

74

THE BLIZZARD

The Sliding Center
Rzhanaya Polyana, Russia

The blue sky confused Pavel Zimalev. He lay on his back. His body hurt badly, his head most of all.

Where am I?

"Mr. President? Can you hear me?" a man near him asked. "He's awake."

"Thank God," a second voice said.

Pavel's personal physician, who traveled everywhere he went, knelt over him, looking shocked.

"Where am I? What happened?" Pavel asked, blinking his eyes and trying to make sense of the situation.

His head throbbed in pain and felt cloudy, like he had the worst hangover ever. He couldn't think clearly. His mind wasn't working properly.

"There was an accident and you hit your head," the second man—his Chief of Staff, also kneeling at his side—told him. "Mr. President, you're badly injured. The helicopter will fly you to a hospital, and we will make sure the spectators never mention what they saw."

He stared at the sky.

So blue. Why is it important?

The invasion! He couldn't recall an accident, but he had to watch for clouds, then snow, and time the attack order perfectly. When the snow came, the West would truly understand Russia's strength—and his own.

The pain in his head grew, becoming unbearable.

"Doctor!" he heard a voice yell, but he no longer cared about the activity around him. He tried to resist the feeling of slipping away but couldn't fight it. Instead, he smiled at the bright white light enveloping him. It felt like the biggest blizzard ever, and he welcomed it.

75

PAYBACK

Rzhanaya Polyana Natural Area
Russia

Haley let out a quiet sigh of relief as one of the men kneeling over Zimalev took off his heavy coat and lay it on the president, covering his face and body.

She looked at Axe next to her watching the scene through his rifle scope. He glanced over and they nodded at each other. They had done it.

Payback is a bitch.

Axe pulled the gun back alongside him and settled his head against the ground. He'd just killed the President of Russia, the man responsible for drugging innocent civilians in Las Vegas and attacking three senators.

That's what you get for coming after the United States of America.

He let out a long breath, allowing his energy to dissipate so he could vanish in preparation for the coming manhunt. Axe released it all—the fear of what he might have to do to Haley, the pride of a difficult job well done, and the satisfaction of eliminating a threat to the United States.

I guess I'm not too old and slow for this kind of work, after all.

76

EGO

The doctor stared down at his coat covering the president's body. He had lost patients before—every doctor had—but for the past two months his sole responsibility had been Pavel Zimalev, the President of Russia. The man who now lay dead before him, his helmet shattered, blood and brain matter oozing from it.

His training took over. He glanced at his watch.

"Time of death: 12:17," he said to Timor, the president's Chief of Staff. "Cause of death..."

Ego, the doctor thought.

He could never put it on an official report, of course. But that's what it was. Stupidity and ego. Instead, he said, "Accidental head trauma."

The Chief of Staff stared at him, in shock. But neither of them had risen to their stations in life without being adept at playing the game of politics.

"This can't get out," the man whispered.

The doctor knew exactly what he meant. They couldn't keep President Zimalev's death a secret. But they could keep it quiet for a while.

"He didn't die doing... this," Timor said, gesturing dismissively at the bobsled track and looking at the doctor to gauge his reaction. Their egotistical president, falling off his sled as he raced down a bobsled track?

"No, definitely not." The trip to Sochi had been the stupid idea of a man trying to relive his glory days of an athlete, not the leader of the greatest country on earth. "But what?"

As they had run to the president's body, the Chief of Staff had ordered the helicopter to warm up, anticipating an evacuation. The pilot must have finished whatever pre-flight checks needed, because the helicopter started, its massive engine coming to life.

"The helicopter," Timor said with a glance toward the helicopter in the parking lot. "A crash. Or..." the man said, "a hard landing. Easier to stage."

"The president hit his head in the helicopter..." the doctor said, thinking it through. There was no way to cover up the massive trauma to the man's skull.

"Yes. A freak accident," the Chief of Staff said, nodding. "A hero's death."

"Absolutely," the doctor said, warming to the idea. "He died on the way to inspect the troops. A true leader. You and I were there, we saw it happen. But what about the spectators?"

The fast-thinking Chief of Staff had also immediately ordered the local spectators escorted out of the building at the start of the run and off the viewing platforms where they had watched the entire debacle.

"Fyodor," Timor called to one of the many men surrounded them at a respectful distance. The bodyguard had a similar build to the president but was much younger. Fyodor moved closer, his eyes locked on the coat-covered body lying in front of him. "Our president died heroically on his way to inspect the troops during their annual winter training. Not here during a sledding accident, understand?"

Fyodor looked at the Chief of Staff with dawning comprehension. "Yes, sir."

"You will go to the locker room and put on the president's coat, hat, and sunglasses. The sled will be brought to you. I will have all the spectators moved to the front of the building," he glanced down at the coat-covered figure, "after we take the president's body to the helicopter."

"Yes," the doctor said, getting the picture. "It will work."

"You will exit the locker room and make your way to the helicopter, holding the sled, waving at the cheering crowd."

"I will pretend to be the president," Fyodor said, "so they will see he is alive and well?"

"Exactly," Timor said. "Will you do this? For the president and the country?"

He stood straighter, coming almost to attention. "Of course." He paused, "But…"

"But what?" Timor snapped, then composed himself. "What?" he added more gently.

"I should limp. They all saw the crash. The president would have been injured at least slightly. They will not believe he is perfectly fine. They may be country people, but they are not stupid."

Brilliant.

"Yes," the doctor said. "Walk slowly, as if you are in some pain. Not too much, though. Limping a little is fine."

"That's even better," Timor agreed. "Our injured but persevering president. Well done, Fyodor. Go now, get ready."

Timor called to another guard as Fyodor hurried off. "You will get the name, address, and a picture of every person here. Confiscate all cell phones and cameras—from the reporters as well. You and your men will tell everyone the president is slightly injured but will recover. To save face in the eyes of the world, they are to not mention the accident to anyone. You and your men say that while taking their pictures and collecting the information. Then you tell them they will be well compensated for their time today."

Perfect. Play on their pride of Russia while threatening them and paying them off. A timeless tactic.

The man nodded and hurried off as well.

"The rest of you," the Chief of Staff called to the nearby guards, "carry the president to the helicopter."

77

DICTATOR 2.0

Gun models make distinct sounds. The Americans' beloved M4 makes a much different noise than the AK. Ivan Ignatov recognized the sound of the weapon fired moments before. He'd used one of the Russian sniper rifles himself as a marksman in a rifle company when he first joined the army. Some of the men patrolling the woods had them.

Only one shot, Ivan thought.

He and his friend Dmitry patrolled together as they had done for years in various hell holes, always watching out for each other.

Despite their experience and time in the great army—or because of it—they weren't officers. They didn't want to be. So instead of getting on the radio and asking for answers, they waited, though Ivan turned to look a quarter mile back along the trail.

No one came on the radio to question the shot.

"Two possibilities," Dmitry began after they'd waited a while for the officers to demand an explanation or issue an alert. His camouflage uniform matched Ivan's. Clean and unwrinkled but not pressed. Neat and squared away, like their gear, attitudes, and heads. As they neared the end of their careers, they had agreed to conduct themselves as the professionals they were, no matter what.

"Three," Ivan corrected his friend.

Dmitry thought for a second, then nodded reluctantly. "Two likely, one unlikely."

It was Ivan's turn to nod.

"One," Dmitry started. "One of the many idiots we work with had an accidental discharge."

In the special operations units, an accidental discharge would be grounds for dismissal. In their unit, it happened a few times per year. Their current duty assignment was no front-line, well-disciplined group. They had been pulled from their nearby backwater military base where he and Dmitry were playing out the last months of their military careers.

It would explain the radio silence. No officer would want to admit one of his men had been so careless; they'd handle it themselves.

"Two," Dmitry continued, "one of the many idiots shot at a deer, bear, or bunny in the woods, thinking it was a danger to our new president and hoping for a medal."

Another reasonable possibility likely handled at the unit level.

"Three?" Ivan asked. He was suddenly convinced there was a fourth possibility.

"Three, one of the idiots killed another of the idiots," he said, shaking his head in resignation.

Unlikely, unfortunately.

"And four?" Ivan asked. His friend looked at him blankly. "One of them fired at our president as he performed his ridiculous stunt for his fawning fans."

Dmitry laughed at him. "You have an imagination, my friend!"

There was a fifth option he dared not mention.

What if it wasn't one of our people shooting at the president?

The odds against it were astronomical. Coming to the bobsled track for the stupid PR stunt had reportedly been a last-minute decision. No enemy could have learned about it and gotten in place so quickly—even a domestic enemy. No, bringing up such a ludicrous idea to anyone would be met with derision.

"Come on," he commanded Dmitry who didn't move, even as Ivan walked along the trail.

"Where are you going?" Dmitry called. With a sigh, Dmitry started toward him. "Where are we going?" his friend corrected himself.

"We passed the perfect sniper position earlier. I want to check it out." Ivan waited for Dmitry to roll his eyes, which he did.

At the very least, I have to satisfy my professional curiosity. Did one of my fellow soldiers—or someone else—attempt to kill the president?

"Fine, it's a lovely day for a hike," Dmitry said. "But when the president is finished with his playtime and all is well, you buy the vodka tonight."

Ivan stopped at the spot. There had still been no mention of any trouble over the radio. In the valley below they heard the helicopter, engine running, ready to leave.

If I had to assassinate the president, I would do it from here.

The shot was difficult, but not impossible.

He and Dmitry stood silently, listening, for a full minute.

Ivan sensed no nearby presence, aside from Dmitry and the remains of the runny nose his friend had had for a week.

Why no mention of the gunshot on the radio?

The question nagged at him. The most likely reason was the officer responsible for the man whose weapon discharged—for whatever reason —hadn't reported it.

Another possibility: the officers didn't hear the shot. They were likely all in the bobsled track building, surrounded by screaming fans with noise-makers, hoping to be noticed by Zimalev. He shook his head at the thought.

Our bold, new president. Stronger, smarter, and more athletic than the last one.

Dictator 2.0, Ivan called him in his head, never daring to utter it even as a joke to Dmitry.

"We should return," Dmitry said, wiping his nose with a pure white handkerchief. He had several in his uniform pockets, especially during the winters when the men traded flu germs in the barracks.

"Yes," Ivan agreed. He neither saw nor felt any of his fellow soldiers here, nor his imagined foreign assassin. Looking downslope, the rocks looked like rocks and the leaves looked undisturbed.

Turning, he looked uphill. From there, the steeper angle equaled a more difficult shot. One none of his poorly trained, backwater fellow soldiers would attempt.

"No, my friend, please," Dmitry said, watching. "I feel horrible. This cold is getting worse." He blew his nose again. "Please don't ask me to hike up the mountain on a fool's errand."

"I won't," he assured his friend, then stopped. Crouching, he examined the ground two feet up from the trail. The moss, still green in the moderate winter climate of the area, looked trampled by a small boot print.

My overactive imagination? Or do I, too, wish to impress the new president and win favor before leaving the army behind?

Ivan unslung his rifle, loaded a round, and flicked off the safety. Another reason an accidental discharge was unlikely—they were forbidden to have a round chambered unless ordered to or in active contact with the enemy.

To Dmitry's credit, they had watched out for one another long enough and seen enough combat that he didn't hesitate. Putting his hanky in a pocket, he unslung his weapon and prepared it for battle. A small line of snot dripped from his nose before he wiped it away on his sleeve.

Ivan started up the slope, his feet finding the small, nearly imperceptible footsteps of whoever had walked there recently.

A few more steps...

The ground in front of him looked somehow different. He stood, trying to determine what made it look... off.

His eyes scanned the area. Then he closed them and extended his senses.

"All units," his radio crackled. "The president will leave soon. Be on the alert, then prepare to return to your vehicles."

Not yet. There is something wrong here.

Below him on the trail, Dmitry kept watch, looking up the trail, down it, then back up the slope to catch his eye.

He will stay as long as I do, risking everything... if I ask him to.

Ivan took a step forward and bent low, touching the leaves, which looked wrong, like they hadn't fallen, but been laid out purposely.

His head turned as he caught the view of the bobsled track and building through the two massive trees.

This is the perfect location for a sniper shot—except for the angle. It's all wrong. The position is too high.

"Ivan?" Dmitry called.

"I'm fine, my friend. Nothing here. I was wrong."

He stood and looked at the spot one last time. His senses tingled.

I'm not the first person to check out this location today.

Another soldier might have missed the signs, but his trained eye noted the disturbed earth carefully rearranged to appear normal.

But the radio had given no indication of anything wrong with the president.

No one had remarked on the gunshot.

And no one would join him here to examine the soft ground with the body indentations, or the perfectly arranged leaves attempting to cover them.

In less than a month, I will no longer be a soldier after twenty years in the army.

He wouldn't make waves, cry wolf, and jeopardize his future—or his army pension—for Dictator 2.0.

The sound of horns, cowbells, and cheering reached them from the bobsled building in the valley below.

The president is leaving. Alive and well.

Without another glance at the ground, Ivan turned and quickly made his way down the slope, slung his rifle, and joined his friend on the pleasant hike back to their vehicle.

He had vodka to buy tonight.

PART 9

THURSDAY, JANUARY 5

78

EXFIL

Airborne Over Europe

Haley flipped the last page of the international newspaper and folded it neatly.

Nothing, but it might be too soon.

Axe took the shot around noon the day before.

It's been twenty hours.

Haley guessed the Russians were either scrambling with succession issues… or creating a better story than the president dying on a bobsled track from an accident.

I'd be covering it up.

She and Axe sat in the business class section of the airplane heading home, unwilling to relax.

The mission isn't done until we're back at base.

She had changed their flight to leave the country as soon as possible, avoiding the danger of capture and the blizzard, which had already started across the north. The huge amount of snowfall predicted proved an excellent excuse to leave after only a brief visit.

When they were on the mountain the day before, the Russian soldiers had loaded into their trucks and left not long after Zimalev's helicopter took off and the spectators' busses drove away.

There was no search. Haley and Axe didn't understand why. They waited hours anyway, until long after dark, before hiking carefully to the rendezvous point to wait for their driver who had instructions to drive by every six hours until they met him.

Through the whole trip back to Tbilisi with their strange, silent Movement contact, they had listened to the news in Russian and Georgian on the radio, waiting for the driver to look at them with wide eyes as he put together what he had helped them accomplish.

He didn't. Nothing urgent sounding had come on the radio.

The driver dropped them off at the airport and left, keeping the sniper rifle, back in its hiding place under the bumper with one round missing. "My friends, goodbye," is all he said in accented English.

Around them on the plane, Axe stayed alert while the other passengers slept, read, or watched movies on the small screens at their seats.

The mission isn't over until we're safe at home. But...

"Excuse me," he called to a flight attendant as she neared. "Could we get two beers?" he asked, naming an imported brand he liked. She brought them quickly.

I could get used to business class. Sure beats a C-130 cargo plane.

"This doesn't break SOP?" Haley asked as the woman moved to check on other passengers. "We're not back at base."

"One beer," he replied. "We deserve it."

Haley nodded and held hers up, looking like she wanted to make a toast but coming up short with the words.

"To the planning," Axe said quietly, holding his beer out to her.

She nodded once, acknowledging the sentiment. "To the execution," she said with a small smile.

Nice play on words, Blondie.

They toasted, and drank.

"*Qui audet adipiscitur,*" he mumbled, wondering if he got the pronunciation right.

Haley looked at him quizzically, then worked out the Latin words.

They toasted again as she whispered, "Who dares, wins."

79

REVENGE

The president had been in the Oval Office only long enough to take a sip of his coffee when the door to the waiting area opened. "Mr. President, Gregory Addison for you," announced Mary Beth, his long-time secretary. Gregory stepped into the Oval Office.

He looks nervous, James thought.

The room had that effect on people. While it wasn't the CAG director's first time, he rarely came in person.

"Please, sit," James said, stepping from behind his desk to the two couches across from each other. He poured Gregory coffee from a carafe into a large mug with the presidential seal on it and set it in front of him. "What is so urgent you have me in the office at six on a Thursday morning?"

Gregory hesitated for a second while he composed himself.

It's not the room that has him shaken. It's what he has to tell me.

"Sir, senior members of my team have discovered a disastrous security breach. We believe the Russians, around one hundred years ago, started a secret sleeper agent program targeting the United States. People were trained, well indoctrinated, and sent to America with financial backing to start various businesses and, most importantly, raise families. Subsequent generations were raised to believe the family owed a great debt to the then Soviet Union."

Gregory paused, and James took a moment to think through the ramifications of the stunning disclosure. "There are third-generation spies who have no obvious connection to Russia, and they're living and working among us?"

"Exactly, Mr. President. And it gets worse. Senator Jonesley's recent death, we believe, was not from natural causes. She was assassinated by a staff member in a way to make it look like a heart attack. Plus, Senator Greenlich's email leak came not from outside hacking, but from his Chief of Staff, who is a sleeper agent."

"Two senators have spies on staff?"

There goes my Thursday.

"Yes, sir, and there's more. You've been informed of the attempt on Senator Woodran's life, of course. But what we've discovered—and I've hushed up until this morning with you—is the chief of her private security detail tried to kill her, apologizing to her before he shot her, and she shot him. He, also, was a Russian sleeper agent."

James stared in stunned silence at the CAG director.

What the hell? I don't even know where to start.

"Assassinating our government leaders is an act of war," he finally said. "How sure are you? What proof do you have?"

If there's even a shred of decent evidence, I'm going to kick some ass. From cyberattacks to cruise missiles, Russia will pay. Nobody messes with the United States of America and gets away with it.

"Very sure, now. This has all only recently come to my attention as well, via... outside sources. But it checks out. We have Senator Woodran's account of the shooting, to start. Additionally, on the grounds of her family ranch were the security guard's younger sisters, both Salt Lake City Police officers, armed and in position to attack the senator. The operation was foiled. And one of the policewomen has confessed to being a Russian sleeper agent, along with her deceased brother and sister. Her story collaborates my team's findings. A sniper was also found dead on the grounds. He was the regional handler of the sleeper spies."

Gregory paused for another nervous sip of coffee.

All he's told me, and he's still scared? What else could there be?

"I haven't put this information into any report yet," Gregory said. "Which is why I'm here so early. We've been putting the pieces together and investigating, but I wanted you to have the information as soon as we were sure. And as far as I know, none of the other intelligence agencies have this—or will, unless you instruct me to tell them. It's completely black and off the books."

What is he holding back?

Thinking it through, James wondered what he might have missed. Reading between the lines of Gregory's story, he thought he had it. "How was the attack stopped?"

Gregory regarded him, his face emotionless.

Yep. Here we go. The meat of the sandwich.

When he didn't respond, James spoke. "Mr. Addison?"

James stared him down, but the man annoyingly brushed off his hard gaze.

"Also, Mr. President," Gregory continued, ignoring the question, "Victor Baranov, whom you know well, has come forward to admit to being a Russian sleeper agent. This too has not been put into a report as yet."

Wait. Victor Baranov a spy? How?

"Baranov?"

Gregory nodded, frowning.

James regarded the intelligence director, unsure what was happening.

He's not answering my questions. And what is he implying about not putting this explosive information into reports?

His anger flared.

How dare he!

"Mr. Addison," James said, his voice ice cold. "If you're attempting to blackmail me, you're—"

The man's shocked face showed James he had misunderstood completely.

"Mr. President, I would never..."

I've misread this. What is he saying?

"I'm sorry," James said. "But you've lost me. We'll get back to Baranov in a moment, but what the hell is going on? Speak frankly and do it quickly." It came out much more forcefully than intended but seemed to have the desired effect.

"Sir," Addison said, speaking more quietly and leaning forward. "At Admiral Nalen's suggestion, I took responsibility for the scene at Senator Woodran's ranch, getting a close, trusted colleague from Homeland Security there to handle it discreetly."

Nalen. I should have known.

"Since we're now speaking candidly," James said, "I can only guess Haley Albright was involved in some capacity?"

Gregory froze, then shifted his eyes uncomfortably before stalling for time by reaching for his coffee.

What now? I've misread this again?

"Sir, I'm sorry," Gregory said after a few seconds. "I thought you knew. Ms. Albright abruptly resigned from the CAG on Friday last week, effective immediately."

Resigned? Why would she—

It clicked.

She resigned because she didn't want her actions blowing back on me.

"I see. Let's return to the disaster at hand. Russian sleeper agents. I'll take your word about Baranov for now. But where else? The government?"

"Yes, sir, and many major industries. And we should call them potential sleeper agents. Innocent until proven guilty."

"Of course."

"My team is running down genealogy, immigration, and population data. So far, they believe the program started in and was contained to one region in Russia—specifically, two towns. Many third- and fourth-generation Russians work in the government, the same as Italians, Koreans, Chinese, and other nationalities. We're investigating, but our hope is only people with families from these two towns during that era are likely to be of concern."

James sat back, his mind reeling at the implications. "How long until you have a list?"

"We're working as fast as we can, sir, but it takes time. I would prefer to keep this information, and the investigation, limited to very few people, and not entered into any databases or reports. Obviously, you needed to know as soon as we were sure, but otherwise, I'd like to keep it with only the two senior analysts at the CAG. They are on it non-stop. We'll have a full list of government people for further investigation, as well as a plan to weed out any potential Russian agents while not damaging the careers of the innocent, as soon as possible."

James frowned but nodded his understanding. It had to be a monumental task.

"Our working assumption, or hope, is not every grandparent followed protocol and passed down to their children the indoctrination they received. And of the ones who did, many of them likely didn't continue the tradition with their kids as they became more Americanized, for lack of a better term. We're hopefully looking at very few."

James considered the possibilities. His tactical mind quickly formulated an audacious plan.

What if we hit Russia where it hurts? Delay the immediate gratification of punishing them for their actions and turn the tables on them instead?

"Let's turn this to our advantage," he told Gregory. "We make the suspected sleepers unwitting double agents."

Gregory sat back, nodding appreciatively, his tiredness showing. "Mr. President, that's brilliant. I'm sorry, sir, I should have thought of it."

James waved his hand. "It's always a team effort. You've had your hands very full, it sounds like."

"Yes, sir. Instead of exposing or punishing them, we can exploit the situation for long-term gain. This could be a major intelligence achievement."

Gregory stared off into the distance, no doubt plotting how to enact the new plan.

James had an instinct there was more to come. Another bombshell the man had saved for last. He took a sip of his coffee, gone too cool for his taste. "Aside from the Russian sleepers, what else do you have for me?"

The CAG director's eyes snapped back to meet James' as the man he relaxed into a blank poker face.

He goes neutral when he should act naturally. It's an obvious tell.

"Don't hold back, Gregory. What's worse than Baranov, my biggest fundraiser, being a spy, and the government being infiltrated by potential Russian moles?"

Gregory hesitated, finished his coffee, then seemed to decide to come clean.

"Mr. President, back in the day, I was once like Haley. Brash, impulsive, intuitive."

Haley—I thought I sensed her hand in all this.

"Yes, she's all that, but much more."

"Yes, of course," Gregory said, backpedaling. "I didn't mean to imply—"

James waved his hand. "Go on. You said she resigned."

"Yes, she did. But what I'm trying to say, sir, is I trusted my gut much more than I do now. Like Haley does."

"'Always trust your gut' has been a motto of mine since day one on the Teams. My intuition saved my life more than once."

"My senior analysts have adopted this 'trust your gut' approach. One of them had a feeling, and some slim data to back it up. It hasn't panned out, but I would be remiss if I didn't bring it up. There may be…"

"What?" James prompted.

"More at play than I'm aware of."

Is he talking about Haley?

The man's vagueness was getting on James' nerves, as was his reluctance to come out and say whatever needed to be said.

"You lost me again."

"One of my senior analysts predicted the Russians would invade Ukraine, Latvia, and Estonia, dividing NATO."

What?

Gregory continued, ignoring James' shock.

"The death of Senator Jonesley; the resignation of Senator Greenlich because of the emails, several of which were made up completely, by the way; and the attempted assassination of Senator Woodran were part of a plan to weaken you and America's ability to respond politically and militarily."

"Hold on. You're saying—"

"If I could continue, Mr. President," Gregory said, interrupting him, which just wasn't done. But the man was finally on a roll, so James let it go.

"We also now know Baranov Brands beer was the culprit behind the rioting and chaos in Las Vegas. If not for the intervention of Admiral Nalen and nearly one hundred retired SEALs and other highly trained veterans, the death toll would have been in the hundreds, perhaps thousands. Your friendship with Baranov would have come to light, further weakening you and causing a crisis in your administration. The Russian invasion would have succeeded."

James regarded the CAG director, stunned yet again.

Baranov behind the disaster in Las Vegas?

"How certain are you of this?"

"Very, sir, thanks to Nalen, Haley, and my team's efforts. We have Baranov in custody, and he's made a full, on-the-record statement. Which we've compartmentalized."

James composed himself, brushing off his shock and thinking through the problem. "The Russians haven't invaded yet. So what's happening?"

"We're unsure."

His nervousness is back. Why?

"Early this morning, the CIA noted some rumors. Nothing definite, but the Prime Minister of Russia may have taken over the running of the country around 13:00 hours their time yesterday, nearly twenty-four hours ago. You'll have it in your daily briefing, I'm sure."

"A coup? Zimalev's only been in charge a few months."

"We just don't know yet, sir. I'm sure the CIA will have a more robust report for you at some point today."

Maybe. At times, though, it seems like half the people at the CIA are much more interested in covering their asses than getting me essential analysis.

The whole damn intelligence community seemed like that.

Except for Haley and the CAG.

"What happened prior to the Russian PM taking over?"

"We're putting it together. Zimalev had planned to fly to a small city in the south to inspect the troops in the area. His schedule didn't officially change, but we have him landing in the city, then taking a helicopter to a mountain resort area near Sochi." He paused and tried to sip from his empty cup. James didn't offer him more coffee.

He's stalling again.

"We think something happened near Sochi, yesterday midday their time. As yet though, we haven't been able to run down exactly what."

"A helicopter accident?" It was one of James' worries, despite the expert mechanics who kept his chopper in top condition.

Helicopters are notoriously fickle machines.

"Unknown, sir, I'm sorry. We're all working on it, though."

"Sochi? That's where they had the Winter Games once, right?"

"Yes, sir. Zimalev was a silver medal winner on the skeleton sled as a teenager—at an earlier games elsewhere—but perhaps he was on his way to stage a publicity event. It's possible they are planning on making another bid for the Winter Games. We don't know yet, but yes, a helicopter accident is entirely possible." He didn't sound like he believed in the idea.

James sipped his cold coffee as he fought to keep his face relaxed. He didn't want to give away his growing realization.

The sledding photo op with the kids happened on Tuesday morning— Tuesday night in Russia. If Zimalev saw me on TV, he would have wanted to show me up. The man has an enormous ego. Everything is a competition.

Somehow, Haley had to be involved. It all fit. Her resignation from the CAG. The letter she sent asking him to trust her and go sledding on the South Lawn.

Gregory also suspects Haley's involvement. But how had she pulled off... whatever she did? And what the hell should I do about it?

80

THE NIGHTCLUB

The After-Hours Club
Las Vegas, Nevada

Mad Dog enjoyed the cold desert night air and the bright neon of the city, easily seen from the outskirts of downtown.

Reminds me of the Sandbox—the air, not the lights, Mad dog thought.

He'd done three fast and furious combat tours, then headed out on his own when his term was up. Private security paid better but wasn't nearly as much fun. He'd had generous clients who were jerks, and some who were kind. Along the way, he'd put a ton of money into investments. Now he could work fun jobs for good people and turn down the rest.

Plus, he'd gotten to live on Kelton Kellison's private superyacht for a few months.

And met Axe and Haley.

Working with them had been the most fun.

Feels like being back on a Team.

He saw the long line of women in short, tight dresses and high heels. The men wore tight pants, tighter shirts, and half of them had high-heeled boots on.

Whatever floats your boat.

They stood, nicely cued, behind a dark red velvet rope. A huge guy, about thirty years old and three hundred pounds of muscle, stood with an earpiece and cord running to a microphone, bored and uninterested in the freezing twenty-something women and men.

Is this club worth freezing your ass off waiting in line at four in the morning on a Thursday? Are they locals or tourists?

No way was he waiting in line. Besides, his black cargo pants and black technical shirt made him look much more like the bouncer than one of the potential bar customers. Though the man at the door outweighed him by at least one hundred pounds and towered over him.

Mad Dog walked slowly to the left side of the door the man guarded. The line of people stretched down the block to his right. The people at the front of the line eyed him suspiciously, unhappy he would try to jump ahead.

He looked up at the bouncer from four feet away, a slight smile on his face.

Let's see if this guy is all muscle, or if he has some brains in his head way up there.

The man gave him an unimpressed stare.

Okay. If you want to play it that way.

Mad Dog dropped the smile and let his eyes change, losing their pleasant look. In a second, he went from short, barrel-chested annoyance to ice cold killer.

The man's eyes flashed with recognition of a predator much more deadly than he would ever be. Still, he held Mad Dog's eyes for a full second before nodding, stepping to the side, and opening the door to the club.

Smart. Not a punk. Good man.

Mad Dog nodded pleasantly at him, and briefly shook his hand as he walked past, slipping him a one-hundred-dollar bill.

Three steps along a darkened hallway led him to another door. Opening it brought a blast of noise. Pulsing bass and wild, flashing lights flooded his senses.

Suddenly, he felt old. It had been years since he'd been to a place like this.

Mad Dog stepped close to the wall and acclimated to the lights, noise, and vibe. A few hundred people were dancing to the hypnotic music. Along the bar to his right, people stood three rows deep, trying to get the overworked bartenders' attention.

It must be one hundred degrees in here. No wonder none of the kids outside have coats.

Near the back of the room were tiny round tables. Along the wall were several large booths covered in purple velvet. A row of dark red stanchions separated the dance floor from the small tables and chairs. Another row kept the patrons at the tables from the more exclusive booths in the back. A huge bouncer guarded each section.

Along the back wall, the guy at the far-left booth, surrounded by two want-to-be tough guys and several attractive women, looked like a younger Victor Baranov and matched the description he'd been given. Thin, sharp nose. Narrow face. Brown hair. Stiff and looking desperate.

That's him.

Mad Dog reached in his pocket and carefully pulled two more hundreds from his stash, folding one into each hand.

Haley better pay me back for this.

He kept to the wall, moving left, staying out of the way of the dancers. He passed the hallway to the bathrooms and kept going until he looked up at the next giant. This one didn't hesitate. He unclipped the rope from the pole and stepped aside for him, smoothly taking the hundred in another handshake.

It pays to take care of the first guy—he always paves the way.

The next bouncer gave him a little more attitude, but Mad Dog just smiled pleasantly and grooved a bit to the music, waiting him out.

After a few seconds, the guard opened his velvet rope as well, accepting the hundred.

Money makes the world go 'round.

Walking up to the booth, Mad Dog put on his biggest smile. "Nicholas!" he called over the music to Baranov's son. "Long time no see!" He smiled at the closest woman for a second, then stretched his arm over the table toward the kid.

Nicholas Baranov shook his hand limply, confused.

Mad Dog winked at the young lady on the end of the bench seat and got her to stand with his outstretched hand. She went along with him, also confused by his familiarity. He took her spot and patted his knee for her to sit down. She glared at him, a drop-dead stare so cold it almost made up for the sweltering atmosphere of the club.

Sorry, miss, but I have a role to play here.

"Who the hell are you?" one of the tough guys yelled across the two ladies sitting between him and Mad Dog.

"Oh, sorry! I'm Dougie. I work for his dad," he yelled. He leaned closer to the guy. "I've got his..." He rubbed his thumb and fingers together, the universal signal for money.

The guy's attitude changed. "It's about time! He owes us."

"Yeah, I figured. Let's go in back and I'll settle up with you." Mad Dog stood. "Come on, Nickie. I'm sure there will be some left over to continue the party."

Mad Dog stood and walked confidently out of the exclusive VIP area, then through the less exclusive secondary VIP section. Stopping by the entrance to the hall, he waited with his arms crossed, leaning against the wall, watching the kids dance.

They'll follow. They want their money. The only question is whether they allow Nicholas to come.

A few seconds later, the group got itself sorted. The ladies slid back into the booth. Tough guy number one strutted toward Mad Dog, followed by Nicholas. The second guy brought up the rear.

The bouncers were suspicious.

Rightly so. They've got good instincts.

"After you—let's get some privacy in the bathroom," he yelled over the music.

This was the crucial moment. If they suspected a trap, they'd make him go first, which he couldn't let happen.

Drug dealer number one, his flabby belly bouncing and his long, dark hair flowing, hesitated for a moment but kept walking. Nicholas passed Mad Dog with a questioning look, then drug dealer two glared at him, his bald head reflecting the flashing lights from the dance floor.

Mad Dog stepped right behind him and put his hand on the bald man's shoulder. "After we take care of Nicholas, can you hook me up?"

The question, yelled into the guy's ear, made him slightly less suspicious.

I don't care if they're worried I'm a cop trying to entrap them.

Mad Dog's big concern was they'd pull a weapon and try to rob him. He'd left his 9mm at the warehouse, figuring it wouldn't go unnoticed by the bouncers. But he didn't see any sign of the two guys carrying.

The club's careful about weapons—I hope.

As soon as their little parade stepped into the men's room, Mad Dog punched the second guy, Baldie, in the kidney. He dropped to the ground in a heap.

Nicholas already stood at the urinal, not paying attention to the action behind him.

As chunky, dark-haired Flabbio turned toward the door, Mad Dog swung his powerful arm, delivering an open-handed slap to the unsuspecting man's face. Flabbio stumbled sideways and stayed on his feet only by leaning against the wall. His head wobbled and his eyes were unfocused.

It was much quieter in the bathroom, deserted aside from the four of them.

"Nicholas, finish up. Time to go." Mad Dog checked on Baldie, who lay moaning inside the bathroom doorway. He turned his attention instead to Flabbio. He slapped him lightly on the same cheek, causing the man to jerk his head away. "Hey! You with me? Nod if you're in there."

The chubby tough guy still looked out of it, but he nodded. "You'll get your money," Mad Dog explained. "Young Nicholas will pay you back in a few days, but I don't have the cash on me. I'm taking him to get it, and you're not going to cause any trouble, are you?" His tone made it clear what the correct answer should be.

"No trouble," the man mumbled.

"Good. Nicholas, you know how to reach these guys once you collect your allowance?"

The kid had finished his business and stood staring at the scene, shocked. He nodded quickly.

"Great. Wash your hands, then we can go."

Nicholas dutifully followed orders, then approached Mad Dog. "Before we go, do you think—"

"No. Your father said you might be hurting, but we'll get you squared away outside, okay?"

Relieved, the kid nodded.

Mad Dog stepped to Flabbio, who was coming around. "If you cause a scene or try to come after us, not only do you not get paid, I'll mess you up so badly you'll spend every cent you have on doctor bills. Do we understand each other?"

The not-so-tough guy looked like he wanted to argue for a second, but then cast his eyes downward and nodded submissively.

"Great," Mad Dog said. To Nicholas, he said, "Let's go."

Mad Dog pushed the kid in front of him, out the men's room door, down the hall, and into the cold night air.

"Come on," he said, escorting Nicholas around the corner to his truck. "Your dad needs you."

81

THE WEIGHT

The White House Oval Office
Washington, D.C.
4:55 P.M.

The president spent the day in the Oval Office, managing the greatest country in the world. Meetings, photo ops with worthy individuals, and more meetings. As always, there were monumental decisions made—some quickly, some after much thought, planning, and input from experts.

Each day presented a new opportunity to help guide the United States in the direction he thought best.

Every day could also be the one he made a mistake that would cost the country dearly.

The pressure rarely got to him, but he always carried the weight of the responsibility.

He packed up his briefcase with yet more reports he needed to read after dinner.

A quick rap on the door was followed by his Chief of Staff, Chad David, entering from the adjacent office. "Mr. President? I have some news you need to hear."

James closed his briefcase, set it on the floor next to the desk, and sat back down in his comfortable leather chair. Chad stood in front of the desk, declining the chair to the side of it.

"Mr. President, the initial intelligence reports were true. We've just been officially informed by the Prime Minister of Russia. Russian President Pavel Zimalev is dead. His helicopter had a mechanical failure as it landed, coming in hard but intact. President Zimalev hit his head, causing massive damage. A freak accident, they're saying. He died yesterday at a hospital in Rostov-on-Don, Russia."

James nodded but didn't say a word for a minute. Chad stood, waiting patiently while he digested the information.

A much better story than whatever really happened.

"I understand," James finally said. "You'll arrange for a condolence call to the Prime Minister?"

"Of course."

"Do we send the vice president to the funeral?"

"We should discuss it tomorrow, sir. There will be time. The Russians will have President Zimalev's body lying in state first."

"Fine. Thank you. Do you need anything else from me tonight?"

He knows I don't want to discuss this right now.

"No, sir. Thank you, Mr. President."

Chad left, returning to his office, where he would undoubtedly work for several more hours.

"Mary Beth?" he called to his secretary on the intercom. "I'm still here for a bit, but I'd like to not be disturbed if possible. Consider me gone for the day."

"Yes, Mr. President. Good night," she replied through the speaker.

He sat back and put his hands behind his head, thinking.

Somehow, Haley and Axe did this.

He felt it in his gut.

And they not only pulled it off, they got away with it.

He desperately wanted to know what they had done, and how. But at the same time, he didn't.

Complete deniability... if I can live with not knowing.

He had mixed feelings about Haley and Axe taking such action without his approval, but knew how they felt—and agreed.

You don't mess with the United States of America.

PART 10

EPILOGUE: ONE WEEK LATER

82

LEGACY

Victor Baranov smiled with pride at his son across the long, narrow office. Nicholas had successfully handled a difficult call with an important customer. He'd kept his cool and resolved the situation to both parties' satisfaction.

"Well done, Nickie—sorry, Nicholas," he called across the room. "Impressive."

His son beamed.

Nicholas had come a long way in one week. Victor's contact at the FBI wouldn't approve Nickie's stay at an addiction treatment program. But they'd arranged for the treatment to come to him.

With me footing the bill, of course, Victor thought.

Victor was quite happy to do it. His son was seven days clean and sober for the first time in years. It was early days yet, but Victor had hope.

This time, it might be different.

Nicholas sat in his rightful place—opposite him on the far side of the office, as Baranov had done with his father, and his father had done with Grandpa Baranov before him.

The only difference is I will never tell Nicholas about our family legacy.

The point had been made clear to him by his FBI handler, who he respected and trusted. He was a decent, smart, committed man.

But deep down, Victor knew who he had to fear if he deviated from his assigned protocol.

The beautiful blond woman who abducted me... and almost made me drink the spiked beer.

He occasionally had nightmares where she stood over him, holding a red plastic cup in one hand and a funnel in the other, his duct-taped mouth and bound hands incapable of stopping her.

The woman—he still didn't know her name—had promised to find him and make his life miserable if he betrayed the United States of America again.

I believe her.

She would know—somehow—and come for him.

When his FBI contact gave him instructions on what to do if—when— approached by a new Russian handler, he paid attention. He would follow the orders to the letter.

It hadn't been expressed explicitly, but Victor knew why he was still free after all the evil he'd done.

They need to know what the Russians are up to with the sleeper spy program.

He was the bait. The FBI was making a deal with the devil.

They will use a little fish to catch the big fish. But then what happens?

He, Dad, and Grandpa only fished the one day—when they revealed his traitorous destiny to him. But he understood the basics.

The little fish almost always gets devoured before the big fish is reeled in.

He smiled sadly at Nickie.

As long as he's okay, whatever happens to me is fine.

The FBI let him play the dutiful Russian sleeper spy while monitoring him from a careful distance. He had become a sleeper double agent.

No problem. Anything to keep Nickie safe and happy—and the blond woman away from me.

His father and grandfather had built the company. Yes, they'd had early guidance and financial backing from Russia decades ago. But all they'd done, all they had built, was because of their hard work.

How much do we owe our past? To what degree do our histories make us... or do we make ourselves?

Nicholas was already on another call. He laughed with the person on the other end of the phone, using a pencil to make notes or doodle as they spoke.

He's checking in with another large customer. He took the initiative. Impressive.

How much of Nicholas' actions were owed to his great-grandfather—and the country he came from?

We're Americans. I should have realized this and rebelled against my father.

But at thirteen, he couldn't have. He had been too young and impressionable.

Which is exactly why the whole plan worked.

Victor had broken the pattern inadvertently with Nicholas because the boy hadn't been mature enough at thirteen.

And now, he'll never have to know. Never have to carry the burden of his family tree.

Victor watched with pride as his son worked the phone, already mastering the family business.

We do not have to be victims of our past.

83

RESEARCH

Maximum Security Facility #8
Dr. Edgar's Lab
Undisclosed Location

Dr. Edgars' back complained as he bent forward to drink, but it didn't matter. He needed the morning maintenance dose, and his body would endure any discomfort necessary.

The pain will be gone momentarily, anyway.

The straw slipped away from his lips as he tried to capture it.

His hands were useless. They shook too much in the morning, and he couldn't risk spilling a single drop. There wasn't much left of his original supply, and they wouldn't allow him to produce more.

He finally caught the straw between his lips. As much as he wanted to savor it, to make it last, his body rebelled.

I should be stronger. I should refuse the drink. Let the pain take me and end it all.

But there was much to do.

He sucked it down in three gulps. The drug, greatly diluted and made palatable by the juice—apple this morning—hit his system less quickly than it had when he'd taken the whole test tube at once a week before, bringing on this instant addiction. Still, it calmed his nerves, and at this dosage, would allow him to function.

There had been an accident on the first day in the prison. He had greedily reached for the paper cup. His shaking hands had knocked it off the small shelf on the inside of his cell door. Minutes later, the guards had shot him with a tranquilizer gun through the small security portal. He had been screaming incoherently, desperate for the drug.

He could still feel the sores on his tongue. He'd licked the juice off the concrete floor, scraping his tongue raw trying to get the liquid into his mouth.

This morning, using the straw to suck up every drop in the small cup, his body reacted quickly. With his need satiated, the tremors stopped.

He got to work, feeling much better. Along the back of his cell, he had a simple but comfortable bedroom layout. Here near the door, under the never-flinching gaze of four security cameras, was his workbench and full laboratory.

The beakers and all other equipment were plastic, instead of glass, but he had all he needed to continue his research.

Not all I need. They still limit my access to the ingredients.

He didn't have the means here to make more of the formula, which frustrated him.

For now, he had been tasked with finding a cure for the affliction. There were at least one hundred people from New Year's Eve suffering like him who needed help.

Today was one more of many until he could continue his true research, but at least he was in a lab, doing what he was born to do.

At some point, they will release me, make a mistake allowing me to escape, or trade me to the Russians.

When one of those events came to pass, he had a brilliant idea for a Level 100 version of the drug he would manufacture.

But it had to exist only in theory—for now.

84

WHAT IF

The Hotel Grand Lagoon
Key Largo, Florida

Axe accepted another ice-cold beer from the friendly pool attendant. The sun beat down, warming him. The occasional cool breeze blew through, keeping the resort pool area from becoming too hot.

Seventy-six degrees and sunny. I could get used to this.

Axe, Haley, and her police officer boyfriend, Derek, had driven down together in Axe's truck. The three of them didn't want to be unarmed and driving made it much easier than flying.

Axe's girlfriend Connie had flown in, unable to get enough time off work to join them for the road trip. They picked her up at the Miami airport and continued the drive to Key Largo.

Connie stood up from her chair and stood over him, blocking the sun, which made her black hair light up like she had a halo. "Happy?"

She looked exactly like his angel from the helicopter eight months ago, when she had saved his life.

"Very."

They clicked as a couple. They each enjoyed the freedom of having their own lives. Both also loved the time, about once every six weeks, when they took several days off to spend together, focused only on making wonderful memories.

"I'm going to the pool bar. Derek's there. Want to come?"

"I'm good here, thanks." She kissed him, rubbing her fingers on his smooth face. She preferred it over the beard he'd finally shaved off. Then she went to sit by the bar for conversation and another round of, "Is Derek good enough for Haley?" They were giving the guy quite the work over, but he seemed to take it well.

Haley stirred from the lounge chair on his other side. She wore a sarong over her bikini and an old, beat-up baseball cap with her hair tucked underneath.

"What?" she asked, half asleep.

"Connie went to give Derek another talking to."

"You guys trying to drive him away?" She sounded more awake now.

"Not at all. But if we drive him away so easily, he wasn't a keeper."

Over the past three days, they'd established a routine. He and Haley woke before dawn for a run or a swim. The hard workouts, combined with discussions about their past missions, helped unpack the difficult emotions they had both stuffed in boxes.

While they were out, Connie and Derek met for coffee until "the boys," as Connie called them, returned from working out.

Derek wasn't thrilled about being one of "the girls" by extension, but he took it in stride. He was used to the night shift and didn't want to work out first thing in the morning.

They did activities together after breakfast, from snorkeling to sea kayaking. Tomorrow, they had deep-sea fishing on the agenda, though more for Derek than the rest of them. Axe would take pictures, hoping to bottle the magic for his summer photography show at the art gallery.

In the afternoons, they lay by the pool, played cards, or sat and talked. The conversation flowed easily among the four of them.

"I had a thought," Haley said, sitting up. Axe had more trouble with the men and women around the pool checking her out than she did. Though, luckily, the middle of January was a slow time at the resort, as Admiral Nalen had said it would be. He'd recommended the place as quiet without being boring, exclusive without being fancy. "You'll love it, I promise," he'd said. And they did. It was perfect.

"We aren't allowed to think on vacation," Axe said, covering his face with his old ball cap.

"Remember your friends in Mexico?"

The ones who disappeared an entire village, shot the scientist I rescued, and spiked Kelton's beer?

He remembered. "Yes."

"What else do you think they were up to?"

"Thinking is your department."

"I don't have a department anymore, remember?"

Her boss, Gregory, had left her messages and reached out via her co-worker Nancy's secure app, but she hadn't responded. She said she needed time to think about her future. Since Sochi, Haley had been unsure about returning to her job at the Central Analysis Group.

She's worried we'll eventually mess up and cause trouble instead of stopping it.

It was something she had to work through. Axe had tried to talk with her about it, but she'd said it was her decision, which he respected. He just hoped she didn't leave the team.

"Haley," he said, removing his hat and looking over at her. "We won. Either let the rest go or get your old job back. In the meantime, though, I'm enjoying the vacation lifestyle. For once in my life, I'm not getting shot at or preparing to be."

Haley sighed and closed her eyes again. "Fine. We'll talk later. After the vacation."

Axe settled back into his chair and prepared to cover his head with his hat. Another nap was in order.

When was the last time I felt this relaxed? This happy?

It had been years. His time with Connie every six weeks came close, but this was another level of pleasure.

Across the sparkling pool, a tall, fit older man with perfect posture adjusted the towel on a chaise lounge, then settled onto it. He removed his perfectly white t-shirt and lay back, relaxed.

That looks like…

Axe sat up and stared, sure his eyes were playing tricks on him.

The man nodded, a small, satisfied smile on his face, and raised a bottle of beer to Axe in a toast.

The sneaky bastard!

A woman approached, and the man stood quickly. He helped her carefully sit down in the chair next to him. Her bright yellow hair shone in the sun. She put a beat-up black cowboy hat on her head and lay back with a relaxed smile.

Admiral Nalen… and Senator Woodran?

Axe picked up his bottle of beer and raised it toward the two of them. The senator noticed and waved.

Way to go, Hammer.

At six the next morning, Axe wasn't at all surprised to see Hammer warming up on the walkway from the hotel to the beach.

"Good morning, Axe. Lovely day for a run." He had a grin on his face.

"Admiral."

"Let's stick with Hammer or William from now on. Nalen is fine, too."

"Yes, sir—Hammer."

Haley jogged down the walkway and pulled up at the sight of the two of them. "Admiral?"

"Hammer," he corrected with a smile. "Mind if I join you?" It wasn't really a question.

Starting at a warm-up pace, they headed south on the firm sand of the beach. There was enough light to see, though the sky was still dark. The Gulf of Mexico water lapped lightly on the shore, a quiet, soothing sound. Nine weeks before and a thousand miles to the west, Axe had joined his former SEAL Teammates in a capture/kill mission in Mexico.

Two weeks before, he'd rescued a nurse being held hostage in the same area, then went north to the cartel-run hotel, starting the mission which had ended in Russia. It felt both like years ago and yesterday.

Time flies when you're having fun.

"First, an update," Nalen started as they ran together along the coast. "Catherine, the police officer and reluctant would-be assassin of Senator Woodran, is in detention. Technically they're calling it protective custody, but since she was about to kill someone, she has to do some time. Her family thinks she, her sister, and brother are dead, all killed in a car accident. Sad, but for the best."

Axe and Haley nodded. Catherine's situation sucked, but it was what it was. At least her family was safe.

"My turn," Axe said, filling in the admiral. "Kelton Kellison is in St. John, US Virgin Islands, on the yacht we 'liberated' from Todd 'The Assistant' Burkley. He's lying low, still recovering from his ordeal in Mexico ingesting the spiked beer. Eventually, he'll be fine, but turning into a zombie and dying hit him understandably hard. Bec and Cody need help running the Movement and he's happy to lend his expertise."

"Smart move," Hammer said as they continued to pound their way down the hard-packed sand near the waterline.

Haley remained silent, running with an easy, natural grace Axe envied.

"On to new business," Nalen said. "I heard some interesting news yesterday."

"Here it comes," Haley mumbled.

"Our little team—what did you call it, Haley, the NHA?"

Axe shook his head, feeling for Haley. She was about to get the hard sell from the admiral.

He knows exactly what it was called.

"It has a new name," Hammer said.

Axe didn't bite, and neither did Haley. Axe could sense Hammer's amusement at their silence.

"It's now the WIA. World Intelligence Agency."

Axe glanced at Haley to gauge her reaction, but Haley stared straight ahead, giving nothing away. She increased her pace. Axe and Hammer had to push for a few steps to catch up.

"We need you back, Haley," Hammer said. "You too, Axe. The world needs us."

They ran in silence for several seconds. Finally, Haley spoke, her voice filled with emotion. "Cards on the table. My big concern is how much harm I could do to the president, and the country, if things ever go wrong." She looked over at Axe. "We took the right actions, but since then I've gone over and over it. The risks..."

"Were manageable," Axe said. "Mitigated."

She frowned, unconvinced.

Hammer looked like he wanted to know what specific actions she meant, but didn't want to ask.

I'm not telling him a thing about Russia unless he makes me. He has to suspect we are responsible for Zimalev's death, but he doesn't need us to admit it or tell him the details.

They ran on, each lost in thought about the past... and the future.

"If you come back," Hammer eventually said, "the president would prefer limited field operations for you, and only in the United States. If you're needed on an operation, you'd be surrounded by a larger team. Mad Dog might be a good addition."

Axe laughed when Haley rolled her eyes. "He's not so bad," he told her. "Funny, if you don't take him seriously."

Haley mulled over Nalen's words.

"Your old boss will lead the unit," Hammer continued. "He'll remain the CAG's director. He's now in charge of all of us, me included. And we're a more official organization, at least until we screw up. Then we're unsanctioned, of course."

The sandy beach turned rocky. The coastline was harder to navigate here, so they turned around and ran back, faster now.

"I'll think about it," Haley conceded after a few minutes.

"Please do," Hammer said formally. "Because I received a report from Gregory." He slowed the pace and spoke even more quietly, though the beach was still mostly deserted. "The five biggest Mexican drug cartels ran out of money last week. It took two extra days for them to pay their people."

"We're on vacation," Axe said, only half joking.

Hammer snorted. "If someone was drowning, would you say that? Or dive in to rescue them?"

"The world doesn't need us to rescue it today," he protested. "Not until Monday morning."

I sound like a little kid not wanting to go back to school yet.

"Never mind him, Hammer," Haley said. "Axe is just looking out for me."

She nailed it... though I'd much rather enjoy the remaining vacation days without thinking about the next mission. I wonder if either of them realizes how much I value this downtime.

"Sorry, Blondie," Axe told her. "I tried."

A few minutes passed. This time, Axe picked up the pace.

Haley looked over at him, surprised. They hadn't pushed this hard the past few days.

"'The more you sweat in training, the less you bleed in battle,'" he quoted.

"Amen," Hammer said, matching his speed.

"How can drug cartels be broke?" Haley wondered.

"Excellent question," Hammer replied. "Nancy and Dave are looking into it, but it has them worried."

"Dr. Edgar's drugs?" Axe asked.

"No," Haley and Hammer answered together.

"At least," Haley continued, "it's not what my gut tells me. It feels more dangerous than drugs."

"A cartel might make, what—a few billion dollars a year in drug sales and other illegal activities?" Axe asked. "How could they be broke?" he said, repeating Haley's question.

Axe turned up the speed another notch. Hammer faltered, then kept up, but he was at his limit. Haley had no trouble.

Ah, to be young again.

"Whatever they're up to, it would have to be big," Axe said.

After another few hundred yards, Hammer slowed to a walk, and they joined him, breathing heavily. They had arrived back at their hotel. A young man set out deck chairs in a perfect line down the beach as the sun rose over the resort.

"The cartels together—in Mexico, I mean—earn approximately twenty-five billion dollars per year. That's more than some countries," Haley said.

"You're saying they've banded together?" Axe asked.

"What?" Haley asked. "No, I'm just saying that combined they make… Wait. What if they did work together for a change?" She looked at Axe, worry on her face.

"It's a scary thought," Axe said.

Criminals who make billions of dollars a year, funneling it into something that's bankrupting them—and cooperating instead of competing?

The admiral looked at them with a small smile.

Hammer knows he has her again—and that I never really left.

One part of the SEAL Ethos came to Axe. He quietly started to recite the line. "I humbly serve…"

Hammer joined in, saying the rest with him. "…As a guardian to my fellow Americans, always ready to defend those who are unable to defend themselves."

Nalen stuck out his hand to Haley. She hesitated, then shook it. He repeated the gesture to Axe, who shook immediately.

Hell yes! We're back in business.

Author's Note

Thank you for reading. Continue with *A Team of Four*, the next book in the series:

What happens when America's enemies join forces?

America is under attack. Saboteurs infiltrate the country to wreak havoc on unexpected - and undefended - targets. And danger strikes close to home, forcing former SEAL "Axe," brilliant young intelligence analyst Haley, and retired Admiral Nalen to fight for their lives.

Mere days after their latest efforts to prevent World War III, the team is thrown back into the fire against mysterious new enemies.

The team is in the dark, struggling to identify their adversaries and uncover the plot against the country.

They're outmatched and outgunned.

But with Haley, they are never outsmarted.

With Axe, they are never out of the fight.

Will the combined forces of America's enemies succeed?

Or can Axe and Haley stay alive long enough to save the United States from an unimaginable fate?

Join them as they put their lives on the line to protect each other... and a country in grave danger.

To view on Amazon, please type this link into your browser (or go to Amazon and search for "A Team of Four"):

https://geni.us/a-team-of-four

(You can also order it from your favorite local bookstore.)

- To read a free short story prequel about Axe's first combat operation as a SEAL and receive exclusive updates about my stories, please visit https://www.authorbradlee.com/operationrapidrevenge
- If you enjoyed the book, please leave a five-star or written review. It helps new readers discover the book and makes it possible for me to continue bringing you stories.
- I'm active on social media, sharing photos (like Axe would take) and writing progress updates. I also occasionally ask for input on character names, plot points, or reader preferences as I'm writing, so follow me and help out. Find me here:
- Facebook: https://www.facebook.com/AuthorBradLee
- Instagram: https://www.instagram.com/bradleeauthor/
- Also, I use the names of real places but fictionalize some details. I also take inspiration from areas but change names and some features to improve the story. My apologies if you live in or are acquainted with one of the areas and think, "Wait, that's

not right." You're correct. License was taken in describing places as well as technology, equipment, weapons, tactics, and military capabilities. Where location details, distances, or technical issues conflicted with the story, I prioritized the story.

Finally, please join me in thanking Beth, David, and Mac for their help. The book is far better because of them.